The Syrian Virgin

by

Zack Love

Copyright © 2015 Zack Love

All rights reserved

No part of this publication may be reproduced, distributed or transmitted in any form or by any means, including photocopying, recording, or other electronic or mechanical methods, without the prior written permission of the publisher, except in the case of brief quotations embodied in critical reviews and certain other noncommercial uses permitted by copyright law.

This is a work of fiction. Any references to historical events, real people, or real places are used fictitiously. Other names, characters, places, and events are products of the author's imagination, and any resemblance to actual events, places, or persons, living or dead, is entirely coincidental.

www.ZackLove.com

ISBN: 978-1508560852

Cover by Cassy Roop and Pink Ink Designs

Contents

Acknowledgements v
Chapter 1: Anissa 1
Chapter 2: Anissa 6
Chapter 3: Anissa 11
Chapter 4: Anissa 18
Chapter 5: Anissa 27
Chapter 6: Anissa 32
Chapter 7: Anissa 35
Chapter 8: Anissa 45
Chapter 9: Anissa 49
Chapter 10: Anissa 58
Chapter 11: Anissa 64
Chapter 12: Anissa 70
Chapter 13: Julien 73
Chapter 14: Anissa 75
Chapter 15: Anissa 86
Chapter 16: Julien 91
Chapter 17: Anissa 94
Chapter 18: Julien 100
Chapter 19: Anissa 102
Chapter 20: Julien 105
Chapter 21: Anissa 109
Chapter 22: Anissa 117
Chapter 23: Julien 120
Chapter 24: Anissa 124
Chapter 25: Julien 129
Chapter 26: Anissa 134
Chapter 27: Julien 138
Chapter 28: Anissa 143
Chapter 29: Anissa 149
Chapter 30: Julien 153
Chapter 31: Anissa 157
Chapter 32: Julien 161
Chapter 33: Anissa 166
Chapter 34: Julien 171
Chapter 35: Anissa 173
Chapter 36: Julien 179
Chapter 37: Anissa 183
Chapter 39: Anissa 192
Chapter 40: Anissa 203

Chapter 41: Julien 211
Chapter 42: Anissa 217
Chapter 43: Anissa 233
Chapter 44: Anissa 238
Chapter 45: Anissa 241
Chapter 46: Anissa 255
About the Author 258

Acknowledgements

I am immensely grateful for the kind assistance and feedback of the following beta readers who helped me to locate errors in my first draft and/or suggested other improvements: author KM Golland, Danielle Goodwin, author Nadine Silber, Jenna Hanson, author Anne Conley, Letty Sidon, author Olivia Hayes, Crystal Solis, Lee Clements Tobar, Daina Lazzarotto, Elena Cruz, Anita Viccica Toss, Author Ker Dukey, Lily Wallis, Janet Wilkie, Jennifer Cothran, and Anima Giraldez.

I am also very fortunate to have the enthusiastic help and advocacy of several wonderful individuals. I am especially grateful to:

Anita Viccica Toss for being such an early, loyal, and hugely helpful fan who has consistently provided tremendous promotional support on Facebook, Goodreads, and other book forums; for helping me to stay organized and upbeat, despite whatever frustrations or obstacles presented themselves along the way; and for readily offering a helping hand with so much research and countless other projects.

Daina Lazzarotto and her awesome company, EPIC Literary Promotions, for organizing a release party and blog tour that were (true to her company's name) epic, and generously giving away a Kindle to help generate buzz, assisting with so many research projects, acting as my de facto publicist in many ways, helping to manage my interactions with blogs, and otherwise promoting my books at every opportunity.

Author KM Golland, for her early friendship; general, mood-lifting hilarity and encouragement; editorial feedback; regular support; and helpful advice.

Author Nadine Silber, for her warm and loyal friendship, enthusiastic support (including countless giveaways and efforts to promote this novel and my other books), assistance with my newsletter, excellent production of promotional materials/graphics, and helpful advice.

Ker Dukey, for her loyal friendship and early support; for conceiving of the brilliant concept behind the cover design for this book; and for her awesome graphics and other generous help along the way.

Letty Sidon, for her early friendship, steadfast encouragement and support of my work, and providing valuable assistance with various research projects.

A friend who modestly insisted on remaining unnamed but

provided some helpful research through her contacts with Syrian Christians and has enthusiastically tried to bring this book to readers in the Middle East.

Jennifer Stevens, for doing such a fast and professional job formatting the paperback version of this novel.

Myriam Judith Perkins for organizing the cover reveal and release launch for this book through her company (Concierge Literary Promotions), and for introducing me to Cassy Roop, who designed the beautiful cover for this book.

These fans who promoted my work with such kind and supportive enthusiasm: Janet Wilkie, Elena Cruz, Verna Mcqueen, Lily Wallis, Jo Turner Field, Alessandra Melchionda, Sarah Mae Zink, Jennifer Pou, Jessica Lynn Leonard, Donna Lorah, Jennifer Cothran, Julie Garlington, Crystal Solis, Maggie Welsh, Jessica Jocher, Erin McFarland, Diana Cardonita, and Renee Dyer.

To the people of Syria. The world let you down.

A shootout ensued and part of me felt too resigned to fate to move – almost as if a preordained defeat had left me stuck to the sofa, waiting to die from a bullet or a knife-wielding Islamist. But then the impassioned words spoken by my father not even an hour ago bellowed through my mind: "…you can do far more for us from America than you can from here, where you're just another defenseless Christian."

I had to survive this nightmare, I told myself. I somehow had to make a difference, from a position of power and strength – not like this. I realized that I had to flee, however I could, in whatever minutes of fighting remained. I dropped to the floor, getting on my hands and knees to stay below the gunfire, as I scrambled further into our house, until I reached the corner, where I turned left towards the stairs. With the sound of fighting and shots still raging on the other side of the wall now protecting me, I stood and sprinted up the stairs as fast as I could to my room, until I reached my bags.

Chapter 1: Anissa
(Diary)

∽ Friday, February 7, 2014 ಌ

To My Dearest,

With mere words, how do I tell you about the destruction of everything in my young life – all that I loved and lived for? How can I explain to you what sustained me through unimaginable evil, when I myself don't know the answer? And after I survived it, but with a soul that was hollowed into a nihilistic ache, how did I manage to carry on, even as unbearable memories pursued me everywhere, like a pack of wolves hounding their prey?

As much as I wish I could tell you everything, there are details that I just can't talk about right now. They're too overwhelming – I'll never make it through the telling. No human being should ever have to remember, much less share, certain events. Sometimes emotional survival means deceiving everyone – including yourself. And ever since that infernal night, on January 18, 2012, I've been trying to lie to myself by pretending that certain things didn't happen – because sometimes it's the only way for me to stay sane. So I don't know if I'll ever tell you those details. With God's mercy, maybe I'll finally believe the falsehoods that I recite to myself every night in bed, in the hope that I can, at last, sleep with some solace. And if that happens, then even you, My Dearest, will never know those details, because the lies of my imagination will be all that I can remember.

For now, I'll begin with the last time that I saw my parents, and my escape from Syria in 2012; then I'll skip to my first years in the United States, and the rays of hope that gradually crept back into my life. Along the way, if I still haven't expunged from my mind the darkest night of all – the one that nearly finished me – maybe I'll summon the strength to share more. Perhaps by trying to recount to you that night sent by Satan himself, I will better understand the hazy madness that my life became – a journey that brought me to the depths of despair and loneliness, but later to a hope and love that I never thought could enter my life after so much pain and darkness. If, one day, I am able to find the fortitude to stare January 18, 2012 directly in the face, and then hand it to you as I see it, then you will know that I somehow began to emerge from this black hole reborn, with a renewed spirit.

But before I try to tell you anything else, let me give you a little background to my story. Until the Syrian Civil War began, our family enjoyed a peaceful and affluent life. We lived in a three-story townhouse in the al-Maljaa quarter of Homs, the third-largest city in Syria. We had a maid from the Philippines named Marisol, who lived in our home since before I was born. Besides maintaining the house, she helped to ensure that we were always speaking English on a daily basis, even when we weren't at school. My father worked as a doctor in the National Hospital in Homs, run by the Syrian Ministry of Health, and had a small but growing business importing medical devices into Syria. He also served as the leader of the Syriac Orthodox Christian community in Homs and was considered one of the city's most important Christian representatives. My mother ran a small pharmacy and her income, combined with my father's, allowed us to live a very comfortable life, and enabled my three siblings and me to attend the most prestigious international school in our city, where we learned English at a very young age. We had a boisterously affectionate but protective German Shepherd named Roy. He would often run around on the grass in our gated front yard, which connected – by narrow, grassy passageways along the sides of our house – to an equally large backyard.

The Syrian Civil War began in mid-March of 2011. At the time, I was fifteen years old; my older brother, Firaz, was twenty-one; my older sister, Maria, was nineteen; and my younger brother, Antoun, was eleven. We were all very close, but also very different. Firaz had recently finished his mandatory, twenty-one-month service in the Syrian Army and was studying business administration. He had grown into a big, strong man, and something of a local heartthrob. But Firaz was very serious and almost the complete opposite of Antoun, who was the family jester. My younger brother was always playing pranks, telling jokes, and generally causing mischief (although that was partly due to his age and the fact that our mother coddled him to no end). Antoun was also obsessed with football, and broke more than his share of windows kicking his ball around. Maria was the family musician: a child prodigy on the violin who went on to study at the Institute of Music in Homs with a bright future as a concert performer. And I was a young scholar who loved to learn, consistently performed at the top of her class, and dreamed of someday attending a university in Europe or the United States. My parents often pushed me towards the future study of medicine, and I would always tell them how much I hated the sight of blood.

But there was a lot of blood from the civil war. By the end of April

2011, about 1,000 civilians and hundreds of policemen and soldiers had been killed. And as the conflict dragged on and world powers did nothing, the violence became progressively sectarian.

Violent clashes between government security forces and protestors intensified, as demonstrators increasingly armed themselves. By mid-May, the military had asserted total control over our city, but the unrest continued and religious bloodshed only mounted, as Syrian Army soldiers defected in greater numbers to join an increasingly Sunni Muslim-dominated insurgency. My happy childhood memories became more and more polluted by images of prolonged street fighting between security forces and rebels, who gained control of several quarters of the city.

The so-called "Arab Spring" had brought a wave of popular protests for greater freedoms across the Middle East, including in Syria. The country's leader, Bashar al-Assad, like his father, Hafez Assad, had always ruled Syria with an iron fist. In the Middle East, the weak perish quickly and autocratic rule seems to be the most effective governing system to combat extremism and overcome so many tribal, religious, linguistic, and ethnic differences. Indeed, the Arab Middle East has no history of successful democracies – Lebanon and Iraq came closest, but both also suffered from chronic instability and bloody civil wars.

Bashar al-Assad succeeded his father's rule in June 2000 with some hint that he would introduce reforms to soften his father's brutal dictatorial rule. But the political realities greatly limited what he could actually do. The Assads hailed from the Alawite sect of Shia Islam and, like Christians, were religious minorities in a country of 18 million people who were mostly Sunni Muslims.

Four decades of Assad rule meant that the Alawite sect comprised the de facto political elite. Syria's 1.5 million Christians were among the religious minorities that supported (and benefited from) the ruling elite, and this made them a natural target for those fighting to topple Assad's regime. Assad and his allies feared not only losing their decades-long hold on power, but also the bloodbath that would likely follow, in a region where major transitions of power are never peaceful.

Our Christian community – and other religious minorities in Syria – also feared vicious persecution by the religious majority. We saw what happened to the Christians just across our border, in Iraq, when the secular regime there ended. After the fall of Saddam Hussein, sectarian killings, persecution of Christians, and an increasingly Islamist political culture, prompted more than half of the Iraqi Christian population to flee an area where Christians had lived for thousands of years. And the same thing could easily happen to us in Syria, if the secular regime were to collapse. Sunni Muslim mobs or terrorist groups could brutalize us with impunity or even tacit government support. Christians had lived in the land of Syria for millennia – many hundreds of years before Arab Muslim conquerors arrived in the seventh century – but our future there was anything but certain.

In the weeks before Christmas of 2011, about fifty Christians in my city had been killed in the anti-government unrest, by both rebels and government forces, while many more were struggling to feed their families as the bloodletting brought normal life in the city to a halt. In one incident, a young Christian boy was killed by the rebels, who filmed the murder and then claimed that Assad's forces had killed him. Another Christian was seized by the rebels, taken to a house, and asked, "How do you want to die?" The man was eventually released, but reportedly continued to suffer from severe psychological distress. Hearing about such callous brutality and cruelty ominously chipped away at whatever sense of security I had felt before the civil war began.

As the conflict ground on, there were more and more guns on the street. The regime's forces increased their presence, but so did other groups of armed men patrolling the streets. Some of these gunmen were army deserters who refused orders to fire on protesters, but many were radical Islamists who wanted to plunge Syria into sectarian chaos. These violent extremists had no interest in the democratic aspirations that motivated the first anti-government protests; they just wanted to bring down the secular Syrian state.

By Christmas 2011, the violence between rebels and government troops had claimed over 5,000 lives in Syria, and almost one-third of those deaths had happened in my city. Not surprisingly, many Christian families fled Homs, leaving behind their possessions, jobs, and homes. Some of those who chose to stay were too afraid to step outside to go to work, and so were suffering tremendous financial hardship. Few dared to be out after 3 p.m. or on Fridays, when the streets were most dangerous. The Christian areas of our city were surrounded by rebels. Insurgents would sometimes try to escape into those neighborhoods, and then would be hunted down there by the army, leaving horrible violence, death, and destruction in their wake.

These were the dark clouds casting a pall over the last Christmas that I spent with my family, as we met for our annual holiday reunion. We tried to pretend that life was normal when coming together with our cousins from Raqqa (in northern Syria), but Christmas of 2011 felt hauntingly different – like it might very well be the last time that we would all be together.

Chapter 2: Anissa

∞ Saturday, February 8, 2014 ∞

To My Dearest,

 I became too exhausted while writing to you last night, but now I'll continue where I left off about the last Christmas that I spent with my family, in 2011. My maternal uncle, Luke, lived in Raqqa with his wife and three children, and would normally take his family on the five-hour drive southwest to our house for the Christmas and New Year's holidays. But in 2011, to enjoy a more peaceful experience away from the violent chaos of Homs, our families traveled to pray at the Saint George de Mishtaya monastery, which is about thirty miles west of our hometown. The ancient site lies in the lush area known as "Valley of the Christians," whose hillsides are dotted with countless almond trees. Across the valley stands the striking Krak des Chevaliers, a beautiful and well-preserved, Crusades-era castle.

 We gathered in the monastery's basilica, built in the sixth century. My fifty-five-year-old father, who stood about five-feet-ten inches tall, wore a white dress shirt and dark slacks. He seemed to be aging faster under the relentless pressures of the war thrashing our city. He had lost nearly all of the hair on the top of his head and his signature brown mustache was sprinkled with some white hairs. My mother, a five-foot-four bundle of energy, was fifty-two years old at the time. She too seemed older, with deepening crow's feet by her green eyes and some white streaks running through her black hair.

 In accordance with tradition, each female covered her head with a prayer shawl and sat on one side of the room, with the men on the opposite side nearby. All of the congregants asked God to restore peace to our country. As the bishop passed along the aisles of the church, blessing those in attendance, we crossed ourselves.

 After the bishop's benediction, we sang the Christmas hymns, which at times seemed discordantly upbeat, given what was happening in Syria. With the music of our singing in the background, I looked at the church candles and thought about the surreal connection between images and memory. The peaceful and joyous candles flickering there during the Christmas ceremony projected warmth, comfort, and familiarity – even though they emitted the same kind of fiery energy as the flames caused by war. How could a conflagration sparked by regime airstrikes or Molotov cocktails have anything to do with a Christmas candle in church? Yet they were both fire: able to illuminate as much as to burn – and now both were part of my life. One moment I could be here with my family, celebrating a religious holiday, and the next moment we could all be in mortal danger from the blaze of sectarian conflict searing through our city. Everything – happiness, memory, and life itself – began to seem so precarious.

Indeed, just two days before Christmas, my father told us how, on his way back home from the hospital where he worked, he was stopped by an armed man who demanded to see his identity card. Upon seeing my father's Christian surname – Toma – the man told him that he had been very lucky. "Had you been an Alawite, I would have killed you right here," he said, pointing to where my father stood and then slowly moving his index finger chillingly across his throat with a sadistic smile.

After that incident, my father called his brother-in-law, my Uncle Luke, and started to plan for the worst. He asked him to house and care for Maria and Antoun, because Raqqa was much safer for Christians at the time. Both my older sister and younger brother would leave with Uncle Luke after our Christmas reunion, so we loaded up our car with their suitcases before heading to the Saint George de Mishtaya monastery. In Raqqa, Maria would continue with her musical studies and Antoun would transfer to a new elementary school. To keep Antoun from trying to bring his football in an already cramped car – our father promised him that Uncle Luke would buy him an even better ball and some private football lessons.

My parents needed Firaz to stay at home and help with their businesses and just for general security – especially with my mother's pharmacy. After her store was looted by rebels in October, it was moved to the ground floor of our three-story townhouse, which was better protected because of its heavy front door and the nine-foot-tall, wrought-iron fence with spear finials surrounding our front yard. No matter how violent the conflict grew, our pharmacy continued to serve all faiths, and my mother would often note that this would help to shield our family and the pharmacy from the growing sectarian violence in Homs. "None of your goodwill can help if Islamists who are not from this area show up," Firaz corrected her, after the incident with my father. "We need to get a gun to keep by the cash register," he said. My older brother was very protective of the women in the house, and would have never agreed to leave – even if our parents didn't need his help. He was too proud, like my father.

But my father insisted that I continue my education in the USA, as soon as possible. The night after he was stopped, he pulled me aside and told me what was on his mind. "Inās," he began, calling me by my Arabic name, as he always did. "You and your siblings are the most precious part of my life. And of all my children, you have the most potential to go anywhere you wish in this world – your test scores and grades have always been among the highest of your peers. But it's clear now that you cannot reach your full potential in Syria. Islamist rebels have been gaining the upper hand in this conflict, and – after last night – I told your mother that I would devise a plan for you to leave Syria so that you can fulfill all of your promise in life. Because if the Islamists take over, we have no future as Christians in Syria. And things are getting worse every day, so we cannot wait another day. A darkness is descending upon our land, and we will bear the cross for our faith as Jesus bore it."

"You're scaring me, Papa. Why are you saying such things?"

"Because this is our reality now – it's becoming clearer by the day. And we must confront the world as it is, and not as we wish it to be. You must leave Syria and get the best education you can in the United States and do what you can for your people and your family. In America, you will be safe and can speak for those of us who have no voice. I am working on your visa and discussing arrangements with my brother in New York to receive you."

My father would work to secure a visa and a flight for me. He had personal connections to Canada's ambassador to Syria, both through his high position in the government hospital, and thanks to some of his Canadian business contacts who exported their medical devices to him. Those contacts would enable him to obtain a visa for me when it was nearly impossible for anyone else to get one, given the number of people trying to leave Syria any way they could. After the U.S. embassy in Syria closed in June 2011, the demand for a Canadian visa grew exponentially. Once I had mine, my father would book a flight for me from Damascus to London, and then from London to Montreal. His only brother, my Uncle Tony, lived in New York and would pick me up from the Montreal airport and find a way to cross the border illegally with me. Once I was in the United States, I would apply for political asylum and stay with him while finishing my high school studies and seeking admission to a U.S. college. I would deeply miss Syria and my family and friends there, but attending university in the United States was a dream I had always nurtured, so it was a bittersweet carrot that my parents could dangle in front of me to lower my resistance to the whole plan.

My father had helped Uncle Luke to establish a medical device import business in Raqqa that the two of them jointly owned as partners. But my dad agreed to give him his share of the business to offset the expense of caring for my older sister and younger brother. And so that his brother in New York would have the funds to cover my needs for about twenty months before I was to start college, my father converted enough Syrian pounds to wire Uncle Tony $10,000 through a bank account that he maintained in France for business purposes. He took that money from his savings account, which dwindled by the day as the war slowed his business (while dramatically raising the cost of everything).

Despite my father's connections to members of Canada's diplomatic corps, everything slowed down around the new year, and it looked as if my visa wouldn't arrive until the second or third week of January 2012. Finally, on the morning of January 18, 2012, I got an SMS from my father: "Got your visa. Bought your ticket. Flight leaves in 2 days. Pack tonight." My stomach turned with nervous excitement at his momentous message. An hour later, I realized that there was no point in staying in class for the rest of the day because I could hardly concentrate and I wouldn't even be showing up again. Homs had descended into unpredictable chaos and mutual suspicion, and I feared that telling anyone of my plans could provoke an envious betrayal of some kind or some other unexpected problem. As much as I loved to learn, it wasn't like there was even much of that happening. I was one of just five students who still bothered to attend school, and sometimes even our teacher didn't show up and we would have to join another class. So I sent an SMS to my mother, letting her know that I would be heading home soon. I snuck out during lunch break without saying goodbye to any of my friends or teachers who happened to be present that day. After spending so many years of my life in that school, I felt oddly unfaithful about ending my last day there with such a surreptitious and unceremonious departure.

With silent farewells still being exchanged in my mind, I made the dangerous trek home from school one last time, using the safer but less direct route that I had found, to avoid the areas where clashes between rebels and government troops were more frequent. As I finally approached our townhouse, its familiar facade – decorated by the Arab medieval style of black-and-white geometric patterns – seemed to call out to me, maybe because I knew that I was just days away from not returning there for a very long time. But what I didn't know, as I opened the black, wrought iron gate and walked towards the front door of my childhood home, was that it was actually the very last time that I would ever do so.

Marisol greeted me at the door and told me that a warm lunch was waiting. I could smell from the entrance that my mother had asked her to prepare my favorite kofta kebab dish of grilled lamb meat, mixed with garlic and parsley, served on rice with assorted dips and salads. It was a mouth-watering scent intimately connected to home, and I couldn't wait to indulge in the deliciousness with my mother.

I walked further into the first floor of our house and saw her locking up some cabinets that were now used for her pharmacy. She stepped away from the area, approached me with a tired smile, and stretched her arms out for a hug. I lost myself in that embrace with my slightly shorter mother, knowing that this moment of maternal warmth and proximity was another thing that suddenly became infinitely more precious as my departure drew closer.

Chapter 3: Anissa

∽ Sunday, February 9, 2014 ∾

To My Dearest,

I wasn't able to finish telling you about the day I got my visa, so I'm resuming from the point where I left off: seated at the dining table next to my mother, where I was enjoying a sumptuous, midday meal with her. I guess I should also mention that when I recount conversations to you, these are just the best approximations of my recall (and not verbatim quotations), although there are certain moments that I remember with vivid precision, even from years ago, like the discussion with my mother during our last meal together.

She tried to put me at ease about staying with Uncle Tony, whom I hadn't seen since he last came to visit us when I was just ten. "He's the same good man who let you ride on his shoulders. But you're older now and he'll have to get used to that. Just focus on your schoolwork and be a top student, as you've always been, and I'm sure everything will be fine," she said.

"Is he going to have kofta kebab like this at his house?" I asked sadly, savoring every bite of that delicious lamb dish as if it were my last.

"Inās, your Aunt Christine is a very good cook," she reassured me. Her sympathetic look told me that she knew how much I was struggling to let go of what I had. She then launched into a long list of reminders, admonitions, tips, and ideas for my coming trip. After that, she mentioned something that surprised me because we had never really discussed the topic much – perhaps because she had secretly relied on Maria for such discussions. "Inās, please promise me that you'll stay away from boys until you marry."

"Mom, if I haven't met anyone I like here in Homs, what makes you think it'll be any easier in America?"

"It's not easy anywhere. But here, you had many people who could guide you and watch your back, and look into someone's background for you. Over there, you'll have Uncle Tony and his family, but it's very different. You're going to have a lot more freedom and you'll be meeting people that nobody knows anything about."

"Why is that such a bad thing? I'm going to be seventeen soon!"

"It's not a bad thing, if you're responsible about it. Just don't start having boyfriends. Wait until you've found your husband."

"And how am I supposed to find a husband if I can't have a boyfriend until then?" I asked ironically.

"No, that's not what I mean." It was clearly an awkward topic for her, so she tried a different approach. "I know that American culture is much more liberal than Syrian culture, but your virginity should be something precious to you, wherever you go. Don't just give it away to anyone. Save it for a man who is worthy. And try to avoid boys in high school – they're usually just trouble at that age. Better just to focus on your studies and keep making us proud. OK?" She gave me that look between bites indicating that she was finished discussing the issue and wasn't going to let us change topics until I expressly agreed to follow her advice.

"OK, Mom."

She smiled in relief. Marisol then brought us a tray of baklava, a pastry made of many thin layers of filo dough filled with ground walnuts and soaked in sugar syrup. It was my favorite Syrian dessert, and I felt the urge to sneak some into my suitcase with me as my mother and I attacked the tray with guilty smiles.

"After lunch, I want us to light a candle for Grandma Marium," she said. I suddenly remembered that it was the anniversary of my maternal grandmother's death. "Then I'll give you something that I want you to pack with you for your trip."

"How much do you think I should take with me?"

"No more than two suitcases. Start with your winter clothes first and then you'll know how much room you have for other things."

That task turned out to be much easier said than done. My mother offered to help with it, but I insisted on doing it alone. I knew that it was going to be a deeply emotional and personal process, and I worried that the sight of my mother helping me one last time would make it even more painful. My body felt heavier as my hands grasped the few things from my current life that would accompany me into a loneliness I had never known. I must have packed, unpacked, and repacked each travel bag at least five times, as tears blurred my eyes with every new attempt to complete the task. The need to decide what to bring to the next phase of my life overwhelmed me, well beyond the guesswork of predicting what would be most useful in such a foreign place. How could I reduce my whole existence to two suitcases, with so little room for any tangible mementos of the place and people I was leaving behind?

I was also upset by the idea that even what I could take with me from my life in Syria would probably be discarded eventually, when I outgrew this pair of pants or wore out that shirt, or realized that some part of my wardrobe just looked too unfashionable for my new environment. An immense sadness and fear about all of the unknowns – and my impending aloneness – suddenly overpowered me, leading to a steady stream of tears wetting my face.

After nearly five hours, I was finally at peace with – or at least resigned to – my packing decisions. I told my mother that I was ready. My two suitcases were left open for her to inspect my choices.

"Is that everything?" she asked with a frown.

I nodded.

"Then you're not done packing," she replied. "Where is that carry-on backpack that I got you for your most important things?"

"Oh, right." I had forgotten about that detail.

"That carry-on bag is also your backup, in case your luggage gets lost for some reason. So make sure you pack at least one warm sweater, a shirt, and two pairs of underwear and socks, along with your toiletries. And put your gloves and hat in the pockets of your coat, along with your cell phone, so that you have all of those things on you."

This of course required some reconfiguring of prior packing decisions, all of which took almost another hour. But by 7 p.m., all of my bags were finally ready to go, with my properly stuffed winter coat resting on my backpack, which contained my laptop, cell phone charger, toiletries, and two days of backup clothes.

"You forgot something," my mother said, this time with a loving twinkle in her eye.

"What now?" I asked.

"You have to take this with you too," she said, opening a box and holding up a silver necklace with the Syriac cross (a crucifix with a budding flower shape on each tip) dangling from it. "My grandmother gave it to my mother, who passed it to me. Now is the right time to give it to you. Not just because you're leaving and will need something that always connects you to your roots, but also because tonight we remember her."

She closed the box and put it in my hand, and I suddenly felt the weight of history and the love of family resting together in my palm. Her smile flooded me with warmth as she wrapped her arms around me and gave me a hug.

She pulled away. "But don't wear it until you have left Syria. It's too dangerous now for that," she warned. "Put it in your backpack."

After I packed the cherished keepsake in my carry-on bag, she led me over to a memorial candle that we lit for her mother. As I peered into the incandescent glow of the flickering candle, I again thought of how the tiny fire on its tip, like that on the Christmas candles I'd gazed at in church, was oddly related to the flames that could consume a building and its residents after a bombing or airstrike.

About fifteen minutes later, my father arrived at our house. When we went to greet him by the door, he seemed worried. He shut and locked the front door, dropped his things on the counter, and looked for his key to open the drawer by the pharmacy cash register in the foyer.

"What's wrong, Youssef?" my mother asked him anxiously.

"Nothing, I hope. But we have to be prepared," he said, as he opened the drawer and took out the pistol that Firaz had bought to protect the pharmacy.

My mother's expression turned grave and distressed. "What do you mean? What's happening?"

"Preparing for the worst," my father replied, trying to sound calm as he nervously stroked the whiskers of his mustache with one hand, while holding the gun with his other. "I also sent Firaz to get a few more guns and some army friends who can help."

"Youssef, stop this mystery and tell me what's happening," my mother insisted in dismay.

"There is a Sunni doctor I had to fire today, after I discovered that he was purloining hospital supplies."

"Which doctor? What's his name?" my mother asked.

"Doctor Omar."

"When did this happen?" she asked.

"About an hour ago."

"And what exactly happened?" she persisted, wringing her hands.

My father started pacing around the foyer a little with the gun still in his hand. "When I confronted him with proof that he had been misappropriating hospital supplies, he admitted that he was transferring them to rebels. And then we had an argument about this."

"What do you mean?" my mother asked, the mounting concern clear in her voice.

"I explained to him that the hospital supplies were for our patients and not for any other purpose. He then accused me of being a supporter of the regime. I replied that I was a supporter of the hospital, and therefore couldn't allow such dishonesty among the staff, or the place would cease to function properly."

"And what did he say?"

"His reply was, 'Are you sure you want to fire me for this, when I know where you live?' I told him that threats won't change a thing and that he was indeed fired, effective immediately. But he obviously has connections to the rebels and does in fact know where I live, so we must now prepare for the worst."

My father stopped pacing, put the pistol down on a counter nearby, and took my passport out of his trouser pocket. "Are you packed?" he asked me.

"Yes," I replied.

"Good. Here is your passport and visa, and some related documents that you'll need for entry into Canada. Put this in your purse and keep it with you at all times."

"Inās, do as your father says. Go put it in your purse, by your bags."

I did as they asked and when I came back, their conversation alarmed me even more.

"She needs to leave tonight," I heard my father say as I was returning. He was pacing about the foyer again.

"What's going on?" I asked apprehensively. "Your SMS said that my flight is in two days."

"It is. But I don't want you to stay here," he snapped back, clearly on edge.

"What do you mean? So where will I stay until my flight?"

"With the neighbor behind our house, Mohammed Rajeh. I already arranged it with him by phone on my way back from the hospital."

"So I'm taking my bags there?"

"Yes, I'll take your luggage there with the car."

"Does that mean he's taking me to the airport too?"

"Yes," he said, still walking about nervously. My father's grim expression only reinforced the sinister tension I felt in the foyer.

"Why, Papa?"

He must have sensed from my voice and expression that my anxiety had – by that point – surpassed his, because he walked over to calm me. My father put his hand on my shoulder and said, "Don't worry, Inās, it will be fine." His reassuring voice and expression eased some of the swelling terror I had begun to feel. "There is nothing to fear with him.

He considers himself first a human, then a Syrian, and only last a Sunni Muslim."

"But I want you and Mom to take me."

"I know. I wish we could do it that way. But us taking you would be dangerous, even before what happened with Doctor Omar. Now, it's impossible. You are much safer going with Mohammed. The Sunni Islamists have been taking over Homs, so I need a Sunni man I can trust to get you out of the city and to the Damascus airport."

My mother agreed. "Your father is right, Inās. Mohammed is a member of the elite and on good terms with the regime. But his Sunni background means that the rebels are less likely to bother him."

"He's a good man – we've been friends since before you were born. And I promised him that upon your safe arrival, my brother would wire him $3,000 for his help – just in case he encounters any risks or expenses along the way."

"And what about you?" I asked my parents, as a foreboding feeling of guilt suddenly descended upon me.

"We are staying, Inās," my mother said gently.

"But why don't you try to leave before it gets any more dangerous? I'm sure Uncle Luke could make room for the two of you and Firaz."

"He has been kind enough to take in Antoun and Maria. That is already too much to ask. I won't be chased out of my own home. And as one of the leaders of the Christian community here, it's not right or honorable for me to flee when danger arrives. I was born in Homs, and I will die in Homs."

"Then I should stay here with you and Firaz, and help however I can," I protested.

"If you want to help, then you'll do as your father says," my mother replied sternly, as if my resistance was only making things worse. "You will give us peace of mind, knowing that you are much safer."

"Yes, Inās," my father agreed, as he took my arms and urgently gripped them. I could almost feel him restraining his fingers from pressing too firmly into my skin. His unease continued to settle upon me as he searched my eyes with an intensity whose message I would remember forever. "And you can do far more for us from America than you can from here, where you're just another defenseless Christian. So if you really want to help, Inās, then you'll go to the very best school you can get into and earn the best grades you can. And, God willing, I'll be able to send you more money by the time you use up what is waiting for you. But take loans if you have to. Work if you must. Whatever happens, don't let anything limit you. And as you rise to the top, guard your values and your purity, and remember your roots and your people – do what you can to help. And I have no doubt that you will. Now come here and give me a big hug before I take you and your bags to Mohammed."

"OK, I understand," I conceded reluctantly but solemnly, as the power of his words seared themselves into my core and I gave him a hug.

Moments later, Roy came running up to me, wagging his tail, moving his head, and then running towards the front door, the way he always does when he wants me to let him outside so that he can do his business. It was as if he knew that this was our last time together.

"I'll do it," my father said.

"Dad, I'm packed and ready to go – let me just take him out one last time."

My father looked as if he was about to insist that he take the dog out, but then his cell phone rang.

As he went to answer it, I grabbed my winter coat and started towards the door, where Roy was waiting, wagging his tail expectantly.

I could hear my father talking on the phone. "Firaz, there isn't much time, so if you have only one armed guard who can come, then bring him now. We can try to get more tomorrow. And make sure you have a good gun for yourself – the one here is too small. I don't – "

That was the last thing I heard from his conversation after shutting the front door and stepping out into the chilly night with Roy. I really didn't want to hear any more. I was already overwhelmed by a thousand thoughts and fears.

For now, that is all that I can tell you about the last time that I ever saw my parents. I just don't have the emotional stamina or fortitude to go into more detail. All I can say is that in the end, there was no car ride to transfer the two large suitcases I had packed with so much tortured deliberation and emotion. I had to get to Mohammed alone, and had the strength to carry only my backpack.

Chapter 4: Anissa

∞ Monday, February 10, 2014 ∞

To My Dearest,

I've been avoiding this moment for about two years, but it's time. Today I spoke with my therapist (Monique – I'll get to her soon) and she told me that I'm ready to share this with you. Or at least ready to try.

I'm actually afraid to write to you now because I know what kind of emotional torment awaits me. But Monique says it's the only way forward. I need to face the ogre head on, and come to terms with it in a safe place, and you are that safe place, My Dearest. So here we go. Please hold my trembling hand as we descend into the ghastly darkness together, because the horror we will visit slithers where no beating heart should go. For the evil that we shall witness there is a shame to all of humanity. Yet – just as a peaceful candle still belongs to the family of energy that can burn down a building full of people – the monsters who did this are still somehow part of the human race.

So let's go back to the night of January 18, 2012, after my father made his emotional appeal and I reluctantly accepted his plan to have our neighbor Mohammed take me to the airport.

I asked my father to let me take out the dog one last time and managed to avoid his objection only because my older brother called him on his cell phone at that moment. I soon heard my father anxiously urging him to come as fast as he could with the armed guard and a gun for himself.

I put on my winter coat and joined Roy by the front door, where he was waiting, wagging his tail impatiently. I stepped out into the cold night and took our German shepherd around to the side of our townhouse, towards the backyard, so that he could finish his business.

A few minutes later, his head suddenly jerked to one side, and he emitted a brief snarl before barking wildly and running towards the gate separating our lawn from the street. I ran after him, my heart pounding with fear at what I might find. When I got to the front yard area, I saw armed men with beards in a Toyota pickup truck – one getting out of the driver's seat, two standing on the hood of the vehicle to step onto the top of our nine-foot metal fence, and two more behind them on the vehicle bed, waiting to do the same.

I screamed in terror as Roy ran right up to the fence, barking ferociously at the bearded men who were preparing to jump down into our yard. The first man jumped and, before he could even reach the ground, Roy had already leapt and buried his teeth into the intruder's calf as he landed onto our lawn. The man groaned in pain as our dog clenched his jaws while growling viciously. Moments later, the other man landed next to him and our dog released the first man and moved to attack the second one. But a gunshot blasted through the winter night and Roy's growls suddenly grew silent. The second man lowered his gun a little. Roy yelped for a moment and then just lay there. Meanwhile, the three other armed men were making their way over the fence and into our front yard, which was when the front door to my house opened and I saw my father enter the chilly night, with a pistol raised and firing. He shot two or three times and hit the second man who killed Roy. The bullet apparently penetrated his waist, causing him to drop to the floor. But one of the three other men shot my father. I heard the thud of the bullet's impact and saw my father wobble just slightly, staggering slowly to the ground. I screamed in horror and ran over to him.

I saw that he was hit in his right shoulder and his gun had fallen from his hand and was on the ground nearby. I almost reached for the gun but stopped myself. I had never used one before so – rather than risk a bad shot that goaded the attackers into a more aggressive response – I tried to pull my father towards the entrance to the house, just steps away. Threading my arms underneath his, I attempted to lift him. But his concrete-heavy frame and weight thwarted my efforts. My failure to move him out of harm's way devastated me even more when he yelled, "Go without me!" But as I stood up to turn and make a run for it, one of the armed men yelled, "Stop!" I froze, realizing that it was too late. Three bearded men stood around my father and me with their Kalashnikov rifles up and ready to mow us down in an instant.

I heard my mother's scared voice from the doorway behind me. "Please," she said in a desperately pleading voice. "Please… My husband meant no harm… He just heard the dog bark and our daughter scream… He reacted to an intruder the way anyone would. He meant you no harm. Please put your weapons down. We can give you medical supplies. Drugs from our pharmacy for your fighters. Whatever you want. Our pharmacy serves every person of every faith."

One of the three men standing in front of us replied. "We can discuss it inside," he said, his words emitting steam in the cold night air.

He gestured to the other two and they grabbed my wounded father under his armpits, lifted him off the floor, and dragged him up the few stairs and into our house. I saw the two men who were injured in the exchange and still by the fence on the ground, slowly getting up and making their way towards me, apparently following their leader into our house. I followed the men who were dragging my father, and I could feel myself shaking and hyperventilating in fear as I entered our house. The two injured men followed me and then shut the door behind them.

My mother frantically unlocked a cabinet and started taking drugs and medicines out for display. "Here. We have so many medicines. Just tell me what you need and it's yours," she said, her voice pathetically unsteady.

"That's not necessary," said one of the armed men. "We don't need you to give these to us because this is now our pharmacy."

His leader corrected him: "No, first we give them a choice." He stroked his beard for a moment, as if he was weighing a proposal in his mind. "If they choose wisely, we don't need to take anything because they are then one of us." He looked at my father, who was sitting up in a chair with two men holding Kalashnikovs standing behind him, and Marisol pressing a towel against his shoulder, trying to stem the bleeding. "As the man of the house, the choice is yours to make," he continued.

"What choice?" my father asked in a voice strained by the pain of his wound.

"You can renounce your faith and convert to Islam, and then you are one of us. Or you can remain a Christian dog, and you will share the fate of your dog outside. He was Christian too, right?"

The other four men snickered and laughed at their leader's joke about Roy.

"Choose wisely, Doctor. Because if you choose to stay a Christian dog, then you are not only an infidel who will get the sword. But you will get special punishment for serving the regime."

"I don't serve the regime. I serve the people of Homs. I help any patient who comes into the hospital – every religion and every political orientation."

"You don't allow Doctor Omar to give us medical supplies, so you are serving the regime, and I should just kill you now for that. But Allah is merciful and has given you the option to live by serving Islam. If you wish to accept His mercy, simply recite the Shahada and your life will be spared. The words are easy to say: There is no god but God, Muhammad is the messenger of God."

"Yes, I know these words. They are the first of the five pillars of Sunni Islam. But I am not Muslim. I am a Christian, and I believe in Jesus Christ."

"You are a brave man. It would be a shame not to have you helping the resistance against the infidel regime." He took out a cigarette and lit it.

"I condemn all atrocities against innocent Sunnis, including those committed by the *shabiha*. And when Sunni victims come to my hospital, I treat them to the best of my ability. I am a human being and a doctor before I am a Syrian. And I am a Syrian before I am a Christian."

"If you become a Muslim, you can continue to work as a doctor for Muslims fighting in the resistance."

"When a bleeding man comes to the hospital, I ask which wounds to suture – not what God he prays to, or whose war he fights. And when a pregnant woman arrives, I ask whether a natural birth or a C-section is preferable, not who her prophet is."

"By embracing Islam, you save your life now, and will heal holy warriors fighting jihad."

"I am a Christian. And as a doctor, I heal everyone. And nothing you can do will change that."

"So you have made your choice and you will die tonight," he replied, resting his cigarette on a piece of furniture nearby. "But first – because you fired Doctor Omar and cut off our medical supplies – we have a special treat for you. Ahmad has fought bravely against infidels in recent weeks and deserves a reward. Especially because he has been looking for a wife."

The two men standing behind my father and Marisol took the Kalashnikovs they were holding and hung them from their shoulders using the strap, so that their hands were now free. They each took out combat knives. One put his blade to my father's throat, and the other started to walk towards me.

"So Ahmad will take your daughter now as his wife and Osama will make sure that you are a witness to this act. Then, if he wants to keep your daughter as his wife and she embraces Islam, then her life will be spared. Otherwise, she will share your fate. The same for your housekeeper and your wife – Osama will choose which one he wants as his wife. But we start with your daughter."

My father and mother screamed out in horror as Ahmad rushed closer, grabbed me, and threw me down on to the nearby sofa. Hovering above me with his knife, he said, "Pull down your pants, or I'll cut them off." Whimpering in terror, I struggled to comply with his command, somewhat constrained by the winter coat that was still on me. Trembling with fear, I willed my fingers to settle on the waistband of my pants, yet fought their movement simultaneously. Thoughts of what I was about to experience had seized my ability to cooperate any further. I froze up. Furious at my noncompliance, Ahmad's eyes flared with an anger that terrorized me even more. Then, a noise I will never forget, sounded – the loud bang of a gunshot pierced the icy, dread-filled night and shocked me to my core. What followed was the unbearable weight of my attacker, crushing my chest as he collapsed on top of me, blood from the wound to his skull splattering all over my face. His weight rested on me and I couldn't endure his imprisonment any longer. I pushed the satanic thing off of me, finding that Firaz had arrived with a security guard.

A shootout ensued and part of me felt too resigned to fate to move – almost as if a preordained defeat had left me stuck to the sofa, waiting to die from a bullet or a knife-wielding Islamist. But then the impassioned words spoken by my father not even an hour ago bellowed through my mind: "…you can do far more for us from America than you can from here, where you're just another defenseless Christian."

I had to survive this nightmare, I told myself. I somehow had to make a difference, from a position of power and strength – not like this. I realized that I had to flee, however I could, in whatever minutes of fighting remained. I dropped to the floor, getting on my hands and knees to stay below the gunfire, as I scrambled further into our house, until I reached the corner, where I turned left towards the stairs. With the sound of fighting and shots still raging on the other side of the wall now protecting me, I stood and sprinted up the stairs as fast as I could to my room, until I reached my bags. Trying to ensure that nothing got lost in my frenzied escape, I stopped to zip my purse shut, sling it across my chest over my coat, and then put my backpack on.

In a breathless panic, I ran back down the stairs while praying to God that none of the attackers had moved deeper into the house. When I reached the bottom step, a temporary and uneasy relief washed over me as I found no intruders there. I turned left to move towards the doorway leading to the backyard. Just as I was about to leave the area and make my escape, I heard an intense volley of gunfire and several different voices yelling "Allahu Akbar! Allahu Akbar!" I shuddered profusely, horrified at the thought of what must have just happened as I flew through the backdoor, sprinting as fast as I could to the six-foot fence separating Mohammed's yard from our own.

Antoun and I had climbed it many times to fetch his football, but a moment of doubt emerged when I realized that I had never tried to do so with my backpack, purse, and winter coat on me. But then my father's powerful words returned to me, and scaling the fence while encumbered suddenly seemed like a small feat. Nothing would stop me. I would climb that fence, and I would survive this nightmare.

I banged on my neighbor's door until it opened just slightly, revealing an armed man with a concerned look, as he assessed my identity for a moment. He ushered me inside, shutting and locking the door behind me. As he led me through the house to the living room, I used my sleeve to wipe the blood off my face.

Moments later, Mohammed arrived looking distraught. "Inās, I'm so sorry I couldn't do more to help. Samir and I together have just two guns and only he is skilled at using one. If we went in to help, we could have easily been killed there or targeted here the day after, and then I couldn't possibly keep my promise to your father to take you to the airport in two days."

I stood there silently, shocked by the events that had just transpired, and trying not to faint from hyperventilation.

"Please forgive me, Inās. As soon as I heard gunshots, I called my regime contacts to the Syrian Army."

I couldn't get my mouth to say anything. It felt totally paralyzed, with my heart racing at a thousand beats per minute. As I tried to catch my breath, Mohammed's wife and his housekeeper arrived. In keeping with Muslim tradition, both women appeared wearing hijabs, in case their unexpected guest turned out to be a man. When they saw that I was a female, they removed their headscarves.

"They said they would try to send some troops but were stretched thin at the moment, with so many battles engaging the army tonight," Mohammed explained, continuing with his apology.

"It's too late anyway," I finally said, between breaths.

"What do you mean?"

"As I was escaping, I heard many gunshots," I responded, stopping for more breath. "And then shouts of Allahu Akbar!"

Repeating those words, I finally broke down in tears.

"I'm so sorry, Inās. So sorry." His voice was full of grief and remorse. His wife came up to me and gently put her hand on my shoulder. "You are safe now, Inās," she said, before holding me in a protective hug.

"Yes, you are safe now, Inās," Mohammed added sadly for emphasis. "But you must not leave the house or stay by the windows for the next two days – until we leave for your flight," he warned me. "It's for your security, just in case."

I was crying hysterically in his wife's arms until she stepped away and looked at me in alarm. "You're bleeding, poor child!"

She turned to their housekeeper and instructed her to retrieve the first-aid kit. She turned to me and gently placed her hand on my arm. "Come, let's clean you up, and bandage your wounds."

I put down my purse and they helped me remove my backpack and blood-stained coat.

"Tomorrow, we will get you some new clothes and a new coat, so that you can go to the airport with clean and proper clothes."

"No," I protested between tears. "These are the only clothes from home that I'm taking with me. My only memories."

"OK, dear – not to worry," his wife said calmly and reassuringly. "We'll wash them out for you. My daughter maybe has some extra shirts that will fit you, just in case you want to take them."

They were so attentive, generous, and kind. They offered to get me a new suitcase full of whatever clothing might fit from their household, and anything else they might be able to find in the day and a half left before my flight, in a war-battered city with few shopping options. But I turned down their offer. If I really was leaving everything behind and starting new, then my clothes might as well be clothes that I picked – not those from another mother who wasn't just murdered.

That night I couldn't sleep at all. The physical pain from my wounds, the emotional trauma of so many horrors in so short a time, and the lingering fear that at any moment, the barbarians just across the backyard from where I was sleeping might suddenly decide to attack Mohammed's house made it impossible for me to close my eyes. I had no way to know if anyone had seen me climbing the fence, and kept imagining the worst-case scenario.

The next day, I spent hours checking all of the usual Twitter and Facebook accounts of local activists, reporters, and neighbors for any more news about what had happened the previous night. It wasn't safe to leave Mohammed's house and calling someone nearby to inquire had its own risks and awkwardness. So checking online was the best option.

Sure enough, that afternoon, I came across the frozen frame of a YouTube link that was an image of what used to be my home. Bracing myself for the worst, I clicked on it – only for the chance to have some closure and learn whatever more could be known about the fate of my parents, my older brother, and Marisol. Like so many other awful videos from the civil war, this one was clearly taken on someone's phone and had that jumpy, grainy, amateur feel to it.

As the footage began to play on my laptop screen, the sound of the cameraman's sadistic glee as he spoke had me fighting the bile that threatened to rise from my stomach. The façade of our home came into view before the camera panned to where my dead dog lay on the front lawn. I swallowed heavily but forced myself to keep watching. I had to. I had to know.

The camera then focused on a bearded man who was laughing and playing with my younger brother's football. The video then panned the yard, stopping and capturing the front door to our house. "Welcome to the Islamic pharmacy center and hotel of Homs!" he announced with a chuckle as he stepped inside, filming the aftermath of the fight that had taken place. There were various cabinets and drawers ajar, most of them empty. Bottles of pills, medications, and other pharmacy materials were scattered about everywhere. Seeing the aftermath on video felt like blades in my chest, as I imagined the struggles that must have caused such destruction.

A voice from afar called out. "Come back here, you didn't show the best part of all."

"Oh, yes! I filmed the Christian dog but forgot to show the retired staff from the hotel and pharmacy," the cameraman replied, with a sickening tone full of delighted sarcasm. He then walked outside where another man added to their evil mockery. "Show them the real Christian dogs," he laughed. "So they know what happens to those who support the infidel regime of Bashar."

My breathing became labored and heat slowly swept across my face. I didn't want to see what they planned to show, for I knew it would be nothing less than the most hideous evil, and I could feel myself about to vomit. But I couldn't bring myself to turn the video off. I had escaped and my family hadn't. I owed it to them at least to find the strength to witness their fate.

Our gate, followed by the fence and spears that topped the finials, came into view as the cameraman walked by, each step that he took mirroring the pounding of my heart within my chest. I knew what was coming – deep down I had no doubt.

Watching with indescribable agony – like a dozen daggers slowly turning in my gut – I saw the video stop and slowly focus in on the heads of my father, mother, brother, and Marisol, each impaled on a spear. That was the last vision I saw of my loved ones before the world turned to black.

Chapter 5: Anissa

∽ Tuesday, February 11, 2014 ∾

To My Dearest,

Writing to you last time was even more emotionally taxing than I expected it to be, and I'm still weary from the effort, but I'm trying to press on with my story. I don't think I will ever have the strength to repeat those details again to anyone else. Somehow, My Dearest, I managed to share with you even more than what I had told my therapist, who had encouraged me to open up to you as much as possible. But it took more strength than you can ever imagine for me to fetch so much of that vile monstrosity from the recesses of my mind. I sobbed the whole time I was writing everything for you, even though I tried to describe each detail as calmly and objectively as possible, so that you could just be there with me, holding the hand of my trembling memory. At times, I had to stop because my hands began to shake uncontrollably and I couldn't type anything on my laptop keyboard. And by the end, my stinging red eyes were bereft of tears – there was simply nothing left to cry out. So I hope you know just how much you mean to me, and what it took me to tell you everything. Besides what little remains of my family in Raqqa, you are all that I have left now, My Dearest. So I am trusting you, and only you, with this horrid secret – if only to feel a little less alone in this world.

There's still so much to cover before I can start to tell you about what is happening now (which is infinitely happier and more normal, and much easier to share), so I'm trying to write to you as much as possible, every day, until we get to the present.

Two days after my entire world was horrifically obliterated, Mohammed drove me to the Damascus International Airport, for my flight to London. Damascus is just a two-hour drive south from Homs, but Mohammed said we had to leave extra early in case of any unexpected problems, checkpoints, or traffic – especially since check-in, security procedures, and border control for international flights meant that I had to arrive two hours early.

About thirty minutes into our drive, Mohammed told me to put on the hijab that his wife had given me, to help remove any suspicions about me. We were getting close to our first checkpoint manned by rebels, he informed me. My hands shook as I fit the headscarf to my head tightly enough to ensure that no hair was showing. A few minutes later, our car was stopped by bearded men with Kalashnikovs, Sunni Islamists, as my father had predicted would happen. My stomach began to churn wildly and fear must have turned me paler than a ghost, as countless horrors from two nights earlier came streaming back into my mind. But I knew that I had to keep my wits about me and act as normally as I could, even though I could feel some nausea building up.

One of the rebels approached Mohammed's side of the car and signaled him to lower the window. I heard some of the rebels behind him joking amongst themselves about how they hadn't killed any Christians or Alawites that night. The man asked for Mohammed's ID and scrutinized it for a moment, before asking him some questions to confirm that he was in fact a Sunni who knew his religion. As I waited nervously in the passenger seat for Mohammed to pass the test, I prayed that they wouldn't ask me for my ID or give me a religious test too, because that would probably be the end of my life.

"Is that your daughter?" the rebel asked him.

"Yes. My mother lives in Saudi Arabia and is very sick. I want my daughter to see her one last time. And, thank you for your brave and tireless efforts to topple this corrupt regime of unbelievers," Mohammed said to the man. "Would you accept a donation towards your efforts?" he asked, offering him about $100 in Syrian pounds. The armed man smiled gratefully.

"Thank you, and go with Allah," the rebel said, letting us proceed on the highway. I exhaled a huge sigh of relief, removed the hijab, and started sobbing while thinking about how my father's foresight and sound instincts had just saved me. Thinking of my father also brought back memories of what happened on that infernal night when he was so savagely taken from me. The horrific flashback and the ever-present danger that followed me as I tried to get to the airport now – where each checkpoint was a potential death crossing – overwhelmed me with a feeling of dizzy nausea. A few minutes later, Mohammed had to stop the car so that I could throw up on the side of the road. He was so understanding, kind, and comforting that I felt ashamed for having ever resisted my father's decision to have him take me to the airport.

We were forced to stop at two more rebel checkpoints along the way, and each time, I put on the headscarf a few minutes before we encountered the men that Mohammed would have to charm and bribe.

But when we were about twenty minutes from the airport, Mohammed advised me not to wear the hijab at the next checkpoint, because it would be run by Syrian troops. I was glad to leave off the headscarf.

Once we reached the checkpoint, the soldier looked at Mohammed's ID and then asked, "You are Sunni?"

"Yes. But I am a real estate developer in Homs and have done work for the Assad family. God bless our president's life and his rule. He has been good to Syria. May God give him the strength to defeat these terrorist rebels – they are destroying our beloved Syria."

The soldier gestured with his gun in my direction. "And who is this girl?"

"She is Christian. Her father also works for the regime, in the National Hospital in Homs, run by the Ministry of Health. He asked me to transport her to the airport because it was too dangerous for him as a Christian."

The soldier nodded in understanding, and waved us through. The rest of the ride was tense but uneventful. Driving into the airport, we were again stopped by members of the Syrian military, and Mohammed gave the same answers.

When I finally walked into the airport, with nothing but my winter coat, my purse, and my carry-on backpack, I finally felt safe. Instead of rebel-manned checkpoints and Islamists, there were regime employees who wouldn't hassle me, and hints of the better life waiting for me overseas: a small coffee shop with magazines for sale, and a relatively quiet and peaceful space.

Panic suddenly struck me again when I went to check in for my flight. The Syrian Air employee kept looking at my passport, flipping through the pages, looking at my photo, and then glancing at me. He scowled at me with suspicion.

"Are you traveling alone?" he finally asked.

I nodded once and tried to respond as calmly as possible. "Yes."

"But you're only sixteen years old. Do you have the necessary documentation?"

"You mean for the Canadian entry?" I clarified meekly.

"Yes, Canadian regulations require us to check these things before issuing a boarding pass. All minors traveling without a parent must have a signed and notarized letter stating the parents' approval of the visit to Canada with the current telephone number and address of the absent parents."

"But I had that letter – it was folded up in my passport," I replied, in alarm.

"I'm sorry, but I looked through your passport a few times and I didn't see any such letter," he explained. "That's why I'm asking you if you have it."

My heart started pounding wildly. Where could that letter have gone? How could some trivial regulation condemn me to the perils of staying in Syria now? Did it somehow get lost while I sprinted through my backyard or climbed the fence to Mohammed's house? I anxiously stood there at the counter, rummaging through my things. My brow furrowed in fear, until I regained hope at the possibility that it fell out of my passport when it was in my purse. Sure enough, that's where I found it. I exhaled deeply and presented it to the airline employee. He unfolded it and read the document.

"OK, this is what I needed," he said. "Don't lose this, because the Canadian border control will ask you for it."

"OK. Is everything fine now?" I asked nervously.

His reply was curt: "No, we're not finished." He flipped through my passport some more and then started talking to his colleagues about the Canadian visa in it.

Finally, he turned to me and asked, "Is this visa to Canada real?"

"Yes, of course it is," I said in annoyed distress. It was as if – after getting this far – some stupid bureaucratic technicality could stop me, and this airline employee was determined to find it. And it wasn't as if I even had an easy way to get back, or anywhere to go, if he found some way to block me at my departure.

"It's just that the Canadian Embassy in Syria officially closed four days ago. They announced that they would no longer be issuing visas as of January 16."

"Yes, but it was processed in Damascus on January 15. My father received it by special courier only on January 18."

He continued to look at me skeptically while his supervisor stood nearby and flipped through my passport.

Were they really going to stop me from taking the flight? It was unthinkable. I had to attack their doubts however I could. "My father has high level connections with Canadian diplomats," I explained. "He emailed me their names and phone numbers, just in case. So if you don't believe me, we can call them right now. I just need to look up their numbers on my phone."

His supervisor looked at me, and then gave a nod of approval to the man who worked for him. Another tremendous sigh of relief. It was over. I would be able to leave Syria.

I checked in to my flight, went through security and border control, and found the gate for my first flight from Damascus to London on Syrian Air. It was my first time flying alone, so I was glad that I had a seven-hour layover, which would give me plenty of time to find my final flight from London to Montreal.

I sat there at the gate for the next ninety minutes, trying to process everything that had happened over the last few days while pondering the countless unknowns waiting for me in the weeks ahead. I spent much of those ninety minutes sobbing – sobbing and thinking.

Chapter 6: Anissa

∞ Wednesday, February 12, 2014 ∞

To My Dearest,

    I arrived in Montreal on the evening of January 21, 2012. I was extremely exhausted, after so much trauma and insomnia over the sudden and horrific murder of my parents, Firaz, Marisol, and Roy. Added to that was the stress of getting to the airport in Damascus, and the international travel – with all of the uncertainties along the way – and the seven-hour time difference. Passing through Canadian border control was again nerve-racking, but the officials seemed very friendly and kind and, in the end, there was no issue with my visa being valid or with the documentation that I carried as an unaccompanied minor.

    The symbolism of clearing Canadian immigration – the last place where I could have been forced to return to the dangers of Syria – overwhelmed me with emotion and I felt tears of relief wetting my cheeks. I had been spared.

    I shuffled past the customs agents, who took no interest in me, and then put my passport and papers back into my purse. After a few more minutes of walking, I stopped before a big sign that said "Welcome to Canada." Other arriving travelers kept moving past me, but I just stood there for a moment. I closed my eyes and thanked God for allowing me to make it out of Syria alive, and then began sobbing at the divine mercy that had saved me. As I wiped away my tears, I trusted that my unlikely survival was part of some greater plan.

    I recomposed myself and resumed my walk towards the international arrivals area of the airport. I prayed that Uncle Tony would be there waiting to pick me up because I had only $300 cash on me and that wouldn't last more than a few days, and I also had no idea how I was supposed to cross the border into the United States without a visa. I figured that, in the worst-case scenario where he didn't show up for some reason, I would need to change money, buy a local SIM card, and try to contact one of my father's connections in Canada. But that would leave me at the mercy of complete strangers in an alien land.

    Fortunately, I was spared that additional hassle and uncertainty because I saw Uncle Tony standing there excitedly among the crowd waiting to see the people arriving. I smiled reflexively, as a weight felt lifted off my shoulders by a familiar face. In his late forties, the hair on top of my uncle's head had thinned out a bit, he had gained a slight potbelly, and his five-foot-ten frame seemed shorter now – probably because I had grown taller since I last saw him. But it was unmistakably Uncle Tony, with his wide grin and jerky gesticulations. Unable to control my overwhelming need for comfort and security, I ran in his direction until I could wrap my arms around him. We hugged for the longest time.

Eventually he pulled away and gave me a puzzled but jocular look, turning his head slightly to inspect the backpack I was wearing.

"What is it, Uncle Tony?"

"I think you just disproved my notions about how females pack when they travel. Is that really all you came with?"

"Yes… It's a long story."

"It must be. OK, well, you'll have to tell me. But let's get you some food first. You're probably starving by now. I drove up here, so I have my car parked nearby."

He took us to a nearby restaurant, where we sat for a few hours talking. First, he asked me to catch him up on all of my siblings – whom he hadn't seen since his last visit to Homs six years earlier. Then we discussed how difficult life had become in my city under the siege, and with sectarian violence raging everywhere across Syria. I skipped over the unspeakable horrors that I had endured, because the memory was too awful, and I didn't have the heart to see Uncle Tony hear these things so soon after picking me up. So I just talked about what a hassle it was to get to the airport and asked him how exactly we were going to get me into the United States without a visa.

"Ah, you have no idea how easy it is. After what you've been through, it's going to feel like a breeze in a lovely, picturesque ride."

"Really?" I said in relieved disbelief.

"Yes. But it's a six-hour drive, so I booked us a hotel stay nearby so you can rest up after such a long trip, and tomorrow we can start fresh. Sound good?"

"Sounds great," I said.

The next morning, we drove for about ninety minutes southwest before reaching a small, unmarked road near lots of farmland. Uncle Tony slowed down to a speed of about fifteen miles per hour.

"Are you ready to be smuggled illegally into the United States from Canada?" he asked with a sudden seriousness that almost scared me, but for his facetious smirk at the end.

"Sure," I said with a hesitant smile.

33

"OK, here we go. We're doing this in broad daylight so be very, very quiet, OK?"

"OK," I replied in amusement. It was so nice just to be with a familiar face and sharing a light moment.

"But I need you to lower your window a little, so that some breeze comes in."

Confused but entertained, I lowered my window a little, so that some of the cold winter air entered the car.

"Good. OK, are you ready to do this?" he asked.

"Ready as I'll ever be, I think."

He stepped on the gas pedal a bit and our speed increased to about twenty-five miles per hour, with the cool air coming in a bit more. After a few minutes, he slowed down again and turned to me.

"Can you believe we made it across?"

"Are you serious?"

"That was a close call, wasn't it? But we made it – give me a high-five!"

I high-fived him and let out a much-needed laugh.

"Welcome to upstate New York. Now put up your window before it gets cold in the car."

Chapter 7: Anissa

∾ Thursday, February 13, 2014 ∾

To My Dearest,

Life with Uncle Tony was good and peaceful. I had my own room in his four-bedroom house in Queens, New York, where he lived with his wife, Christine, and two daughters: Sarah, who was thirteen, and Katrina, who was my age. He wasn't overly strict with me, and quickly realized that trying to control my conduct wasn't even necessary because I had no interest in boys or going out, or any of the other things that are typical of U.S. teen-age girls, including his own daughters. I was what most people would call "a nerd" and wasn't at all bothered by the idea. When my cousin Katrina eventually worked up the nerve to ask if I had ever had sex, I told her that I was proud of my virginity and intended to save it for someone very special – someone worthy of it.

My studies consumed me, not just because I've always loved learning, but also because the pursuit of knowledge for its own sake seemed pure and honest and good, and I no longer knew what else was – apart from Uncle Tony and his household, Mohammed Rajeh and his family, and my surviving relatives in Syria. Of course, there were also the powerful exhortations of my father, the last night I ever saw him, urging me to succeed and not to forget my people in Syria.

The day after I settled into Uncle Tony's home, when I had a moment of privacy, I called my sister, Maria, and Uncle Luke on Skype and told them that my mom, dad, Firaz, Marisol, and Roy were all murdered, but that I had made it out alive. I asked them not to say anything to Uncle Tony because I didn't want to upset him or talk about the event with anyone, even him. Maria also wisely decided that we should keep the truth from our younger brother because his move to Raqqa was already challenging enough for him; she would need to find the right time to ease him into the terrible news.

There weren't many more conversations with people in Syria after those post-arrival calls. On so many levels, speaking to my relatives there was too much for me to handle emotionally. On top of that, there was a certain survivor's guilt that haunted me – particularly because, in the weeks after my arrival in New York, I read news reports about more than eighty percent of the Christians in Homs fleeing. Most were forced to abandon their homes because of armed Islamists who gave them a grim choice: leave Homs or die. This trend only worsened and, by the third week of March, there were an estimated 50,000 Christian refugees forced from their homes, after armed Islamists reportedly went door to door in the Christian neighborhoods of Hamidiya and Bustan al-Diwan, telling homeowners to vacate immediately or be shot. The Islamists then photographed some of their victims' corpses and sent them to Arabic news outlets, claiming that the Syrian government had killed them. Those of my faith who managed to escape in time did so without any of their belongings, desperately fleeing to mountain villages thirty miles outside of Homs; the militants then claimed their homes and possessions as "war-booty from the Christians."

It was horrendous and the world seemed completely indifferent – all of which reinforced my general feelings of weakness and passive vulnerability. So there was little point to following the news out of Syria, or even talking with people who were likely to share it with me. I desperately missed my family, and tried to talk to Maria and Antoun on a regular basis, but each time I did, I was deluged with countless painful memories and a terrible feeling of guilt that I was now safe and they weren't.

I also tried to stay in touch with Mohammed and his family, and made it a point to call them every year at the end of Ramadan to wish them a happy Eid al-Fitr. They truly embodied goodness and generosity – like angels sent to save me in my hour of greatest need. Mohammed had risked everything to keep a promise to my father. He and his family saved not only my life, but also my faith in others. They were always happy to hear from me, and had become like close relatives, which made me feel guilty that I didn't call them more often.

After everything that I had been through and lost in Syria, and given the daily, ongoing traumas there, I eventually recognized that I just needed to disconnect from the place a little – at least long enough to adjust to my new reality and regain a sense of normalcy and confidence. That was the recommendation of my therapist, Monique, whom I saw a few times a week at the insistence of Uncle Tony. My uncle noticed during the first weeks of my stay that I was severely traumatized and depressed, and realized that I needed professional help – especially after I told him about the car accident that killed my parents. I had to invent that fabrication on the spot, when he suggested that we call my parents together on Skype. To help me cope with so many daunting psychological challenges, he recommended Monique, a nice lady in her fifties who had arrived in the United States in 1985, back when she herself had been a Christian refugee from the Lebanese Civil War.

Her similar life experiences and ethnic/religious background – coupled with her doctorate in psychology and her powerful intuition – made Monique uniquely qualified to help me. I felt as if she truly understood me, had my best interests at heart, and knew the steps I needed to follow to improve my emotional state during the difficult adjustment period after my arrival in New York. She advised me to gravitate towards people and activities that could boost my sense of security and self-empowerment, and recommended that I explore a self-defense class. She also encouraged me to start running as a sport.

So I supplemented my disciplined study routine with a focus on both sprinting and distance running, while researching options for a self-defense class that felt comfortable to me. Running seemed to purge my system in an almost meditative way, when I managed to follow Monique's directions. She called it "restorative imagination" and her technique involved healing myself in a way that combined the physical and the mental. When I succeeded at getting into "the zone," the way she instructed, all I could feel was the rhythm of my breath, as the ground below my feet seemed to vanish under my willpower. I imagined the rotten past being sucked out of my inner core, transpired through the pores of my skin, and then later washed off in the shower.

Sprinting on my high school track or in the park also felt like a boost of my defenses – it would get harder and harder for anyone to catch me. As if to confirm that feeling, our biology textbook mentioned how walking on two legs helped early humans flee certain predators more effectively by running. There was also something optimistic about running – the road ahead is a wide-open horizon, and becomes the future you strive for as you dash towards it.

Another technique of "restorative imagination" that Monique gave me was specifically designed to manage my recurring nightmares. I would light a candle and hold the necklace that my mother gave me when we remembered Grandma Marium on my last night at home. I would imagine my grandmother reassuring me, "Don't worry, Sweetie. It will all work out. We have suffered for our faith for thousands of years – going back to when Christians were thrown into the Roman Coliseum." She would then remove from her neck the silver necklace with the Syriac cross and place it gently into the open palm of my mother's hand. Then, with an optimistic sparkle in her eye, she would add, "But we're still here, aren't we?" And then my mother would smile at me, saying "It will all work out, Inās. You come from a long line of survivors and strong women. So everything will be fine in the end. And we are always with you in spirit, to guide you and love you."

If, despite that exercise, I still wasn't able to sleep, I would then imagine myself with my parents on the last night that I saw them. Monique encouraged me to embrace the car accident lie that I had told Uncle Tony because it was a way for me to normalize the death of my parents, Firaz, Marisol, and Roy, since countless people die in vehicle collisions every year. In a hushed voice (so that others outside of my bedroom wouldn't hear), I would beg them aloud not to enter the car, and then I would imagine them listening to me. I would then go back further in time, to one of my happy Christmas memories from before the war, when we were all safely in church and enjoying our time together. With enough practice, that technique eventually helped me to avoid the nightmare most of the time.

My razor-sharp focus on school, running, and self-healing, meant that boys were easily dismissed as an irrelevant distraction. After everything that I had been through, the boys whom I met in the eighteen months that remained of my high school years usually seemed annoyingly immature to me. Every now and then, I had some random interactions with men in their twenties – usually while on the bus, in a store, or getting some pizza – and even they seemed as if they had barely lived compared to what I had been through in my much shorter life. After what I had endured, I felt as if I had aged a good decade, if not more.

The one exception to my disinterest in members of the opposite sex was Michael Kassab, a twenty-six-year-old graduate student whom I found on Facebook. We connected virtually there while I was seeking recommendations for a place that taught self-defense. For my first three months in New York, I avoided all online forums and groups about Syria, Mideast Christians, etc., but towards the end of April, I made an exception just to find out where I could study martial arts with members of my own community. I figured that I'd be more comfortable learning to fend for myself around others who could relate to the experiences that led me to seek out such classes in the first place. And so began my secret crush. I even signed off my messages to him as "Inās" to create a certain cultural familiarity with him, since it was clear from his posts that he was fluent in Arabic.

Everything about Michael fascinated me and drew me in closer, even as he kept me at a distance. In fact, his tendency to break off our chats well before I wanted to sometimes drove me crazy. I would stalk his Facebook page and just marvel at the man – his smoldering good looks, his strength of character, his inspiring vision, and his bold leadership powers. He would have attracted me, even without his handsomeness, after I saw the cogent articles he wrote and published, the photos of political rallies that he led and organized, and the breadth of knowledge he displayed in his posts. But in his posted pictures, I would stare at his powerful, scruffy jawbone; his dark, Middle Eastern features; his piercingly intense brown eyes; and what I could see of his impeccably sculpted body, which attested to his fitness addiction and martial arts routine.

He was earning his Ph.D. in Political Science and Middle East History at Columbia University. So our chats were always enlightening and planted the seed of Mideast Christian power and self-determination in my mind. From his assertive boldness when it came to his identity, I could scarcely recognize that he was a Syrian Christian. While my own father and older brother were both strong men who stood up for our community, they still operated from the mindset of a vulnerable minority. Michael had this abundant strength to him that made anything seem possible for our people. I remembered that there was something very special about the name "Michael" in the Bible. So I went back to research it, and what I found only reinforced his mystique: "Michael" means "who is like God" in Hebrew and, in the Book of Revelation, Michael leads God's armies against Satan's forces during the war in heaven, and ultimately defeats Satan.

He also opened my eyes to countless things – including what an amazing country the United States is. Where else could I find a martial arts school owned and run by a Syrian, an Egyptian, and an Iraqi teaching an Israeli martial art? Granted, they were all Christian (which was exactly what I sought out in this case) but Michael assured me that, if I wanted to, I could just as easily find examples of multi-religious businesses, schools, organizations, etc. Indeed, New York City fascinated me with its cosmopolitan variety – it seemed like every language, ethnicity, creed, race, ideology, profession, philosophy, political persuasion, and combination thereof was miraculously crammed into the same tiny space, and yet somehow everyone seemed to get along.

But I digress. Michael told me to go to his cousin's martial arts school, where he used to train before moving for his studies to the Morningside Heights area of Columbia University (where he continued his training with a student club). Owned and managed by Kassab (Michael's Syrian-American cousin), Moshi (an Iraqi Christian), and Saad (an Egyptian Copt), the KMS School of Martial Arts was based in Brooklyn. When I went to see them, they recommended that I start with an introductory course to Krav Maga, mostly because it was a relatively simple combat system that could work for just about anyone (since all Israeli conscripts had to have some basic training in it). But KMS also taught many other styles, and I ended up training more in Brazilian Jiu-Jitsu and Muay Thai.

As a result of my experiences in Syria, I tended to dichotomize the world's men into two categories: those like my father, uncles, older brother, and Mohammed Rajeh, and all other men. Either you were a good man who could be trusted, or you weren't. And since nearly all of the violence, brutality, and sheer evil that I had witnessed and directly experienced in Syria were perpetrated by men, I tended to distrust men I didn't already know through family or friends. But Michael and the owners of KMS established early on that they belonged to the class of men like my father and Mohammed.

Absurdly enough, my interactions with Michael never left Facebook – presumably because he knew that I was still in high school and ten years younger than him. I also thought he had a girlfriend – just based on the fact that I always saw this one very pretty woman, who was also a Columbia University student, constantly interacting with his posts, leaving her likes and comments almost every time he posted, and he would sometimes do the same to her posts – more than he did with any other woman's posts.

Paradoxically, the more Michael kept me at a distance, the more I trusted him – perhaps because he was always willing to help me with tips and introductions even though he wanted absolutely nothing from me (and never reciprocated my nosiness with personal questions of his own about me). It's bewildering to me how you can just start chatting with a complete stranger on Facebook, and – next thing you know – it seems as if there's some intense connection with the person – or at least you feel that closeness and hope it's mutual. Maybe it's the immediacy of these online chats and other interactions, combined with my deep loneliness and surprised excitement at discovering a new and fascinating person. But then, in the case of Michael, when he wouldn't show any interest in me, I started to think that this whole "connection" was just in my head. I mean, we had never even met and I had no idea how we'd really get along in person or whether we'd feel any special chemistry… But I still found myself daydreaming about him on study breaks or while riding the bus. Maybe it was just a welcome escape from my otherwise intense daily routine of studies and physical training. Or maybe I was just excited and relieved to know – for the first time in my life – that I could feel this way about a man.

In general, my life in New York was filled with a forlorn emptiness and personal struggle to move on from the past. Around the end of 2012, Monique advised me to stop trying to maintain my Facebook relationship with Michael. That was supposed to be my New Year's resolution of sorts, after I finally acknowledged that this unrequited infatuation with an unattainable man was just reinforcing my dejected loneliness. But it took me another six weeks to implement the decision. And as hard as it seemed at the time to cut Michael off completely, May 13, 2012, the day I turned seventeen, was infinitely worse.

My birthday felt irredeemably sorrowful without my parents or siblings there, and I became terribly depressed. The same thing happened on Christmas and New Year's, about half a year later. I felt utterly alone in the world. The people who had been there with me through all of my most important moments – of joy, pain, pride, sadness, and countless other emotions – were now either dead or too far away to see any time soon.

Nothing felt the same any more, and a suicidal despair would often stalk me mercilessly. But the one thing that kept me from stepping over the precipice each time was the powerful memory of my father's impassioned plea on the last night I saw him. He would have lost all respect for me had I taken my own life, when so many others – far less fortunate than me – were suffering through so much more, praying for the day when someone with my opportunities could somehow help them. So I stayed. Because killing myself would be the easy way out, and would selfishly fail those desperate souls in my community who were counting on someone like me to give them hope. I overcame the urge to leave this world, even though there often seemed nothing left to live for. I continued to endure the most horrific nightmares that woke me up in gasps of terror almost every night of my first year in New York. Even during the day, at the most random moments, I had visions of the horrors that took my parents and older brother.

My therapy sessions with Monique, and the various techniques she prescribed, were critical to maintaining my sanity through all of this. Over time, she managed to improve my mood, outlook, and sleep, but it was clear that it would take years for my wounds to heal – especially because the situation in Syria only deteriorated with each month. Sadness from the daily tragedies in Syria had this way of popping back into my life, no matter how much I tried to hide from them.

For example, in late October, just as I was in an unusually stable frame of mind and trying to embrace the relative fun and silliness of Halloween, news from Syria showed up while I was on the Internet. I learned that the last remaining Christian in the center of Homs had been killed. An eighty-five-year-old, Greek Orthodox Christian refused to leave his home because he had to take care of his handicapped son, even though he knew that his life was in danger. The circumstances and self-sacrifice that led him to stay in Homs – despite so much danger to a man of his age – struck me as horribly tragic. But what really upset me was the symbolism of this tragedy: our community in the center of Homs was reduced to these two poor souls, and now they too were gone. After reading that, there was no hope of trying to partake in any Halloween festivities.

I also continued to worry about what was left of my family in Syria. My younger brother and older sister were staying with Uncle Luke and his family in Raqqa, and the situation there seemed to deteriorate every time I could bring myself to call them. The northern city's population had quadrupled to over a million by early 2013 – overwhelmed by the influx of refugees forced to flee the violence in other parts of Syria. Uncle Tony, who hadn't lived in Syria for decades, didn't react nearly as strongly as I did to the bad news coming out of our home country. So he usually stayed much more current than I did and would sometimes fill me in on anything that he thought was particularly important. In early March 2013, he told me that there had been heavy fighting in Raqqa, so I immediately called my sister for more details. She told me how the city was overrun by rebels. After days of fierce fighting between the rebels and regime troops, the insurgents had acquired near-total control of the city – marking the first time in the two-year conflict that the rebels held a provincial capital. Soon afterwards, anti-regime activists released amateur video footage of people destroying the city's statue of late President Hafez al-Assad (Bashar's father) – a powerful symbol of how the government had indeed lost control of the city.

When I spoke to my sister again in mid-May 2013, she told me how the al-Qaeda-affiliated al-Nusra Front brought in a radical cleric from Egypt to set up a sharia court in the city's new sports center. By all accounts, he was also now preaching at Friday prayers, which would only fuel the rise of extremism among Sunni Muslims in the city. There were also recent reports that Islamist thugs had ravaged one of the two shops that sold alcohol. The black flag of al-Qaeda now flew over Raqqa's main square in front of the governor's palace, with its former occupant now in prison. Adding to all of the chaos, there was an active rivalry between al-Nusra Front and another – even more extreme and barbaric – rebel group, known as the Islamic State of Iraq and Syria (or "ISIS").

My sister was in tears for most of that Skype call in May. "There can be no music in a place like this," Maria whimpered, recognizing that her dream of a musical career belonged to a more peaceful era that had irretrievably slipped away. The whole idea of a life devoted to music seemed laughably quixotic in a society where even one's basic dress was strictly monitored and regimented under the threat of public lashings.

"How is Antoun holding up with all of this?"

"He can't even play football any more – Uncle Luke is too afraid to have him playing outside of the house."

"This is all so awful," I said, once again feeling that terrible helplessness that I had felt so many times during my last year in Syria.

"It will only get worse," she warned. "Now they have steady sources of income and can pay salaries. They control the city's main flour mill, so they supply bakeries, and have even seized a few. At night, you can see long queues of women waiting to buy their daily ration under the strict eyes of al-Nusra guards. And they have taken the oilfields in the neighboring Deir al-Zour province and sell the oil to the local market, which also helps to keep them well funded."

"Can't Uncle Luke move somewhere else? Maybe Damascus?"

"No, it's too dangerous and complicated with so many people in his household, plus Antoun and me. And he still has a medical device import business to run here. If he leaves, then he will lose that, and his home, and everything else. And where would we all go? Who will take in so many people? All of his extended family and in-laws are already hosting more immediate relatives who became refugees in the last year – and it's not always that much safer where they are. So this is the best we can do for now. We just have to pray that somehow things get better.

Maybe the world will wake up and resist this evil cancer that is spreading across our beloved country."

But of course, things didn't get better. They got only worse, which made it increasingly difficult to stay in touch with my relatives in Raqqa. Our talks were always full of crying, anxiety, and despair.

Chapter 8: Anissa

∽ Friday, February 14, 2014 ∾

To My Dearest,

    Happy Valentine's Day! Tonight I actually have a date with my longtime crush – and I even seem to be developing an interest in someone else in recent weeks. Thus, as you can imagine, I'm getting really impatient to tell you about everything that's been happening to me in the last few weeks – maybe because I'm generally starved for happy news and "normal" kinds of life excitement.

    So I'm going to cover my last year of high school (from September 2012 to June 2013) with far less description – especially because the time between my arrival in Montreal and when I started college wasn't that interesting (at least not to me). And my senior year – as far as I was concerned – was mostly about getting into college, and then preparing for it. So I'll just summarize the highlights that come to mind now, as I write this to you.

    My academic performance in the United States was substantially enabled by the excellent education that my parents had worked so hard for me to receive in Syria. I was grateful to have studied English for all of my schooling there and virtually nobody in the United States could guess from the way I spoke or wrote that I had arrived in the country for the first time only recently. Since my arrival in New York, I used the language so much that it began to feel like my native tongue. By the end of my first full year in the United States, I even began to count and dream in English (unless I was dreaming about Syria, in which case the dream was in Arabic). But despite my fluency in English, there was one thing that powerfully separated me from everyone else in high school: my "refugee reality." I could barely relate to many of my classmates, who were often caught up in high school dating dramas, drug and alcohol experimentation, celebrity gossip, professional sports news, the latest fashions, and other such trivialities that preoccupy teenagers enjoying a relatively pampered and safe life – especially the ones suffering from "senioritis."

    Even the more serious students who were ambitious about their futures and getting into college still understood nothing about the madness I had fled. But it was probably those very horrors that led me to take my studies more seriously than even the most competitive honor students – maybe because my education was what my parents had so wanted for me and what was most tied to my future. My schoolwork also provided a hopeful escape from my past (along with running and martial arts).

Uncle Tony lived in a relatively suburban part of Queens – almost an hour from Manhattan by subway – so many students in my high school eagerly wanted driving lessons and a car, and most thought it was odd that I resisted the idea. When one of my teachers heard about my aversion to driving and then asked me about it privately, I shared with her my made-up story that my parents and brother were killed in a car crash – an event that had tainted my view of cars and driving. In therapy, Monique also tried to address my driving phobia, but I insisted that there were more pressing issues – like my general distrust of men. Monique's theory about my unrealistic crush on Michael was that I was purposely pursuing someone I knew I couldn't have, so that I'd never have to deal with my fear of men. But I maintained that there just wasn't anyone for me in high school and that I was still open to the possibility of meeting a more attainable version of Michael in college.

Indeed, the prospect of meeting more serious, mature, and accomplished men only reinforced my already high motivation to get into a top college. And in the end, my driving-free, ascetic lifestyle of rigorous studies and athletic training paid off. I graduated with a 4.0 grade point average (GPA), won a track medal in the New York State Track & Field Championships my senior year, scored in the top 1% on my SAT college admission exam, and was admitted to every school where I applied: Stanford, MIT, Harvard, Columbia, Yale, Princeton, University of Pennsylvania, and NYU. I was also admitted to a few "safety schools" that were public, and much less expensive. There were plenty of students whose academic record was just as good as mine was, but who were still rejected by some of those schools, so I suspect that my background and life story may have also helped. I wrote an emotional essay about my refugee experience and the American Dream. My application made it powerfully evident to each admissions committee that it was deciding my future like no other group of people could.

There was a bittersweet joy each time I read a new college admissions offer, because it reminded me of the promise that I had made to my parents. While the accomplishment seemed almost hollow in their absence, I felt their spirits looking down at me, acknowledging that I had reached an important milestone in keeping my word to them. Indeed, every offer felt as if it should have been addressed to Dr. and Mrs. Youssef Toma – because it was for them that I had made this dream come true, and they would have been proudest of its realization.

When deciding which college to attend, I wanted to remain as close as possible to New York because I preferred to stay near Uncle Tony and, more generally, was falling in love with my new city. But to honor my father's wishes for me, and to give myself as many future opportunities as possible, I also wanted to attend the best university I could. So I was torn between Yale, Harvard, and Columbia. In the end, Columbia gave me a full merit scholarship, so that – coupled with the fact that it was in New York – made the decision for me (I tried to convince myself that Michael being a student there was not at all a factor!). The full merit scholarship was crucial to me. Now that I had no parents to send more money after the first $10,000 ran out, I would need that kind of assistance even more. And I could actually save that money from my father for my younger brother's college education (in about five years), if he ended up leaving Syria and joining me.

Once I sent in my acceptance of Columbia's offer, a certain closure let me breathe a bit easier for the rest of high school. But – despite my relief about the next phase of my life being settled – I still wasn't partying like some of the other seniors in my honors classes. They considered an Ivy League acceptance to be the informal end of high school. But unlike them, I felt as if I had made it onto the Olympic team, which meant that I now had to train even harder to take full advantage of this special opportunity and hopefully win a medal. So my attention soon turned to "college prep" concerns: doing what I could to excel in college and trying to figure out what my academic focus would be. There were so many things that I wanted to study – each for a very different reason. Economics interested me because I wanted to understand money and wealth, and because it seemed to be a gateway to the lucrative finance jobs – all of which could better position me eventually to help my people. Psychology also intrigued me – primarily because of my deep desire to understand both my own psychological wounds and the psychopathic hatred that inflicted them upon me and so many members of my community. But I was just as drawn to political science and Middle East history – mainly because a command of those subjects might enable me someday to advocate for my community through journalism and/or politics.

Ironically, judging from how my second college semester has gone thus far, I will probably end up spending my first year deliberating far more over which man to choose, than over which major to pick. Anyway, I have to get ready for my Valentine's Day date now. See you very soon!

Chapter 9: Anissa

∾ Saturday, February 15, 2014 ∾

To My Dearest,

    Yesterday I had my Valentine's Day date and I'm dying to jump into the heart of the matter (literally) and tell you all about it! But I still need to summarize for you my first semester of college at Columbia University, just to set the stage for all of the latest developments in my life.

    My first college term – which began with the New Student Orientation Program (last August) – was a positive experience overall. I continued to benefit from therapy sessions with Monique, but only once every two weeks because of the greater distances involved (now that I was living on campus) and my rigorous study schedule, which still included some running and martial arts training.

    When applying for my first-year housing, I wanted a hall that was comprised mostly of first-year students but that offered single rooms. I wasn't comfortable with having a stranger for a roommate – mostly because I didn't want someone else to see my pre-bed ritual, holding my necklace in front of a candle, and sometimes also whispering to my parents aloud not to enter their car. Such moments were too personal and potentially embarrassing to be shared with anyone. I explained all of this in my housing application and I guess it helped, because the housing administrators gave me my top choice: my very own room in Furnald Hall, on a floor with only female students on it. The rooms are arranged in a corridor along the halls, and the building is generally well kept and quiet, facing the South Lawn of the main campus. In some ways, the student residence felt more like a hotel – judging from the only one that I had ever stayed in (in Montreal, with Uncle Tony). The entrance to Furnald was inside the campus, near Broadway and 115th Street, with easy access to Butler Library, where I did most of my studying.

    My first semester I had a relatively heavy course load because I wanted to stay focused on school while satisfying as many of my graduation requirements as possible. I took University Writing, the first semester of Masterpieces of Western Literature and Philosophy, Frontiers of Science, and the History of the Modern Middle East. For the first of the two required Physical Education courses, I took Judo, which I had always wanted to learn. And I passed the swimming test required for graduation about a month into the semester.

The students I met impressed me – they were very well read, intelligent, and generally motivated – and the professors I encountered were brilliant and inspiring on many levels. The campus culture was full of vibrant debate and stimulating diversity – a marvelous mix of ideas, perspectives, and experiences that all came together to clash, yet coexist, in one special place. Indeed, the neoclassical architecture of the enclosed space spanning from Butler Library to Low Library, the verdant lawns and trees inside, and the pensive-looking sculptures placed throughout the area – all offered an almost surreal serenity relative to the big city bustle of Manhattan just outside the gates of College Walk on 116th Street.

But my dark past still haunted me and made it difficult to embrace certain aspects of college life – especially "Greek life" and the whole fraternity and sorority party culture. It all just seemed like senseless debauchery – young people getting drunk out of boredom, or to add some artificial drama or interest to their lives. And the values surrounding the norms of dating were so different from what I was used to in Syria, where sex between unmarried men and women was taken much more seriously. Couples that had sex outside of marriage normally hid such events in a conservative society where a woman's reputation was everything. But in college, with so much booze everywhere, students had sex as casually and easily as people shaking hands, and often shared details or even images or video from their escapades. Sexual relations also rarely implied exclusivity because – far from their parents for the first time – many of my classmates were suddenly proud to be "liberated" or "exploring."

I also heard that a surprisingly large number of female college students were paying for school by "seeking arrangements" with older men whom they met online. The tough economy meant that their parents were able to help them less, and there were fewer student jobs available for them to take. So I actually felt sorry for girls like that, especially because desperation might have forced me to resort to similar solutions, had I received no scholarship and then failed to find a job.

But I could neither respect nor understand the unabashed gold-diggers – the girls whose whole life plan seemed to be the seduction of an older man whom they could marry primarily as an economic arrangement. These girls would dress to look older, wealthier, and more sophisticated, and go to certain bars and hotels that very wealthy men were known to frequent. The whole concept was distasteful to me: fawning after some man they don't particularly like, just because he buys them nice gifts, takes them to nice dinners, and maybe – in forty years – could leave them all of his money. That's like being sentenced to forty years in a golden cage. Isn't it better just to make your own money, and then spend it how and when you want, and with dignity?

Beyond the cultural differences that reminded me how much I was still an alien in so many ways, the horrendous news from Syria – which I tried to avoid my first semester – disconnected me from my classmates more than anything else, whenever it happened to reach me. With a timing that was curiously similar to the year before, the worst incident happened around Halloween of my first semester.

But even before that, towards the end of September, Maria told me on Skype about the latest developments in Raqqa. Jihadist rebels burned two Catholic churches in the city, and I again worried for her safety and the rest of my family there. ISIS fighters entered Our Lady of the Annunciation Greek Catholic Church, destroyed sacred icons and church furniture, and removed the cross from the church. Activists in the city demonstrated against such bigoted vandalism, and carried the cross back to the church, but this prompted deadly threats against the woman who led the protest, and she was forced to flee the city for her safety.

Armed Islamists repeated the same crimes at the Holy Martyrs Armenian Catholic Church, where they destroyed the cross on the clock tower and replaced it with their al-Qaeda flag. As their rampage continued, they reportedly decimated Shiite mosques and Christian churches, summarily executed Alawites, and kidnapped priests and bishops.

Even had I not spoken to my sister about the situation in Raqqa, I would have surely had Syria on my mind anyway, because around that time, it was all over the news as the U.N. Security Council debated how to remove Assad's chemical weapons arsenal – a move I fully supported. Such horrific weapons cannot be left in the hands of illegitimate governments – especially when they could be toppled at any moment by extremists. Assad's army had already committed countless atrocities, but gassing hundreds, maybe thousands of civilians – like the chemical attack last summer on the Ghouta suburbs around Damascus – brought his war crimes to a new level of outrage. Whatever protection he may have offered to Christians and other religious minorities – just to strengthen his grip on power – and however more secular and rational his regime might be relative to the fanatics trying to overthrow him, nothing could justify his use of chemical weapons on innocent Syrian civilians. Not only was it morally reprehensible, but it would only make the rebels fighting him that much more bloodthirsty. And if they ever got their hands on those same weapons, I can't even imagine the kind of bloodbath that would ensue. So I was all for their removal.

Then, in late October, Uncle Tony emailed me some articles from Christian and Syrian news sites. I often ignored his emailed news updates precisely because they would distract and depress me. But this time I clicked on some of the article links and read a report about forced conversions to Islam, churches being desecrated, and clergy being abducted throughout my hometown province. Another article described how a large number of Christians were forced from their homes and farms in villages in the Homs area.

Islamist militias invaded and occupied the Christian town of Sadad around the third week of October. For one week, as battles between jihadi insurgents and the Syrian regime raged on, the Islamists held 1,500 families, including children, women, and the elderly, as hostages and human shields. Some Sadad residents managed to flee on foot for about five miles to al-Hafer to find refuge. About 2,500 other families escaped with only their clothes, and became refugees scattered throughout Damascus, Homs, and other areas.

The Syrian Army recaptured the town about a week later, enabling Christians who had fled the terror to return. To their shock, they found two mass graves filled with dozens of corpses – the bodies of their relatives and friends. According to eyewitnesses, forty-five civilians, including women and children, were killed by militia gangs of the al-Nusra Front and ISIS, and then dumped into mass graves.

I read that Sadad is an ancient Syriac village located in the region of Qalamoon, north of Damascus. It dates back to 2000 B.C. and has fourteen churches, a monastery, temples, historic landmarks, and archaeological sites. But most were damaged or desecrated, including the Syriac Orthodox Church of Saint Theodore, where some of the militants took cover during battles with the Syrian Army.

Upon returning to the ravaged city, the Syriac Orthodox Archbishop of Homs reported that there was no electricity, water, or phone service; houses were looted; and churches were damaged and desecrated, with their old books and precious furniture taken or destroyed. Schools, government buildings, and the hospital were all destroyed. He called what happened in Sadad the biggest massacre of Christians in Syria and the second largest in the Middle East, after the Iraqi one in 2010, when an al-Qaeda-linked Sunni group, the Islamic State of Iraq, attacked the Church of Our Lady of Salvation with a mass shooting that killed about sixty people, including scores of worshippers.

Some web sites tried to explain these attacks by suggesting that Sadad and other targeted villages quietly supported the regime. Other reports indicated that, while there were residents on each side of the conflict, most were neutral and just wanted peace and quiet. But jihadists apparently didn't care about such nuances. They harassed all Christians in their path of conquest and destruction, and preyed on women in particular. According to news reports, jihadists regarded Christian women as their right and would touch and molest them on the streets. Some were with the al-Nusra Front terrorist organization, and others were foreign Islamists who had flocked to Syria from North Africa, Europe, and other places. There were accounts of jihadis who had kidnapped, gang-raped, and then killed some Christian women, leading many families to flee their villages for fear that their daughters would be next.

And through all of this evil, the world stayed silent and everything went on as usual, as if nothing wicked and barbaric were afoot. I saw no world leaders discussing the issue, and no major protests on campus or anywhere else in the city, except those organized by the Mideast Christian Association (MCA) – the nonprofit that Michael had founded and was actively growing just before I stopped chatting with him last February. How could everyone else remain silent? Maybe because these horrors weren't even reported by the mainstream media. Most of the planet doesn't follow the Middle East and Christian news sites or social media activists who cover such atrocities, so they can't really be blamed for not speaking up. But unfortunately, the ignorant silence of the masses enables the hateful slaughter of vulnerable minorities to continue. And what about the world's two billion Christians? Surely, some of them must have read these awful reports. Why didn't more of them at least try to raise awareness among other Christians and the rest of the world?

All of this weighed on my mind as everyone else was running around frolicking for October 31. While students in silly outfits and disguises were out reveling in Halloween parties, I was in absolute anguish, reliving nightmarish memories and feeling guilty about not doing anything to help. I began to resent all of the boisterous, party-going students in costumes, even though I knew that it was obviously not their fault for having happy, carefree lives. I just wished I didn't have to be so exposed to their mindless mirth just as I was hearing this gut-wrenching news out of my home country.

After Halloween, I was more tempted than ever to reach out to Michael, even though I had managed to avoid him for about eight months. While we were now on the same campus and I was a bit older, I assumed that he would still be as unattainable as ever, even in the unlikely scenario that he didn't have a girlfriend. I also worried that he would suggest that I get involved in the MCA. After everything that had happened in Syria around Halloween 2013, I was actually quite eager to become active in a group like the MCA – especially because they were the only group on campus trying to raise awareness with protests and other activities. But I also feared that such an organization – and meeting Michael – would quickly monopolize all of my time and attention, before I even had a chance to prove to myself that I could excel in college. I wanted to have at least one semester of top grades before branching out into extracurricular activities – whether it was the MCA or meeting Michael.

So instead, I messaged him again on Facebook in a way that allowed me to maintain my intense focus on what I considered my most important semester – the one that would give me the academic confidence I needed for the remainder of my college career. Here's what I wrote to him (in early November):

Hi Michael,
I know we haven't been in touch in about eight months and I actually wasn't planning on contacting you before the start of spring semester, but the recent massacre in Sadad really affected me. I'm sure you heard the news, and I hope you don't have any family or friends who were in some way affected by the savage rampage through that town (or other areas recently overrun by Islamists).

I feel terribly guilty that I haven't been involved in the cause of protecting and helping our community, but I just need to get through my first semester of college. A successful first term should be enough for me to get the hang of things here and feel more confident about participating in non-academic activities – especially ones that will have a powerful emotional impact on me. I really want you to know how much I appreciate the work that you and the MCA have been doing, and I hope to join your efforts early next year.

In the meantime, I have a simple question for you: how do you get other people to care about the Syrian Christians being victimized by violent Islamists every day? The number of atrocities only seems to increase with time, yet most people still appear to be ignorant or indifferent. What do you say or do to make others care?

Inās

As I suspected would happen, I experienced a bit too much excitement each time there was a notification about a new message waiting for me, and – when it wasn't from him – the wait for his reply started to become torturous. But a week later, he finally sent me this reply:

Hi Inās,

Thanks for your message and for your deep concern, which I of course share. History shows that the battle for a just cause all too often involves a struggle against the ignorance or indifference of the masses.

This unfortunate fact was poignantly captured in a poem by Pastor Martin Niemöller (1892–1984), who wrote about the cowardice of German intellectuals following the Nazis' rise to power. So whenever I need to rouse to action those who think that this issue is not theirs, I often send them his poem. You may want to do so as well, when you encounter those who don't know or don't care. Here is his poem:

First they came for the Socialists, and I did not speak out—
Because I was not a Socialist.
Then they came for the Trade Unionists, and I did not speak out—
Because I was not a Trade Unionist.
Then they came for the Jews, and I did not speak out—
Because I was not a Jew.
Then they came for me—and there was no one left to speak out for me.

His words poignantly capture the risk of apathy, so I hope that they help you to combat it. Best of luck with the rest of your fall term, and I hope to see you at an MCA meeting next semester.

Michael

Reading the poem Michael shared with me sent chills up my spine – especially because it is so relevant to what is happening today in the Middle East, with totalitarian Islamists who murder anyone who dares to think or pray differently.

Even the offshoots of Islam, like the Alawites, are at the mercy of these evil thugs. The fanatical Sunni extremists will determine someone's religious identity by asking the person to recite a certain prayer. So in a moment of terror, looking at the barrel of a gun, an Alawite is compelled to pray the only way that he knows how to, and – the moment he has failed to say the Sunni Muslim prayer that will save his life – he has been marked for torture and death. So these barbarians are literally discriminating based on what is in a person's mind or heart – not on race, language, ethnicity, or anything else. Therefore, they represent the end of free thought, and that should rouse everyone in the civilized world to action. And yet it doesn't.

I was skeptical that this German poem would ultimately help much because the fact that world powers had allowed such horrific cruelty to go on for so long suggested a more disappointing truth about human nature: the lessons of history are rarely taken to heart – including when it really matters. Or maybe the real problem with human nature is not our failure to learn history as much as it is our tendency to shy away from it. Even with the Holocaust, it took the death of six million Jews and several million others before the world was finally united enough to confront and defeat the Nazi terror that had swept across Europe. And the Holocaust was itself a repetition of the Armenian Christian genocide that happened not even three decades earlier, when world powers again cowered from history until it was too late. Hitler himself was clearly aware of how forgetful and fearful world powers were: after achieving total domination of Germany, Hitler decided to conquer Poland in 1939 and famously told his generals, "Who still talks nowadays about the Armenians?"

Indeed, when I think about these things on a psychological level, I don't really blame anyone for failing to act against a seemingly remote threat – humans are naturally inclined to choose the path that seems easiest and safest. Last summer, while I was studying some textbooks on my own, to prepare for college, I read a little about decision theory and the psychological phenomenon of "loss aversion," which refers to people's strong tendency to choose the avoidance of losses over the acquisition of gains. I found the concept and the related experiments fascinating. Loss aversion was first demonstrated by Amos Tversky and Daniel Kahneman. In 2002, Kahneman received the Nobel Prize in Economics for the work he did with Tversky. Incidentally, it seems unfair that Tversky didn't share the honor only because he died in 1996 and the prize is not awarded posthumously… But I digress.

The insight of their work boils down to this: something in human nature makes us experience greater "pain" at the loss of $100 than the amount of "pleasure" we experience by winning $100. And obviously for military battles on faraway continents, there is far more to be lost than gained. So it's no surprise that the United States would avoid spending so much money and risking so many lives to fight a relatively remote threat overseas, whether it's the Nazis murdering Jews and Gypsies in Europe, or Sunni Islamists murdering Christians and Alawites in Syria. World powers that consider a threat to be distant and/or minor will not be moved to stop that menace until it becomes sufficiently serious and imminent – a very human inclination, but one that condemns countless innocent people to suffering and death along the way.

Wow. I just realized that I still haven't arrived at the potentially romantic developments that I was so excited to share. But if I don't stop writing now I'm going to collapse on my laptop from fatigue and will end up cheating you out of some important details, so I have to stop here… But I promise to continue as soon as I finish with some of the studying I have planned for tomorrow. And the good news is that you're just about caught up to what's happening right now!

Chapter 10: Anissa

∽ Sunday, February 16, 2014 ∾

To My Dearest,

I am extremely tempted to tell you about my Valentine's date two nights ago, but I'm still processing how it went and what it all means, so I'm not quite ready to share my thoughts about it. And there are still some key background details that you need, in order to understand all of the subtleties involved.

So I'm going to continue filling you in on the recent past. But now it's the very recent past because there really isn't much to tell you about the rest of my semester. After what I shared with you about Halloween and the messages exchanged with Michael, I resumed my intense academic focus. My very first college final exams were just before Christmas and quite stressful – mostly because I didn't know what to expect and became obsessively concerned with performing well. Well, to my immense delight and relief, I actually got an A in all five of my classes! And I enrolled in a slightly lighter course load for my spring semester: Psychology and Markets, the second semester of Masterpieces of Western Literature and Philosophy, Economics, Introduction to American Government and Politics, and Karate (to finish my physical education requirement).

My fall semester results left me much more confident about my ability to excel in college. After basking in the satisfaction of seeing my hard work pay off, I thought about how I could either maintain the same level of focused intensity and try to graduate valedictorian, or relax a little and diversify my collegiate experience, even if it meant getting slightly lower grades. I quickly realized, during winter break, that I was going to be opting for the latter option. I had been depriving myself for too long of two things that I really wanted to do: meet Michael, and get more politically involved in efforts to help my surviving family and my persecuted and beleaguered community in Syria. If that meant that my cumulative GPA for my first year would drop from a 4.0 to a 3.7, then so be it. I could always reprioritize next year, as needed. My therapist also helped me realize that I've been fixated on my grades to a fault – partly as an escape – and now that I'm off to such a good academic start, I really need to turn my attention to some of the more important things that I've been neglecting.

So now, let me tell you about an exciting moment that I have impatiently awaited for a very long time.

There really could not have been any more nervous anticipation preceding my meeting with Michael. My Facebook privacy settings allowed virtually no one to see my photos and – as if to further confirm that he wasn't romantically interested in me – he never once asked me to send him any pictures of myself during the year or so that we were chatting there. So I had no idea if he would even find me remotely attractive. I was also a bit self-conscious about how much more he knew about Mideast history and current events than I did.

For all of these reasons, I wanted to meet him under the most casual circumstances possible – with no hint of a date or any interest on my part. The most natural way to do that was to attend the rally that he had scheduled for the MCA on the very first day of spring-semester classes.

So, on Tuesday, January 21, 2014, I met Michael Kassab in person for the first time, after he confirmed that he was not going to cancel the rally because of the snowstorm in New York that day. The email that he sent out earlier that morning, confirming the rally, asked simply: "Should a foot of snow stop us when so many of our brothers and sisters must endure far worse winter conditions without basic heating in their homes? I'll see you on College Walk at 4 p.m."

I saw him standing on the College Walk sundial, with a wool winter cap pulled snugly over his head and ears, speaking passionately into a megaphone in front of a crowd of about ten people, as snowflakes fell all around us. Most of the people gathered there looked like they were Christians from the Middle East, judging from their generally dark features, the bits of Arabic that I heard here and there, and the crucifix necklaces that many proudly displayed over their winter sweaters. Some were holding placards that read, "Stop the Genocide of Christians" or "Your Silence is Killing Us."

Michael looked like he was on fire when he addressed the small crowd. His bold voice and message boomed throughout the campus, shaming the university community for its apathy. "How many of our women must be abducted and raped before you join us at this rally? How many of our priests must be beheaded before you write to Congress and demand military intervention?" His eloquent ardor and unwavering conviction commanded the attention of anyone who walked by. There was something incandescent about this naturally compelling leader, and no passerby could ignore him, even in the middle of a blizzard. "How many of our dead children must be thrown into ditches before you care enough to take action? How many?" he asked rhetorically.

After he finished, a few more people spoke into the megaphone, while some of those gathered in the crowd – including me – tried to solicit signatures and donations from anyone passing by in the freezing cold. With anyone else leading the rally on the day of a snowstorm, I doubt even three people would have shown up, much less stayed and tried to gather support for as long as they did. But under Michael's leadership, everything seemed different. He had a way of inspiring everyone and ensuring that morale remained as high as possible.

And then something embarrassing happened – especially because Michael was nearby, watching the entire incident. I saw this older man, probably in his mid-thirties, walking in my direction. He was bundled up against the snow, except for his hand exposed to the cold so that he could type something into his phone. As he approached, I saw that he was wearing a trench coat over a stylish men's suit, with black galoshes for the snow. A black leather briefcase hung from his shoulder by a strap. His right hand was holding a state-of-the-art smartphone, and a shiny, silver luxury watch graced his wrist.

Trying not to overthink my first attempt at political activism, I accosted him in a polite and straightforward way with my request. "Excuse me, Sir, can I get you to sign our petition in support of U.S. military intervention in Syria? Or maybe donate something towards our efforts to help Syrian Christians?" I asked.

"I'm sorry, now is really not a good time," he said, clearly annoyed as he lifted the phone to his right ear and picked up his pace.

I blushed and tried to pretend that I hadn't just been brusquely rejected, while hoping that Michael hadn't noticed.

"Don't feel bad," Michael said, startling me a little, as I realized that he had just witnessed my first failure as a political activist.

"I'm not off to a very good start," I replied, turning to look at him. "I probably shouldn't have approached him just as he was making a call – and on such a snowy day. But it's not like there were many alternatives," I said, gesturing with my gloved hand at how few people were out.

"He's just a rich asshole. He'll never give a penny. Not on a sunny day, and not when his hands are free and he's making no calls."

"Why do you say that?" I asked with curiosity, trying not to stare at the way his lips moved when he spoke.

"Because that's who he is… I've approached him myself many times just for a signature. Not five dollars – just a little signature. All he cares about is his money and things like that Rolex on his wrist."

After about forty minutes of approaching people in more or less the same way, I saw that most people would end up giving me a similar reaction, although I did manage to score a few signatures and even one donation. By 5 p.m., our group had dispersed and I went to Butler Library to warm up a bit, check my email, and figure out where my spring class schedule required me to go next.

About an hour later, I made my way to room 702 of Hamilton Hall, where my last course for the day, Psychology and Markets, would be starting at 6 p.m. The course, taught by Professor Julien Morales, combined economics and psychology, and was exactly the kind of interdisciplinary subject that I found most interesting. But even getting into the class was a bit of a challenge because I hadn't taken any of the course's prerequisites in psychology or economics. So I had to get special permission from the chair of the psychology department to enroll. He granted me an exception on the strength of my overall academic record (including from high school) but warned me that the course is notoriously hard.

I picked a seat towards the front but not too close, where I might have felt overly exposed or self-conscious. More students entered the class, filling the seats around me as winter coats, umbrellas, book bags, and other personal items came off and began to litter the floor, wall hooks, and a few empty desks and chairs in the back of the room.

Moments later, the very same man in his mid-thirties who had disagreeably rebuffed my appeal, just ninety minutes earlier, entered the front of the classroom and put down his black leather briefcase on an empty desk by the podium. He was Professor Morales.

"Oh my God," I thought to myself. "Could this get any more awkward?" As he unpacked his lecture notes, I felt myself shriveling up in my seat, trying somehow to shrink my body mass so that it would be fully blocked by the students sitting in front of me, in the hope that he might not notice me. "Would he recognize me without my winter cap and coat?" I wondered, trying to find the angle at which his view of me would be most obstructed by other students sitting nearby.

The chatter amongst the hundred or so students gathered there gradually quieted down, as they realized that Professor Morales was about to start, even as some stragglers continued pouring into the room.

"Good evening, everyone. Thank you for braving the elements on this snowy Tuesday for our first day of class. For those of you who aren't sure if you're in the right room or the correct class, this is the Psychology and Markets course, which meets on Tuesdays and Thursdays from 6 to 7:30 p.m." He paused for a moment and scanned the students in the room. "If any of you have just realized that you're supposed to be somewhere else, I won't be offended if you leave now," he added with an ironic smile. A few students grabbed their things and awkwardly left the room.

"OK, to the rest of you, welcome to Psychology and Markets. As you can surmise from the name of this course, we will be exploring behavioral economics, including decision theory, and how psychological peculiarities, or paradoxes, impact market behavior – whether it's in the context of consumer marketing or financial markets. To understand why financial markets react as they do to rumors of a housing bubble, or what makes consumers react as they do to a rebate offer, we use the same fundamental, behavioral tools of analysis.

"But before we dive into the substance of this class, a few more housekeeping items are in order. My office is located in Uris 1405, over at the Business School, and I'm there on Fridays from 6 to 7 p.m. I see students there on a first-come-first-served basis, unless you schedule a meeting in advance with my TA for this class. And her name is Elise, by the way," he said, pointing to a beautiful, slim, blonde-haired woman in her early twenties. She rose from her seat to give a quick, somewhat shy wave to the class before sitting back down. "Elise has a bachelor's degree in both Psychology and Economics from Princeton, and is getting her MBA here at Columbia, with an emphasis on Behavioral Economics. So I'm delighted to have her assistance with this class, and she will certainly be helpful to you – both throughout the course and when preparing for your exams.

"And while I'm on the topic of exams, I should mention something about the midterm exam for this class that has become something of a tradition. As some of you may have heard, in my spare time, I run a twenty-billion-dollar hedge fund and financial products firm in Midtown known as JM Analytics & Trading, or simply 'JMAT.'" There were some laughs at his understatement. "As you can imagine, that kind of extracurricular activity requires a lot of help, and my office is always looking for new talent. So I started inviting the top three students – as judged by their performance on the midterm exam – for a special tour of the JMAT office. I do the same thing for the top three grades on the final."

There were some whispers of excitement around the room.

"I founded the fund with an algorithm that tracks market sentiment on trading platforms and social media, and generates trading ideas accordingly, so top performers in this class are a natural fit for the organization. Of course, being invited to the office tour doesn't guarantee you a job offer, but in recent years, JMAT has hired both student interns and recent graduates who have excelled in this course – including nearly everyone who was invited to take the office tour. And in case that's not enough of an incentive for you to take this class seriously, I should point out that our starting salary for a fresh graduate is $90,000, plus a discretionary, performance-based bonus. And for star performers, sometimes that bonus can be higher than the base salary."

There was some more muffled excitement and I could see how every student's face seemed to be wondering who the top performers would be and what this class could mean for their future.

While Professor Morales spent most of the hour and a half lecturing, he did interact with students a few times, either asking them about situations to get them thinking, or answering the questions that they asked him. But fortunately he never addressed me and I'm fairly certain that he didn't even notice me during the class, thanks to my constant efforts to keep my head down or blocked from his view. I was, however, able to get a better look at him while he was addressing several students just beyond me. With no winter clothes on him or snow flurries in our midst, or the awkward pressures of soliciting a stranger's support for my cause, I could clearly and calmly spy his handsome looks. His slim physique rose just under six feet, and he wore a stylish suit and tie, and genuine leather shoes. With the better lighting of the classroom (compared to the snowy conditions outside), I could see his olive-colored skin, dark eyes, and well-trimmed eyebrows. His thick, black hair was coiffured neatly and parted down the middle, like what I had always imagined the hairdos of European or Latino bankers to look like.

At 7:30 p.m., he concluded his lecture and, as several students went up to him with questions, I scurried out with a crowd that was leaving and managed to exit without being seen by him. My hope was that by the next class, he would have forgotten our very first, and somewhat unpleasant, interaction on College Walk.

Chapter 11: Anissa

∽ Monday, February 17, 2014 ∾

To My Dearest,

In the days that followed my first meeting with Michael, I communicated with him regularly on Facebook and started using Twitter to help raise awareness about the plight of Christians in Syria. I would often retweet articles that Michael either authored or shared and – when I saw how prolific he was, and how involved he was in so many activities – I marveled at how he could possibly be getting his Ph.D. at the same time. This twenty-eight-year-old student was a renaissance man of sorts. In addition to his doctoral program, he served as the managing director of the MCA (which he had founded alone and had steadily grown to over one hundred members in under a year), while still participating actively in several other Christian and Middle East nonprofits. He also worked as a freelance journalist, owned a small public relations company (with a few, mostly political clients), and trained in the martial arts.

Naturally, my curiosity about him continued to grow and I was excited to see him again on the Friday of the same week when we first met. Our second, in-person encounter was at an MCA meeting held at the student center in Alfred Lerner Hall – a giant glass building on campus that hosted various student activities and organizations. Unlike the first time we met in person, my view of Michael was not obscured by his winter cap and clothing or the falling snowflakes that kept me blinking more than usual. Now, under the bright indoor lights, and in the warm comfort of the student center, I could get a better look at him, while he led a group planning and strategy meeting about protests and other political activities for the coming weeks. He sported the same five o'clock shadow that he had in most of his Facebook photos, but his black hair had grown out to almost his shoulders, which hadn't been so apparent with his winter clothing on. His eyes were a deep brown, but seemed almost radiant when he spoke. The rigorous fitness routine that he maintained was only hinted at because of the sweatshirt that he was wearing above his blue jeans. His ruggedly handsome look seemed to cast a spell on me, and I found it hard not to look at him, even though doing so made my heart beat faster.

During the meeting, I volunteered to help him photocopy some fliers that we would be posting around campus to raise awareness about the mistreatment of Mideast Christians. While my initial motivation to join the MCA was the desire to help our beleaguered community in Syria, Michael soon made me realize that Christians across the Middle East – and the rest of the Muslim world – faced varying degrees of persecution. As a fellow Syrian, he shared my concern for what was happening there, but convinced me that we needed to join forces with other Christians from the region in order to grow our numbers and have a bigger impact on public opinion and eventually public policy.

So, after the meeting adjourned, I helped him to clean up, and then, after putting on our coats and gloves, we walked over to the photocopy shop nearby. During this time together, I had a chance to learn more about Michael's background.

His father had immigrated to the United States from the Syrian city of Aleppo in 1978 and settled in Boston, where he worked as an accountant for two years before starting a business consulting practice. His mother hailed from Cairo, Egypt, but moved to New Jersey in 1980 for her graduate studies in business administration at the Newark campus of Rutgers University. In 1982, she met her future husband, who had come down from Boston to look for new hires. After finding a few potential candidates on campus, he started his drive back from Newark to Boston and then stopped, on a whim, to visit a quaint Coptic Orthodox Church that he saw on the way. Within minutes of entering, he saw Michael's lovely mother. He gave her his business card and noted that he was in town looking to hire recent graduates willing to relocate. She was drawn to this handsome Syrian businessman and curious about Boston. Within two weeks, she was working for his fledgling company, and three years later, she gave birth to his son.

Michael was born and raised in Massachusetts, but he traveled to Syria and Egypt many times while growing up. Most of his pre-college education was at a Boston-area, Syrian-Christian school, so he was well versed in our prayers and religious doctrines. Nevertheless, he considered himself an agnostic and didn't share my faith in God or other beliefs inherent in the Christian religion. But he greatly valued our traditions and our history.

Despite all of his theological doubts about organized religion in general, Michael still seemed like an exponentially more powerful leader for the cause of persecuted Christians than most of the Syrian clergymen

I knew in Homs. They tended to embrace Jesus' principle of "turning the other cheek" and their answer to every threat was to urge us "to pray"; they never showed any kind of assertive strength and always seemed so vulnerable, compliant, and dependent on the goodwill of the regime and the Muslim majority in our city. Michael showed me a Syrian Christian that I had never before seen: defiant, strong, and ready to fight for our rights. I think this difference is partly explained by the fact that he never had to experience the kind of weak vulnerability that Christians in Syria must accept every day. While Syrian Christians are just as much a minority in the United States, or even in cities like New York and Boston, where they are more numerous, there is no implied threat from the majority against them. Not only is the majority religion in the United States Christian, but religion in general isn't as linked to survival here. This amazing country is, generally speaking, a successful melting pot of cultural, racial, and religious identities, without the kind of sectarian hatreds of the Middle East that constantly need to be contained by a powerful, autocratic leader. So someone like Michael – who was raised in a country of tremendous freedom, where anything is possible – could develop the confidence to grow into a fearless leader who advocates for a new and bolder kind of Middle East Christian. Michael could speak and act on behalf of our community with a dignity and strength that continually inspired and awed me. He wasn't taught from his earliest years to stay quiet, avoid confrontation, "know your place," and just accommodate whatever the more powerful groups around him wanted.

Whereas I was raised on the idea that the Assad government is the friend and protector of Syrian Christians – mainly because the alternative was so much worse – Michael viewed the Assad regime with nothing but scorn and disgust. "Four decades of brutality and undemocratic rule by the Assad dynasty is the reason Syria fell apart," he argued, as we waited at the photocopy shop for the fliers to be printed. His unabashedly critical perspective would have been unthinkable for Christians in Syria, because their personal security depended on the Alawite clan that controlled Syria.

"He has committed genocide against Sunni Muslims," he continued. "So it's no surprise that they're now behaving in the same way against Alawites and any groups that were protected by the Assads, including the Christians. But it didn't have to happen this way."

"It's true that the early protests, in March of 2011, were peaceful," I timidly agreed, as we stood by the counter with the sound of photocopying machines humming in the background.

"Exactly. Those demonstrations were completely justified demands for more freedom. At that time, Assad still had an opportunity to start a meaningful national discussion about reforming the Syrian state. Yes, it would have been risky for him to give more power to the majority Sunnis, but doing so would have probably produced results that are far better than the bloody mess we have now, with an imploding country overrun by countless Sunni extremists and fragmenting along every ethnic and religious fault line. And I just think – "

"Hey, look at that," I said, cutting him off and slowly stepping around him while pointing to the TV screen that was hanging by the cashier area. Michael gave me a slightly annoyed look for interrupting his diatribe, before turning to look at what had grabbed my attention.

"Yeah, so what?"

"That's my professor!" I remarked in excitement.

"He's your professor?"

"Yes!"

"That's the same asshole who blew you off at our rally last Tuesday."

"I know. Thank God, he didn't see me in his class after the rally… But I can't believe Professor Morales is on TV," I said, still in shock, moving closer to the television.

"You've never seen him on TV before?" Michael asked, slightly amused at my cluelessness as he followed me. I really knew nothing about my professor before I had enrolled in his class. I just thought that Psychology and Markets seemed like a fascinating course that would simultaneously explore some of my different academic interests.

"No, not really, I…" Suddenly I realized that he was being interviewed in Spanish on a Latino news channel. "Wait, what's he saying? I don't speak Spanish."

"Really? You need to learn it ASAP."

"Why?"

"Because it's the most important language in this country after English. And any major political effort needs to ally itself with the Latinos."

"So you speak Spanish too?"

"Yes."

"Really? When did you learn?"

"I started studying it in junior high school and it just grew on me over time."

I tried to conceal how impressed I was at his polyglot talent. From our other conversations and my Facebook stalking, I knew that – in addition to native English – he spoke Arabic, Kurdish, Aramaic, Armenian, Hebrew – and now Spanish.

"So what's he saying?"

"He's discussing the Fed policy of quantitative easing, and the effect that it has on Latin American economies."

"Gracias, Señor Kassab," said the Latino store clerk, indicating that Michael's fliers were ready. Michael went over to pay for them, as they exchanged some friendly chitchat in Spanish. I eventually left the TV and walked over to the counter to help Michael carry the large stacks of fliers.

We put our winter coats and gloves back on and headed out into the cold carrying the boxes of flyers to his apartment nearby. Michael lived on West 112th Street, about half a block west of the beautiful Cathedral of Saint John the Divine. We had just arrived at the front door of his building, and were resting the heavy boxes of flyers on the floor so that he could get his keys, when some awkward bad news showed up.

"Hey, Michael," a young woman's voice called from behind us, just as Michael had taken out his keys and was about to open the front door. We both looked around, a bit surprised.

"Oh hi, Karen," Michael said, a little clumsily but with a smile. He went up to her and gave her a hug and then a brief kiss on the lips. She was an attractive Asian-American, roughly my height, wearing a sweatshirt and black spandex that showed off the form of her gracefully long and toned legs.

Michael turned and looked back at me. "Anissa, this is my girlfriend, Karen. Karen, this is Inās – or Anissa, in English. She became involved with the MCA last Tuesday and was just helping me with these flyers."

"Hi Anissa. It's nice to meet you," she said, extending her hand cordially. I shook it politely. "I really should start going to those meetings as well," she replied, apparently addressing both of us.

"Nice to meet you… Aren't you cold like that?" I asked lightly, trying to make some friendly small talk.

"Yes, I am actually," she replied with a smile. "I wasn't planning to stay outdoors for long – I just needed to make a quick stop here on the way to my yoga class a few blocks away." She turned to Michael and continued, "Sweetie, I left my mat at your place two days ago, when I came by after class, and I really don't want to use one of the school's mats."

"Ah yes, you'll be freaking about germs for at least a week, if you do that. Sure, come on up." He then turned to me and said, "Inās, don't worry about helping me get these up to my place – Karen will take it from here."

"Um, OK, well… " I replied, looking down for a confused moment.

"Thanks so much for your help," Michael said, apparently sensing that I needed some kind of departure cue.

"My pleasure. Let me know if you need any help getting members to post them up… Nice to meet you again, Karen," I said awkwardly, not really sure how I was supposed to say goodbye to either of them.

"Bye," they said pleasantly, thinking nothing of the matter.

I nodded politely, turned around, and walked back to my dorm room, feeling utterly mortified and foolish.

Chapter 12: Anissa

∾ Tuesday, February 18, 2014 ∾

To My Dearest,

I was very disappointed to learn that Michael had a girlfriend and that she wasn't even Syrian. Somehow, that tarnished my image of him a little. I know that New York is a very liberal place and ethnicities mix here more freely than they do perhaps anywhere else, but – after that incident – I couldn't help thinking, "if he's really going to be the future leader of Middle East Christians, then he should act the part." Then again, it's not as if he indicated some definite plan to marry this woman, so maybe I was just being jealous with those kinds of thoughts.

Whatever the case was, I was a bit down because of the whole thing and rescheduled my session with Monique to meet with her earlier than originally planned so that we could discuss these latest developments with Michael. I also wanted to tell her that the recurring nightmare about the murder of my parents suddenly returned, after it had left me alone for nearly two weeks.

In therapy, Monique interpreted the nightmare's temporary disappearance as a sign that Michael had made me feel safer about the threats that still haunted me, and it returned once I realized that I can't have him. It made sense, although my dreams are never really that predictable or rational. I also told Monique how I was concerned that I might convey some kind of jealous energy the next time I encountered Michael, and she wisely suggested that I completely reframe the way I view him. Monique reminded me of the primary reason why I reconnected with Michael: so that I could become more active in my support for Syrian Christians. She rightly pointed out that if I just considered him as my organizational conduit to political activism, while allowing myself to develop an interest in other men (now that I was broadening my horizons beyond schoolwork and physical fitness), I could more effectively "move on" from him, as she put it.

So, "moving on" from Michael for now, I'll tell you about my third time going to Professor Morales' Psychology and Markets course the following Tuesday. I finally mustered the courage to speak in class. I figured that, after a week of maintaining a low profile, he probably wouldn't recognize me if I now entered the spotlight by responding to one of his questions. The class lecture was about self-perception and lies, and some of the fascinating insights and experiments about prevarication and dishonesty that have been done by Dan Ariely, a Duke University behavioral economist whose studies have shown that we're not quite as honest as we'd like to think. Fortunately, his brilliant work is required reading for our course, but unfortunately, that assignment came only after Tuesday's lecture. Had I read those materials before class, I would have completely avoided my embarrassing exchange with Professor Morales that night.

It all began when he introduced the topic in class with a simple question: "Who here has never lied?" With my stomach nervously churning, I raised my hand, hoping that I'd be inspired to say something insightful or at least intelligent-sounding.

"Yes. We have a bold confession here. What's your name, truth-teller?" he asked playfully as the class laughed.

"Anissa."

"Well, congratulations, Anissa, on telling your first lie in this class – but certainly not in your life! How can you possibly believe that you've never lied?" he asked in amusement.

"Um, what if by lying to myself, I can convince myself that several untruths are true, and then I tell those 'truths' to the rest of the world?"

"So your theory would seem to be that lying to yourself is no lie at all because you haven't deceived any third party. And if you then convince yourself of those lies, you'll believe them enough to repeat them to others with the genuine conviction that they're true."

"Something like that," I conceded uneasily.

The class laughed some more.

"But there are two major flaws in that reasoning. The first is the assumption that you can't lie to yourself. I don't think that lying, by definition, necessarily means that you are lying to someone other than yourself. It just means to convey a false image or impression in general – whether to yourself, in a form of self-delusion, or someone else. And secondly, even if it were impossible to lie to yourself, the fact that you then repeat those lies to others under the false belief that they're true, after deceiving yourself, does not prevent you from conveying a false impression to someone else. In other words, genuinely believing something false does not make it true."

I felt myself sinking further into intellectual humiliation and had to redeem myself somehow.

"But there is at least one definition of lying that has the element of intent," I argued. "In other words, deliberately trying to deceive someone else about what is true. And if I genuinely believe the lies that I've told myself, then when I repeat those lies to others, I actually think that I'm telling them the truth and therefore can't possibly intend to deceive them."

The class was silent for a moment, considering my rejoinder.

"That's a fair point, Anissa. Your analysis sounds more like it's from the realm of law or philosophy, where moral and legal judgments hinge on notions of intent, but you make a valid point, nonetheless. But then – if we go back to your impressive claim about never having lied – how can you genuinely believe all of your lies, if you recognize them as false?"

"Well, I don't think they're lies. But I was explaining how it could be theoretically true – how what starts as a self-deception ends as honest dishonesty with others, if there can be such a thing."

"Honest dishonesty. That's quite the oxymoron – but I like the originality that you've brought to bear in the art of rationalization. Maybe you should consider becoming a lawyer," he added jokingly.

I smiled and the class laughed some more. But afterwards, I felt so embarrassed. I was trying to be clever to impress him, and came out sounding completely foolish and possibly like a pathological liar. The only good news was that I didn't detect anything in his voice or expression suggesting that I looked familiar to him from that first encounter we had on College Walk a week earlier. I had been thinking of talking to him some time during his office hours, but – after our exchange in front of the class – I lost the courage to do so.

Chapter 13: Julien
(Journal)

Tuesday, 1/28/14 at 23:49.

    One of the students in my class tonight sparred with me a little on the issue of lying. Most noteworthy from our somewhat amusing exchange was that, as we debated the question, I suddenly recalled seeing her a week earlier on College Walk, when she randomly asked me to sign a petition. I actually had noticed her in the class the Thursday after that and looked at her for a moment (trying to figure out where I had seen her) when she was looking down at her phone. I wonder if she realizes that I'm the same person who curtly blew her off that day. Now I feel a bit guilty about it – especially since there's something very sweet and innocent about her – despite this weird confession of hers about self-delusion. Not sure what that's about. She's also quite beautiful in a subdued and natural manner. She carries herself in a very dignified and somewhat conservative way – not like so many of these slutty girls I see on campus or around the city. And that dark hair and Mediterranean look – just gorgeous. And, from what I can tell through the winter clothes, she has a sexy figure – curvy but firm and fit. But who am I kidding? She's clearly very young – and my student. Getting involved with her would be exactly the kind of scandal that would instantly derail any plan to be promoted to a full professor by next year. And my love life is complicated enough as it is.

    When I was back home after class tonight, Areli came over briefly for our usual hot sex, but then she rather dramatically tried to change the terms of our arrangement. Every woman who has ever approached me about being in my circle of lovers knows that I'm a bachelor with no plans to get married. Thanks to New York's tabloids, it's practically common knowledge. And, to avoid any possibility of doubt or misunderstanding, I very clearly told her from the start what I tell every potential lover: I don't date anyone exclusively. Ever. So why, after just a month of dating each other non-exclusively, would Areli suddenly expect me to agree that we're now exclusive? I told her that we need to cool things off because we clearly see things differently, but then she had the audacity to demand a "breakup fee." I told her that her behavior amounted to tacky coercion and the fastest way to ensure that she never sees or hears from me again. But I worry that she's not going to get the message, even when I stop returning her calls and texts. How did I not see her for the opportunistic, gold-digging bitch that she is? Clearly, her stunning looks dulled my intuition into some kind of kneejerk, male stupidity. I just hope she's not as unstable as I'm beginning to think she might be.

I'm discovering that being a quasi-celebrity has problems of its own that I'm still getting used to – particularly in an era where video recording is practically ubiquitous. After class, at around 7:45 p.m., while walking back to my car and driver, I passed a young woman who was filming her friends on her phone. She apparently recognized me from one of my recent TV appearances (I overheard her say something like, "Hey, I saw him on TV yesterday!"), and suddenly decided to make me the focus of her filming. Fortunately, I was just a few minutes away from my car, so there wasn't much of me to film, but the severe reduction of my privacy – without ever really signing up for that loss – is frustrating. In a sense, nobody opted to live in a world in which we are all subordinate to the constant impulse of someone to record some moment that we might happen to walk into. But being viewed as famous only makes you that much more of a target. And we seem to live in an era now where people are inclined to record every moment, and turn every second into a performance of some kind, to be viewed and commented on later by someone or many. Whether driven by narcissism or nostalgia, the increasingly present possibility of recording life leaves no moment safe from permanent preservation for later consumption by unknown eyes, and potentially multitudes.

I think I need to start seeing a therapist again. I'm going to ask Raegan to start vetting candidates. I'm very lucky to have someone so discreet and trustworthy as my personal assistant.

Chapter 14: Anissa

∽ Wednesday, February 19, 2014 ∾

To My Dearest,

After I finally spoke out in Professor Morales' class, I decided that I had better go back to maintaining a low profile in his course, to spare myself any more embarrassing exchanges. My new strategy for his class was just to focus on being one of the top performers on his midterm exam – if only for a chance to visit his hedge fund office and maybe get invited to interview for a job there.

Coincidentally enough, a few days later, it turned out that a new friend of mine from my Economics study group, Maya, had actually taken Psychology and Markets a year ago. We hung out for a bit after our study group meeting ended. So naturally, I had to ask her about how hard the exams and grading are in that class.

"He's a tough grader," she warned me, as the others students in our group left the area. "I got a B- in his class – my first of only three college grades lower than a B, actually. But he started inviting me to his parties. And as far as I'm concerned, that's way better than getting an A+ with no party invites," she added.

"Really?" I said, trying to imagine these parties hosted by my professor. Maya definitely seemed like the kind of girl who would be invited to VIP parties. She was a beautiful, mixed-race black woman who had no qualms about dressing in a sexy way – like so many other American girls I had met in the two years that I had lived in the United States. But Maya managed to do so with a certain degree of class and style. And there was a charming sophistication to the way she carried herself, so I could see how she might be someone to invite to a VIP party – where attractive women are always welcome, from what I hear. But I still couldn't imagine that Professor Morales really throws such soirees.

"Yeah, they're actually really fun parties. He has the most amazing, triplex penthouse apartment, and the networking there is top-notch. And so are the bachelors. It's a really high-quality crowd."

"Sounds like it," I said, trying not to sound too intrigued or eager. And then, in a moment of candor that surprised even me, I said something that needlessly revealed just how inexperienced I am. "But I don't know if I could handle that crowd – I've never even had a boyfriend before."

Maya looked at me in surprised amusement. "Really?"

"I know. I guess I've been too much of a nerd up until now."

"Well, girlfriend, we need to get you out more!" she said moving her head from side to side as she spoke, for extra emphasis.

"But I'm not even legally old enough to drink yet," I protested feebly, as we started to head out of the room and down the stairs towards the building exit.

Maya laughed heartily. "Oh, you are precious, Anissa. You say that as if that fact ever stopped anyone. I'm only twenty myself. That's why God gave humans ingenuity – so that they could do things like invent the fake ID."

"I'm not even nineteen yet."

"Well, then you're at the age of conscription, Honey. And if you're old enough to die for this country, then I say you're old enough to have a drink in this country." Maya chuckled at the whole conversation again. We reached the ground floor and she stopped by the exit, sensing that this was a longer conversation.

"Want to grab a cup of coffee and some treats at The Hungarian Pastry Shop?" she suggested.

"Sure." I had heard great things about that neighborhood café, but had never been there.

A bit later, nestled into a comfy corner, with the scent of coffee and pastries on the small table before us, our conversation became more personal. Maya's tone grew a bit more cautious and respectful but still lighthearted. "Now I'm wondering about something very private. I think I can already figure it out on my own, but I don't want to assume anything about such important details."

I sensed that she wanted to ask me if I was still a virgin, but was trying not to ask the question explicitly. She saw me blush and avoid her gaze for a moment, which made her calibrate the buildup to her question.

"OK, I know we haven't known each other that long, but this is how I roll, Baby – I'm all in. If we're friends, then I'm an open book with you – just ask me what you want to know about me and I'll tell you. And I expect the same of my friends. I mean, if you don't have total trust in your friends to speak freely, then why bother having friends, right?" she asked.

"Right. All right, I know where you're going with this. And I haven't really told anyone at school this, so this really is just between us as friends, OK?"

"Of course, Honey."

"OK, well," I paused for an awkward moment – still unsure if I wanted to admit such a private fact but aware that it was already painfully obvious to Maya what the truth was, even if I tried to conceal or deny it. "Yes, I am."

"Aww, isn't that just so sweet," she replied affectionately but respectfully. "Well, don't feel bad about it, Honey. You'll know when the time is right."

"I just never really met anyone in high school – they all seemed so immature and not that interesting."

"Oh you don't have to tell me about younger guys. Last year I discovered the virtues of a solid decade or more of age difference, and it's amazing how much men eventually grow up. But even then, there's no guarantee!"

We shared a good laugh.

"I also really wanted to do well in my first semester of college, so I just haven't socialized much," I continued with my explanation, between sips.

"I hear you. This school costs too much not to take it seriously. And this is our future. So I'm all about working hard. But you do need some balance in your life."

"Yes, I sort of realized that over winter break, so I am trying to loosen up a bit and diversify my college experience a little."

"So now that you've been diversifying since winter break, is there maybe someone who's caught your eye? On – or off – campus?"

"Actually, there is someone. But I recently found out that he has a girlfriend."

"Oh that's a shame," Maya responded, putting down her cup. "How long have they been dating?"

"I don't know yet. I mean, I don't know. I'm trying to move on now, so I probably won't even bother to find out."

"Makes sense. Well, maybe I can see if I can get you into one of Julien's parties. He lets me call him Julien now that he's no longer my professor."

"Really?" I asked, feeling a mix of excitement and intimidation at the idea. "Do you think he'd even say yes, knowing that I'm one of his students?"

"Oh, he can't know that, Baby. If I tell him that upfront he'll almost certainly say no. I need to say only that I want to bring a beautiful friend who's never been to one of his parties. He trusts my judgment now because every time I say that to him, he's pleased with the guest I bring. So he'll probably say yes – but you have to just play dumb when you see him, so that it looks like I didn't know that you're his student, and you didn't know that he's the host of the party."

"It does sound tempting."

"Honey, this is probably the single best private party you can be invited to in Manhattan. You will leave with a ton of business cards from the city's business and power elite. I have girlfriends who don't speak to me anymore because I haven't tried to bring them to a Julien party yet."

"Really?" I asked, somewhat flattered and surprised. "So why me? I mean, we just met."

"I don't know. Because I like you. I'm very intuitive. I can tell that you're a very decent and genuine person – not like some of these annoying social climbers who are always trying to get something out of you. Like those old girlfriends of mine I don't talk to any more."

"Well, I still wouldn't know what to say around a bunch of older, successful men."

"Just be your usual, sweet self, Baby. And don't worry, I'll be your wing woman. But first let me see if I can even bring a guest to the next party, and when it is."

"OK, well no pressure – like I said, I'm not even sure if I'm up for it. I'm much better at being a nerd than socializing with the elite," I said with a simper.

"I gotcha, Babe. And it'll be fine. I just need to get the details on the next opportunity. Sometimes he has much smaller gatherings and then I can't bring anyone. Hell, sometimes I'm not invited either, and I hear from someone else that he had one of those super-exclusive parties."

We stayed at the café chatting for a good hour, and it felt great to connect with a new friend on a more personal level.

Then, over the weekend, just as I was getting excited about maybe meeting some new men, I saw Michael again. Our chance encounter happened on Sunday, while I was buying groceries at the Westside Market on Broadway, between 110th and 111th. He was wearing a hoodie and winter running pants that showed his powerful legs, and it looked as if he had just finished his workout, judging from his wet hair. As fate would have it, we ran into each other by the store's delectable selection of Middle Eastern dips and desserts.

"Hey, Inās," he said, startling me a little. "I should have figured that we'd end up meeting in the best neighborhood place to get some hummus and baklava."

I smiled, as he joined me in the line where I was waiting to get some baba ghanoush and other goodies that reminded me of home. "How's it going?" I asked.

"Good – actually, I meant to apologize for last time. I didn't expect Karen to just – "

"Oh, no apology needed. It's not like you owe me anything," I replied nonchalantly. "We're just all working for the same cause, right?" I asked.

"Right… I just…" He seemed a bit awkward, which suggested to me that there was more going on, as far as he was concerned (although this may have been wishful thinking on my part). "Well, I guess I should have mentioned that I had a girlfriend at some point, when we were talking."

"No worries – it's not like you can share every single fact about yourself right away. Details come out gradually, in whatever order seems most natural, right?" I replied, with a casual wink.

"True," he said, sounding a bit more relaxed and relieved. "Maybe I wasn't sure what you'd think about me dating an Asian woman."

"Why would I have anything against Asians?"

"No, that's not what I meant – at all." More awkwardness. "I guess a part of me feels as if I should be dating a Syrian Christian, or at least a Middle Eastern Christian. If I'm going to lead the fight for our survival, then me dating someone completely outside of our community might send a mixed message."

"Now you sound like you're advising one of your public relations clients," I replied playfully, trying to put him at ease.

He smiled in amusement. "Yeah, well, it's something that I still struggle with on occasion… But Karen is incredibly supportive and completely believes in our cause. She's actually a much better Christian than I am. Koreans have a huge and very active Christian community."

We shuffled forward a little as the queue advanced. "Well, I can't imagine that you would date anyone – Asian or otherwise – who wasn't, at the very least, enthusiastically supportive of your main cause in life!"

"True. And she really is. She's just a great girlfriend all around."

"Seems like it. How long have you been dating?"

"It's funny, we met just before you messaged me around Halloween." He removed the hood that was covering his dark, wet hair.

"That is funny timing," I responded as casually as I could, while pondering whether his budding relationship with Karen was the reason it took him so long to reply to my message last November. I also wondered whether Michael and I could have been dating all this time, had I prioritized the struggle for our people from the start of college, rather than wait until January.

"How's that asshole professor of yours?" he asked, thankfully changing topics.

"He's actually not that bad," I corrected him.

"Oh really?"

"Well, I obviously don't know him that well – we've had only four classes so far. But he seems like a good man."

"Well, there's a very apt Edmund Burke quote that I could cite in response to that."

I could feel a confident smirk on my face, as I realized the exact quote he had in mind and recited it for him. "All that is necessary for the triumph of evil is that good men do nothing."

Michael flashed a smile suggesting that he was surprised and impressed that I knew what he had in mind. "Did you do some research after I sent you that Martin Niemöller poem?"

"I've done some reading since November," I replied with a playful wink.

"Very good. So you see that it's not enough just to be good. You have to do something about it."

"Yes, you do," I affirmed.

"And what good is massive wealth in the hands of someone who cares only about his own comforts and luxurious lifestyle? You can't take any of that stuff with you to the grave."

"True… So what will you take with you to the grave?"

"Do you really need to ask me that?" he replied, almost offended, as if I had just suggested that he might have no greater purpose.

"I mean, obviously I know how dedicated you are to our cause, but how does that translate into a lasting legacy?"

"Ah. Well, there's Antioch. In the end, I will live and die for Antioch."

"Antioch? What do you mean?"

"It's the name that I think I'm going to give the new Christian state in the Middle East."

"What do you mean, 'new Christian state?'" I asked, intrigued.

"Well, this is an idea that has only recently come to me, so it's still very much in its embryonic stage… Can I trust you not to tell anyone? Because you're literally the first person that I'd be sharing this with."

I was beyond flattered that he would trust me with such an idea. "Of course, you can trust me. I won't tell anyone – it will all stay strictly between us." Just saying those words suddenly felt as if some intimacy was being created between us.

"Good. So I mean exactly what it sounds like I mean. I think it's time to create a new state for the Christians of the Middle East, and I have decided that I am going to lead that effort."

"Really?" I asked, in awe.

"Yes. There are twenty Arab Muslim states in the Middle East and North Africa, and if you add the non-Arab states of Turkey and Iran, that's twenty-two Muslim states in the region. So why can't there be a single Christian-majority state in that region – a place where Christians control the government, the army, the borders, and the laws? It doesn't have to be a big state. It can be small. Even very small – look at tiny Israel. It's the size of New Jersey, and it's still managing to survive and even thrive in that crazy neighborhood."

It was already my turn in line to give the store attendant my order, but instead I stepped out of the line because I was completely mesmerized by the boldness of Michael's vision and didn't want to interrupt what he was saying. He moved with me out of line and kept speaking.

"So why can't Christians have the same thing that the Jews have? We have far more people than they do. They're only about fourteen million, and we're about two billion. So can't we have a state too?"

"Well, there are plenty of Christian-majority states in Europe and elsewhere," I pointed out.

"Yes, but what do Christians have in the Middle East? Nothing – nothing but pathetic persecution in the very lands where Christianity was born – centuries before the Arab Muslim conquerors showed up in the seventh century and took over by force. Ever since that time, we've been living as a persecuted minority in our ancestral home. Undergoing forced conversions, mob riots, and attacks on churches with no protection from the police. Forced to pay an extra "jizyah" tax to Muslim authorities because of our "dhimmi" status. Often unable to get basic justice and suffering constant discrimination – like not even being able to repair churches without special permission. How is that fair? We deserve better than that. We deserve to live in dignity, in a sovereign and independent state of our own in that region. There are enough of us in the Middle East who have lived under enough persecution without a state to justify its creation."

"Wow." I was stunned at the boldness of his vision, and was still trying to understand how this could even be possible. "A Mideast Christian state is a powerful and revolutionary idea – I just don't know how you'd get the world powers to agree to it."

"I didn't say it would be easy. The Jews didn't exactly have an easy time creating or preserving the State of Israel. But that didn't stop them, and the challenges of creating the first modern Middle Eastern state for Christians shouldn't deter us either. Just as the genocide of six million Jews made it painfully obvious to them – and to the rest of the world – that they needed a state of their own, in their ancestral home, so too do Christians. We have also lost millions to genocide."

"You mean the genocide of about two million Christian Armenians committed by the Muslim ultra-nationalist Young Turks?" I clarified.

"Yes, that genocide is the most well-known, but unfortunately there are far more cases that most people don't know about, so the total is closer to three million slaughtered, if you include all of the Christians of the Syriac, Armenian, and Greek Orthodox denominations who were killed in the same context. Between 1914 and 1923, there was a genocidal campaign against the Christian minorities of the Ottoman Empire – Armenians, Assyrians, Pontian Greeks, and Anatolian Greeks," he said.

"And then you have all of the Christians murdered at the hands of Muslim extremists in the hundred years since the genocide of Armenians," I added, thinking how many in Syria alone had died just in the past few years. Michael noticed that I was getting tired of holding my basket of groceries.

He took the basket out of my hands. "Here let me hold that for you," he said. "If I'm going to make you review Middle East history in a supermarket, the least I can do is hold your groceries for you," he added wryly.

"Thanks," I replied with a chuckle.

"But you're right," he continued. "You have the Islamist slaughter of Christians in Syria, Iraq, Egypt, and other places year after year. The atrocities against the Christians of the Middle East and Africa have continued unabated for centuries – even though most aren't covered by the mainstream media."

"That drives me crazy," I vented. "I read about horrible things in Syria and nobody else seems aware of them."

"I know. And that's just one more reason why the genocide of Christians runs into the many millions, and far worse than most people realize."

"It doesn't surprise me, given how vulnerable we are. We have no military strength anywhere."

"Well, this goes back to my core point. Except for Israel, every single state in the Middle East and North Africa is a Muslim-majority state where Christians live as second-class citizens. Even in Lebanon, where Christians are about forty percent of the population, they are hardly secure or confidently in control of their own fate. So Christians desperately need at least one state of their own in the area. We've lost enough blood for not having one."

"Well, you convinced me on that point," I affirmed with a smile.

"That's a start. Now I just need to persuade the rest of the world," he noted, raising his arms for emphasis, with the weight of the basket in each of his hands making his biceps bulge through his hoodie.

His joke made me chuckle at the absurd grandiosity of his whole plan, which he himself clearly recognized.

"But why do you want to call this new state 'Antioch?'" I asked.

"Because it symbolizes a more universally Christian state, whereas 'Assyria' emphasizes more the historical and geographical territory and is perhaps more fraught with political complications."

"Why do you say that?" I asked.

"Because Assyria enters part of Iraq, Turkey, and Iran, whereas Antioch is more of an ancient city... Although, if the new state includes the Nineveh Plains – near Mosul, Iraq – where Assyrian Christians make up a slight majority, then Assyria might very well be a better name."

We stepped out of the way of some other shoppers who were trying to get by.

"It seems like Iraq is doomed to disintegrate anyway," I added.

"I think so too," he agreed. "There's already a de facto Kurdish region in the north, a Shiite region in the south and much of the rest of the country is Sunni. So carving out a Christian state using parts of the country that have been historically Christian areas could be the way to go. Although the name 'Antioch' still has a lot of symbolic meaning."

"In what way?"

"Well, the ancient city of Antioch played a major role in early Christianity, and is considered the cradle of Christianity," he explained.

"Oh, interesting. The name did ring a bell, but I didn't remember that detail. Where was it located?"

"At the very northwest corner of today's Syrian border with Turkey. So we'll have to see precisely where world powers can be convinced to create this new Christian state, before finalizing a name. I guess this new state could also be called 'Osroene' to avoid political complications."

"Osroene? You may want to talk to some branding experts about finding something that's easier to pronounce and write!" I joked.

Michael chuckled. "Very true. But Osroene was the first Christian state in history, and a major center of Syriac literature and Syriac Christianity. So it could be a good name too."

"Wow – it's funny to think that we plotted to make history while waiting to get some hummus at the Westside Market," I noted in amusement.

"I can't think of any other place I'd want to plan a revolution! At least this way, we're inspired by the food that awaits us there."

We shared a laugh, and then he returned us to the original topic that caused this massive digression: Professor Julien Morales. "So you see? That is what will be my legacy. I will live and die for that dream, so that Mideast Christians can finally live in dignity and security. But what will your professor have lived and died for in the end? Only himself and his fancy lifestyle. And that's a selfish and empty life."

"Well, we don't know that he's really like that."

"I've been at Columbia for a few years now, and he's one of the wealthiest men ever to be associated with the university, and I've never heard of any big donations from him to anything."

"Maybe he donates anonymously – to avoid being solicited by all of the charities out there."

Michael stopped to think about what I had just said. He was silent for a moment – apparently trying to find some kind of rebuttal. But instead, he surprised me with a concession!

"That's a fair point, Inās. Maybe I've unfairly judged him without really knowing all of the facts."

"I like that you can admit when you're wrong – it gives me hope about men!" I retorted jokingly.

"Hahaha – well, don't get too used to this dangerous idea that I might be wrong some of the time!" he bantered back.

It was a completely unplanned, magical moment with Michael – and right after I was supposed to have reframed him as just a friend. Instead, it felt like we were co-conspirators plotting some wildly ambitious plan to redraw the map of the Middle East and change the history of our people forever. It's funny how you can resolve to do one thing with your therapist, and then life can throw some scenario or conversation at you that neither you nor your therapist could have possibly imagined – rendering all of the advice completely irrelevant and outdated.

Chapter 15: Anissa

∽ Thursday, February 20, 2014 ∾

To My Dearest,

We're now just two weeks away from the present, which will make keeping you up to date much easier. I wish I had the time and energy to capture everything in one sitting, but it's far too much to write. In any case, I left off at February 2, when I unexpectedly ran into Michael at the market, and – like a ping-pong ball – I now swing back to Professor Morales, whom I saw two days later in class.

As usual, his lecture was both fun and fascinating. He started with the role of psychology and subjective value on consumer demand.

"We're going to try a quick experiment now," he began. He pulled a package out of his briefcase and held it up. "For those of you sitting in the back who can't see what I'm holding, this is a brand new pair of men's underwear."

There were some laughs and whispered jokes in the room. "Where on Earth is he going with this?" I wondered.

"Now we're going to have a classroom auction, and the winning bid will get to take the tighty whities home. And no, they've never been used and their packaging is still hermetically sealed."

The room erupted into laughter again.

"OK, so who's willing to pay one dollar for these? Raise your hand if you'll bid one dollar. They're 100% cotton, by Calvin Klein."

There were some chuckles and whispers as nearly every single hand in the room went up. Professor Morales addressed the student next to me raising her hand.

"What's your name?"

"Kelly."

"Kelly, do you normally buy men's underwear?"

The class laughed some more.

"Well, no, but it's such a good deal, that I'd get it for my brother. Or my boyfriend, if I had one."

"Now that's one lucky boyfriend, if you're already looking out for him before he even exists!"

Student laughter again filled the room (including mine). I wondered if the professor was in an unusually good mood or if this was all part of his pedagogical plan somehow.

"OK, very good. Now what if I price the underwear at seven dollars. Any takers?"

Now all of the female hands dropped and there were maybe only one-third as many male hands still raised.

"How about for thirty dollars? Let's not forget – these aren't just any undies. They're Calvin Kleins."

There were some chuckles as all hands came down.

"OK, so no takers for a thirty-dollar pair of Calvin Kleins. I'm relieved to see that rationality still prevails in this class. And there you have just witnessed the price elasticity of demand for brand new Calvin Klein underwear. Now let's try something different. What if I told you that this same Calvin Klein underwear is not brand new at all. It's been used. Any takers at our first price of one dollar?"

The class was clearly amused at the idea that anyone would pay for used men's underwear, and of course, no hands went up.

"OK, I'm glad to see that this class is not only rational but also concerned with basic hygiene and avoiding unnecessary exposure to other people's germs. But watch now how this will change completely with one minor detail added."

We waited in suspense to see how any detail could change our disinterest in paying anything for used men's underwear.

"What if I now told you that this pair of Calvin Klein underwear was used by Brad Pitt during the entire filming of the movie *World War Z*? And not only that, he autographed the label on the waistband. All of this has been authenticated and certified as true by forensic experts who work for our auction house. Any takers at one dollar?"

Every hand shot up in an amused uproar. And then he kept raising the price by hundred-dollar increments, and there were still hands up at five hundred dollars, including Kelly's. He addressed her again.

"Kelly, the curiosity is overwhelming me. Are you still buying these for your brother or non-existent boyfriend?"

"Neither," she replied, reddening.

"I see," he replied, clearly amused by the exchange. "Well, shall we have the auction house wash them before delivering them to you? Or do you prefer to wash them yourself, Kelly?"

"I'll wash them myself," she replied with a giggle and even more blushing.

After the class laughter died down, he put the pair of underwear down and got to the point he wanted to make.

"What you all just witnessed was the impact that subjective value has on consumer demand. Because underwear that was worn by Brad Pitt is subjectively viewed as valuable, it can command a far higher price, even though there is nothing objectively better about used underwear. Indeed, because it's used, its objective value should actually be lower than a brand new pair. But consumers can irrationally ascribe a much higher subjective value to something that they consider unique or special, and this is particularly true in a culture that idolizes celebrities."

There was some self-conscious chuckling and murmuring, as students wrestled with this irrefutable proof that they too placed an irrational value on movie stars.

"Indeed, subjective value is the fundamental basis for the entire collector's market – from antiques, to paintings, to autographs, to the personal stuff of famous personalities, and other such rare items," he continued.

We then discussed a fascinating experiment that we were supposed to have read about before class. Like so many other hugely important and groundbreaking studies in the field of psychology, this one was conducted by Amos Tversky and Daniel Kahneman. In their experiment, the subjects were told the following story: "Linda is 31 years old, single, outspoken, and very bright. She majored in philosophy. As a student, she was deeply concerned with issues of discrimination and social justice, and also participated in anti-nuclear demonstrations."

The subjects were then asked this question: "Which of the following two statements is more probable?"

1. Linda is a bank teller.
2. Linda is a bank teller and active in the feminist movement.

Most of the respondents chose the second option, even though such reasoning exemplifies the conjunction fallacy. That is because every time the second statement is correct, the first one also is, but not vice versa. Hence, without knowing anything else about Linda, the first statement is more likely to be true.

Professor Morales summarized the explanation that Tversky and Kahneman gave for why most people answer this question incorrectly. The cognitive bias stems from our tendency to think in terms of representative categories. The description of Linda does not fit our image of a bank teller but does seem very representative of a feminist activist. The respondents therefore tend to focus on the second attribute (feminist) and less on the first one (bank teller), which then produces their error in judgment about what is more likely.

As we discussed these topics, I began to think to myself, "Wouldn't it be fun just to be an academic who thinks about these questions all day, coming up with clever experiments that reveal the amusingly irrational ways in which humans think and behave? If only that could lead to the kind of wealth or influence that I need to support – on a much bigger scale – Michael's quest to help Mideast Christians... Then again, Professor Morales gets to think about these things a lot and has exactly that kind of wealth and influence... Maybe I should talk to him during his office hours someday, to see if he has any practical tips from his own experience." And, at that point, I regained my courage and resolved to see him that Friday.

The next day (Wednesday, February 5), my thoughts were back to Michael. Just three days after we ran into each other at the market, I saw him again at an MCA meeting. This time Karen was there, and it was very awkward. She seemed to allow her body to come into contact with his quite a bit and I would occasionally catch her looking at me and then at Michael, as if she was trying to see if there was any kind of subtle communication or romantic energy between him and me. I could tell that he wasn't entirely comfortable with how much she was clinging to him – not just because I was there, but probably also because he didn't want others in the group to know that he was dating someone who clearly was outside of the community. Even though Michael had opened up the MCA to anyone who was sympathetic to the cause, there were still just a few non-Middle Easterners at the meetings.

Actually, there's even a Sunni Muslim member of the MCA now – a chemistry student named Yazid Khalid. I had no idea he was Muslim, until he introduced himself by speaking in front of the whole group, with Michael's permission. Yazid spoke fondly of the Christian friends that he had cherished as a child growing up in Iraq, and declared that it was his moral duty to do what he could to help. He also wanted to show that there are Muslims who take a stand against Islamist terror.

After the meeting, when everyone had left except Karen, Michael and me, I went over to chat with them a little, in the hope of creating some kind of normalcy. But as soon as I approached the two of them, I could feel the tension in the air, so I just said politely, "See you guys next time."

And in a somewhat masochistic stalker moment, I lurked around in the area, where I could observe them without being seen, and waited to see how they interacted as a couple, now that they had privacy from the rest of the MCA members. I ended up following them almost all the way to Michael's apartment because they still hadn't done anything, and I wanted to know where things were going between the two of them... Then, at around 115th Street and Broadway, I saw Karen put her left arm around Michael's waist, which he soon reciprocated by wrapping his right arm around her shoulder. When I saw his arm go around her, I felt a physical pain in my chest – as I was again reminded of what I want but can't have, after getting my hopes up again just a few days earlier.

Michael was an emotional rollercoaster for me, and with each abrupt dip and turn of the car I was in, it seemed as if I might just be hurled out of my seat for a very painful, if not mortal, crash to the ground below.

Chapter 16: Julien

Thursday, 2/6/14 at 22:10.

Haven't seen or spoken to Areli since 1/28/14, but she still texts me two to four times a day. Her first texts are always gentler, asking when she can see me. But then, after I don't respond to her all day, by the evening her dark side comes out and she warns of "consequences" and repeats her demand for a "breakup fee." I'm just lucky that she's not a student at the university or she could have caused even more damage by reporting some bogus charge to Dean Butterworth and generally tarnishing my reputation on campus. She somehow crashed one of my house parties and charmed her way in, and – with her looks – I let my guard down. Feeling pretty stupid about the whole thing now.

My mood has definitely been deteriorating. The fund's returns have taken a dip and profits this quarter may not be as good as the last few quarters. There have also been several big redemptions from investors whose lockup period expired, bringing total assets under management down to 19.5 billion. Raegan says that we should have some new hires for my approval in investor relations and marketing soon, so hopefully that will help.

Class was fun and engaging last Tuesday (with the Brad-Pitt-underwear example), but tonight felt forced and dull. Maybe because students were expecting more of the same playful atmosphere from the prior class –even though tonight's lecture had to focus on more technical and challenging concepts in behavioral economics. So a drier and more focused approach was needed, but it still felt like a letdown somehow. At the end of class, that student who had jousted with me over lying, Anissa, told me that she planned to come by during my office hours tomorrow. I'm not sure why she would need to see me this early in the semester, but the last thing I need is more drama or complication in my life.

The fact that I haven't been sleeping well lately may be contributing to the general deterioration in my mood. I definitely need to see a therapist. I've narrowed the search down to two candidates (Lily and Olivia) and will pick one of them tomorrow.

There's a lot on my mind in general, but exacerbating everything is the fact that my nightmares seem to have gotten worse – like how they were a few years ago. Sleep has become more difficult because I've been waking up gasping for air at 4 a.m., throwing the blanket off me in terror. In my nightmare, it's a down comforter full of razor blades, and it cuts deep into me every time I move, spilling my blood everywhere until I'm drowning in my own vital fluid, gasping for air, and that's when I wake up hyperventilating, and tossing the covers off me.

Apparently, the nightmares started to get worse last week, after I accidentally clicked on a YouTube link while reading the news out of Syria that morning – something that I generally avoid reading or looking into, because it can be so gruesome and depressing… I'd much rather learn about new real estate opportunities, catch up on Latino news, read about the latest film projects of my Hollywood friends, or look at my fund's portfolio results (although even that can be stomach-turning on a bad day in the market). All of that is better than following the bloodbath that is the Middle East. Why focus on grim realities over which I have no control? But I somehow ended up reading about the carnage in Syria and then unintentionally activated one of the related videos embedded in the article.

That made me think about how we live in an era of far too much knowledge. The same omnipresent video cameras on everyone's smartphones that destroy our privacy are also eliminating our blissful ignorance of this world's ugly cruelty. The full scale of human horrors has been uncovered like never before. Barbaric crimes have always happened somewhere on the planet at any given time, but only recently have we all been made privy to each atrocity from the comfort and privacy of our home Internet connections or phones. There is a surreal disconnect between the ghastly reality that is shared for all to see, and the place of relative safety from which this unfathomable barbarism is observed. When the modern technology of smartphones meets the primitive brutality of sectarian Middle East conflicts, the congenital defects of humanity – the child rapists, the beheaders, the mutilators, the immolators – are uncovered for all of their grisly ugliness. With more of our unembellished nature exposed, the mirror screams ever louder for our higher selves to stop that vile dark side from pushing humanity ever closer to wanton self-destruction. But how exactly can any of us stop the collective madness over there? And I wonder how much we're possibly being desensitized – in general – just by being able to see any act of violence or sex on our phones at any time of our choosing.

I was happier in my blissful ignorance. I want nothing to do with the nightmare that is the Middle East. If my Internet reading ventures outside of financial news or academic work, then I really need to avoid the sickest parts of our world and stick to Europe or the Americas. Especially Latin America – whose food, music, language, culture (and women) I so love. Not that Latin America hasn't had its own ugly chapters of history. But it's also my heritage, and the worst period of violence, in the eighties and nineties, seems behind us (except for Mexico, which still has serious issues with drug-related violence). And the violence that sometimes hits Latin America doesn't stem from ancient sectarian rivalries. We don't have clashing tribes and religions engaging in an endless battle of tit-for-tat violence, and viciously settling scores like medieval savages.

The bottom line: I'm done reading about the Middle East.

Chapter 17: Anissa

∾ Friday, February 21, 2014 ∾

To My Dearest,

Picking up where I left off the last time I wrote to you, on Friday, February 7, at around 6:15 p.m., I went over to the Business School and found Professor Morales' office. There was another student meeting with him and two ahead of me in line to see him, and none of them looked familiar, so I assumed that they were all from the other course that he teaches at the university.

By the time it was my turn to meet with him, there were only fifteen minutes left in his office hours, although I was hoping that maybe at 7 p.m. he would have to walk somewhere and we could continue talking if I accompanied him. But I couldn't be sure if we'd have enough time for a complete discussion of my original question (how to leverage my academic fascination with psychology into major financial success), so I decided to save it for another time.

I stepped into his book-filled office, realizing that I needed something to discuss with him or it would look strange that I was there. "Hi, Professor Morales," I began, without really knowing what I would say next. I was confident that he would recall my face from our mini-debate about lying – especially since only yesterday I had given him a heads up about maybe coming to his office hours. But I wasn't sure if he would remember my name from the few hundred students collectively enrolled in his two classes.

"Hi, Anissa. What brings you here today?" he replied, to my surprise. He was leaning back in his chair, with some spreadsheets and statistical charts open on his desktop computer nearby.

"Well, I, um... I guess I was hoping that you could share your psychological expertise on something that has been... interfering with my concentration at school." I couldn't believe I was moving our conversation in this direction.

"I can try," he replied sympathetically, while looking at the wall clock near us and then adding, "But you haven't left me much time."

"I know, I'm sorry. OK, I'll try to make it quick... Well, I'm a refugee from the war in Syria and I lost a lot of relatives there... But I still have some family left in a town called Raqqa... And sometimes the stress and worry of it all is too great. I've tried everything. I've been seeing a therapist ever since I arrived here about two years ago... And for most of the time that I've been here, I've managed to avoid reading about Syria altogether. But every now and then, it just comes back in some unexpected way, and suddenly I can't sleep or concentrate... Or even enjoy the most basic things... I'm sorry, I don't even know why I'm telling you this... It's obviously not your concern... But I guess maybe I just want you to keep it in mind if you notice that my performance in class is slipping somehow."

"I'm really sorry to hear that you've gone through such hard times, and that they continue to impact you like this..." He seemed to have been caught off guard – not at all expecting to hear what I had just told him, but now adjusting accordingly. He continued: "Actually, just yesterday, I accidentally clicked on a YouTube video while reading about the conflict in your country and it just horrified me. With so many smartphones capturing so much of human life and all of its varied experiences, we now have easy access to things that are probably better kept far away from our minds... Atrocious acts that should never happen – much less be recorded and shared – are now there for everyone to experience. So our narcissism has bared forth an unflattering nakedness that shames our species. But this is humanity. This is our condition."

"Wow, that's a tough but poetic way to sum it up," I remarked.

"Yes, sometimes I get that way, but don't tell anyone," he said with a half-smile.

"Well, you're lucky that you can just turn it off so easily. It's not really your fight."

"No, thankfully, it's not my fight. But I can't run from it completely. Events in the Middle East impact oil stocks and other parts of our fund portfolio that are sensitive to certain geopolitical risks. And, more importantly, if our species is ultimately doomed to self-destruct in a nuclear holocaust or some other form of collective stupidity, there will be no escaping that either."

"True, but these are still relatively remote issues for you – not deeply personal, as they are for me. I can't ever fully disconnect from what's happening over there, no matter how much I try. And it's affecting my ability to concentrate in school. So I thought maybe you'd have some suggestions for how I can manage the problem better. You know, drawing on your expertise in psychology, maybe you have a tip or two for me," I added.

"Anissa, there are no easy answers for the types of traumas and concerns that are undoubtedly weighing on your mind. I'm sure that your therapist has told you that such things can take years to resolve, if they ever do. But I guess one small tip that I would suggest – if you haven't tried this already – is to keep a journal."

"Really?" I asked, a little surprised.

"Yes. I find that they can be extremely helpful in ordering and clarifying your own thoughts and concerns. And then of course you have a personal record of your own emotional evolution, which you can trace and analyze later, as needed."

His computer pinged lightly. "Excuse me for a second," he said, as he took a moment to respond to whatever had just demanded his attention. He consulted some data and then typed a quick response, as I wondered about the countless things he must be working on: academic research, managing his hedge fund, seeing students like me, and staying on top of so much scholarship, as suggested by the innumerable books vying for a space in his small, crowded office with a nice, fourteenth-floor view of Manhattan.

"I'm sorry. Go on," he said, looking back at me, and leaning back in his ergonomic office chair a little. "We were talking about keeping a journal."

"Yes. Well, actually, I used to keep a handwritten diary in Syria. My mother bought it for me when I turned eight. And I used to write in it almost every night, and – by the time I was fourteen – there were several volumes. I really wish I still had it to reread – both for nostalgia and self-understanding. But it was lost with everything else in my life when I fled. And it's been too difficult to think about everything that's happened to me since then, so I've just avoided the project of starting a new one."

"So maybe this meeting can be your impetus to do just that, for this new chapter in your life."

"I don't know if I'm up for it...It's so difficult to revisit certain memories..."

"I can imagine," he began sympathetically. "But you don't have to write about those... You can just start with the recent past, or whatever you're able to write about without the memories bringing you down too much."

"I suppose that's a good approach," I said, warming up to the idea.

"I honestly can't recommend it enough. In fact, I don't normally tell people this, but I'm fairly obsessive about keeping a journal myself," he added wiping a speck of dust off the screen of his computer.

"Really?" I was somewhat surprised by the revelation and flattered that he would trust me with it.

"Yes. Sometimes it feels like my private mental sanctuary. That place where I can explore everything that an efficient workday forces me to ignore."

"How exactly does it let you explore?" I asked. "Sorry, if that's prying too much... I'm just really curious about how others keep diaries." I glanced down at my fiddling fingers, a little embarrassed for prying but hoping to reassure him that he could open up to me more.

"Well, that is very personal," he noted, looking away. Professor Morales suddenly stood up out of his chair and walked towards the window and looked out at the view.

"You're right, I'm sorry – I shouldn't have asked that," I said, shifting in my seat a little, worried that I had taken liberties with a quasi-authority figure I barely knew.

"That's OK," he reassured me, still looking out the window. "I suspect you need a journal much more than I do, and I just recommended that you keep one."

He turned towards a large globe of the Earth, tilted on its axis, and gave it a flick with his finger, and reflectively watched it spin under the force of his movement. "Let's just say that in a journal you can recreate interactions with others and try to understand them better than when you were just trying to get through your day as quickly and productively as possible."

"I like that approach. But doesn't it take forever to recreate entire conversations?"

He looked up from the globe at me. "Yes, it does. That's one of the ironies of life: the more time you spend recording it, the less time you have to live it."

Just as the globe came to a rest, he gave it another turn, as if to emphasize the rest of his thought. "And even reviewing what you recorded takes time, so there's no winning the war against time. Which is why I rarely try to recall a whole conversation verbatim. I just attempt to reconstruct the words and actions that seem most representative of the moment I'm recording."

He walked back to his chair, sat down, and looked at me again. This time, his speaking style was rather matter-of-fact, as if he were reading from an instruction manual: "Usually that involves remembering the gist of what each person said, how I or others responded, and the approximate sequence of the exchange. I often don't have time to analyze whatever I've recorded, but at least it's there, if I ever want to go back to it."

"So, if nothing else, you have a record of what you thought was worthy of being recorded," I recapped, realizing that this made Professor Morales more sentimental than I had imagined him to be.

"Exactly," he affirmed, pointing his index finger at me for emphasis, as if to confirm my realization about him. "Of course, everyone has their own style, but that's what works for me."

"I really like that," I replied. "I just don't know when I'll find the time for it with all of my schoolwork."

He put his hand down on his desk with conviction. "You have to make time. Just like you make time to sleep and eat, even though neither activity is part of your schoolwork, you should consider journaling a priority – especially given what you've been through and what must be on your mind."

"I guess," I agreed, looking away, thinking about how he had no idea just what I had been through and how hard it would be to recount those things in a diary. But I didn't want to get emotional just as our meeting was coming to an end. "Time management is definitely one of the biggest challenges in college," I noted.

"Not just in college. Time is all you have, so you have to manage it well throughout your entire life. Keeping a journal didn't become any easier for me after college. During the week it's actually quite difficult. But usually I devote part of every Sunday to it, and sometimes during the week, if needed."

"And you never fall behind?"

"Of course I do. But I always feel guilty when that happens. After all, my journal is the oldest and most loyal friend I have. And it never interrupts me when I'm speaking," he added, with a boyish grin.

I laughed a little and we shared a smile. Then he looked up at the wall clock and I saw that there was just one minute left before 7 p.m.

"Well, I think you just talked me into it," I said. "Thanks for your time."

I stood up and started to leave.

"Sorry I couldn't solve Syria for you." He shrugged and gave me an apologetic grin. "But I hope I helped in some small way."

And then, just as I got to the door, I turned towards him with a question that was carelessly impulsive, because I had no idea why I would ask such a thing just as I was leaving his office.

"Oh, one other thing, Professor. Who do you blame for what is happening in Syria right now?"

He gave me a puzzled look for a moment and then rubbed the back of his neck. "My mother taught me never to discuss religion or politics, and that has served me well in life," he said with a smile, as he diplomatically dodged my question.

I left his office feeling very foolish for having put him on the spot like that, and with no time for him even to explain whatever answer he might have opted to give to a potentially complex and controversial question. But I knew why I did it: a part of me just wanted to know if he was ultimately sympathetic to my community there. I wanted to prove to myself – and above all, to Michael – that Professor Morales did care and might even be willing to help in some way. Nevertheless, those were still just my selfish hopes – he's hardly under some obligation to sympathize with the Christians of Syria and I really shouldn't have pressured him with my question the way I did. It was stupid and hardly an effective way to advance the cause with him.

Chapter 18: Julien

Sunday, 2/9/14 at 4:45.

Still getting harassing texts from Areli – that bad decision that just won't go away.

Had a new girl over here last night. She wanted to stay in my bed afterwards (as they all do), but she's in one of the guest rooms. I explained to her that I've been sleeping alone for years because of work reasons and that my policy isn't about to change for anyone. Sometimes I wish I could just share the truth: that my insomnia and violent nightmares are the real reason I can't let anyone sleep in my bed with me. But then I'd start to get all sorts of questions about the meaning and cause of these nightmares, and – more generally – there would be some risk that such personal and potentially embarrassing details about me could be leaked to others, including the gossip-hungry press that seems to have taken a greater interest in me in recent years.

And, sure enough, here I am hanging out with you, my loyal insomnia buddy, at 4:45 a.m. But this time something peculiar seems to be haunting me. When I came home from my office hours last Friday night, I was talking on my cell as I got out of my car and accidentally stepped on a sparrow that was sitting by the curb. I felt so bad about the whole thing – perhaps because its wing was so small and fragile under my shoe, and it was entirely my inattention and carelessness that ultimately broke its wing. Had I just put the call on hold long enough for me to watch where I was putting my foot on the way out of the car, I would have avoided the poor bird. But when I realized what I had done, I cut the call short, put my phone away, scooped up the injured animal in my hands, and brought it up with me into my apartment. I had the housekeeper find an appropriate cage for it and call a veterinarian to come and examine it. The vet said that I had actually injured the bird's leg as well, and its full recovery could take several months. Sigh.

I even named the poor little guy "Icarus" – after the hero in Greek mythology whose wings were melted by the sun. Not that this poor creature could have had any hubris that might be responsible for his injury – this was entirely my fault. But with this sparrow, as with Icarus, a wing was rendered useless by a more powerful force.

Maybe I'm also up thinking about Anissa, the student who came into my office today. I got a closer and longer look at her than on previous occasions. Her emerald green eyes somehow radiated with a wisdom beyond her natural age, yet with the pristine freshness of youth. She has long brown hair that seems to accentuate her slender frame (which seemed about five-foot-six). She was modestly dressed in dark jeans and a beige, earthy top that was just tight enough to hint at her round breasts. And she's exactly what I don't need in my messy life right now.

What I do need is a therapist, and I'm relieved to have finally found one. Raegan found some hot ones with great credentials and, after interviewing the two finalists, I settled on Lily. I even tested her honesty by leaving twenty one-hundred-dollar bills clumped together around a messy part of my office floor, near the guest chair where she sat. They were clearly in her view when Lily entered my office and took a seat, and it would have been easy for her to snatch one of the bills when I told her that I was stepping out for a bathroom break. There were enough bills there for her to assume that I wouldn't notice if one was missing when I returned. So I was pleased to see that she didn't give in to the temptation towards dishonesty, although she might have also assumed that this was some kind of test and purposely restrained herself to get the job. In any case, I'm meeting Lily for our first session today, in about ten hours, and hopefully I'll manage to get some sleep before then. I didn't want to be away from the office during market hours, and nights are often busy with my lecture schedule and socializing, so I tripled her hourly rate to make it worth her while to see me on Sunday afternoons. At six hundred dollars an hour, even a junior lawyer will see you on a Sunday.

Chapter 19: Anissa

∽ Saturday, February 22, 2014 ∾

To My Dearest,

The day after I saw Professor Morales during office hours, I met up with Maya for lunch at the John Jay Dining Hall (one of the university's student eateries, just a few minutes from my dorm).

"Guess what?" she began, with an almost mischievous excitement, as we put down our trays of food on the table we had chosen. "I have good news!"

"What is it?" I asked with sudden curiosity, taking a seat.

"You're invited to Julien's next party!" she beamed, as she sat down next to me.

"What?!"

"Yep. It's official – you have an invitation. The party is two weeks from today, so mark it on your calendar – the night of February 22."

"Wait, so you specifically asked if I could come?" I was still trying to make sense of this unexpected sequence of events. "I mean, you mentioned the name 'Anissa' in your request?"

"Oh no, Sweetie. I just asked him if I could bring one of my lovely friends. As I told you before, if he knew that I wanted to bring someone who's a current student, he'd definitely say no, so you have to pretend like you didn't know that it's his party when you show up."

"Ah, OK. That makes more sense, because I just saw him yesterday at his office hours and there was nothing to suggest that this might happen."

"Don't you worry – this one is all me, Babe," she said, putting her hand on my shoulder just as we were about to start eating.

"Well, that's very exciting," I responded enthusiastically, even though I felt ambivalent about the whole thing. "But I think you should take someone else."

"Why? Are you crazy? Do you know how hard it is to find someone else who can bring you to one of his parties?"

"Well, I wouldn't want to go with anyone else. I'm just not ready."

I started eating, and Maya followed suit.

"Why not, Sweetie?"

"I need to see how I do on his midterm first," I answered, between bites. "Was it a hard test when you took it?"

"Hell yes! I got a C on that test. So I had to study my ass off for the final and only managed to bring up my final grade to a B-. His tests are really hard and tricky and the grading curve is tough."

"I was afraid you'd say that!" I remarked, slumping back into my seat a bit.

"You'll be fine, Anissa. I also wasn't as serious as I should have been about studying for his class. You're one of the most disciplined students I know, so just keep doin' what you're doin' and I'm sure you won't have any problem."

"Well, I don't want to go to his private party uninvited – especially before I know whether I'm even doing well in his class. I prefer to feel like I'm in good standing if I'm going to show up like that. You know what I mean?"

"Actually, what you're saying makes perfect sense, Anissa. For an eighteen-year-old, you've got a very good head on your shoulders, I must say."

"Glad my instincts pass the Maya test," I replied lightly. "So how about this: I'll go with you to the first party that he throws after my midterm exam results come in, provided that I do fine on that test."

"With that head of yours, I'm already making the arrangements to bring you," she said with a smile.

On Sunday, February 9 (the day after my lunch with Maya), I saw Michael at another MCA meeting. To my relief, Karen wasn't present, although I kept thinking she might show up at any moment. In the end, she never showed up, but Michael seemed distant and his interactions with me were very short. At times, he also appeared impatient or disappointed when it became clear that I didn't know certain details of Mideast history. I could tell that he was in a bad mood, and when I tried to stay after the meeting to talk to him, he snapped at me.

"The meeting's over, Anissa. I need to focus on a few things alone now."

"Was there something I did to upset you? Or can I make you feel better somehow?" I asked.

"Sorry, I'm just not in the mood to talk right now," he said.

"OK," I replied, meekly, and began to make my way out of the student center. As I walked away, feeling hurt and confused, the sound of hurried footsteps from behind caught my attention.

"Inās, wait!" Michael shouted, as he ran up from behind me. "That was rude of me. I'm sorry, my head is just in a fog right now," he apologized. "I broke up with Karen yesterday, and I'm still just sorting through the related emotions and issues. Maybe we can catch up properly in a few days, once the dust settles a bit more?"

"Sorry to hear that you're going through that," I said. "I'll be happy to talk with you again, whenever you're up for it."

"Thanks, Inās."

Chapter 20: Julien

Sunday, 2/9/14 at 18:45.

Saw my new therapist at 3 p.m. Even though we had met for a good twenty minutes when I first interviewed Lily in my office, I noticed her beauty much more this time – maybe because meeting in her office made her seem more powerful. Or maybe it was her sexy outfit, or our more personal conversation this time. Whatever the explanation, Lily is a hot, leggy redhead with pouty lips, nice round breasts, and sparkling blue eyes. She also maintains a very professional demeanor, which only enhances her sexiness.

"Thank you for agreeing to come to my office," she began. "I know it's a bit of an inconvenience, but I find it easier to maintain a professional focus this way."

"Yes, I agree. And it actually feels a bit more private than my office, since neither of us will run into any of my employees here, and they do sometimes come in on weekends."

"That was quite the selection process you put me through," she noted lightly.

"You should see how hard it is to get a job at my fund."

"Well, I'm honored to have been selected as the therapist for an expert in human psychology and behavior."

"It is an honor – mostly because I have issues with trust and don't open up to people very easily, or very often. But, as with the observer effect in physics, I also know that in the realm of psychology, the observer often impacts the thing being observed."

"Very true, Julien. But that means that I will impact you while observing you no less than you might impact yourself during self-observation."

"Indeed. We'll just have to see exactly what your impact is. I already know what my own impact is. And clearly I have concluded that I need an external observer to see if the results are any better."

"What areas, in particular, are you looking to work on?"

"They both relate to women: trust and self-control. In fact, that's one of the reasons why I had Raegan, my personal assistant, find therapist candidates whom she knew I would find attractive."

"I don't follow," she said, with a slightly suspicious tone.

"Well, you can consider yourself a complete failure as a therapist –

and I can consider this entire engagement a massive waste of time – if anything sexual happens between us," I clarified, with a temerity that practically dared her to breach her professional code of ethics.

She raised an eyebrow, with her expression unfazed. "Isn't that a rather extreme and dramatic description for such an outcome?"

"I have a known weakness for beautiful women, so what better way to tackle that issue than to hire such a woman to cure it? This way, if I ever feel myself tempted to change our arrangement, we can analyze those feelings, as they happen. And I know that it's your professional duty to maintain your distance, so hopefully that will be enough to stop any temptations I may feel. But if not, we'll be able to discuss and analyze the situation."

"That sounds like a reasonable approach. But you may also have to get used to the idea that I'm going to be in control of our sessions too. I suspect that could make you feel uncomfortable."

"Well, there's very little in my personal or professional life that I don't control. So yes, your suspicion is correct."

"I suppose that's one of the advantages of being independently wealthy. But, as I'm sure you know, wealth can quickly vanish for all kinds of reasons. And, even if it doesn't, there are some very important things that no money in the world can control."

"Genuine love being one of them," I agreed.

"Exactly. Have you ever experienced that?"

"I don't think so – certainly not after I became wealthy."

"And when was that?"

"I made my first million at twenty-five and my wealth has only increased since then. Today I'm thirty-nine, with a few billion in the bank, plus about twenty billion dollars of investor money under management."

Lily glanced down at the yellow pad in her hand and scribbled some notes with her pen before she looked back up. "That must make you feel like a kind of captain of the world."

"It does. Especially in a place like Manhattan – where wealth is everything. Money is the standard, universal metric upon which the city's social hierarchy is based."

"And yet you aren't able to find a satisfying relationship with one woman," she said. Her tone had a hint of smugness it in – the kind sometimes displayed by service providers who suddenly realize just how much you need them.

I felt myself getting slightly defensive. "Putting aside the issue of trust for a moment, I've never been convinced that monogamy is the best lifestyle for me. I simply love variety too much. And if you can afford variety, then why not enjoy it?" I asked rhetorically.

"Why do you enjoy it so much?" she explored.

"When I was younger, it was mostly about the chase. The feat of finding and seducing the hottest women I could find. And once that conquest was achieved, the attendant challenge was suddenly gone."

"And when you grew older, that changed?"

"Yes. Because my wealth made it far less of a challenge. I went from being the chaser to being the chased. But the intrinsic delight of variety was still there. I think it has to do with virtually living many more lives."

"What do you mean?"

"Well, I think licentiousness may be hardwired by evolution in some weird way. A thousand years ago, the average man could sleep with maybe one or two women in his lifetime. If he was the most powerful man in the tribe, maybe he could have ten over his lifetime – because his life was short and his contact with sexually desirable women was limited by the small number of women in his tribe. And of course, sleeping with a woman usually meant fathering another child, which could have all sorts of unwanted consequences of its own."

"True," she noted, intrigued by my analysis.

"Now contrast that with today's reality for men. We live many more years now. We can meet, seduce, and sleep with far more women during our longer lives – especially with the help of the Internet and smartphones, which make it that much easier to meet new people. This city's huge and constantly changing population further ensures a steady stream of new sex partners. And thanks to modern contraception, there's almost no risk of unwanted fatherhood from all of this sex. But most of these changes came about only in the last few decades, all while our brains are still programmed to think of sex as a big deal, based on the conditions and circumstances of our prehistoric ancestors. Sleeping with so many women gives you the heady illusion that you're experiencing the equivalent of many lifetimes worth of sex from an earlier era of human history."

"That's a rather elaborate theory you've developed to rationalize your promiscuity."

"Yes, I doubt most men who sleep around think about it in such evolutionary terms. They probably just feel great and their manliness seems validated. But I suspect that this relates to the outsized way in which, for evolutionary reasons, sex with a new woman inflates a man's ego. A thousand years ago, it was rare to sleep with a new woman, and maybe the related thrill was programmed into our brains over time – so profoundly that it still influences our sexual behavior today."

"Scientific explanations aside, are you happy this way? Do you think that you can find deep, long-term satisfaction with this kind of approach to women and relationships?"

"I don't know. I guess if I met the right person, maybe the joy and fulfillment that I found with her would be greater than the intrinsic pleasure of variety... Even the novelty of variety can wear off, I suppose. Although I do wonder how likely such a development is, if it hasn't already happened in over two decades of dating."

I didn't mention to Lily that I think I'm developing a tentative interest in Anissa. It's really too early to conclude that. Besides, as my scandalously younger student, she's untouchable. Not sure how much I really want to tell Lily about that. Maybe that means I'm growing interested in my therapist too?

Chapter 21: Anissa

∽ Sunday, February 23, 2014 ∾

To My Dearest,

On February 12, I officially exchanged cell phone numbers with Michael. Up until then, we had always communicated via Facebook or email. I think we had never traded digits before then because he had always wanted to maintain a certain distance from me. The first year of our interactions, he probably thought of me as just a kid, and then, after we finally met in person last month, he was dating Karen and it might have seemed too risky and/or inappropriate for us to be calling each other. But all of that changed on Wednesday, when – after far too much typing between us, he finally wrote to me something charmingly funny: "You know, there's this amazing technology called a telephone, and it would enable us to talk to each other rather than have to type everything out all day. I just need your number to use this technology." I laughed and sent him my number. He called me a few minutes later, and I stored his number.

About ten minutes into our phone conversation, Michael again amused me with a similar line: "You know, Anissa, it turns out that there's a technology even better than the phone. You know what it is?"

"What? Skype video?"

"Even better! And it was invented before any of this stuff – it's called the face-to-face meeting."

"True, but it's quite cold out right now," I replied in amusement.

"You should know by now that bad weather is never a good excuse, as far as I'm concerned. I'll swing by in about ten minutes."

And so he braved the wintery elements for the short walk from his apartment to my dorm, and from there we sauntered together to the John Jay Dining Hall. We filled our meal trays with hot pastrami sandwiches, some salads, tea, and desserts (I opted for a brownie and he chose the strawberry ice cream).

Michael sat across from me, and we started eating. At one point in our conversation, I finally found the boldness to ask him what I had been wondering since I last saw him in person.

"I know it's none of my business, but I just hope that I didn't somehow cause your breakup with Karen."

"Is that because you were secretly hoping we'd stay together?" he asked playfully.

"No, I wouldn't put it that way," I replied with some amusement at my understatement of the week. "But you just seemed to be going through a tough time when I saw you last time, and I wouldn't want to be the reason for that."

He put down his cup of tea, as if to focus more on what he was about to say.

"Well, we were starting to grow close. You know, the comfort and familiarity that develops when you start dating someone exclusively. You get used to seeing them, talking to them, laughing with them, having sex with them, eating with them – you know, everything that comes with a relationship."

"Actually, I wouldn't know, but I can imagine…"

"Oh…I see," Michael paused for a moment to process everything that I had implicitly just communicated to him with that simple response. He then continued, trying to seem as nonchalant as possible about the disclosures that I had just shared: "Well, that's how it is," he informed me. "You get used to the person."

We each took some bites of food.

"So why did you end it?" I asked.

"I still struggle with that question myself – I mean, it's not as if she did something bad to deserve a sudden breakup… I guess I just worry that we're not really compatible in the long run, given the path that I seem to be on now with Antioch."

"Because she's not from the Middle East?"

"That's definitely a big part of it. I mean, as much as she supports me and the MCA, I just don't think she'll ever feel as passionate and invested in the cause as someone like you or me who is directly impacted because our families are from there."

"And you might be unfairly judged by others from our community."

"I've thought about that too and it saddens me a bit, but that's the reality. The issue could become a distraction or even a political liability – particularly if my leadership of the movement is ever contested and I need to persuade members of our community to support me."

"I still can't believe that you really plan to do this… I mean, it's such a grand vision."

"Yes, it is."

"Don't you ever worry that it might just be too monumental a project to pursue?"

"Well, to quote someone whose dream was no smaller, 'If you will it, it is no dream.'"

I loved how his eyes radiated full of hope and determination when he spoke about his vision. "I really like that…Who said it?"

"Theodore Herzl."

"Who's that?"

"He led the movement to create a state for the Jews in their ancestral home. And our movement will create a state for Christians in their ancestral home. So as we take this arduous journey, we should remember those inspiring and fearless words: 'If you will it, it is no dream.'"

His Adam's apple appeared more pronounced as he repeated that powerful refrain, and I felt a privileged proximity to him – as if I could have been a journalist interviewing an important political activist over lunch.

"It's so strange how you seem to admire and support Israel and the Zionists. Growing up in Syria, I always heard about how evil they were in school and in the media – occupying Syria's Golan Heights and oppressing the Palestinians."

"Well, you were clearly raised on a lot of misinformation. Of course, Israel has made mistakes and done some bad things – like every state. But the real picture is very different from what you'll hear in Syrian schools and news broadcasts," he asserted, taking another bite of his sandwich.

"Maybe. But as Jesus said: 'Render unto Caesar what is Caesar's, and unto God what is God's.'"

"What do you mean? How is that relevant?" Michael asked, amused as to why I would mention that quote in this context. He took a first bite of the ice cream dessert on his tray.

"Whether in the form of taxes, political allegiances, or anything else concerning the state, we generally supported the Syrian government. And that includes its hostility towards Israel and the Zionists."

"Yes, but that kind of weak and unquestioning compliance is exactly what I want to end by creating Antioch. I'm tired of Mideast Christians being forced into quiet and undignified submissiveness because their physical security depends on the mercy of a Muslim majority. And, as you diversify your sources of information, you will see that we actually have much to learn from how the Zionists built their state."

"Really?" I asked, with skepticism tempered by my desire to stay open-minded – especially because I felt so drawn to the man in front of me.

"Yes. Growing up in the USA, with a free and diverse press and open debate, I was exposed to a lot of information that you probably missed. The education and media of a corrupt and illegitimate government naturally tries to distract its population with external enemies. So of course you would hear lots of negative accusations and misinformation, without any positive reports or details about Israel."

"Well, I do know that the Israelis have taken in many injured Syrians and given them medical treatment, so obviously they can't be as horrible as we were taught."

Michael and I had finished eating everything but our desserts. I was already half done with my brownie, but I started eyeing his strawberry ice cream. I blushed a bit when Michael noticed.

"Here," he offered, with a smile, holding up the bowl to me. "Try some."

I dipped my spoon into the cold, strawberry-flavored treat. "Thanks," I replied, with a guilty smile, realizing that he was now far more interested in our conversation than any of the food in front of us.

"Enjoy," he said, trying to slow himself down, but clearly too eager to continue. "You probably also didn't know that twenty percent of the Israeli population is actually Arab, including a Christian Arab who sits on Israel's supreme court and others in the Israeli parliament."

"Really?"

"Yes, it's a real democracy, with full rights for women and religious minorities."

Michael saw how much I was enjoying his ice cream. "You're welcome to finish it," he added with a wink before leaning back in his chair, as if to confirm that he was done eating.

"Sorry for stealing your ice cream – this was much better than I expected," I apologized.

"Well, that's all the more reason for you to finish it because it wasn't doing that much for me," he noted with dry irony.

"We should eat together more often," I joked. He chuckled, but I could tell that he wasn't finished speaking. "I'm sorry – go on with what you were saying."

"In Israel, a Muslim can openly convert to Christianity, or any other religion. Or just renounce religion and God altogether. And that kind of freedom is no small thing. In the rest of the Middle East and North Africa, doing something like that can get you killed."

"Wow," I mumbled with a mouthful, experiencing a bit of an ice-cream headache. "I've never heard such things before," I admitted.

"Exactly my point about the information you grew up with. You know what, Inās?" He looked at me playfully. "I'm going to give you a homework assignment, just to counter the toxic narrative you were obviously fed as a child."

I smiled in curiosity. "What is it?"

"I want you to read the novel *Exodus* by Leon Uris. It's a powerful book that will help you to understand the real story behind Israel – why and how it was created, and what it represents."

"Are you serious?" I looked at him as if he was crazy. Yet there was something tantalizing about his readiness to think so freely and independently.

"Completely. It's an epic book – translated into over fifty languages and made into a movie starring Paul Newman. And it's relevant to the project of building a Christian state in the Middle East."

"Why?"

"Because like the Jews who founded Israel, we Christians have been persecuted for millennia, have survived genocide, are indigenous to the Middle East, and will build a tiny, democratic state for ourselves there – despite whatever enemies and challenges we may face along the way in that tough neighborhood."

"So you want me to read about this in Exodus?" I asked, as I came dangerously close to finishing the ice cream.

"Yes. You need to reframe your thinking about certain things. And then, I want you to read *Startup Nation* – just to learn about what an incredible, high-tech economy Israel became, despite so many enemies and threats. We can do that too."

"More reading?" I asked in amused disbelief.

"Yes. These books can open your mind and inspire you to see what we can do for our own Christian state."

I showed Michael the empty bowl of ice cream with a childishly sad and silly face.

"Shall I get you some more?" he offered, with a good-natured smile.

"OK, I realize that you want me to read these books, but are you trying to bribe me with ice cream now?" I asked lightheartedly.

"Whatever it takes," he replied unflappably. His charismatic confidence is perhaps what drew me to him most. He could have asked me to do a handstand in the dining hall, and I might have considered it.

"You do realize that I have a ridiculously long reading list for three of my classes this semester."

"Just be glad I'm not asking you to learn Hebrew now, although I will need a Secretary of State who is fluent in all of the languages of the Middle East," he joked.

I laughed. "Yes, if you were adding that to the list, I think I could just drop out of Columbia and enroll in Michael University."

He chuckled briefly but soon transitioned back to his usual intensity. "All kidding aside, Inās, our future Christian state will be a natural ally of Israel in the region for many political and geostrategic reasons, not to mention shared values."

"Well, I'll try to keep an open mind as I do some more reading on the subject."

"Good. And you have to start getting used to the idea that the Christians of the Middle East can be strong, like the Jews there. We have to learn to defend ourselves, the way they did. The Christian doctrine of turning the other cheek isn't helping us, because we've run out of cheeks."

Michael looked like a rock of determination when he spoke about our cause. Sometimes I could feel myself wanting to anchor to him – to latch my arms around him and feel his sturdiness and strength. It was a new feeling, and one that I preferred to suppress until I understood it better.

Instead, I forced myself to stay focused on the topic at hand. "There is a part of me that couldn't agree with you more. I mean, 50,000 Christians were expelled from my hometown. Islamist animals committed unspeakable evils in Homs – including to me and my family – that I'm still trying to erase from my mind."

"It pains me every time I hear you say that, although I still have no idea what exactly happened to you and your family."

His expression softened, as he searched my eyes for a clue into my past.

"And I don't know if you ever will," I admitted sadly. "I'm still trying to heal those wounds…" I looked away. "And right now I need to think about those memories as little as possible."

"I'm sorry," he said gently.

"No, it's OK," I looked back at him. "But even after everything that I've been through, and all of the reasons I have to think that we should stop turning the other cheek, I'm still not convinced that violence is the answer. As Jesus says in the Book of Matthew, 'all who take the sword will perish by the sword.'"

"Well, you know that I don't share your faith in the existence of God and the truth of the Bible. But I did study Christian texts and they aren't entirely pacific. The Bible also says that the sword can deliver justice. The Book of Romans states, 'if you do wrong, be afraid, for he does not bear the sword in vain. For he is the servant of God, an avenger who carries out God's wrath on the wrongdoer.'"

"True," I agreed. I loved how he could recite verses from the Bible. "And there is another part of me that thinks our community must embrace the idea of self-defense like never before. So many Christians – from the time of the Romans until today's Middle East – have faced the worst kinds of persecution with peace and love. It's beautiful and inspiring on some level, but if we're all dead in the end, what good does it do anyone?" I asked rhetorically.

"There'll be no one left to live by any Christian values, much less share them," he recapped my point. "And in a brutal region like the Middle East, pacifism dooms us to extinction, and only empowers the violent extremists. As Christians, we have a duty to stop evil as best we can," he added.

"Sometimes violence is necessary to prevent even more violence," I concluded, almost as if it were an epiphany.

"Yes. Some Christian values, like protecting the vulnerable, resisting evil, and seeking justice, become impossible without force."

"So Antioch would have to be set up as a highly militarized state. At least initially, right?" I asked.

He leaned forward, as if we were now huddling to plan the most crucial details of our future state, and his eyes looked at me with total certainty. "Definitely. It would need enough military strength to survive in the world's toughest neighborhood. So, yes – especially if Antioch ends up being as small as Lebanon."

"But would it still be set up as a democracy?"

"Of course, although merely defining it as a liberal, voting republic won't suffice to make it a true democracy. Just look at the Mideast countries where elections have been held over the last few years – Iraq, Egypt, Tunisia, Iran. As a Christian or other religious minority – or even as a modern, free-thinking individual – would you want to live in any of those places?"

"Definitely not."

"We have to create democratic institutions and a culture that tolerates dissent. We need a free and independent press, a vocal opposition, freedom of assembly and religion, and an independent judiciary – all of the freedoms that we have here in the USA… "

"You really think that Antioch can bring all of that to the Middle East? Even as a highly militarized state?"

"Israel did it. Why can't we?" He looked at the time on his cell phone and it was clear from his expression that we had stayed far beyond what he had planned and a thousand forgotten tasks suddenly came back to visit him. We stood up together and prepared to leave.

"I guess we can," I said, trying to hit an optimistic note.

"If you will it, it is no dream," he affirmed, with a twinkle in his eye.

"That does have a nice ring to it," I said.

"You know what else we can do?" he asked, momentarily stopping for dramatic effect.

"What?" I asked, curious.

"Go ice skating on Valentine's Day."

"Really?" I felt my face light up in a smile, happy to transition back from the grandiose "big picture," to that much smaller and more personal moment between Michael and me.

Chapter 22: Anissa

∞ Monday, February 24, 2014 ∞

To My Dearest,

    At 3 p.m. on February 14, the security guard for my dorm called me with a cute message from my visitor. "There's a Mr. Kassab downstairs who wants to know if you'll be his Valentine today." I quickly looked in the mirror one last time before leaving, and felt butterflies in my stomach as I closed the door and made my way to the elevator.
    When I arrived in the lobby, I saw that Michael was waiting for me by the door. He held it open for me and we exited the building into the crisp New York air.
    As we walked towards the subway stop on 116th Street, I lightly shared a small confession: "Do you realize that this is officially the first date of my life?"
    "Wow. Well, it's good to know that there's no pressure on me here!" he replied ironically.
    I playfully elbowed him. "None at all."
    "And that means it's also a good thing that I brought these goodies for you," he said, taking a small bag of Baci chocolates out of his coat. "But – since this is your first date – I should warn you that most dates do not come with chocolate! You know, just to manage your expectations a little."
    "And why shouldn't they all come with chocolates?" I replied with a teasing smile.
    "I guess that's a fair question. But if you got chocolates on every date, then getting them on Valentine's Day wouldn't seem very special, now would it?"
    "I think I'd be OK with that," I said, amusing us both with my understatement as we arrived at the subway entrance.
    We passed through the turnstile, went down the stairs, and stood by the track, waiting for the downtown train to show up. Our flirty banter resumed as the area gradually filled up with more New Yorkers heading downtown in sweaters, scarves, hats, and gloves.
    "Well, I think there may be a compromise arrangement we can work out," he replied, looking down at me with a smile.
    I glanced up into his brown eyes, curious. "What's that?"

"You see, Baci literally means 'kiss' in Italian, so I think you could fairly expect some kind of kiss on every date."

"Will I ever get both chocolate and non-chocolate kisses on the same date?" I responded, glimpsing at him coyly from the side.

"Are we getting greedy now?" he joked. "Ten minutes into your very first date ever? I guess you may need to make up for some lost time," he said with a teasing glint.

"I might."

"Well, your odds of getting both kinds of kisses are probably best on Valentine's Day, so there may be cause for optimism."

And just as it seemed like the space between us was subtly starting to shrink, the train arrived. But we soon stood even closer to each other on the crowded subway car. As we traveled downtown with countless strangers, we were at times pressed up against one another during the twenty-minute ride to the Columbus Circle station. At 59th Street, we got out of the subway and walked over to the skating rink in Central Park.

February 14, 2014 brought with it a few firsts, and ice skating was one of them.

Michael was comfortable and experienced on the ice but went very slowly so that he could effectively serve as my training wheels while I clung to his arm to avoid crashing every other minute. Thanks to his support, I fell only every ten minutes or so, and sometimes brought him down with me – usually with some silly or self-conscious laughs along the way. He always helped me up, and a few times, I felt his big palm cup itself around my hip when lifting me to my feet.

After holding onto him so much while ice skating, it felt almost oddly distant for us not to be holding hands after we left and headed back towards the subway together. But the tension surrounding if and when our hands might clasp again (without any external cause like ice skating) proved to be a good distraction from my sore behind. After I jokingly complained about it, Michael replied, "Next time we visit a rink, remember to stuff your pants with lots of toilet paper, or some other butt cushion."

A few minutes later, I saw the subway station in the distance, and figured that we probably weren't going to hold hands again. I reasoned that there wasn't that much time left before we'd have to stop holding hands in order to go down the stairs and through the subway turnstile, and that might make it seem even more awkward or silly to have held hands for so short a time before that. Of course, we could resume holding hands on the subway platform, but then we'd have an audience and it wouldn't be as cold, so the reason for our hand-holding would be more obviously a growing intimacy rather than, for example, a way to keep our palms warm.

"How are your hands doing?" Michael suddenly asked, as if he had read my thoughts. "Are they warm enough?" he inquired, taking my hand into his.

"They are now," I replied with a smile.

Chapter 23: Julien

Sunday, 2/16/14 at 20:45.

Had another session with my cute shrink. There's definitely something sexy about Lily – and it's not just because – as my therapist – she's formally off-limits and therefore taboo. She's like a psychological chess partner of sorts, constantly trying to extract information out of me, as I try to conceal it. There's something intimate about watching her process each of my personal disclosures, sometimes noting her thoughts and impressions about our exchanges on her yellow notepad.

"Tell me more about Areli. Why do you think she's still calling and texting you?"

"Maybe it's ego. Maybe she wants to feel as if she's somehow different from the countless other women I've had flings with."

"But don't you think that's a normal reaction for women who might not want to think that they've just had casual sex? Or who quickly form emotional attachments after sex, as many women do?

"Yes, I agree that ego or neediness alone can't explain it or this sort of thing would happen with many of my other lovers. Maybe she has some kind of psychological imbalance in her. Or maybe she's just an opportunist and wants to see what she can get out of me. It wouldn't be the first time."

"So women have taken advantage of you before?"

"Yes. They know that I'm wealthy and have influential connections, so women have tried to leverage our sexual relations into all kinds of nonsexual favors. I actually don't mind it, to some extent. I'm happy to help someone – especially if she's added some pleasure to my life. But I don't like to feel pressured or threatened into it. That only backfires, as it has with this girl."

"How often does something like this happen to you with one of your flings?" she asked, as if she were just gathering data for a survey.

"Enough times that I've been thinking about making girls sign some sort of contract before entering into any sexual relations with me."

"This incident with Areli has made you consider implementing this policy?"

"Yes."

"You really think it would help?"

"It's certainly worth trying. I'm sure you know about the

psychological research that confirms the wisdom of such an approach."

"You mean the studies showing that when people sign a promise to answer truthfully – before they fill out a form – there is an increase in the percentage of forms filled out accurately?"

"Yes, exactly. So perhaps, for that reason alone, I should institute some kind of contract – not because I'd ever sue one of these women for breach of contract, but just so that they're more likely to respect the rules of the arrangement."

"But when you refer to it as an 'arrangement,' it sounds very much like a transaction, which is telling."

"All relationships are transactional."

"Do you really believe that?" Lily asked, as she noted something on her pad. "What about parent-child relationships?"

"Well, I've never been a parent. But I'm obviously familiar with the unconditional love that children are supposed to receive, and that I received from my own mother. But I think people idealize just how unconditional that parental love really is."

"What do you mean?"

"I think the vast majority of normal parents have some minimum expectations for their children and would stop loving and supporting them under certain conditions. For example, most parents assume that their child will try to live by the basic rules of society. But imagine a mother who is attending a family picnic when her son shows up with a machinegun and senselessly guns down her husband, her two daughters, her parents, and another twenty random victims in her family. Would this mother still love her son? It's hard to imagine how she could, after such a heinous act resulting in such devastating and permanent losses. But even if she somehow could still love him, if he later sought refuge in her house from the authorities, wouldn't she still turn him in to the police, even though she knows that he may ultimately face the death penalty?"

"You know, Julien, I've noticed that when you talk about parent-child relationships, you've mentioned some very dark scenarios."

"It was just an extreme hypothetical, intended to illustrate my point about the transactional nature of all relationships."

"I might have believed that, had you not avoided my questions about your father."

"I'm not ready to talk to you about him. And I'm still waiting for you to concede the truth of my observation."

"Regarding all human relationships?"

"Yes. Except in relatively rare scenarios. Like when children are disabled or too young for the person helping them to expect anything of them or their conduct. Then you could say that the person loving or caring for them is doing so unconditionally. Or, when an adult or elderly person is receiving love and care, because of some medical incapacity or other exceptional scenario and cannot possibly be expected to reciprocate. Anyone who cares for such a person without compensation or even recognition does so out of some absolute love that has no transactional expectations attached to it. But outside of uncommon situations like that, human interactions are essentially transactional – including ours."

"Would you feel better about our interactions if they weren't transactional?"

She unfolded her legs and changed her expression ever so subtly, so that – if I wanted to – I could have interpreted that look as inviting me somewhere we hadn't yet gone.

"Well, there is the sense that you care about me only because you're being paid to care about me. And that ultimately makes me dispensable – replaceable by any other client who will pay you a similar rate for similar services."

"I could say the exact same thing. You could just as easily replace me with another therapist who will charge you similar rates for similar services."

"Exactly. In the end, we are all just participating in exchanges that we think will in some way make us better off."

"But you say this in a way that sounds almost disappointed – as if, contrary to what you've said in the past, maybe you really are seeking some kind of deeper and more absolute connection."

"Maybe I am. But there's something absurd about entering into a transaction with a therapist so that she can help me to find a non-transactional relationship."

"I can appreciate the irony of your observation, but you describe my services far too narrowly. I'm not trying to help you find true love. My goal is to help you to understand yourself better, so that you can show yourself the best way forward – with relationships and any other issues that you want to focus on."

"Yes, I know. I'm just joking. I think I just enjoy sparring with you about these issues. I don't get to have such conversations very often."

"Maybe you've grown bored because you're always the boss – always in complete control."

"It's funny because sometimes I do think that I'm getting bored of women, but you've described things much more accurately."

"Yes, I don't think you're bored of women – just the kinds of relationships that you've been having with them. So, if nothing else, our sessions can show you another way to relate to women. Simply by empowering them and opening up to them, as you have with me, it can change the dynamic into something that you find more satisfying and meaningful."

Chapter 24: Anissa

∞ Tuesday, February 25, 2014 ∽

To My Dearest,

    I'm so pleased that I finally caught you up to the present (given that there isn't that much to tell you since my Valentine's Day with Michael)! Now if I can manage to write to you on a regular basis, each update should concern the last few days, and not events that happened months or years ago.

    I haven't seen Michael since February 14 because the next day he took a special trip to Damascus to meet with local Christian activists, to get a better sense of what's happening on the ground, and to help however he can. I've been quite worried for his safety, but he says that he's gone to Syria a few times over the last few years on similar missions. He told me that he's able to re-enter the United States with a special permit that he secured from the State Department, in exchange for sharing whatever intelligence he's able to gather for them about the regime, the different rebel factions fighting it, and the state of Christians and other minorities, etc. He also reassured me that he's developed a reliable and extensive network of contacts there, both in the regime and among moderate rebel fighters, as well as in the Christian community. So I pray that he'll return safely as planned tomorrow, and I'm grateful that he's been sending me periodic updates via email and Facebook.

    But my nightmare about January 18, 2012 has returned and tormented me every night since Michael left for Syria. No matter how many contacts he has, it is still Hades where he now moves about – and just the thought of him there reawakens my horrid memories from Syria, and all of the dangers that might take him from me – as if the infernal war there hadn't already taken enough from my life. Desperate to avoid the nightmares that haunted me the first few nights after his departure, I tried the techniques that had often helped during my first year in New York. Before going to bed, I would light a candle and hold my necklace while imagining my grandmother reassuring me as she handed it to my mother, who then also tried to calm me while giving me the necklace. I would picture my parents listening to my plea not to get into their car; and I would then reminisce about one of my happy, prewar, Christmas memories with them, when we were all safely in church, enjoying our time together. But my attempts at "mind management" haven't helped at all over the last few days: in my dreams, my parents don't listen to me; they get into their car, pick up my brother, and I get a call informing me that they have all been burned to death in a horrible collision. Sometimes I am in the car with them, watching them die. Other times I am holding a shovel, digging their graves. Still other times, I relive the ghastly events of January 18, 2012 exactly as they happened. I just pray that these oneiric vultures finally fly away and leave me in peace upon Michael's safe return to New York.

And there hasn't been much to report about Professor Morales – except that the last two classes from this week were as interesting to me as his lectures have always been. But I'm writing to you about him now because earlier today, when I saw Maya at our Econ study group, she shared some juicy gossip with me. It was somehow a welcome diversion from my latent but growing anxiety about Michael being in Syria.

Once our study group had disbursed, we made our way to the university gym, where we had planned to go running together. As we walked towards the Dodge Fitness Center, Maya's voice suddenly became a bit more hushed. "You know what I heard the other day about the TA for your Psychology and Markets class?" she began.

"You mean the pretty blonde woman? Elise?"

"Yeah, her."

"What about her?" I asked, mildly intrigued.

"Well, rumor has it that she's been sleeping with Julien."

"What?!" I stopped in my tracks and she followed suit, as my mouth stayed speechlessly agape for a moment as I tried to digest the information.

"Mm hmm," she confirmed with a suppressed grin, as if trying not to let any judgmental thoughts slip out.

"How did you find that out?"

"Oh, I can't tell you that, Honey. But I have my sources and they're very reliable."

"When did this happen?"

"Apparently it's been going on since last fall, when Elise first applied to be his TA."

"What?!" I said again, as shocked as I was the first time.

"Mm hmm," she repeated with the same self-censoring look, before releasing a belly laugh at our repetitive conversational pattern.

"I still can't believe it," I finally remarked, as we resumed our stroll towards the fitness center. "I mean, they both seem so serious and professional when they interact with each other in class – you'd never guess that there was anything like that going on outside of the classroom."

"Well, that's the word on the street. But you didn't hear it from me. Actually, you didn't hear it at all. You're kind of becoming one of my besties now, so I wanted to tell you – especially since you're in his class. But I need you to promise me that you won't share this info with anyone else."

"I promise you. Honestly, I think I'd rather forget it. Because having such thoughts in my mind during class will only disrupt my focus."

"Ohh, you envious now, ain't ya?" Maya teased me with a playful elbow.

"Hahaha, well I didn't mean it in that way. I just think it'll be harder to take them both seriously if I'm imagining them in bed together while I'm supposed to be taking notes on whatever he or she is saying in class."

"Come on, you can 'fess up to me. It'll be our little secret if you have a crush on Julien. You definitely would not be the first!"

"No, I promise you, I don't. I mean, he's an interesting man, but I – "

"An interesting man?" Maya burst into chuckles. "Now *that* is the understatement of the year, I think. He happens to be the most sought-after bachelor in all of New York City but, to Anissa, he's merely 'an interesting man' – you know, like he's got potential but not quite up to her standards!" she chortled.

I indulged her levity for a bit, as we left the cold air behind us for the warmth of the fitness center we had just entered. And when she was done teasing me, I set the record straight.

"Actually, you'll be pleased to know that I finally went on my first date! On Valentine's Day, no less," I told her with a smile.

"Well, look at my Syrian virgin go! High-five, girlfriend!" she exclaimed playfully, as I raised my palm to slap her hand victoriously. "So who's the lucky fella? I want all the details!"

"His name is Michael and he's a Ph.D. candidate here."

As we walked towards the dressing room area, we passed various sections of the fitness center, each with people doing different things: yoga, weightlifting, aerobics, and other activities.

"What's he like? I mean, tell me all about him! Don't make a sista' fish for the details!" Maya complained teasingly.

"Tall, very handsome, athletic, and born to lead. He's probably the most important leader of Middle East Christians in North America. In fact, he's in Syria right now."

"Look at you, Anissa! I'm so happy for you. I just hope he's staying safe over there."

"Yeah, me too. I got an email from him this morning, so that was a relief."

"So what happened on your date?" she asked.

"Well, it's very new, so I'm still not even sure what it all means."

"What do you mean?"

"Well, Michael didn't even kiss me on our first date. But he did take my hand at one point, on our way home. And he walked me back to my dorm, where there was definitely some awkward tension when we were saying goodbye by the entrance, as if he wanted to kiss me. But I guess he didn't want me to feel embarrassed by the security guard who would have seen us, not to mention all of the other students who were coming and going in the area."

"Aww…So he was being a gentleman."

"Yes. But he recently broke up with his girlfriend, so maybe that has something to do with it too. Maybe he's not quite ready, so he's taking it slow."

"Could be."

"I also think he understands my cultural background and is very sensitive to it."

We reached the women's dressing room, found two adjacent lockers, and started to change into our workout clothing.

"Does he know that you're a virgin?" Maya asked.

"He knows that he was my first official date ever," I replied, slightly self-conscious. "So maybe that's part of it too."

"Yeah, I'm sure it is. He'll probably take things nice and slow, if he really cares for you and is a gentleman."

"That's kind of a relief. I mean, it seems like there's so much pressure around here to have sex."

"You mean here at Columbia? Or in the city?"

"Both, I guess. Things here are just so different from the norms in Syria, where there's a real premium placed on virginity – it's hugely important."

"Well, it can be important here too. Just depends on the girl and her upbringing. And some girls are really smart and shrewd about losing their virginity."

"What do you mean?"

"There have been a few that auctioned it off on the Internet for ridiculous amounts of money."

"Are you serious?" I asked, in disbelief.

"Look it up. Some Brazilian girl sold her virginity on eBay for almost $800,000."

"Really? When was this?"

"I think it was about two years ago. But she wasn't the first. And she won't be the last. You hear about this sort of thing at least once a year. It probably happens much more than that, but it's only when there's a huge sum of money involved, like with that Brazilian, that everyone's talking about it."

"Well, selling your virginity for almost a million dollars certainly seems like a better way to honor it than going to some frat party and getting so drunk you don't even realize or remember the man who took it from you."

"Amen to that, my Syrian sista'. You are on a roll this evening with the understatements. First you call Julien 'interesting' and then you note that selling your virginity for almost a million dollars is better than losing it to some drunk slob you can't remember."

We shared a hearty laugh and finished changing into our running clothes.

"There are definitely some hos on this campus," she began. "And plenty more in this city. And the fact that you're so different from those types only makes it that much more likely that you'll fetch a nice figure on eBay for the popping of your cherry," she joked suggestively.

"Well, I would never do something like that – unless of course the only alternative was the frat party option."

We laughed again and left the dressing room.

Chapter 25: Julien

Sunday, 2/23/14 at 22:06.

Had another session with Lily today, for about ninety-five minutes. Around twenty minutes into our session, we talked a bit about how Areli continues to harass me.
"Why don't you go to the police?" she asked.
"Is it just me, or do I detect some concern in your voice?"
"Well, it's my job to be concerned about the things that concern my clients. And you seem concerned about this."
"Ah yes, transactional concern."
She rolled her eyes, knowing not to indulge that discussion again. "So you're not going to report her to the authorities?"
"There's something emasculating about that," I replied. "It's not as if she poses any physical danger to me or threatened anything specific. So there aren't even legal grounds for the police to take action against her. She's just a nuisance – or maybe a good reminder of the risks attached to some of my bad habits."
"That's a good way to reframe it, I suppose. So there's really no harm that she can cause you?"
"Oh, there's always some kind of potential harm that can happen the minute two people share a room alone," I said looking suggestively at her closed office door. She chuckled, trying to contain a playful thought.
She finally released it: "Do you think we're safe from each other here?"
"Well, we've now done this three times and we both still have all of our limbs, so I'd say that we're off to a pretty good start."
"Indeed. So what sort of harm do you think Areli could cause you, now that she can no longer share a closed room with you?"
"Never underestimate the imagination of a spurned woman," I replied. "But for now she hasn't threatened anything in particular, so she remains in the nuisance-you-can't-do-anything-about category."
"So why haven't you at least blocked her from your phone?"
"Oh, I did. Yesterday, as a matter of fact."
"What took you so long?"
"Well, for a while I thought that blocking her could deprive me of whatever early warning she might inadvertently signal while harassing

me. But then I realized that she's going to do whatever she's going to do because I refuse to give in to threats or blackmail on principle."

"What could she use to blackmail you?"

"I'd rather not get into the details of it, unless it actually comes up. But the bottom line is that I'm not going to pay her even one dollar to make her go away. On principle. And so for the same principle, why even let her have any effect on me with her calls and texts before she does whatever it is that she's going to do? And, of course, if she's not actually going to do anything, which could very well be the case, then there's even less reason to receive her communications."

Lily seemed to acknowledge the merit in my approach and we eventually moved on to other topics. At one point, I told her about Icarus, the injured bird that I took in, after accidentally breaking its wing.

"Why do you think that nursing him back to health makes you feel that way?" she asked, after I described how caring for the bird brought me a certain solace.

"It's sort of silly, but in the absence of a family of my own, the sparrow gives me some sort of answer, when I'm staring down the nihilistic abyss."

"What do you mean?"

"I have dark thoughts. I've had them since my mother left my father and took me with her."

"How old were you?"

"Nine."

"So it was 1984 – the year I was born," Lily noted coyly. And then suddenly my mood shifted for a moment, and I felt myself leaving the sparrow and the darkness and was totally in the moment with Lily – her vivacious smile, her long legs, her perceptive blue eyes.

"Yes, you're almost young enough for me to date you," I joked. "But we do have this professional relationship now."

"Indeed, we do," she said cordially. "So I'll resist your invitation to banter, and return our focus to the question at hand. Although that does raise the question: why do you prefer younger women?"

I wondered whether Lily realized that she had just telegraphed her own interest in me. Ironically, she further digressed by asking me a date-like question just as she was noting the need for us to return our focus to the injured sparrow and how it helps me to escape the darkness. I indulged her tangent, as if it were unquestionably the clinically correct approach for her to take at that moment. I was curious to see where doing so might lead.

"I've thought about that question enough to know that there's more to my preference than the typical reasons why older men like younger women."

"You mean because men generally think that younger women are more beautiful? Or because younger women are less likely to pressure a man into a serious commitment since there's more time on their biological clock? Or because getting a much younger woman is usually harder for a man, and therefore provides more of an ego boost?"

"Yes, those are all fairly typical reasons."

"And none applies to you?"

"Well, I do think that younger women are generally more attractive to me, but there are always exceptions," I noted, with a suggestive smile.

"Excuse me, but I am very much a woman who is younger than you!" she retorted in amusement. "But we all have our cutoff points, I suppose."

"Yes. We do. And what is yours?" I asked, genuinely curious.

"This isn't about me. So that's not an appropriate question," she asserted, apparently realizing that her professionalism had lapsed. "This is therapy, not a date – remember?"

"Fair enough. But there's something about you that sometimes makes me forget that," I teased her. "I'm sorry, where were we? Oh yes, youthful beauty is definitely one reason why I prefer younger women, but the second reason doesn't really apply to me. As I've told you before, I'm not opposed to a serious commitment, if I find the right woman. And the third reason about the ego boost also doesn't apply."

"Because a younger woman has never rejected you for being too old, so there's no age-related challenge to boost your ego. They all focus too much on your financial success and stature to care about your age."

"Exactly."

"OK, so what's the less typical reason behind your preference for younger women?"

"Well, I don't know if it's less typical per se, as I haven't conducted any kind of scientific study on this question. But the desire for immortality isn't typically cited by older men when they explain their preference for younger women, although I'm sure it may be present for many, at least subconsciously."

"You want to live forever?"

"I'm not sure. But — unless I'm struggling with the darkness within — I like to sustain the illusion that death is actually much farther from me than it really is."

"So it's more a denial of mortality than a wish for immortality."

"Precisely. For me, attracting a twenty-year old woman allows me to nurture the illusion that I'm no closer to death than I was at the age of twenty. For those few hours when we're together, I'm hearing her fresh laugh, feeling her unblemished and tight skin, enjoying her youthful vigor, and hearing her inexperienced outlook on life, all of which makes me forget for a moment that I'm actually thirty-nine. And the fact that this much younger woman feels the same attraction to me as she might feel to a twenty-year-old man, effectively transforms me into a twenty-year-old man. Thanks to that magical moment with her, I become a thirty-nine-year-old mind reincarnated in a twenty-year-old body, or me as a twenty-year old somehow transported from 1993 to 2014. A much younger woman is a psychological time machine to the older man she likes."

I expected Lily to say something but she was just taking notes on her pad with a slightly raised eyebrow. She flipped back to an earlier page of her notes and then finally looked up and spoke: "Older women tend to be far more confident, sexually comfortable, and assertive than much younger women — which is why middle-aged men who prefer females half their age often have self-esteem problems."

"Yes, that is often the case," I agreed. "But I don't know of too many self-made billionaires with low self-esteem," I pointed out. "Their problem tends to be outsized ego."

"Which can mask deep insecurities," she countered.

"Fair enough," I conceded with a friendly smile. "I'll let you decide, since I've hired you to do that, right?"

"Right," she smiled back. "OK, let's go back to what you said earlier: 'the sparrow gives me some sort of answer, when I'm staring down the nihilistic abyss.' And then you mentioned that you've had dark thoughts ever since you and your mother left your father. Why did she leave him?"

I looked at my watch, and was relieved to see that we had already met for more than the ninety minutes we had agreed upon for this session.

"I'm sorry, Lily. We're actually five minutes over, and I have a ton of work to do on some new trading strategies that my firm's investment committee is meeting about tomorrow morning. We'll have to continue next time."

Lily looked at her watch and seemed to return herself to reality. "Right, I lost track of time." I could tell that she wanted those answers. But I wasn't ready to give them to her – or maybe anyone.

Chapter 26: Anissa

∽ Sunday, March 2, 2014 ∽

To My Dearest,

I was so relieved to learn that Michael had returned safely from Syria last Wednesday, as planned. I really wanted to see him as soon as he arrived, but he was jetlagged and behind on everything in his life: his doctoral work, responding to his PR clients, and some freelance articles on Syria that were due within twenty-four hours of his arrival back home.

But last night I finally saw him for a few hours, and I guess it was officially our second date. He had heard that there was a special screening of the movie *Exodus* on campus, and invited me to watch it with him. Michael figured correctly that I hadn't finished reading the six-hundred-page book in the two weeks since he had recommended it to me (on top of all of my school work), so he wanted to accelerate what he called my "deprogramming" – a joke he made as we walked through the chilly evening to the screening room.

"It's not as if I was in a cult or something," I protested lightly.

"Well, there is a certain cult of Israel-hatred and most people who were raised in the Arab world belong to it, unfortunately." His breath formed puffs of steam visible through the shining night lamps. "But you'll have a very handsome man to look at for three-and-a-half hours, so it should be relatively painless," he added with a playful smile.

"Oh, I didn't realize that you were starring in this movie," I replied in a flirty tone. I couldn't resist.

He chuckled. "Well, I'm flattered that you think I could look like this in 2014, even after starring in a 1960 film."

"You mean you're not over seventy years old?"

"Thanks to my special cocktail of nutritional supplements, I have pharmaceutical companies around the world begging me to sell them my secret recipe."

We shared a laugh.

"OK, so who is this hunk from another era?" I asked.

"It's Paul Newman." Michael noticed my non-reaction to his answer and added, "I guess you've never seen one of his movies."

"No. Isn't it strange how his name can mean nothing to a person my age, even though he apparently meant so much to so many people before either of us ever walked this earth?"

"It is strange. But you'll get to meet him tonight, and then his name suddenly will mean something to you."

"I guess that's the benefit of making history in some small way. You sort of live forever."

"Yes, but that's not always a good thing."

"Why not?"

"Look at Behaeddin Shakir, a Turk who was trained as a medical doctor. Was he remembered for healing countless people? No."

"So what is he remembered for?"

"For his role in the Armenian Genocide. He ran the so-called 'Special Organization,' which oversaw the mass slaughter of deported Armenians. I'd rather live a decidedly ordinary life than make history like that."

"Right. I see what you mean," I said. "I wonder if Assad ever considers that he'll be remembered as the man who presided over the destruction of his country and the death of over 100,000 people?"

"Tyrants are much more preoccupied with the present than with future history," he opined. "It's really the only way they can survive."

"Well, maybe if you end up leading Antioch someday, you'll be remembered for having set a different example in the Middle East."

"It's sweet of you to root for me, Inās," he began. "But, unfortunately, Antioch is still just an idea. And turning it into a reality will require the help of countless people beyond me."

We arrived in front of the building where the film was being screened and stopped. He turned and looked at me with that fire that builds in his eyes whenever he starts thinking about Antioch.

"I alone am nothing. I need others who will be remembered for many contributions. I need idealists, including you, if you choose to be a part of it," he said, beaming at me, with his winter cap pulled halfway down his forehead and the brown stubble on his strong jaw now more visible in the light of the building. He opened the door for me and added, "For now, though, I'm just going to be remembered as the man who deprogrammed you with Exodus."

We shared a chuckle, and I walked in as he held the door for me.

The film really did open my mind a bit, as I had always viewed the Zionists as foreign colonizers, rather than as an indigenous and persecuted people who returned to their land and made it flourish. It also made me reflect on how the media controls the point of view and narrative that the masses consume and quickly accept as true. Here I was, raised in Syria to view Israel negatively in every possible way, now seeing those who built that state in a completely different light – from the perspective of their struggles and journeys, all of which could indeed inspire the quest for a Christian state in the Middle East. And my tendency to analyze things in terms of psychology kept returning me to a very basic but frustrating conclusion: "It is the media that perpetuates public ignorance of Christian suffering in Syria and other parts of the world." Those who control the most-watched broadcasts and widely read newspapers still decide what most people will know and discuss. And in a world that is ultimately controlled by just a few, very powerful forces, if the small web sites read by the vulnerable Assyrians and Copts are the only news outlets that cover an atrocity, then it's as if it never happened, and so the atrocities can continue.

Paul Newman turned out to be very handsome indeed, and – absurdly enough – actually reminded me of Michael in some ways (beyond just his smoldering good looks). They both seemed to have the same unstoppable intensity and boldness of purpose. And even though the film was so obviously from a different era – from the large and clunky cars to the funny fashions and speech mannerisms – there were a few times when I oddly felt as if Michael and I were in a contemporary, Christian version of that movie together. That could also be because at one point during the film, our hands found each other. And when I felt Michael's middle finger caress the inside of my palm, it sent a tickle up my spine. A delicate exploration began, as we took turns tracing the contours of each other's hands.

At one point, I felt his arm resting around both of my shoulders, prompting me to snuggle into his left side and happily place my hand against his muscular chest. Feeling the warmth of his presence, I looked up at him, finding his gaze peering down upon me. I smiled timidly, which was when he brought his mouth near my right ear, so as not to disturb the others in the audience. "How are you enjoying the deprogramming process?" he whispered suggestively. He pressed his left fingers gently into my left shoulder, and his right hand took mine. I felt my heart pounding faster with building excitement.

"I've enjoyed watching your acting performance from over fifty years ago," I whispered back with a smile as our hands caressed each other. Michael pivoted more towards me, and I couldn't help but turn more towards him too, so that we were almost facing each other.

"That kiss you saw me do in the movie was with the wrong girl though," he said with a steady and intent focus, slowly moving his head toward mine. As he drew ever closer, a flurry of butterflies fluttered about in my stomach, their wings flapping more feverishly as his lips gently brushed mine. I instinctively reached up and delicately glided my fingers across his five o'clock shadow.

He gently caressed my leg as his lips nibbled on mine, and the tip of his tongue began asking permission, teasing me with short licks that suggested so much more. And I wanted more. I could feel myself breathing heavier as heat surfaced across my cheeks, until he slowly pulled away with a look that lingered on the lips he had just caressed so beautifully with his own. "We still have a film to watch," he whispered with a wink, before settling back into his seat.

Chapter 27: Julien

Sunday, 3/2/14 at 22:55.

Some notes from today's session with Lily. When she opened the door to her office, her white blouse shimmied in a way that hinted at her perky breasts. Could she tell that I was privately feasting on her sexiness?

"Hi, Julien." She was wearing glasses for the first time, and had her hair up in a lovely chignon that somehow accentuated her appeal. She gestured for me to enter.

"Hi, Lily. What is this, your sexy librarian look?" I asked her playfully. I took a few steps inside and sat on her couch, as usual, wondering if maybe I was just horny because I hadn't had sex in a few days.

She picked up her yellow notepad from her desk and sat across from me, flipping through some pages until she stopped at what she was looking for and glanced up. Her tone became more focused and professional. "If you don't mind, I'd like to continue where we left off just as our session came to an end last time."

"Ah yes. I told you that nursing Icarus back to health gives me some sort of answer when I'm peering down the nihilistic abyss."

"Yes. I want to understand better why the sparrow does that for you, what the abyss is, and why you've had dark thoughts ever since you and your mother left your father."

"Shall we also cover the two-hundred-year history of the New York Stock Exchange in the next ninety minutes?" I asked sarcastically.

"I know it's a lot. Let's just see how far we can get. Tell me about the nihilistic abyss. What do you mean by that term?" Lily placed the end of her pen on her bottom lip, her eyebrows furrowed while she waited for my response. For a moment, I wished that pen was my cock.

"It's how I refer to that sinking feeling that none of this matters. Not the money. Not the academic prestige. Not the fame or influence. Not the beautiful girls. Not anything. It's all meaningless in the end."

"Why?"

"Because in the end, we die. It's like Chekhov observed in his play *Uncle Vanya*: 'in two hundred years, no one will even know we were here.'"

"Well, objectively speaking, you have a much better chance of being discussed in two hundred years than the vast majority of the people out there."

"Maybe. But I won't be around to know it, so what difference does it make? In the end, this life is the only one we can experience. And we struggle to get through it, we survive pain and hardship, and we have our journey, growing attached to people, places, and projects. And then it all ends, usually in some unceremonious or undignified way, with painkillers and tubes connected to us. And so – no matter what we did, or where we went, or whom we loved while we were here – it ends badly for all of us. On some grand scale, it's all rather pointless. But we go through the motions as if this life actually has meaning, because that's how we were biologically programmed to think and behave. Our species was designed to survive – despite its many self-destructive behaviors – so we march on, and try not to think too much about the essential futility of it all. And I normally don't – except when the nihilistic abyss rears its head for one reason or another."

She tapped the pen on her lip before speaking and, again, I had thoughts of my cock in her mouth. "You mention getting attached to people, but you don't strike me as someone who forms deep emotional attachments very often."

"I don't. But I was extremely close with my mother. And then she died on me, my last year of high school. Cancer."

"That must have been very hard on you."

"Hardest day of my life. And all I have now are fading memories, a few short video clips, and photos that my mind can only try to animate with my imagination, because there's no way to have any new experiences with her. That's what her life has been reduced to: a collection of moments that her son struggles not to forget and can never share fully with anyone who never had her as a mother. And as little as she means to everyone else on the planet, she meant the world to me when she was here."

"You sound almost bitter about it."

"I am. Life is a cheat. A tease. If you're born into a happy or comfortable existence, then you grow attached to it and one day it's taken from you for one reason or another. And if you're born into suffering, then things are that much worse. No matter how your life begins or unfolds, as Jim Morrison so poetically put it, 'No one here gets out alive.'"

"Do you think that the loss of your mother made it harder for you to achieve intimacy with women?" she asked, crossing her legs.

I raised my hand to my face and massaged my jaw as I watched her legs change position. "Well, it certainly didn't help, that's for sure. It probably planted the notion in my psyche that anyone I get close to can be taken from me – or leave me – at any moment. And of course, I've since had various women try to take advantage of me for my money or influence, making trust that much harder for me to establish."

"So is your nihilistic abyss what leads to the dark thoughts?"

"Sometimes. But they are different. And sometimes they complement each other."

"What do you mean?"

"The dark thoughts are usually related to some truly horrible moments in my past that my mother saved me from. Sometimes those memories turn my neutral nihilism into a dark one."

"How so?" she asked, uncrossing her legs and momentarily distracting me yet again. I needed to fuck, and soon.

"Well, neutral nihilism is more of an objective, philosophical conclusion about the fundamental meaninglessness of life. But dark nihilism is the further conclusion that this life is actually not a gift but a curse, because of all of the senseless evil and suffering that it contains."

"So dark nihilism leads to suicidal thoughts."

"Exactly."

"How often?"

"It used to be frighteningly often, when I was still a child. But my mother helped me through that period. Until she died. And then, my nightmares tormented me like never before. And now they come and go. Fortunately, I'm generally too busy with life to indulge the darkness much, but it's always there, lingering in the shadows of my mind."

"Do you think your drive to succeed in finance and in psychology was in some way an escape from the darkness?"

"Very much so. And I think sex with beautiful women is too."

"Why do you say that? Because of the pleasure principle?"

"Yes. And it's an escape that overpowers everything else. In the same way that sex with a much younger woman fuels the illusion of ageless appeal and immortality, the all-consuming pleasure distracts my mind from the bleakness of it all. Sex reduces us to our most primal function, in a way that tricks the mind out of existential ruminations. Dark nihilism becomes irrelevant when you're looking at a hot woman who's bent over, waiting for your cock."

Lily's left eyebrow rose ever so slightly. She uncrossed her legs and then crossed them again, switching the thigh that was on top, in a way that suggested both discomfort and arousal. As she wrote down some more notes in her yellow pad, looking up every now and then, she seemed to be saying to herself, "Holy shit, who is this guy? And why hasn't he wrestled me to the floor and ripped off my panties with his teeth yet?"

There was something very intellectually intimate about therapy. And it allowed me to express vulnerabilities that no one else knew about. I suppose there's even some kind of erotic appeal to it because it allows me, for a change, to feel exposed and weaker than my interlocutor. Just as powerful men sometimes fantasize about a dominatrix who punishes them because they need some reminder of what it's like to be subordinate to someone else's power, Lily exposes a weak – even pathetic – side of me that no one else sees. As with all pleasures, power can't be truly understood and savored without experiencing its absence. And Lily reminded me of what it's like to be vulnerable – something that's easy to forget when you're rich and powerful.

She finally looked back up and composed herself while formulating her next question. "Tell me about your father. Why did your mother leave him? What exactly did he do? And were you always much closer with your mother than your father?"

"I'm not ready to discuss any of that with you."

"Don't you think that's a basic part of your story that I need to know, if I'm going to help you?"

"Those are details that I've shared with no human being. You haven't earned that kind of trust from me." I realized that I must have sounded a bit defensive – maybe even disdainfully standoffish, but there was something invasive about how she just expected me to open up about so many painfully personal details so quickly.

"How long do you think it will take before you can trust me enough to talk about something that's so fundamental to how you developed as a person?"

"I don't know."

Lily pursed her lips in slight frustration. She finally exhaled, as if to concede that there was no point in pushing me further on this now. She adjusted her posture a bit and returned to a line of questioning that she rightly suspected would produce less resistance.

"What about Icarus?" She looked down at her notes for the exact words she had recorded. "Why did you say that, 'nursing the injured sparrow gives me some sort of answer, when I'm staring down the nihilistic abyss?'"

"There's something very simple and decent about nursing him back to health – especially because I accidentally broke his wing."

"So it's a kind of substitute for fatherhood?"

"In a sense. As a parent, you don't ask your children for permission to bring them into this crazy world. You just do. And then you're obligated to help them survive as best you can, because it's the least you can do after imposing life on them. At least that's how I imagine parents view their duties when the going gets tough and they feel like giving up. Similarly, the poor bird didn't ask to have his wing broken by my careless step, so the least I can do is take care of him now."

"And that simple act of kindness and compassion restores your balance?"

"To some extent. Because I then remember that there is goodness in me and I'm acting on it. And that, in turn, reminds me that such goodness exists in others, and that the world can't be that bad. And once those thoughts are in my head, I start to think that maybe my nihilism – whether neutral or dark – is just a useless cacophony in my head, drowning out the symphony of goodness and joy that life is trying to play for me and that I should be cherishing."

Those were the more intense moments of our session. And, once again, the end of our ninety minutes caught us both by surprise – flying by much faster than either of us expected.

Then there was the goodbye afterwards, which seemed as awkward and abrupt as ever. I imagine that saying farewell to a prostitute must feel very similar. You've paid a stranger for some brief intimacy and then your time is up and you part ways. It's always been like that with the few therapists I've had; but with Lily, that feeling is somehow more pronounced.

Chapter 28: Anissa

∽ Tuesday, March 4, 2014 ∾

To My Dearest,

In my excitement to tell you about what happened on my movie date with Michael last Saturday, I forgot to mention one thing: class last week with Professor Morales definitely felt a bit different. I kind of wish that Maya hadn't told me that rumor about him sleeping with Elise. Every time I looked at him, I would start with his smoothly coiffured, slightly wavy hair, and then move down, searching for his hazel eyes through the stylish, vintage eyeglass frames that he wore that day. I tried to see if I could somehow descry his true character through those lenses. Could he really be having sex with our TA? But no matter how hard I stared, I couldn't read any more into him. And then I would look at the blonde-haired Elise, who that day happened to be wearing a short skirt with sexy winter stockings, and would try to see if there was anything about her demeanor or her reactions to Professor Morales that could somehow confirm that she was in fact sleeping with him.

And then I had an eerie feeling about the strange reality that is everywhere around us. I kept returning to this new and bizarre question: is there *anything* that actually is as it *seems*? Is anything perceptually straightforward? Maybe that's inherently impossible, because impressions are, by their very nature, cumulative – the sum of all your interactions with and perceptions of things. And since these evolve constantly, as new information is added or your emotional state changes, whatever we observe seems a little different at any given moment. Even when I hold the silver necklace from my mother, my experience of it varies from time to time. Usually it calms me, but sometimes it conjures a memory that brings distress or despair. And one day I could learn something new about its history, or do something unusual with it, and that could somehow further change its meaning. In the end, I followed almost none of Professor Morales' lecture that day. But I concluded, from my own meandering thoughts, that our experiences can be reduced to our ever-shifting impressions, and the constant struggle to make sense out of new information that so often contradicts everything we thought we knew or understood.

The surprise of reality contradicting prior impressions happened again with Professor Morales today, about forty minutes before my class with him started. The entire thing felt like déjà vu from the very first day of the semester! I was at another rally on College Walk with Michael, although this time, we had a bigger turnout (perhaps because there was no snow), even though it was still a very cold twenty-nine degrees out. About twenty members of the Mideast Christian Association showed up, along with a few others not from our group who had stopped to listen. Michael was standing on the sundial, addressing the crowd, through a megaphone, while some of the protesters gathered around him held up placards like, "2014: the Last Year of Syrian Christianity?" and "Christian Blood is Not Cheap!"

Michael stood on the sundial, holding his megaphone and addressing the few people in the crowd who weren't from the MCA. "I know that most of you are busy with your schoolwork. But today the evil sweeping across the Middle East was covered even by some of the major media here in the USA." His voice boomed with anger. "Fox News reported on how the Islamic State of Iraq and Syria, or ISIS, announced that they had signed an agreement with twenty of Raqqa's Christian leaders. Let me read you the Fox report." Michael raised his hand so that he could read from his smartphone, as a few students walked by indifferently.

He continued, reading from his phone: "Faced with losing their lives or denying their Christian faith, the community opted for dhimmi status – suppression as a 'protected' minority – which requires them to submit to an array of demands, including the notorious jizya tax, which can be compared to Mafiosi protection money: purchasing their safety, but under strictly enforced regulations. Raqqa's Christians are now subject to an extreme version of Islamic Shariah law, which among other things forbids them to repair their war-torn churches, worship or pray in public, ring church bells, or wear crosses or other symbols of their faith. Bearing arms is, of course, forbidden, as are alcoholic beverages."

Michael put his phone down and looked around. I also surveyed the crowd to see if any more people had joined our gathering. But hardly anyone had stopped to listen to our protest. Nobody seemed to care. Sometimes it felt as if there was a list of politically correct causes that mattered on campus (in terms of generating large rallies and local media coverage), and the persecution of Mideast Christians just wasn't sexy enough to make the list.

Undaunted, Michael continued addressing the crowd: "Now Raqqa,

Syria may seem far away to many of you, but there is actually someone here with us in this crowd whose sister, brother, and uncle live there." He looked at me and I just nodded back at him, holding back tears, as he acknowledged the conditions afflicting what was left of my poor family.

"And it's not just Raqqa. This scene has played itself out countless times in Syria and across the Middle East since Muslims conquered Christian lands there about 1,400 years ago. Mideast Christians need a state or they will forever be bullied, second-class citizens, with no dignity or security. Historical justice demands it, after so much persecution and so many massacres of Christians in their ancestral lands. And we – as Americans – should wake up to the menace of radical Islam because it threatens everyone, as we were reminded on September 11th. That was thirteen years ago, but the threat has actually grown worse since then."

Michael put down the megaphone for a moment, as he surveyed the crowd again. Two new students holding hands were walking by and stopped to listen. Michael addressed those two, as if he were now pleading his case to the two most influential members of Congress.

"I know that you two probably don't read the local papers in the Middle East. But a Lebanese paper today reported that in Hasake province, a mainly Kurdish town in northern Syria, jihadists destroyed a Sufi Muslim shrine. ISIS thugs blew it up, and then burned a mosque and a police station. You see, it's not just the Christians who are at risk. It's any Muslims who think differently than the Islamic State. And that means Sufis, Shias, and moderate Sunnis who prefer to live in a secular state. Whether you're any of those things, or Alawite, or Christian, or Jewish, or Buddhist, or Hindu, or atheist, you are their enemy. And if you are silent when ISIS slaughters others in the Middle East, then ISIS only grows stronger for the day they come to slaughter you here in the USA."

The couple he was talking to seemed moved by the urgency of his message, as one of our group members approached them with a clipboard containing our petition. The others at our demonstration started chanting, "Stop ISIS now! Stop ISIS now!" Michael stepped down from the sundial, chanting the same thing into his megaphone, as he walked towards me in the crowd. He put down the amplifier and stopped by my side.

"Amazing job, Michael," I told him. "Thank you. Thank you for giving my family a voice here!"

"You're welcome, Anissa. But no thanks are needed. This is really the least we can do. Let's just hope that someone here is listening."

"Well, I'm sure our message is getting through to some people. And I'm not going home today until I reach two hundred signatures, even if I have to come back out here after my next class," I declared, showing him my clipboard with one hundred eighty-five signatures.

"Wow – great work, Anissa!" he beamed.

"And I already have two hundred dollars of donations from the last two days. My goal is three hundred by tomorrow."

And just as he said that, we noticed Professor Morales approaching. He was talking on his cell phone.

"Well, *he's* certainly not going to help you get there," Michael joked, sarcastically referring to my professor.

As he approached us in his stylish suit, elegant dress shoes, and trench coat, with his black leather briefcase hanging from his shoulder by a strap, his eyes met mine and I heard him say, "Let me call you back in a few minutes." As he put away his cell phone, the Rolex watch on his wrist flashed a glint of silver. When he was about five feet away, he slowed down, as if to greet me. "Shall we try this again?" he asked me with a wry smile.

I grinned and played along, as if we were suddenly on stage, in front of a small audience that just gave us another chance to improve upon our last improvisational performance. "Excuse me, Sir, can I get you to sign our petition in support of U.S. military intervention in Syria? Or maybe donate something to our efforts?" I asked with a smile.

"Well, I try to stay away from politics – especially when it concerns military interventions in the Middle East."

Given that he initiated our interaction, I was slightly surprised and disappointed by his response. And I could tell that Michael was quietly restraining himself from replying – only because he knew that this was my professor and he didn't want me to have any problems with him. Meanwhile, the crowd around us from the rally was starting to disperse.

"And even when it comes to the Latino causes that I hold dear, I rarely sign petitions," he continued. "They may nurture the belief that our political efforts can change big things, but rarely do they actually effect that change."

Despite my disappointment in his response, I was secretly amused to see Professor Morales breaking into this quasi-psychological lecture on the whole thing, as if he was completely oblivious to the community leader standing right next to me, who was clearly a bigger and stronger man and a passionate believer in the efficacy and importance of political activism. Fortunately, Michael continued to remain diplomatically quiet, although the sneer on his face seemed to say, "I told you so. He's a cheap billionaire. And he's too full of himself and his academic bullshit to care about anything outside of himself."

I was about to say something to make Professor Morales feel better about not supporting us with a donation or a signature when he suddenly continued. "Having said that, I really don't like to see my students freezing in such cold weather. And I see that you're out here quite frequently for this cause."

"It's not just my cause – it's my family," I pointed out firmly but cordially. "So maybe that's why."

"Well, your dedication is impressive, to say the least. Especially in this weather. So, can I make a small donation towards the purchase of an outdoor heater for your winter efforts?" he asked. The right side of his mouth curved into a mischievous half-smile, as if he was amused by misleading me into thinking that he would offer nothing.

"Sure!" I exclaimed in surprised delight.

He gave Michael and me a cordial smile and then handed me a one-hundred-dollar bill. "Here you go. That should cover it. But the bad news is, you can't miss any classes for being sick from the cold now," he joked. "Speaking of which, I need to prepare for today's lecture. I'll see you in class." He looked at his watch. "In about forty minutes."

"Yes. Thank you so much, Professor Morales. See you soon."

He smiled, gave us both a charming nod of his head, and continued on his way.

"Look at that! He just brought me up to three hundred – a fifty percent increase in minutes. Normally that could take me a whole day of effort."

"Yes," Michael agreed reluctantly.

"See? He's not that bad."

"Well, let's not forget that he would have never given you that if you weren't his student. So it's not like he really cares about the cause."

"But it's the biggest donation we've ever received when soliciting out here. Nobody ever gives more than ten or twenty dollars."

"OK, but what's a hundred dollars to him? It's like a dime to me."

"Yes, but it's still a hundred dollars to us!"

"Fair enough," he conceded. "You're right – and you did a great job in getting him to open up his wallet," he added with an approving smile.

"Did you just admit that I was right again?"

"Haha… Yes, I guess we can add this one to your scorecard," he agreed, bringing me into his arms. "Come here. You deserve a hug for being right so often. And I'm going to have to be your outdoor heater now because we need that hundred dollars for more pressing things."

I savored the warmth of his chest against my cheek for a moment. "Well, if losing the outdoor heater means you have to keep me warm like this, how can I complain about such an efficient use of funds?"

"We certainly can't have our fundraiser-in-chief turning into a popsicle," he bantered.

I could have stayed there in his embrace forever. But any longer and we'd be kissing in public, a step that neither of us was ready to take just yet. And I wanted to make sure that I was extra prepared for class after what just happened.

"Will my new, personal furnace excuse me so that I can review my notes in time to impress our latest benefactor?"

Michael gradually released me. "I guess that's a good idea. It would be rather awkward if you were now unprepared for his class."

I broke away and we shared a parting glance. "Call me tonight," I said.

"I will."

Chapter 29: Anissa

∽ Saturday, March 8, 2014 ∾

To My Dearest,

In February, I was writing to you almost every day, but this month has been less frequent, and that's mostly because of school pressure – every second I have, I've been cramming for the big midterm in Psychology and Markets this coming Tuesday. Professor Morales reminded us that it's forty percent of our final grade, but I actually care about this exam less for my GPA and more for the opportunity to be invited to a tour of his office and maybe a future job interview at JMAT. For that reason alone, this will be the most important test I take since leaving Syria. In fact, I made the strategic decision to prepare less for some of my other midterms so that I have extra time for this one.

The idea of lining up a job at Professor Morales' hedge fund would be a dream come true on so many levels. I can only imagine how proud it would have made my parents to learn that I was offered a position in such a selective and prestigious firm. And I'd no longer be freezing my butt off begging strangers for small donations for the cause when I myself could donate thousands of dollars from my own six-figure paycheck. And of course, as an employee at JMAT, I'd be in the company of so many super smart and successful people that if I ever did solicit anyone's support, the donations would be far bigger than the twenty-dollar bills I now get so excited about. I might even have the resources to try to get Maria and Antoun out of Syria and over to New York, where they could stay with me.

That is the power and beauty of this country – the great United States of America that so generously granted me asylum during my time of greatest need. Here I am – a young Syrian woman orphaned in the Hell on Earth that I barely escaped – and I'm potentially just one exam performance away from the American Dream. There's something so exhilarating and liberating about the thought that my destiny is now (finally) entirely in my own hands, and that I have a second chance at building a happy life. The only thing that matters now is how I spend my time between this moment and the test on Tuesday and, of course, how I use that preparation to perform on the exam itself. Our midterms are submitted anonymously (with only a number that is randomly assigned to each student), so when Professor Morales grades them, he has no idea whose answers he is evaluating and there's no chance of the results being influenced by personal favoritism, prejudice, or anything else that could be unfair to a student. The only thing that counts will be what we each write on the exam.

I went to the review session that Elise held for us yesterday (which meant skipping my Econ study group), and I've been spending every free moment preparing for the exam. That involves memorizing the details of every psychology study discussed in his class, reviewing all of the assigned reading and notes from his class lectures, and making sure that I know all of the relevant psychological terminology and concepts. I've also been taking practice tests from prior years that have been released (and then reviewing the correct answers to understand any questions that I missed). Lastly, I need to go over all of the previous problem sets.

So I haven't really done that much outside of studying every available moment in Butler Library. I even cut back on my fitness routine. But there were a few study breaks and other moments that are worth sharing with you now before I go back to my intense cramming mode.

I saw Michael only twice this week and not much really happened with him because each encounter was relatively brief and inherently limited by the circumstances. The first time was last Wednesday when we went jogging in the evening. It was the first time that we had ever worked out together, and there was something intimate about running in lockstep around the Dodge Fitness Center track, our pace and breaths in synch as we completed three miles of laps in about twenty-four minutes. For that brief time, all of my exam stress dissipated and any thoughts of the past or the future just merged into a blissful moment of calm focus on the simple present. My mind felt liberated from all thought except the sound of our feet clicking on the floor below, with the surroundings flying by in an irrelevant blur, as the engines of our lungs and hearts pumped away.

After we finished our run, we basked in our post-exertion endorphins for a bit, and there was something almost erotic about the musky smell of Michael's sweat so near, his toned and muscular body glistening with perspiration. I told him that once the weather warmed up a bit more I wanted to run with him in Central Park or Morningside Heights, where the breathtaking scenes of Manhattan all around us would make the moment even more magical.

"We don't have to wait for the weather," he replied. "We just need to get some winter running gear."

"Well, then it will have to wait until I'm done with this test because shopping for anything is the last thing I have time for now," I said, suddenly sounding a bit anxious.

"Don't worry, Inās – you got this one. I can just tell."

"How?"

"Your intensity. Your determination. Nothing will stop you."

"It's funny, that's exactly what I think of you, whenever I hear you talk of Antioch."

"Well, you're right. Nothing will stop the creation of a Mideast Christian state. I may not be a man of faith, but I do believe in history and purpose, and this is an idea whose time has come."

"I'd say it's actually long overdue," I agreed.

"Yes. And I get so excited about it because, for the first time, it looks like realizing this vision may actually be within our reach. The conditions on the ground may eventually deliver this birthright of ours. And with every day that passes, I'm increasingly convinced that I was put on Earth to make it happen, if it's the last thing I do. So that our people can finally live in dignity."

I repeated that quote that he had shared with me. "If you will it, it is no dream."

"Exactly," he affirmed with a smile. "And that goes for your test this Tuesday. So just keep it up and you'll get there."

The other moment with my budding love happened just yesterday and awkwardly involved Professor Morales. I knew that Michael was holding an important rally and – even though he told me not to come so that I could concentrate on preparing for my midterm – I took a short study break to show up briefly, just to give him and the other MCA members some moral support. And, as luck would have it, Professor Morales happened to show up just as Michael was standing behind me with his arms wrapped around my shoulders to keep me warm in the chilly outdoors.

With a touch of dry humor in his tone, Professor Morales, who was walking past the part of the protests where Michael and I were standing, remarked, "Is *this* the outdoor heater you got with my donation?" We let out a bit of a nervous laugh at the awkwardness of the moment. It felt mildly uncomfortable because we hadn't expected him to see that the two of us were now openly a couple and that we apparently hadn't used the funds he donated in the way that he had requested. His joke also seemed eerily omniscient – as if he had placed some kind of listening device on me the last time he had encountered us, thus hearing the joke Michael had made (about being my personal heater) after Professor Morales had left us.

But he seemed to sense that we were a bit uneasy and then genially added, "Well, as long as you're staying warm – one way or another."

"I'm definitely looking forward to spring at this point," I replied with a smile.

"That makes two of us. And we're supposedly moving the clocks forward for spring this week, but at the moment it feels like maybe we should be moving them back an hour!"

I chuckled at his joke, relieved that nothing had apparently changed in how he viewed me, but was still waiting for him to leave so that the awkwardness could end. He seemed to sense that in me and started to move on, but then stopped for a moment.

"Are you planning to attend the review session with Elise later today? Or are you feeling prepared enough for the midterm to focus on political activities instead?" His tone was friendly but sounded slightly skeptical, as if he doubted my abilities and/or judgment.

"No, I'll be there. I was just taking a quick study break for the bigger picture. But I'll be returning to my own, much smaller picture very soon," I reassured him.

"Glad to hear it. Good luck on Tuesday."

"Thanks, Professor Morales."

Chapter 30: Julien

Sunday, 3/9/14 at 22:55.

Last Friday, I ran into my student, Anissa, who was protesting in the cold again. This was the third time our paths had crossed in this way; the last two times I noticed that she was in the company of a good-looking man who seems to be the leader of their group. I think he's also her boyfriend, which is something of a relief, as I had sensed a certain attraction from her, and a student-teacher romance is really the last thing I need right now, although I still haven't mentioned her to Lily.

Today in therapy I did tell Lily about my office romance with Raegan.

"When did your sexual relationship with her begin?" Lily asked.

"Raegan received her bachelor's degree from Brown at the age of twenty. I hired her as my personal assistant when she graduated in 2008. About three months after she started working for me, our fund was hit with a series of large redemptions due to the financial crisis at the time. Our office went through enormous stress and I had to lay off about thirty percent of the JMAT staff at the time. But I kept Raegan on as my assistant, and I think she never forgot that – maybe because she came from a family of modest means and was carrying a lot of student debt. We had a normal, professional relationship for the first two years, when she was still dating her college boyfriend. But then, one day, around July of 2010, she had recently broken up with him and was working late at the office, helping me to prepare a presentation to a big Saudi sovereign wealth fund. She saw that I was quite stressed out and just sort of intuited what I needed."

"What do you mean?" Lily asked, now very curious.

"Well, I was just leaning back in my office chair, exhausted and feeling a bit burned out. And she was nearby, on her hands and knees collating some papers together for the presentation." I purposely stopped recounting the incident, as if to tease Lily.

"Go on," she nudged me on, after a moment of awkward silence. Her impatience to hear the rest of the story gave me all the permission I needed to shock her with a more detailed account, which was exactly what I wanted to do.

"And then she looked up at me and said, 'You look really stressed, Julien. Do you mind if I relax you a bit?' as she slipped her hand just under the hem of my trousers, and on to my calf. I looked at her succulent lips and seductive, doe-eyed face, eager to help and comfort."

Lily's eyebrow rose a little, as I paused for a brief moment. "There was something irresistibly good and delicious about Raegan's offer, and I just nodded slightly in response to her question. I was too tired and dazed to answer verbally. She gradually made her way up my thighs, until her small hands had unzipped my suit pants. My tie had already been loosened, but I took it off completely and flung it to the floor, and then opened a few more buttons towards the top of my shirt."

Lily adjusted her posture. She made eye contact but then looked just below at my throat area as I continued.

"And before I knew it, Raegan had my hard cock in her hand, moving it gently and deliciously in her palm as I became increasingly aroused. She slipped the tip between her lips, sucking the pre-cum that was beading there. Raegan looked stunning on her knees, and now slightly naughty, with a sensual expression that practically compelled my decision to let her help me 'relax a bit.' Moments later, I felt the glide of her wet lips and tongue as they slid down the length of my shaft. At first, she started moving her head slowly, but soon increased her bobbing with a hungry vigor. As the watery warmth of her mouth slid up and down on my cock, I got even harder until I felt my balls tingle. There was a hot pulse making my cock throb against her tongue, warning me that I might come down her throat if I didn't pull out."

"OK, Julien, I think I get the picture," Lily said, trying to regain her focus.

Like on so many other occasions during our sessions together, Lily seemed both aroused and uncomfortable. She apparently wanted to hear every detail for her deeper understanding, prurient curiosity, and maybe for other reasons, but she was also cognizant of the need to maintain a certain decorum, even though therapy was supposed to be a totally open experience.

"So what happened after that first time at the office?"

"Right, sorry about that – I wasn't trying to make you uncomfortable. I just figured the details might give you a bit more context."

"No, it's OK. Go on. I mean, continue with what happened after that first time at the office."

"OK. Well, needless to say, that first time definitely relaxed me. And our presentation the next day to the sovereign wealth fund actually went extremely well – they invested five hundred million dollars with us."

"And then what happened?"

"Well, that's just it. Nothing happened. I mean, I hadn't even been thinking straight when I acquiesced to Raegan's tempting offer. I was too tired to resist the idea and a part of me almost didn't care about the consequences because I was that burned out from work. So it was clearly reckless on my part and I'm quite sure that, had I thought through that choice in advance, I would have never allowed any sexual relationship to develop with any of my employees, given the many risks involved. But none of those risks materialized with Raegan. There was no drama and, besides the occasional, inside joke about relaxation being key to securing big investments, it was business as usual. Nobody at JMAT ever suspected anything, and there was never any jealousy between us. She told me about her dates and sometimes helped to arrange my dates. And yet, every now and then, we'd lock the door to my office and enjoy a release of some kind."

"How often did you release together?"

"During periods of high stress, maybe a few times a week. Sometimes not at all, if one of us had a busy social schedule that week, or if there were many people who might need to see me during a certain period or project."

"Why do you think it's been so uncomplicated with her?"

"It's a bit of a mystery to me sometimes. I think it's a combination of extreme loyalty, practical level-headedness, and having the emotional intelligence to understand that we could never actually be a serious couple. So she knows the limits and never really tests them."

"It sounds like she may just be very good at compartmentalizing."

"I wouldn't say that. Compartmentalization is an unconscious psychological defense mechanism employed to avoid cognitive dissonance. But it's not as if Raegan experiences mental discomfort and anxiety caused by her conflicting values, thoughts, or emotions about me or within herself."

"So how would you explain it, in psychoanalytic terms?"

"Well, I think it's more the phenomenon of isolation. She can separate thought from feeling in a way that prevents her from growing too emotionally attached to outcomes. She can rationally see the various benefits to herself and me of indulging sexual encounters, and then enjoy them without feeling that the sex means we should become romantically or exclusively involved with each other. And she knows that I can be extremely generous when it comes to rewarding loyalty and good work."

"So she's never let your sexual relations interfere with her performance or otherwise done anything to betray your trust?"

"Never. She's done too well and she enjoys her position at JMAT too much to jeopardize it like that. She just bought herself a nice, two-bedroom condo in Tribeca last year. How many twenty-six-year old New Yorkers can do that?"

Chapter 31: Anissa

∞ Saturday, March 15, 2014 ∞

To My Dearest,

My apologies for neglecting you for an entire week. Lately, it just seems like I've been too busy living life to write about it! Just as, in a magical moment of Zen-like concentration, I can become perfectly present while running or sparring, sometimes the demands of life require such constant and total attention that the time just flies by without any chance to think or write about it. The nonstop pressure related to my midterms also makes writing to you seem like a luxury that I should postpone until my exams are finished, because the stakes are so high. But you're very important to me, My Dearest. Writing to you has really helped me to adjust to my exciting new life here in New York while continuing to heal from the traumas that marked my last year in Syria. And the good news is that there's a lot to fill you in on because there have been so many developments in the last week.

First, let's start with the biggest news of all: I took the most important exam since I came to the USA – actually, maybe the biggest test of my life, considering the potential rewards for excelling on it. Well, not only did it go brilliantly well, but also I got the highest grade in a class of 110 students. For a moment, I was in ecstatic shock and disbelief. And when I finally realized that I wasn't dreaming, I couldn't have been more elated, and was practically doing cartwheels and victory laps all over campus for a good hour after I found out the news.

"Congratulations to the three of you," Professor Morales said last Thursday, when he announced the midterm results to the class. "You are each invited to my hedge fund's midtown office this Monday morning for a private tour. Please come to JMAT in business attire, as you'll also be meeting the head of our HR department. There are a few more logistical details regarding your visit, so please see me after class for the rest of the information."

At that point, I was so euphoric that I couldn't focus on anything else that he said for the rest of that class. I texted Michael a message, asking him to meet me after my class on the South Lawn, by the entrance to Butler Library, for some surprise news.

When I told him about my grade, it was already dark out, but the campus lights illuminated the area enough for me to see how much his face lit up with a huge smile. "That's amazing news – I'm so proud of you!" he exclaimed, opening his arms to give me a hug, at which point I literally leapt into them.

It's a good thing he's big and strong enough to catch me, because a smaller man might have stumbled backwards and taken a tumble from all of the energetic elation I hurled at him. But his muscular chest absorbed my celebratory jump, as my arms caught his neck while my legs wrapped around his waist. He spun me around as we shared a triumphant yell that felt endlessly happy. He eventually brought us down to the grass where he gently laid me, his hands still on me, as our faces moved towards each other for a kiss. This time, after our lips pressed against each other, his tongue grazed the tip of mine, and our mouths moved even closer together, until both of our tongues passionately unleashed themselves, exploring freely as we indulged in a long and deep kiss on the lawn.

I was so thrilled about my grade that I wanted to share it on Facebook and tell other students (and pretty much the whole world), but my mother had always been suspiciously circumspect about sharing good news, urging me to keep it to myself. "Don't invite envy to your house – you never know who will show up," she used to warn me. So I told only Uncle Tony and Monique (in a brief email) and no one else except Maya.

"You got the top midterm grade in Psychology and Markets?" she repeated, in disbelief with a hint of envy, when I told her after our Economics study group finished its meeting.

"Well, I'm sure my grades in some other classes will suffer because I spent 90% of my study time preparing for that midterm."

"I think at this point all you need to worry about is not flunking out of college because that should be enough to get you a job at Julien's fund."

"Well, there's still a final exam, you know."

"Yeah, but somehow I think my Syrian sista' is gonna do all right on that one," she replied, with a cocky wink.

"Let's hope so! That would be really awkward if I bombed the final."

"Nah. You're gonna own that exam like you did this one... I'm really impressed, girl. I barely got a C on that test and I think the class average my year was a B-. His exams are no joke and everyone knows that. Nobody takes his class to boost their GPA!"

"Well, I did study for it 24/7. And I doubt I did well on my Intro to Politics midterm the day after – I just didn't have enough time to study for that one."

"You did the right thing, strategically. You have gold in your pocket right now, Anissa."

"I still can't believe it actually. And I've been a little out of focus ever since, almost as if midterms were over. But I have to keep up the cramming mode for a little longer, even though I'm a bit burned out at this point."

"How many do you have left besides our Econ test next week?"

"Just one – Masterpieces of Western Literature and Philosophy. And I still have a solid two days of catch-up reading to do because I fell behind."

"OK. Well, you're welcome to my notes, if you want. I got an A in that class, but that was with Professor Mulholland, so just keep that in mind. I don't know if your professor focuses on the same stuff."

"Thanks, Maya. I may take you up on that offer at some point."

Her eyebrow rose in a slightly suggestive way, and I knew she was about to change the topic. "So are you coming to Julien's party now that you no longer have to worry about a poor midterm performance? There will be many eligible men there."

"Well, I've seen Michael enough times now that... I'm not so sure *I'm* eligible!"

"Oh, is that right? Do tell! You've been holding out on me, girl!" she added playfully.

"Well, there isn't that much to tell, except that he's a really good kisser, and that it feels like he's my boyfriend now."

"Look at my Syrian virgin represent!" She high-fived me. "Well, just remember that the men at Julien's parties are only one of many reasons to go. Probably the biggest reason to go is the networking with all of the VIPs there."

"And how exactly do I fit in with the VIPs as a first-year student at Columbia?"

"Oh, I think getting the highest grade on Julien's midterm definitely qualifies you as a mini-VIP."

"Maya, are you going into politics? Or at least sales?"

She chuckled a bit. "I don't think so, but you never know."

"I think you should seriously consider it. You've got a powerful two-punch combo with that charm and persuasion!"

"I'm just bein' real with you, Anissa. You need to be at that sexy soiree. But we may have to take you clothes shopping. You kinda have to dress the part a bit, if you know what I mean."

"As long as you promise to stay by my side at the party the whole time – and take all the blame if Julien gets mad that I showed up."

"Oh, I will, don't worry. But I can't imagine that he'd get mad now that you're the star student in his class. He'll probably be delighted. But you still have to play dumb and act surprised when you see him, as if you had no idea that he was the host and I had no idea that he was your professor. He just assumes that I'm bringing someone who's not a current student, so he can't know that I told you it was his party. Otherwise I'll get in trouble with him."

"Of course, I'll play along."

"I mean it, Anissa. It is hard as hell to get those invitations, so I will burn down your dorm room if you screw this up for me. You cannot tell him that you knew it was his party when you get there."

"Don't worry, Maya. I promise I won't say a word. Besides, the whole thing will be very surprising to me anyway, so it shouldn't be too hard for me to act surprised when I run into him there."

"OK, cool. So, when are we going shopping?"

"Well, I need to go shopping for business attire anyway because I don't really have anything to wear for the office tour this Monday."

"Sounds like you and I are going to be reviewing Economics at Macy's. Which isn't necessarily the same as economizing, but we'll start there."

"I'm sorry the timing is so bad, but I feel like we're both pretty ready for the Econ final next week."

"Yeah, I'm just teasin' you. It'll be fine. As long as we don't spend more than forty hours shopping for you this weekend!"

I laughed. "Trust me – I want the process to be as fast and painless as possible!"

"Amen to that, Sista'!"

"Thank you so much, Maya. I really appreciate you helping me with this stuff, and bringing me to the party."

"It'll be epic. Just wait."

Chapter 32: Julien

Monday, 3/17/14 at 3:45.

    Can't sleep. I tried watching and feeding Icarus a bit, which sometimes helps, but not this time. Too much on my mind. I told Lily about my nightmares in far too much detail (when we had our session about twelve hours ago) and now those disclosures are making me avoid sleep, wary of the torment that awaits me as soon as I succumb to the fatigue that's now drooping my eyelids. But the thing that's probably weighing most on my mind is the fact that Anissa is coming to tour my office tomorrow. HR has a full program for her and the other two midterm superstars. So I'm not planning to spend more than ten or fifteen minutes with them, but I'm still thinking about it now.

    I'm already seeing the whole scenario play itself out in my head. She had caught my eye early in the semester, even as I tried to suppress any thoughts about her. But after her recent exam performance, I'm much more impressed and intrigued by her. This is one very special, intelligent, and fascinating young woman. And she projects a simple and pure kind of beauty that is breathtakingly rare – especially in a jaded, materialistic city like New York. And, as if God wanted to make me a passenger on this train wreck many miles from the final collision, I could see her growing gradually more interested in me in those first weeks of class. Yes, she now has a boyfriend from the political cause she's so involved in, but that never seems to change the way she looks at or interacts with me when he's not around. And after the office tour (in about seven hours), she'll be that much more interested in me, if the experience with prior female students on that office tour is any indication.

    This is just the kind of trouble that I would end up in… The New York tabloids make their living off powerful men who impulsively submit to their weakness for women, and who, in one stupidly brash act, bring their world crashing down. But this situation isn't quite as bad as the scandals that sell so many newspapers – I'm not a politician or otherwise violating some kind of public trust. In the worst-case scenario, I'd lose my university position and maybe a few investors would leave because of some temporary public outcry. But most investors are making too much money with my fund to divest in protest – certainly those who have been with the fund for at least two years. The more recent investors will be disappointed with this next quarter and could try to use even the hint of a scandal to justify some kind of early exit.

But it's not as if I would be breaking the law: her university registration details indicate that she's eighteen years old, and the age of consent in New York State is actually seventeen. So, if this does end up going where I fear it will go (and secretly want it to), this wouldn't be statutory rape – just an inappropriate relationship with an embarrassingly young woman who happens to be my student.

Maybe I can somehow deflect my reckless libido by focusing on a much safer yet still somewhat taboo target: Lily. Psychologically, she doesn't offer quite the same level of extra excitement and allure produced by the forbidden fruit that Anissa represents. But because of Lily's professional duties, and how strictly she has maintained a propriety-driven distance from me, she too involves a certain challenge and enticement to pursue the proscribed. In the worst-case scenario, I'd lose her as my therapist, which is hardly an ideal outcome, given how helpful she's been and how much I enjoy our sessions. But we could still continue to see each other, perhaps as lovers, if she were so inclined. And losing her as my therapist still seems far better than being caught having a sexual relationship with my eighteen-year-old student.

And I have been starting to feel a certain intimacy towards Lily – if only because I've told her things that I've shared with no one else (like the detailed description of my nightmares that I gave her yesterday). Granted, I know very little about her, beyond the information that Raegan gathered for me when I was deciding whom to hire as my therapist. But after having shared so much of myself with her, I'm becoming increasingly curious about this person receiving, analyzing, and forever holding some of my deepest secrets, thoughts, and fears.

I had never shared with anyone in such vivid detail what my recurring nightmares look like. But Lily baited me into doing just that.

"Why don't you trust me as a professional?" she asked. "You know as well as anyone that I'm bound by confidentiality obligations, and that none of this can ever leave my office."

"Yes, in theory. But your office security is not infallible."

"Even if someone broke into my office and knew which notepad corresponded to you, do you really think they could make any sense out of my chicken scratch? Sometimes I myself can't read what I've written and have to reconstruct it from other bits that I do recall or other notes that I am able to read."

"Yes, but you're still human. You could accidentally slip and share something that you shouldn't – maybe over a glass of wine, or a forgetful moment of indiscretion when talking to a trusted friend or relative."

"That hasn't happened yet. In almost seven years of practice."

"Would you tell me if it did? Don't answer, because I can't possibly know whether your answer is truthful."

"Why not?"

"Because I'm the one answering all of the questions. I know almost nothing about you, beyond what I learned before hiring you. And it's only by learning far more about you that I could eventually form a judgment about your truthfulness in general and your level of discipline and discretion when it comes to client confidentiality."

"So how do you trust any therapist?"

"Well, I haven't really. It's a process. And you may have to open up about yourself at some point for me to share more with you."

"We both know that isn't appropriate, considering that you are the client, and this is not at all about me."

"Yes. But I'm just highlighting how you're assuming a certain level of trust that you may not be able to achieve with me."

"Then I guess, at some point, we may hit an impasse, where we have to conclude that these sessions are no longer productive. You still refuse to tell me anything about your father, or why your mother left him, or any details from your early childhood. And if you can't even tell me anything about the very nightmares that you say are one of the reasons you've sought out my professional help, then we may have already reached a dead end."

"I've told you far more about myself than I've revealed to anyone else. That should count for something."

"And it does. What you've told me is helpful to a certain point. But if that's the most that you'll be able to share with me, then I'm not sure we can make much more progress, and this may have to be our last session."

There was a heavy pause as I felt the power play implicit in her ultimatum. By threatening to walk away, she actually intrigued me more and pushed me slightly past my comfort zone, forcing me to trust her sooner than I might have otherwise.

"OK," I finally acquiesced. "I'll tell you about the nightmare that comes back most often."

She leaned back a little and exhaled, as if she was relieved that the most dramatic confrontation between us had passed. She looked up at me attentively, her pen poised to take notes.

"The dream can start in any number of ways – from my childhood, my teen-aged years, my college and graduate school years at Yale, my early career on Wall Street, or from the recent past. But no matter who is in the dream or what era of my life is depicted, it always ends with me wrapped in a blanket."

"What do you mean by that?"

"I'm literally bundled in a blanket – often inside a coffin, buried alive. But sometimes it's not in a coffin. I can be in the bed that I sleep in now, or my bed as a child, but I'm always enveloped in the same blood-drenched blanket."

"Why is it drenched in blood?"

"Because at some point, when the experience stops being a dream and becomes my recurring nightmare, the threads of the blanket will usually turn into sharp hooks, or blades – razorblades, kitchen knives, or even a blanket woven of small daggers. And the hooks or blades catch onto bits of my skin, piercing or cutting me open, until blood is everywhere on the blanket. And sometimes…" I paused for a moment, horrified at the image of what I was about to share.

"Go on, Julien."

"Sometimes, a blade or a hook will cut open my carotid artery," I said, pointing to it in my neck. And so much blood will spray out, with nowhere to escape because it's enclosed in the blanket, that the blood starts to pool and gets into my mouth and nose. And then I'll start to feel as if I'm choking on my own blood, gasping for air, and struggling desperately to take the blanket off me, even as its hooks and blades sink ever deeper into my bleeding flesh. And the harder I try to remove the blanket, the deeper the blades or hooks enter my skin, and the harder it is for me to breathe."

Lily raised her eyebrows a bit, as if to adjust to what she was hearing. "And what happens next? Or is that the end of the recurring nightmare?"

"That's the end. If I'm inside a coffin, then my struggle with the blanket is even more violent. But the nightmare always ends with me desperately gasping for air and violently throwing the blanket off me before bolting upright in my bed, at which point I see that I've hurled my blanket to the floor and I realize that I've had that horrific dream again."

I still can't believe that I shared all of that with her. But I didn't want to lose her as my therapist. And how the fuck am I supposed to sleep now, after writing all of that down? It's 4:15. And I just feel miserable all around. I hate taking sleeping pills and almost never do it, but I may have to resort to them this time. I'll give Icarus one last visit – maybe seeing that little guy again will somehow help. Actually, Lily had suggested bringing him into my bedroom, and I think that idea is worth trying to see if it brings me any extra solace when trying to sleep. I wonder what birds would choose, if God offered them the ability to dream but with the caveat that they might end up with nightmares.

Chapter 33: Anissa

∽ Monday, March 17, 2014 ∾

To My Dearest,

    Today ended up being even more exciting and unforgettable than I imagined it would be. As the only female among the top three midterm grades in Psychology and Markets, I felt as if I would stand out no matter what I wore to the JMAT office tour this morning. But as I sat in the reception area with the other two students, excitedly waiting for the head of HR to show up for our tour, I was suddenly glad about the shopping time and money that I had reluctantly spent yesterday. My beautiful new dress gave me a boost of confidence and seemed to signify a new phase in my life somehow. After obsessing for hours over way too many options at multiple stores (and wishing I had more than a student's budget to work with), Maya helped me to pick out two dresses: one for the office tour and the other for the VIP party. For my visit to JMAT, we chose a black Danny & Nicole Polka Dot Jacket Dress.

    "Can you believe this view?" Xavier asked, pointing at the floor-to-ceiling glass window next to us, overlooking Manhattan from forty floors above ground. He had earned the second best score on the midterm and sported that clean-cut, athletic look that seemed so prevalent among the guys in my Economics class whose post-graduation goal was a corporate finance job.

    "Yeah. I wonder if there will be any kind of Myers-Briggs or other testing from HR," Nicholas replied, a little nervously. He was sitting between Xavier and me, playing Tetris on his smartphone. He definitely looked like the classic "nerd," with thick glasses, pasty skin, some pimples, and curly hair that needed a good trimming – all of which seemed to offset whatever elegance his ill-fitting suit and tie was supposed to add to his appearance.

    "I hadn't thought of that possibility," I replied. "But I have a feeling that if Professor Morales was going to have HR test us in some way, we wouldn't even know it."

    "Very true," Xavier replied. "But if they're going to measure our enthusiasm for the office environment, they really shouldn't make it so easy to fall in love with the place."

    "Exactly. I love the marble floors and kinetic sculptures in this waiting area," I enthused.

And then a petite, attractive woman appeared. She had big blue eyes, porcelain-like skin, and long brown hair tied back into a simple braid. "Hi everyone! I'm Raegan, the personal assistant to Julien Morales – or Professor Morales, as you probably refer to him. You must be Anissa," she said as she shook my hand. "It's nice to meet you."

"Very nice to meet you, Raegan."

"Now, which one of you is Xavier?"

"Right here," Xavier replied, as he shook Raegan's outstretched hand.

"Welcome, Xavier," she said. "So then you must be Nicholas. Welcome to JMAT," she said, shaking Nicholas' hand as well. "Professor Morales mentioned that the three of you got the highest scores on his recent midterm, which I've heard is notoriously hard, so congratulations to all of you."

"Thank you," we each said, not quite in unison, but all clearly proud of the accomplishment.

"I'm going to be giving you your initial tour of the JMAT office, starting with the trading floor, which guests always enjoy visiting – almost as much as our food pantry and recreation rooms. Then, I'll bring you by Professor Morales' office so that he can chat with you for a few minutes, and then I'll take you to Daina, who's the head of HR, and she'll take over from there. You should be done with the tour in about three hours. I know that you were asked to come in business attire today, but you should know that our office is actually very relaxed about such things – unless you're working in investor relations, financial products, or other departments that have client or investor meetings. But if you're in research, analytics, or trading, you can show up in flip-flops if you like."

As Raegan led us around the office, it felt – in every possible way – as if we had entered a very special and elite world, populated with the brightest and most talented people, surrounded by an aura of wealth, comfort, organization, creativity, luxury, art, and an ineffable feeling of abundance. The entire place seemed designed to make you never want to leave. There was a giant aquarium with all sorts of exotic fish; a karaoke room; a giant recreation room with Ping-Pong tables, video games, chess sets and other games; a fitness room with every type of workout machine; a shower area; and a cushioned room with two full-time massage therapists working there. There were healthy snacks everywhere, in addition to several spacious food pantries that featured juice bars and food prepared by gourmet chefs (although Raegan pointed out that meat is never served or even allowed onto the JMAT premises – a rule that struck me as a bit odd).

As we toured JMAT, which occupied the top fifteen floors of the fifty-story midtown office building, the three of us were speechless. And seeing so many young, smart, beautiful women working there made me realize, more than ever, that Professor Morales could literally have any woman he wanted.

Later that night, I saw Michael at Alfred Lerner Hall, where I caught the last half hour of his MCA meeting. Showing up so late can't have helped the lousy conversation that we ended up having. But, after losing about three hours at JMAT, plus forty minutes to get there and back (in the private car service that Professor Morales had arranged for Xavier, Nicholas, and me), I couldn't really make it to the entire meeting.

My tardiness only exacerbated the tension between Michael and me after the MCA meeting adjourned. I kept gushing over my experience at JMAT, but the more excited I seemed to get about that office and possibly working there someday, the more Michael seemed to grow distant – almost jealous or resentful. I couldn't quite tell. I know it wasn't envy, because he had turned down plenty of lucrative job opportunities to pursue his political activism. Money means nothing to him personally – he just needs it for the cause. Actually, I think that's why he often secretly resents the very donors he has to bootlick; they usually represent that self-centered path of comfort and luxury that he forsook for a higher calling. And yet he needs them. That must be so frustrating: to need the very people who only enrich themselves while you slave away for some greater good. And I think he already started to see me as becoming one of those people.

Or it might have been jealousy, or some combination of the two. But it was too awkward for me to ask him if he was jealous of Professor Morales, and I was afraid that doing so might give him new ideas that he hadn't considered before. So I stayed away from that possibility in what became our first real quarrel.

"I just wish you could have been there to see what I mean," I enthused at one point.

"Oh no, that's fine, I really don't need to see it – I'll just take your word for it," he replied, with a tone that was borderline disparaging.

"Why do you sound like you're not actually happy for me?"

"No, that's great, Inās. I am happy for you. I just hope that you don't get swept away in some materialistic American dream that makes you forget your roots," he finally admitted aloud.

"Michael, I don't even know if I'm going to get a job there. And if I did, it wouldn't be before this summer, and a full-time job couldn't happen for about three more years. So we're getting a little ahead of ourselves, don't you think?"

"Judging from the way you speak about it, I don't think we're getting ahead of ourselves at all. This is already the only thing you've been talking about for the last few weeks."

"That's not fair, Michael! The last few weeks I was totally in midterm-cramming mode. And the goal was to win the prize that I enjoyed receiving this morning. Can't I just celebrate that victory for five minutes?"

"Of course you can. And I really am happy for you. But I'm just worried that you'll quickly grow intoxicated by all of that wealth, comfort, and luxury that seduced you on that tour this morning. Those are actually not the things that matter, Inās."

"You have a lot of nerve telling me that! You have no idea what I lost in Syria. How much evil I personally witnessed."

"Well, maybe if you told me, I would know."

"How do you expect me to open up to you when you say something like that to me? And where do you get off judging me like that? You, who grew up in this comfortable American life, who never had to hide that he was a Christian – who never witnessed any friends or family die because of their Christian faith. How dare you judge me for enjoying, for the first time in my life, all of that American opportunity that you've always taken for granted because you knew nothing else?"

"Are you joking? How many humanitarian missions to Syria have you been on? You only left Syria. But I regularly go into the very danger that you fled. I'm trying to help our community there survive, even if I grew up here. And I never once was impressed by all of this money bullshit. My parents raised me to care about education and good morals – not money."

"As did mine! Listen, this conversation is just upsetting me. I need to go. I have my Econ midterm tomorrow and this is definitely not helping me to prepare for it."

And after that, I just stormed off. As I headed back to my dorm, hot tears filled my eyes and spilled on to my cheeks before falling away. Frustration and anger tightened my chest into an uncomfortable heaviness. Michael didn't even run after me as I left. Or call me afterwards. And that only made me cry more, because I so wanted to celebrate this day with him.

So here I am at 4 a.m., writing to you now because I can't stop thinking about everything, even though I have my Economics midterm tomorrow. If I heed my mother's advice "not to invite envy to my house," who can I talk to about my JMAT visit? Who can share my excitement without growing covetous? The only people who can genuinely and harmlessly participate in this little triumph are Uncle Tony and Monique. So I guess I'll tell them. Of course, Maya will want to hear all about it, and she won't get envious like some of the other students I know here. She's a real friend. But I wanted to enjoy this win with Michael more than with anyone else, and somehow it highlighted differences between us that hadn't been there before.

I'm going to attempt to go to bed now. I was too sad and hurt to focus on studying Econ after the fight with Michael. I'll just try to wake up in a few hours and somehow make up the lost study time.

Chapter 34: Julien

Friday, 3/21/14 at 2:19.

    Last Sunday night, when I was having trouble sleeping, I decided to follow Lily's advice and relocate Icarus into my bedroom after writing my last journal entry. He chirped and flapped his wings about in alarm as I moved his birdcage onto the marble shelf by the window overlooking Manhattan. Then I gave him some more seeds to eat, and watched him peck away at the food while looking at his damaged wing, which did seem to be healing a little. We both stared out at the New York skyline together – as if to contemplate the heights where he belongs. "At least you're still up high now, with a good view, and not limping around with a broken wing in a New York gutter," I whispered to him, as if he could understand me. And finally, at around 5:30 a.m., I left the window where I had brought Icarus, and walked over to my bed nearby. I fell asleep without any pills, although I awoke about three hours later from that awful nightmare.

    I think having Icarus in my bedroom definitely helps. But some kind of tension with Anissa continues to build and I suspect that it's now the main thing keeping me up at night. I saw her briefly last Monday, when she, Xavier, and Nicholas all came to JMAT for the office tour, and then again in class on Tuesday and Thursday. I can see that she's feeling increasingly comfortable around me, smiles more readily, and speaks more freely, and I seem to be encouraging it wherever possible, rather than maintaining my distance, as I had before.

    I may soon have to speak to Lily about this because it feels as if it's getting a bit out of hand. I even wondered how many times she might have tried to add me on Facebook, as so many of my prior students (and lovers) have, but was frustrated by the fact that my friend count is already at the limit of 5,000, making it impossible for anyone to friend me. I even thought about unfriending some people just so that she would be able to friend me the next time she tried, but – because others could quickly take whatever "friend spots" I freed up – I'd have to let her know that I'm friendable now. But then I might as well just friend her myself, although that could definitely seem inappropriate to any outside observer. And, more importantly, it would probably be interpreted by Anissa as a huge signal of interest from me, effectively accelerating the very process that I'm worried about and probably need to decelerate.

    I decided that the best way to deal with it for now, is to pursue someone who might be a rough equivalent to Anissa but not a student of mine. And a party at my place is always the easiest way to draw in some new hotties, often with help of Maya or Verna. I sent them both this text message an hour ago: "Small VIP party this Saturday at my place. 9 p.m. Just 30 invited. Bring a hot, smart, young babe with you." Maya sent me a reply text about five minutes later: "Done. I have the perfect girl to bring." And Maya probably knows my taste better than anyone else does, so there is cause for optimism.

Chapter 35: Anissa

∽ Friday, March 21, 2014 ∾

To My Dearest,

This last week has been something of a rollercoaster. First, the heady excitement of my visit to JMAT, then the emotionally draining fight with Michael, followed by my last two midterms, and then tons of other stuff that I'll tell you about.

Going to my Psychology and Markets lecture after the visit to JMAT definitely felt different. Thanks to our midterm performance, the whole class already looked at Xavier, Nicholas and me with more respect. But after our tour of JMAT, many students also sought out the three of us with questions about the work environment there, what Professor Morales was like at the office, etc.

Interestingly enough, my new status in the class also may have indirectly confirmed for me that Elise was indeed having some kind of secret relationship with our professor. Up until I was mentioned among the top three, the vibe from her had always been straightforward and friendly, her wide smile generally putting me at ease and making her seem more approachable. But the Tuesday after the JMAT tour, I sensed a subtle shift in the energy that she projected, as if she suddenly viewed me as some kind of rival.

I also felt more confident about speaking in class and approaching Professor Morales afterwards, when he normally took some questions from students on his way out. It felt almost as if an unspoken familiarity was now starting to develop between us, thanks to my admission into his elite club. For both of the class sessions this week, Xavier, Nicholas, and I seemed to enjoy a new admiration and friendliness from Professor Morales, but he appeared to be warming up to me the most (although that could also just be in my head – some kind of wishful thinking maybe).

That class was the only bright spot for most of the week. My last midterm, in Masterpieces of Western Literature and Philosophy, was on Wednesday and it wasn't a disaster like my Econ midterm, but wasn't anything too stellar either. I'll probably get a B+ or maybe an A-, if I got lucky on some of my answers.

My quarrel with Michael (from last Monday) festered for far too long. Yesterday, there was another MCA meeting scheduled, and I almost chose not to go out of spite. But then I realized that this was wrong on several levels. Most importantly, the cause is far more important than any petty differences among MCA members, even if that means swallowing my pride a little. Also, I didn't want Michael to be the one to decide or control what my involvement with the MCA would be. As much as I admire him and view him as the natural leader for the organization, I should be able to support it as an active member regardless of what my current relationship with him is. Lastly, I thought it might actually be good for us to see each other in person, and for a purpose that might remind us how we found each other and why we are naturally good together.

But then, to my substantial and very jealous dismay, I saw his ex-girlfriend at the meeting! Just as I had convinced myself that the MCA should be about the cause of Middle East Christians and not about personalities or relationships or anything relatively trivial like that, I found myself getting jealous and angry and wondering why Karen was suddenly at an MCA meeting when I hadn't seen her at one in about six weeks. To make matters worse, it became clear in the meeting that she had volunteered (last Monday) to help find additional large potential donors in North America – a key research project that would virtually guarantee that she and Michael would need to be in touch on a regular basis.

As much as I wanted to confront her and Michael about the whole thing, I had to control myself – both for my self-respect and for the sake of the MCA (which really needs a business-like and drama-free environment that stays focused on the life-and-death issues facing our community). I didn't want either Michael or Karen to think that I cared enough to get publicly upset before I even had all of the facts.

After the meeting, I was relieved to see Karen promptly leave the area, without lingering around Michael, so that we didn't have to go through any extra drama or awkwardness. When Michael and I were alone in the room, he said, "I'm glad you could make it tonight. I know how busy you've been with midterms and after last Monday night, I wasn't sure if you'd come today."

"Well, believe it or not, Michael, this cause really does matter to me. More than you may realize. But what was Karen doing here? It's not as if she's been consistently involved with the MCA. I haven't seen her here in about a month and a half."

"Actually, she was here for the first part of last Monday's meeting – the part that you missed."

"Well, why are you letting her volunteer for a project like that?"

"What do you mean?"

"That's something that I could have easily done."

"I would have happily assigned it to you last Monday, had you been here when the most pressing tasks were in need of volunteers. Her hand went straight up when I asked who wanted to help with that."

"Of course it did," I snapped back.

"Inās, what did you want me to say to her? 'No, you can't help me with that because someone who's not actually at the meeting now might want to volunteer for it later?'"

"Why don't you see her interest for what it obviously is, Michael?"

"Inās, this organization, and the work it's trying to do, is much bigger than any one person's motives. If I have to let personal issues get involved in every little decision, we'll never get anything done. Besides, you're more than welcome to help with the exact same project. We can just divide up the North American territory so that your efforts don't overlap."

"So you can't give the project to me alone now?"

"You want me to reject someone's help just because you question her motives? What kind of signal will that send to her? Or anyone else who might end up hearing about it? And how can we progress efficiently as an organization with a management style like that? I asked for help, and someone generously volunteered it. There's nothing more to it than that."

"You really expect me to believe that, Michael?"

"Inās, I hadn't been in touch with Karen since I took you ice skating on Valentine's Day."

"You were in touch with her that day?" I asked in dismay.

"Well, she just sent me a text wishing me a happy Valentine's, and I just sent her back a text saying thank you. I didn't even wish her a happy Valentine's Day back. Just a polite and short thank you."

"So you didn't tell her that you spent it with me?" I clarified, still upset.

"That would have been needlessly cruel on Valentine's Day, don't you think? Anyway, the point is that I haven't been in touch with her at all. And I never asked her to come to the meeting last Monday. But she showed up. I'm not going to tell her that she's not welcome. It's not as if

175

she's done anything wrong. You know as well as anyone that people show up and help when they can, including you. We don't know what else was happening in her life during the time she was away. So just give her the benefit of the doubt, rather than jealously assume the worst."

"It's not jealousy. It just looks very suspicious," I replied, aware that I probably still sounded as territorial as I felt.

"I can see why you might think that, but there's really no cause for drama," Michael reassured me, trying to soften the tone of our conversation. "How did your Economics midterm go yesterday?"

"Terribly. Not that this was any surprise – I knew as I was taking the exam that I missed some important questions."

"I'm sorry to hear that. When do you get your grade?"

"They posted it today. I got my first C in college."

"Oh that sucks. I know how disappointed you must feel. But it's just the midterm, so you can make up for it on the final."

"At this point, there's no way I'll be able to get even an A- in the class."

"Well, you can thank Professor Morales for that, since you spent all of your study time on his class," he replied, with a touch of defensiveness and insecurity in his voice.

"Now who's jealous?"

"That's not being jealous – that's just stating a fact!" He again adopted an edgy and defensive posture. "You yourself said that you were sacrificing your other classes to do as well as you could on his class. And you did – you couldn't have done any better."

"Yes, but I was also crying all of Monday night, instead of studying," I admitted, feeling myself start to get upset again.

"I know, Inās, and…" he started, putting his hand lightly on my shoulder. Michael suddenly softened in his tone and facial expression again. He reached for his backpack and took out a wrapped box.

"I didn't think you were going to make it to tonight's meeting, so I was planning to leave this for you with the guard at your dorm. But since you're here, I'd much rather give it to you in person."

I took the box from him, curious about its contents, while suspecting that the welling hurt in my chest was about to dissipate thanks to this surprise gesture. He winked and nodded with his head, signaling me to open it. I removed the wrapper and found a small box of Baklava with a Baci taped to the top of the lid, and a small, heart-shaped paper underneath it. I took the paper and read the handwritten note on it: "I'm so sorry for upsetting you, Inās. You're as beautiful on the inside as on the outside, and the last person I'd ever want to hurt. I'm grateful for every moment we have together."

My face lit up, my heart skipped a beat, and all was forgiven as he wrapped me in those big, warm arms of his. Soon our mouths were pressed together in a passionate kiss. I felt his palms gradually make their way down my back, and then, just when they got to my butt, his hands moved towards each other until his fingers met at the curve of my spine, and wandered back up to my neck. Our make-out session felt like it could have lasted forever, if there hadn't been another student meeting that was just starting to set up around us.

As if all of that weren't enough of a crazy ride for this week, a few hours ago I was hanging out with Maya after our Economics study group and she completely surprised me. "Guess what?" she began with a suggestive smile. She was clearly in a good mood – probably because she had received an A on the same Econ midterm that I had flopped. I mean, I don't think she's competitive like that – she doesn't seem like the kind of person who is happier only if her friends are worse off than she is. But I'm sure she secretly feels at least a tad vindicated, after I got the top grade on a midterm that she bombed.

"There's almost something mischievous in the way you say that, so I'm not even going to try to guess. Just tell me," I replied lightly.

"You're coming with me to Julien's party tomorrow night."

"What?!"

And then she showed me the text that she got from him: "Small VIP party this Saturday at my place. 9pm. Just 30 invited. Bring a hot, smart, young babe with you." And I saw her reply to him, five minutes later: "Done. I have the perfect girl to bring."

"So soon?" I was in a bit of nervous shock. "I mean, I thought this would happen a bit later in the semester."

"So did I. But he sent me this late last night. And with Julien's parties, you just go when you're invited. You don't ask him to reschedule," she added with a chuckle.

"I know, but I just saw him at the JMAT office on Monday."

"How was that, by the way? Is it as epic as everyone says?"

"You can't even imagine," I replied, with an excited smile.

"You better make friends with the people in HR and hook me up!"

"It's not like I already have a job there! Besides, you're on his VIP party guest list – isn't that better than knowing HR?"

"Well, he's a bit obsessed with the idea of meritocracy, so he's quite strict about the procedures for getting in. There are really only three ways to get a job there: on-campus recruiting, applying through HR, or being one of his top students. He doesn't play favorites with anyone. And if he saw me trying to leverage my friendship with him for an interview, that could totally backfire, and then I might also lose the party invitations."

"I see."

"Anyway, aren't you glad we got the shopping part out of the way? Now you're already all set for tomorrow night," she remarked with a playful wink.

Chapter 36: Julien

Sunday, 3/23/14 at 11:05.

Last Friday night I couldn't sleep much. I was too anxious for Saturday night to arrive – curious as to whom Verna and Maya would bring to my party – especially Maya, who claimed to have "the perfect girl to bring." I was eager to develop an interest in someone other than Anissa, and that would mean a very smart, young, innocent, and exotic beauty. I knew the odds of finding that were rather small, but somehow Maya's text gave me hope and had me imagining some new babe that offered the kind of excitement that thoughts of Anissa generate, but with less risk.

I tried talking to Icarus, but that didn't help. I finally took some sleeping pills at 5:24 a.m. and was very grateful that I could sleep in the next day. Even better – there was no nightmare involved and I managed to get about six hours. But I regret using the pills and have resolved not to resort to them again for at least a month. I just wanted to be reasonably alert and amiable at the party that I was hosting the next night, and that required getting at least a few hours of sleep.

All of the usual VIPs showed up, including some of my closer friends. It was supposed to be just thirty people, but there are always a few extras and it ended up being over forty. I included all of my customary treats and everyone seemed to be having a good time. At 9 p.m. sharp, just when the party was getting started, Verna showed up and brought a cute twenty-five-year-old, Cuban-American girl with her, but she didn't really have that uninitiated look and feel that Anissa had made me crave. She had studied fashion design at FIT and was working in retail, and – from our brief conversation – didn't strike me as having anything like Anissa's intellect.

There were probably ten other new women who showed up with my male friends (who were allowed to bring more than one guest only if they were single females). But none of these girls impressed me very much either. And at around 10 p.m., I started to feel some disappointment settle in as I realized that it may have been foolishly optimistic of me to assume that a single party could solve my ridiculous bachelor problems – problems that just about any man on the planet would kill to have. I rolled my eyes at myself, thinking, "Julien, what the fuck is wrong with you? Your personal net worth as of yesterday exceeds

4.2 billion dollars. You can fuck your cute assistant any time you want. You've got fan mail from countless girls who see you on TV and endless opportunities to hook up with young hotties at one of the nation's top universities, where you are a professor and – if you play your cards right – could get promoted and become a full professor next year. You live in this obscenely beautiful penthouse triplex. Oh, and there's the hot grad student who's your TA for Psychology and Markets whom you've bent over the lectern in your Hamilton Hall lecture room on a few occasions, not to mention all of the times she came over here. And yet, somehow, you have the ungrateful audacity to be disappointed that a suitable replacement for Anissa has failed to show up at your place in less than forty-eight hours of first seeking her out. You really do need to see a shrink. Oh wait, you are seeing a shrink and may try to sleep with her as a last-ditch attempt to solve these so-called women problems. Who are we kidding? You are one fucked up guy with zero perspective on life and totally twisted values."

I shook my head and sort of chuckled at myself while pouring some wine. As I put the bottle down, I realized that Maya hadn't yet arrived, and suddenly my absurd hopes were revived, and I went to check my phone to see if she had sent any update. And sure enough, there was a text message from her twenty minutes earlier, at 9:45 p.m. "Sorry, hun. Running a bit late. We just now got in a cab. Be there soon!"

Ten minutes later, my doorbell rang. I opened the door and it was Maya, but I couldn't see who was with her because there were a few other late arrivals crowding the doorway next to her. And then, as they made their way in, Maya says, "Julien, I'd like to introduce you to a good friend of mine, Anissa," and my student steps forward into plain sight, slightly blushing and surprised.

She looked absolutely ravishing in a sexy but very classy white dress. In class, her dark brown hair was sometimes messy, and usually blocking her face a little, as if she had forgotten to bother with it because of too much studying or something. But tonight her hair was pulled back in a French braid that seemed to spotlight the youthful beauty of her face. I was totally speechless. At her breathtaking looks and elegance. At the shock of seeing her again. At the fact that Maya had in mind exactly the woman I wanted but was hoping to forget. And at the realization that I would now be getting closer to – rather than farther from – Anissa. Amusingly enough, Anissa was also at a loss for words. So the three of us just sort of stood there for an awkward moment, trying to figure out how to proceed.

"You – what are you doing here?" she asked me, finally, laughing nervously.

"What am I doing here?" I suppressed a laugh at the absurdity of our exchange. "I live here! What are you doing here, is the question!"

"Well, Maya just…mentioned a party and – "

"Wait, you two already know each other?" Maya chimed in, looking equally amused at the serendipity of the whole situation.

"Yes, she's my student," I explained, still in disbelief about the whole thing.

"Your top student," Anissa added coyly.

"For now," I corrected her. "There's still a final and some more problem sets, you know."

"Yes, of course," she conceded reluctantly.

"And she came to a tour of my office just last Monday," I told Maya. Then I turned to Anissa and tried to play it cool while saying something cute: "Speaking of which, aren't you sick of me by now? I mean, you saw me on Monday, Tuesday, and Thursday. And now *tonight?*"

Anissa paused for a moment, and responded with a certain amused indifference. "You know, you're right," she conceded, as if the truth of my observation had just dawned on her. "Maya, I can always see Professor Morales in class next week."

My jaw dropped at her ballsy remark. So did Maya's. "What do you mean?" she asked Anissa, slightly nervous about how she might reply. I also braced myself for a potentially embarrassing moment. The three of us were still somewhat awkwardly standing by the doorway, so – in spatial terms – Anissa had very clearly not yet committed to staying at my party and was optimally positioned for a quick escape. She answered Maya. "Well, you said tonight was all about getting me out into the city to meet some new people. And you mentioned that there were a few parties that we could stop by tonight, right?"

"Are you serious?" Maya responded, practically gawking.

"Well, I'm not sure if it's really appropriate for me to be at the party of someone who is currently my professor and who didn't even invite me."

I couldn't believe my ears. "Yes, but you are now as officially invited as a guest can be," I quickly pointed out, worried that she might still now leave with Maya to some other party – an outcome that would be humiliating on multiple levels. But Anissa didn't seem convinced that she should stay, so I kept going. "Even though we've already seen each other three times this week, this would be the first time that we're doing so in a more casual setting, so I'm delighted that Maya decided to bring you," I continued. "Here, let me get you both a glass of wine," I added.

"Wouldn't that be intoxicating a minor?" Anissa quipped playfully. And with the slightly impish smirk on her face, it became clear that she was going to stay. I let out a hidden sigh of relief.

"OK, how about a glass of cranberry vodka without the vodka?" I replied.

"Much better!" Anissa replied.

With my mind at ease and now more hopeful than ever, I led the two towards the bar area of my living room.

But for the rest of her time at my party, Anissa seemed to mingle with everyone except me, as if she knew that this would drive me totally fucking crazy. It was sheer torture – especially because I had to play it completely cool and look as indifferent as possible while I played host. But as I flitted about from one guest to the next, each interaction – especially with females – only increased my desire to speak to Anissa. And – ironically enough – her teasing avoidance of all interactions with me (other than those required by politeness) subverted my entire purpose for the party! She trounced my plan to forget her by making herself so unforgettable that I could think of only one thing: I had to have her.

Chapter 37: Anissa

∽ Sunday, March 23, 2014 ∾

To My Dearest,

All I can say as I try to write to you about last night is: WOW! Just like my tour of JMAT, everything about the party last night was beyond my wildest expectations, and conveyed the idea of abundance and endless possibility.

Everything about the night just felt "on" – as if I was in the zone, like when I'm running or sparring, and perfectly focused. But before I recount my experience at Professor Morales' party last night, I should tell you about my lunch date with Michael that occurred several hours before.

My Saturday actually began rather early because Friday night I couldn't fall asleep out of so much anticipation about the party. So I ended up taking all of that restless, nervous energy, and going for an early-morning run in Riverside Park.

The spring weather had already started to arrive, but at that pre-sunrise hour, it was still chilly out. I hadn't had a chance to buy any special winter running gear, so I just improvised and wore some sweats, a winter cap, and gloves.

There was something perfectly peaceful about jogging through the park alone, with the rest of the city still asleep. In the early morning light, the trees and river passed by to the sound of my steady breathing, as I imagined the horrors of my past seeping out of my soul through the sweat on my skin, and gradually falling away.

When I reached the peak of a hill in the park, I stopped to recover from my final sprint, basking in an endorphin-filled glow as I watched the sun rise over the skyscrapers dotting the eastern side of the city. It was a glorious moment that somehow calmed me, telling me that everything would be fine.

When I got back to my room, I took a long, hot shower, and then made myself some warm oatmeal and berries. With my stomach satisfied, my body exhausted from intense exertion, and the previous night of no sleep gradually hitting me, a wave of drowsy relaxation descended over me. I crawled into bed and slept like a baby for a solid four hours.

At 1:30 p.m., Michael took me out for a falafel lunch and we talked about my invitation to Professor Morales' VIP party. At first, I wasn't sure if it was wise to mention it – especially after all of the drama with him from the previous week. But we had reconnected the previous night in such a loving and reassuring way that it felt safe to discuss it. And the issue wasn't going to go away any time soon, since I still had a few months left of Psychology and Markets and was quite keen to work at JMAT now. So I told him.

"Why wasn't I invited?" he joked. I couldn't tell if he was insecure or jealous.

"Well the truth is, I wasn't invited either. I mean, he has no idea I'm coming – he thinks Maya is bringing someone else," I explained.

"I'm just teasing you, obviously. I doubt I'd enjoy mingling with the type of people who go to his parties."

"You promise you're not jealous?"

"Do I have any reason to be?" he asked genuinely, with a hint of vulnerability.

"No, you don't, Michael," I reassured him, as I looked directly into his eyes and put my hand on his.

"Good," he replied, with a relieved smile. "Just promise that you'll get closer to him not just to advance your career, but also to help the cause."

"Michael, you really don't need to remind me to do that."

My hand was still on his, so he took his other hand and placed it lightly on my shoulder, as if to emphasize the praise he had for me. "I know, I know," he conceded. "You brought in the biggest outdoor cash donation from him," he noted, rubbing my lower neck gently as he proudly gazed at me. "But I've just seen what money has done to some of my friends – male and female – so I worry sometimes. And a part of me wants to know that you'll always be by my side in this important mission."

"I will be, Michael. I promise. And not because it's you – although obviously that's a huge bonus," I added with a reassuring smile. "But because it's the last thing my father requested of me."

"What do you mean?" Michael asked, withdrawing the neck massage he had started giving me as his dark eyebrows furrowed a bit, trying to imagine the details behind the story I had never told him.

I took my hand back to feel a bit more control over what I was about to say, which was not the truth. Only Monique, and you, My

Dearest, can have that. So I told him what I had told Uncle Tony about January 18, 2012.

"Before my parents got into the car, never to return alive, they – " I began, when he interrupted me.

"They died in a car crash?" he clarified.

"Yes, but that's all I'm comfortable sharing about that night. I saw them a few hours before that happened, and my dad said words that I will never forget. I repeat them any time I feel the slightest temptation to give up on any endeavor."

"What did he say?"

"As you rise to the top, guard your values and your purity, and remember your roots and your people – do what you can to help. And I have no doubt that you will."

Michael was silent for a moment, almost out of respect for the words of my father, as if his spirit had been there at our table, sharing our hummus and falafel, imparting the wisdom of his experience.

"Wow. I didn't realize that he said something like that to you, and on the last time that you saw him. Now I feel quite embarrassed – even stupid – for reminding you not to get seduced by all of the wealth around us in this city."

"It's OK," I said. "There's still a lot about me that you don't know."

"Very true," he conceded in a humble tone. "But can I still give you some advice for how to get the most out of this party?"

"You mean for me? Or for the cause?"

"Both," he replied with a smile. "The same strategy applies, whether you're trying to advance yourself or the MCA, because – either way – you will be more effective if you keep your professor's psychology in mind while you're at his party."

"I'm intrigued. What's your advice?"

"You have to be completely different from all of the other women he meets. And, in many ways you already are – without even trying."

"Because I'm a Syrian refugee? And a virgin?"

"Yes. I'm sure he doesn't meet either of those very often. Not to mention the top student in his class. But there's more that you can do to set yourself apart from the others in a way that takes your influence with him to a whole other level."

"What do you mean? What should I try to do?"

"How does every woman act around him?"

"With admiration. Awe. And usually some fear of saying or doing the wrong thing around him."

"So now you know what not to do."

"You want me to disrespect him?"

"Not quite. Be polite. But carry yourself as if you're indifferent to the man. Interact with him as if he needs you more than you need him. Let him chase you."

I smiled at the devious boldness of Michael's suggestion. "I think I can do that tonight," I replied with a smile.

"Good. Make him realize that you're complete without him. And, unlike the countless beauties throwing themselves at him every day for his money or power, you don't actually need or want anything from him. You just showed up with your friend who promised you a good party."

I liked the idea even more because it might help me to normalize someone I was secretly starting to worship on some subconscious level – something I could never admit to Michael. "So I'll just be polite and friendly, but show much more interest in the other people at his party," I recapped.

"Exactly. And by doing that, you will remind him of something he forgot long ago: what it's like not to have power over a woman. And if you return him to that position of need and potential rejection, you'll command his respect and his eagerness to please you far more than anyone else can."

"Well, I'm glad that you and I are now so comfortable in our relationship that you can advise me on how to increase the attentions of my professor," I joked.

"Honestly, I'm not entirely comfortable with this scenario." Michael admitted, gazing into my eyes for a moment. He took my hand. "But I can trust you, right?"

I stared back into his brown irises for a dreamy second and then nodded my head to answer him, while putting my other hand on his.

He continued: "And increasing his attentions is fine, as long as it doesn't go any farther than that and makes him want to write big checks for the cause."

At 7:30 p.m., I took another shower, put my hair into a French braid, and put on the white Elie Tahari Erin Small sleeveless dress that Maya had helped me to pick out. By 8:30 p.m., I was ready to go, since Maya told me that we would leave around that time to arrive punctually at 9 p.m. But in the end, she was running late, so we ended up getting into a cab and heading downtown only at around 9:40 p.m. We arrived a little after 10 p.m. And at first, I was worried about arriving so late, but then I remembered my chat with Michael and told myself, "All of the other girls worry about showing up an hour late to his parties, but not you. You're just stopping by on your way to something better."

But my newfound aloofness towards Professor Morales was briefly tamed by our entrance to the apartment building of his residence rising sixty-five floors above Madison Square Park. The majestic lobby had high ceilings, stylishly dimmed beams of light, and a waterfall behind the security guard and doorman, who had just finished admitting some party guests and greeted us moments after we entered.

"Hi Maya," he said.

"Hey Ethan, how's it going?" she replied. They clearly knew each other from her prior visits here.

"Good, thank you. I assume you're here for Julien's party?"

Maya nodded in response.

"OK, let me just make sure your name is on here, plus one, because he told me that it's a stricter guest list this time." He looked over his list and found her name. "OK, you're all set. You know the way – have fun," he added with a smile.

Maya led me past the waterfall area, to a long hallway that ended with two large elevator shafts. "Ready to be blown away?" she asked with a smile.

"Sure," I replied.

We entered the elevator and she pressed the button for the 63rd floor. "That's the main entrance, but it's a total of three floors," she explained. "They're connected by a stairwell, but the elevator also stops on each floor."

When we arrived, I was indeed astonished, but I did my best to hide it, and – as Michael had shrewdly suggested – I practically ignored Professor Morales, and interacted with him only enough so that he couldn't accuse me of being a rude or ungracious guest. But secretly I could not have been more impressed by everything – his palatial and impeccably designed apartment, the kind of company he keeps, the other beautiful women who showed up to his party, the artwork everywhere, and the list goes on. His living space conveyed the same ideas as his office: unimaginable wealth, creativity, luxury, art, comfort, state of the art technology, and a general feeling of plenty. The views of Manhattan from the sixty-third floor were absolutely breathtaking –

particularly because his entire apartment was made of glass walls that, with a push of a button, became opaque with whatever background theme one selected. He also had a high-powered telescope for stargazing or eavesdropping.

The artwork in his private collection clearly cost a fortune, and included not only a Rembrandt and a Salvador Dali painting, but a variety of sculptures and fixtures, including some fanciful, floating glass bubbles that hung from the ceiling and staircase, and made the space feel even more magical.

Before Maya and I began mingling in earnest with the other guests at the party, she gave me a quick tour of his place, describing everything with the detail and enthusiasm of a real estate broker. His 8,000-square foot triplex apartment included a game room, a bar, two deluxe kitchens, five bedrooms, six bathrooms (some with Jacuzzi baths), a spa, a private gym (in addition to the building's Olympic pool and fitness center), an entertainment room with a projector that had a film beamed onto the wall (almost like in a movie theater), and a massive wraparound terrace with trees and stunning views of every part of the Manhattan skyline.

The gourmet food tasted positively delectable but oddly included no meat of any kind (like in the JMAT office). There was about one server for every four guests, so nobody had to hold trash for very long or walk too far to get the next hors d'oeuvre.

And the networking there was out of this world – unlike anything one could probably find anywhere else. As I worked the room with Maya, I met a former U.S. Senator, the head of New York's top hospital, Chile's ambassador to the U.S., a TV newscaster on a major financial news network, the New York State Attorney General, and several extremely wealthy individuals (tycoons of real estate, high tech, venture capital, and finance). There were also several top models, including a former Miss Mexico and Miss Argentina.

We stayed for a few hours, although I could have easily lingered there all night, talking to the other guests, enjoying the delicious food and drinks, and marveling at this man and his world. But I purposely told Maya that I wanted to make it to one other party before heading home, figuring that this might get back to Professor Morales at some point.

Maya and I were actually among the first to leave. I sensed a smattering of disappointment in Professor Morales, when we came by to say thank you and good night.

"So soon?" he asked. "You can be honest and just tell me if you thought there wasn't enough space or food." He released an ironic smirk.

"It was lovely." I looked at Maya and then back at him. "Thank you so much for having me, even though I was somehow smuggled into this VIP party."

"Anyone who gets the highest score on my midterm is a VIP in my book."

"Well, there's still a final and some more problem sets," I quipped with a wink, throwing his own line back at him.

"Touché!" he conceded with a smile.

He hugged Maya goodbye, and there was an awkward stiffness as neither of us seemed to know whether to part by shaking hands, hugging, or just tipping our heads in a friendly acknowledgement. We both took the safest route and chose the last option.

Chapter 38: Julien

Monday, 3/24/14 at 3:16.

Another night hanging out with Icarus and the Manhattan skyline. Can't stop thinking about Anissa since she was here a little over twenty-four hours ago. And to make matters even worse, at one point Maya whispered into my ear a fact about Anissa that made her even more special and rare: she's a virgin! As if I needed anything else to ensure that I would obsess about her. I'm not a very good Catholic, but the absurdity of the situation may have strengthened my belief in God just a hair – if only because I saw Him at that moment, laughing hysterically at me.

I had to get some answers before seeing her in class this Tuesday, so I used the only discreet conduit that I had: Maya. I called her a few hours ago to get her take on things.

"Did she have fun?" I asked.

"I think so. She thought you had a cool crowd."

"Is that all she said?"

"Pretty much."

"And you went to other parties after you left my place?"

"Just one. She's not that much of a party girl. I don't think she's really into the scene, but I'm trying to get her to come out more and expand her social horizons a little."

"I see."

"Why? What's wrong? You didn't like her?"

"No, she's great – I just couldn't tell if she enjoyed herself. We barely spoke."

"Oh, I'm sorry about that. I'll mention it to her, in case there's a next time."

"No, please don't. That's not necessary." The last thing I wanted was for Anissa to sense that I desired or needed her, but unfortunately – from that kneejerk reaction – Maya immediately detected my posturing.

"Ha. I knew you'd like her!" she replied. "Don't worry, I won't tell her."

Maya and I are as close as we are because she's always been very discreet, so I wasn't too worried about her saying anything to Anissa, but I still tried to downplay my interest as best I could.

"Well, that was the first time that we'd ever seen each other in a more casual setting, so I was curious to get to know her better in that context. But that never really happened because of the party setting."

"I have an idea."

"What?"

"Why don't I bring her thirty minutes early to your next party, and then I'll go off to the bathroom so that you can just chat with her alone for a bit?"

"Thirty minutes early? Isn't that wishful thinking, considering you came an hour late to the last party?"

"Julien, you know I'm not usually late. It won't happen the next time, if you like my idea."

"Yes, I do like it. I'll let you know when I'm thinking of having the next party. It might even be this weekend or next."

Maya's strategy seemed ideal precisely because it allowed me to play it very cool with Anissa until we meet again under casual circumstances. In fact, I'm going to feed my new obsession some of her own medicine. I won't call on her in class unless she's the only volunteer to answer a question. I'll avoid even looking in her direction during my lecture, and afterwards I'll give priority to any other student who wants to speak with me. If she tries to see me during office hours, I'll be very short with her, pretending to be extra busy. If – like when we first met – I can seem a bit more reserved and distant to her than I have been lately, then she may come around and warm up to me again. But I can't go too far with my tonal adjustment; I still need to be nice enough so that she doesn't get intimidated or discouraged, because then she might just decline Maya's invitation to join her at my next party.

Chapter 39: Anissa

∞ Wednesday, March 26, 2014 ∞

To My Dearest,

Michael organized a demonstration earlier this afternoon in Union Square, but I arrived about thirty minutes late because it started just after class finished. As I was approaching the gathering from the subway, I saw Karen speaking to Michael. I think she noticed me from the distance because, within a few minutes, they stopped talking and by the time I reached the crowd, she was handing out signs for people to hold up. The placards each displayed one of four messages: "U.S. Stop Islamist Terror in Syria or You're Next," "Stop the Genocide of Mideast Christians," "ISIS: Syria and Iraq Today, the USA Tomorrow," and "Protect Religious Freedom in the Middle East."

I greeted Michael and some of my other friends who were there.

A few minutes later, Karen came up to me and offered a sign, saying, "Would you like one?"

"Thanks," I replied, taking it from her and holding it up.

A few minutes later, Michael went up and addressed the crowd of about one hundred people.

"The United States may not enjoy being the policeman of the world, and the wars in Iraq and Afghanistan certainly cost this country a lot of blood and treasure. And mistakes were made. But we cannot completely withdraw from the world. Because where the powers of good are absent, evil is free to take root, as we are witnessing today in Iraq and Syria."

There was some applause, including from people who weren't from our group, so that was nice to see for a change.

"And eventually that evil grows in power," Michael passionately warned into his megaphone. "It comes back home to you – in the form of two one-way flights into the Twin Towers, or a Nidal Hasan, who gunned down thirteen U.S. soldiers in Fort Hood, Texas. We must act not only out of our long-term self-interest, but also out of a moral imperative to fashion this world into a more humane place that is worthy of future generations."

More applause. I wondered if the crowd was so supportive and responsive because a different demographic frequented Union Square, or because awareness about the threat of ISIS among the general population was gradually increasing.

"As most people remember from their childhood," Michael continued, "when children are left alone in a playground, the bigger kids often start to bully the weaker or less popular children, and it isn't long before cruel impulses lead to repugnant behavior – even among the very young. But with some adult supervision, the peace and decency of the playground is maintained. And that is what is needed in Syria and Iraq. Peace and decency. Because violent Islamists are savagely destroying everything that the civilized world stands for. And as long as no greater force intervenes to stop them, their terrorist capabilities will increase and the atrocities will grow. Is that the world we want to live in? Where Christians and Shiites are beheaded for their faith? Where secular Sunnis are tortured to death as apostates? Where churches are burned along with every freedom that we care about? How much more evil and carnage must we witness before we say 'enough' and do something? They are taking over Iraq. Just last week ISIS displaced about 300,000 people from Fallujah and Ramadi. Shall we just hand them the whole country, after all that the USA sacrificed for Iraq?"

There was some applause as Michael concluded his speech and walked towards my area of the crowd. But then I heard the sounds of another group chanting nearby. And by the time he reached me, it was clear that a group of counter-protestors had set up next to us. There were about twenty people holding signs and shouting slogans like "No U.S. Intervention in Syria" and "No More U.S. Wars in the Middle East." They seemed to be associated with some kind of leftist/anarchist group, but there were also many wearing keffiyehs.

"Who are those guys?" I asked.

"Ignorant assholes," he snapped back, clearly growing angrier by the moment.

One of the counter-protestors wearing a keffiyeh came up to me and yelled, "Have you no shame asking the U.S. military to attack Syria?" He was apparently responding to the sign that I was holding, which said, "U.S. Stop Islamist Terror in Syria or You're Next."

"So you want the slaughter there to continue?" I shot back at him.

"Stop invading Muslim lands!" he shouted.

"They're not just Muslim," Michael corrected him.

Then another guy who was protesting with him, also wearing an Arabic headscarf, jumped into the fray, shouting, "Yes, they are. Those are Muslim countries and the U.S. should mind its own business."

"You like it better when Muslim extremists are free to bully the religious minorities around them?" Michael replied sarcastically. "Why should the U.S. spoil the party, right?"

Hearing their empty slogans made my blood boil. "This is about justice and dignity for Christians in their ancestral lands," I added angrily. "We have rights too. And we call on all decent powers to defend them."

Then a third one accosted me. He was very big – maybe two inches taller than Michael – and he yelled back at me, "Enough with your Christian imperialism. Take your infidel crusade somewhere else!" he roared at me. But – because of his size – I was too intimidated even to respond, and seconds later, he spat down onto my face, and snatched the sign out of my hand, ripping it up.

And then everything happened very quickly, even though, in my head, it seemed to unfold almost in slow motion. As I was wiping off the man's spit from my face, I saw the placard in Michael's left hand fall to the grass, as his right hand closed into an angry fist. Then I saw his clenched hand barrel thunderously from his side until it landed smack on the nose of the giant guy who had spat on me. I actually heard the thud of the impact, and the man just collapsed to the ground from the force of Michael's blow. He was out cold.

"Come on, shitheads – who's next?!" Michael shouted at the first two counter-protestors, gesturing them to step up for a fight. By then, their entire group had gathered around, so Michael was even more outnumbered. But his dangerous rage was palpable – as if he alone could destroy everyone there. More of our protesters also started showing up, after hearing or seeing the commotion. But they weren't needed in the end. The counter-protestors raised their hands in surrender and backed away in fear of this large man who just knocked out an even larger man with a single punch. "OK, OK, take it easy. We're leaving," they said.

"Apologize to her. Now!" he boomed, ready to rip them to shreds. The first two protesters looked at me meekly.

"We're sorry…We're sorry, ma'am, our friend got out of hand."

"Yeah, he shouldn't have done that."

"Now get the fuck out of here!" Michael commanded.

"It's cool, dude, we're leaving," one of them said, as the two of them picked up their dazed comrade with a bloody and probably broken nose, and left the area with him stumbling between them.

About twenty minutes later, our rally ended, and Karen went

around collecting everyone's signs for reuse at the next rally. After taking a placard from someone who was next to me, she turned to me and beamed, "He's quite the fighter, isn't he?"

"Yes, he is," I replied curtly.

"Last November, I actually saw him at another rally like this that turned into a mini-brawl. He ended up taking on three guys at once."

"Really?" I asked, as I suddenly recalled that they had been dating back when I was still ensconced in the academic shell of my first semester.

"Yeah. He left all three of them on the floor in about five minutes."

"Well, he's definitely not your typical Ph.D. student," I replied.

"No, he's not... I nicknamed him my Christian Lion," she said with a slight swoon.

"Well, that was last November," I said, feeling a catty impulse that I just couldn't repress any longer. "We're in March now, and he's *my* Christian Lion."

"Easy, Anissa. No need to get so territorial. Besides, he's the leader of an ever-growing organization with a grand vision, so he's really a lion for all persecuted Christians out there."

I was getting angry but didn't want to make a scene or add any more drama to the day. And she was obviously correct on some level.

"Right. Thanks for helping us with this event," I said curtly but cordially.

"No need to thank me. It's a cause I very much believe in, and hope to find the time to get more involved."

I felt an ugly, bitchy urge to say, "What's the real reason why you're trying to get so involved? You're not even one of us – you're Korean." But I held my tongue and realized what a horrible thing that would have been to say – because how hurtful it would be to her, and because how stupidly provincial it would be to limit the cause to Christians from our region when it's really a human rights issue that should concern all people, of every faith and race. And saying something like that could be extremely damaging to our organization, if word ever got out that we somehow mistreat or discriminate against Christians who aren't from the Middle East. Not to mention that Michael would kill me for speaking like that to anyone, much less his ex. So I bit my tongue and managed to be painfully nice and diplomatic (almost as if I were punishing myself for even thinking of saying such things to her).

"Well, the MCA is very lucky to have so many dedicated members,"

I replied. "And that means you too. See you at the next meeting."

But right after saying that, I went over to Michael and very conspicuously put my arm around his waist. I then pulled him in for a long and intense kiss, as if our future together depended on it. After a few minutes, we finally came up for air, and my face felt flush with impatient passion. "Let's go back," I said. As we walked to the subway, I had my arm around his waist, hoping that Karen might spy us walking off together, in case she happened to miss our kiss.

I got out of the subway at his stop (110th Street), instead of mine (at 116th). We didn't even discuss it. Somehow, it was just clear to both of us that I was going back to his place after the rally.

After we entered his apartment, we removed one layer of clothing to adjust to the cozy temperature there. He took my jacket along with his and tossed them both onto the living room sofa nearby. My heart rate increased in nervous anticipation as Michael lingered by his sofa for a moment – like he was aware that something momentous was probably about to happen but he hadn't yet come to terms with it. As he stood there quietly, Michael suddenly seemed much too far away and the silence began to grow unbearable, so I was relieved when he offered me a drink.

"Yes, I'm feeling kind of thirsty," I replied. "Some water or juice would be great, if you have any."

He came back with a tall glass of apple juice. I took a big gulp and handed it to him. "Thanks," I said, after quenching one of the thirsts I was feeling. He drank from the same cup and then put it down on a nearby shelf.

"Well, this is my apartment," he noted awkwardly. "I'm not sure how we ended up here. I mean, I wasn't trying to bring you back here. But I guess we just – "

"I'm glad we're here," I said, taking the tips of his fingers in my hand. My heart raced as he looked down at me for a moment, his eyes full of desire. I pulled him towards me for a kiss.

His warm, full lips pressed heavily against mine before his tongue forced them to part, exploring my mouth expertly with wet, rhythmic swipes. My cheeks heated and butterflies danced up my spine, causing my nipples to pebble and rub against the fabric of my bra until they practically ached. His toasty apartment and the mounting passion made our sweaters feel much too hot, so I began to remove mine when Michael took over, lifting the garment up and over my face before our lips met for some more kisses. His wandering hands began to caress my hips, back and shoulders. It felt wonderful, and I wanted to give him that same feeling, so I helped him remove his sweater too.

As I lifted it over his head, the seam of his T-shirt rose with it for a moment, making me breathe faster and heavier. Below his T-shirt, I explored the newly exposed skin of his abdomen with my hands and couldn't believe that I was touching a man's upper body for the first time. It felt strong and warm. No longer able to control ourselves, we tore off each other's shirts, so that only my black bra was left, and his chest was completely naked.

An anxious unease turned my stomach at being so exposed before a man for the first time. But I felt emboldened when I saw Michael breathing more heavily as he feasted his eyes on me, looking almost dazed by what he saw. "You're even more beautiful than I had imagined," he confessed, as he held me by my hands, with his arms fully extended for a better view of me.

I drew nearer and took one of his forearms into my hands, feeling its warm, muscular shape. I moved up the contours of his well-sculpted arm towards his shoulder, and then turned him a little, curious to see more. With my first view of his shirtless back, I noticed that it was adorned with two tattoos, one of a Coptic cross, and the other of a Syriac cross – both of which were situated just below his shoulders. It was a powerful and beautiful reference to the different Christian roots from each of his parents: his Egyptian mother and his Syrian father.

"You really are the Christian Lion, aren't you?"

He looked at me surprised and slightly embarrassed. "Did Karen really tell you about that nickname?"

"It's just a shame that she had the opportunity to think of it first, because it fits so well that it's going to be hard for me not to call you that," I lamented jealously but playfully.

"Well, I'm with you now, so you can call me whatever you like."

"Really?" I asked, relieved at his reassurance.

He took my hand in his. "Yes, really."

"So what nickname should I give you?" I asked with a smile.

"I wish you could call me your 'Christian F-16.' But I don't think I'll ever have the chance to train as a fighter pilot who then takes out ISIS."

"How about just 'my Christian Hero?' You were totally my hero today," I said, as I continued admiring the sculpture of manly perfection in front of me.

"It would be an honor to be Anissa's Christian Hero," he affirmed with a smile.

My eyes savored every detail: his powerful forehead and his dark, intense eyes; his tough jaw with the cleft in his chin; the silver cross that he wore around his thick neck; the patch of short dark hair blazing between and across his large, chiseled chest; the bulging muscles of his biceps; his ripped abdomen. I had never wanted someone to take me so badly and the physical craving left me ready to be devoured by him right there.

I couldn't resist him for another second. I flung myself towards him and he caught me, lifting me up higher onto his hard chest as my legs straddled his waist. His hands held me up while my lips pressed against his. Our tongues once again caressed each other during a long and passionate kiss. My arms wrapped around his nape as my fingers ran through his thick, brown hair – all while his musky scent drove me crazy. My bottom sat firmly in the palms of his big hands, as I stayed suspended in the air, supported by his rock-like strength while we kissed so passionately that I felt breathless. Minutes passed in a flurry of lingering kisses. I savored his taste as our tongues were unleashed on each other like never before: playing, battling, and dancing. I could feel myself gasping as heat coursed through my body.

He carried me over to his bed and placed me down by the edge, which he sat on next to me. We kissed some more and his fingers lightly traced around the clasp of my bra.

"Can I take this off?" he asked. I was tempted to show him but felt insecure about fully exposing my breasts to a man for the first time. "Please?" he added with a boyish grin full of desire. I nodded with a nervous smile, giving him permission. He removed my bra and my nipples hardened, as they were fully exposed to the air of the room.

We slowly leaned back together until I was lying on his bed and he was hovering over me a little. He pressed his cheek up against my chest and closed his eyes, slowly caressing my skin with the tip of his nose, as he seemed to breathe me in. A small, satisfied smile crept across his face before he gently took my nipple into his warm mouth. I gasped in pleasure at the heightened sensation spreading across the area. I felt his fingers groping my inner thighs as his tongue danced around my left breast before moving to my right one. I moaned in delighted arousal.

My hands pressed against his upper body and explored his every inch, noting the warm but firm feeling below my fingers. I traced his marvelously chiseled physique downward and felt his ripped abdomen contract slightly as I passed over it. I could see the swelling of his erection bulging through his pants, and felt both intimidated and curious. Did I really want to see it? Was I ready for what would probably follow, if I did? He exhaled his pent-up desire in a deep breath, and I couldn't hold back. I started to unfasten the top button, and then he took over.

He began to fumble with my jeans until I raised my hips, so that he could strip them away. And then I had on nothing but my panties. My chest was rising and falling with each excited gasp for air, as he stalked my body with his own. The sprinkle of hair exposed from the open top button of his jeans made my teeth sink into my bottom lip. I craved more and wanted to see all of him. His body lingered over mine, and I felt his hands fondling my every curve, softly caressing my breasts, and working their way around my back and spine, and then down over my bottom, around my inner thigh, and all while his mouth savored mine – kissing me relentlessly in a passion-fueled frenzy. I was getting wetter by the moment as his tongue explored my neck, behind my ears, and again down to my hardened nipples. His hand continued caressing my waist and over the contours of my lower stomach, until it slipped under the top of my panties. I let out a moan that begged for more, as my heart pounded within my chest, feeling exhilarated by our closeness, and the movement of his fingers so close to my –

And then everything suddenly came to a halt. I felt a mix of confusion, frustration, and relief as the moment changed from erotic exploration to personal questions that we had never fully discussed.

"What's this?" he asked, his face a bit concerned, as his index finger traced the scar that had been hidden by my panties.

"That was from Syria," I answered timidly, suddenly feeling more exposed. "I don't want to… Can we not talk about it? I'm… I'm still not ready."

Moving his hand away from that area, he conveyed a gentle empathy with the slight tilt of his head. "I'm sorry."

"No, don't worry about it – it's just something that I'm… that I'm still dealing with."

"I totally understand. We don't have to get any more naked than this," he reassured me with kindness in his eyes. "I just got a little carried away, I think."

He reached for a shirt nearby, and he suddenly felt distant.

"No, but I want to. I want to do this with you," I replied, as if this were suddenly the last chance.

"Oh, believe me, I want to do this with you even more," he said gently, as he put his shirt back on.

I covered myself with a nearby blanket. "But...?"

"But I'm not sure it's a good idea. At least not right now."

"Because I'm a virgin?" My throat tightened a little in dread, but I had to know the truth.

"Well, that's certainly a big part of it," he admitted, getting a bit closer and sitting next to me. He genuinely searched my eyes, trying to anticipate my reaction.

I diverted my gaze, as a twinge of embarrassment and disappointment settled within. "I had a feeling this was going to be an issue eventually."

"Well, don't feel bad about it," he reassured me, putting his hand on my shoulder. "There's nothing to be ashamed of here."

"No, I know. I'm actually kind of proud of it, in a funny way."

"And you should be."

"But in one respect, I sort of wish I had done it already."

His hand on my shoulder tightened slightly. "Why?"

"So that it wouldn't be such a big deal for us to do it."

"Well, that's OK. There's no rush here," he noted, loosening his grip and caressing my shoulder gently.

A self-deprecating snicker escaped my mouth. "I know. But sometimes it seems like such a big deal that it will never actually happen."

"It'll happen when the time is right," he said, running his fingers gently through my hair.

"But it seems like such a major step – especially because of our culture – that I'll always wonder whether the time is right."

"Well, it is a major step. And that's why we should both be really ready and confident that this is right for both of us and that we're going to end up together."

"You're not sure if we're right for each other?" I pushed his fingers away from my hair.

He took his hand back. "Well, Inās, if we're being totally honest and objective about things, we met in person for the first time only about two months ago, and started dating only about one month ago –

right after I broke up with Karen."

"Why does that matter? Are you saying that you're still in love with her or something?"

"Well, I don't know if I was actually ever in love with her, but we grew very close. And I still have some feelings for her – I mean, you can't just turn these things off from one day to the next. I've actually known her more than twice as long as I've known you."

Tears pricked the back of my eyes, my throat constricted, and my chest tightened as insecurity and anger washed over me. "So what are we doing here? Why don't you just go back to her?"

"No, it's not like that, Inās. I want you much more than her. On every level. And that's why you're here and she's not. And that's why I'm with you. But I'm not a machine – I don't just stop caring for someone I was involved with – especially when she never wronged me in any way. I just wasn't sure that Karen and I were compatible."

"And what about us? Are we compatible?" I asked, not even sure that I wanted to hear his answer. I was so confused.

"I think so. It feels like it. But we're still just getting to know each other, right?" he asked with a smile.

The blanket was still covering me, but I couldn't help crossing my arms over my chest. "I guess."

"If anything, the fact that I'm not rushing to bed you now should reassure you that I actually care about you. And if I'm going to be your first, then I want us to make love when we're both truly ready – and not just when we're feeling passionately explosive."

"Right."

"And I also don't want us to have sex for the very first time just before I'm leaving on a dangerous trip to Syria. If I am the one who takes your virginity, then you deserve to be sure that you're actually going to see me again."

"You're going to Syria?" I asked, sitting up in alarm. "Soon?"

Michael cupped my cheek. "Inās, I'm flying to Syria tomorrow, and I – "

"How long have you known this?"

"I got a call this morning," he admitted, dropping his hand and turning his gaze away from mine. "Things are very bad and I'm needed on the ground there. And I have to bring my people there some things."

Whatever pain I thought was tightening my chest until that moment suddenly felt like it was strangling me. "What do you mean?"

"I'm bringing some of the local activists some cash, about ten small tablets with data plans, some solar chargers for areas without electricity, and some other things to facilitate communications with the local community leaders and activists."

"Why now?" I asked, tilting his chin so that he would have to look me in the eye when he explained. "Didn't you tell me last week that you're supposed to defend your dissertation in about a month?"

"Yes, but the situation keeps getting worse and I need to do what I can…"

As I looked at the smoldering warrior-leader in front of me, I marveled in awe at the risks that he was taking, and the sacrifices he was making to help total strangers. I suddenly felt painfully ashamed. I dropped my hand and turned my back to him. "Oh God, I've been a terrible sister and niece," I confessed.

"What do you mean? Why do you say that?" he asked, placing his hand on my shoulder to coax me back to face him.

"Because I haven't been in touch with my relatives in weeks." I truly felt terrible.

Michael's fingers flexed, gently kneading my shoulder. His touch was reassuring. "Why not?"

"I guess I… I just felt guilty talking to them when so many good things were happening in my life."

"Well, you should check in with them," he said, replacing his fingers with the soft press of his lips.

"You're right. It's the first thing I'm doing when I get home."

Chapter 40: Anissa

∽ Friday, March 28, 2014 ∾

To My Dearest,

    Terrible nightmares haunted me the last two nights, after Michael left for Syria again. To make matters worse, because of the time difference and I guess just bad timing, I never saw anyone from Uncle Luke's household on Skype and nobody answered when I called their landline. So I started to fear the worst, especially after searching for updates on the Internet and learning that ISIS had recently abducted and murdered Christians and even carried out some public crucifixions in the very city where my family lived. And the more time that went by without me reaching someone, the guiltier I felt about selfishly focusing on myself and forgetting my family that was still so vulnerable in Syria. I shuddered as my mind pondered the unthinkable: what if I lost everyone? What if Michael died on this trip and my relatives in Raqqa were killed? Would I still have the strength to carry on? Would my promise to my father be enough to keep me going?

    But then, yesterday afternoon, I finally got through to someone at Uncle Luke's house, and I let out a huge sigh of relief. I suddenly saw Antoun log onto Skype and I immediately called him. We chatted a bit over video, and it was amazing how my baby brother, who was now thirteen, appeared more grown up each time we spoke. But I also noted that he didn't joke around nearly as much as he used to, and seemed to be more serious and withdrawn now. After we talked for about twenty minutes, Maria took over his seat by the webcam so that she and I could catch up.

    Maria confirmed the news reports that I had read online and said that Uncle Luke was desperately developing options to leave the city within the next few weeks. He was still researching the best place to go with his aging parents and one grandparent, together with his wife, three children, Antoun and Maria. The options were Turkey, another city in Syria, or maybe Lebanon, where Christian Arab communities were still relatively safe. The logistics of relocating so many people – especially finding a safe way out of Raqqa and to their next destination – were daunting. And he had to figure out what to do with his family's personal and business property, although Maria said that if he couldn't find a buyer in the next few weeks, he was just going to abandon everything because the situation had gotten so bad.

"Try to be in touch every day," Maria urged me. "Because once we leave, I don't know when we'll have a chance to talk again. And it's more dangerous than ever for us now. Every day that we stay here is risky. And leaving brings other perils."

"This is so awful," I said, starting to cry.

"I'm just glad that you're safe there in New York, doing exactly what Papa would have wanted for you."

"No… I should be there with you… helping somehow," I protested between tears.

"How could you help us here? We can't even help ourselves now. Just make the most of what you have there, Inās. Make Papa's spirit proud."

"I'm really worried about all of you," I replied, fighting back more tears. "I'm going to help you. Michael, my boyfriend – or my friend – I don't know what he is really… But he's a good man – a really strong and powerful Syrian-Coptic Christian with connections… He should be arriving in Syria very soon – I think his connecting flight gets in early tomorrow. When I talk to him, I'm going to ask him to get in touch with you to see if he can help Uncle Luke somehow. He knows many people there – Christians, moderate Sunni rebels, people in the regime, and others. He's an activist, Maria. A real leader."

"I don't know if anyone can help us, Inās. We have only God now, so we keep praying."

"No, Maria, please don't lose hope!" I begged her, bursting into tears. "I'm… I'm praying for you too… And… And everything will be all right… Please… Please just have faith," I implored her, choking up as I tried to get the words out. "Please promise me, promise me you won't give up."

"I'll try, Inās. I promise."

I desperately needed to escape the looming darkness, so I went for a run at Dodge Fitness Center, which helped me clear my mind temporarily. My Psychology and Markets class also provided an interesting diversion – at least for the bits of it that I could focus on. For most of Professor Morales' lecture, I struggled not to let my mind wander anxiously back to Syria. And I sensed that he was avoiding me in class, as he had the previous Tuesday. His renewed distance made me suddenly doubt my behavior at his party, thinking that maybe I had taken Michael's recommended strategy a little too far, and now I had simply lost Professor Morales – just when I needed him more than ever. I was tempted, if I could catch him alone at the end of his lecture, somehow to reassure him that I actually did admire him. But I held back, trying not to act rashly out of a sudden insecurity. "Just keep doing what you're doing at least for this class, until you talk to Michael, to see what he suggests," I told myself. So after Professor Morales ended the class, I just walked out without showing the slightest interest in him. But as I shuffled out of the room with the first students to leave, I secretly prayed that my recent aloofness hadn't just irrevocably pushed him away.

Finally, today, I had two bits of good news. The first came when I was hanging out with Maya after our Economics study group, as the other students started to leave the lounge area where we had gathered. She told me that Professor Morales invited her to another party tomorrow night, and, when she asked if I could join her, he said yes! What a huge relief. It actually suggests that Michael's recommended approach is working exactly as intended: Professor Morales apparently wants me to think that he's not interested but still wants me at his parties because he secretly is interested.

Once Maya and I were the only people left in the room, we sat down on the nearby sofa and I told her about what happened at Union Square and then back at Michael's place.

"No wonder you were all over him back at his apartment. A man looks sexiest when he's protecting his woman."

"But what do you make of the fact that he was able to stop himself so easily? Do you think it really was just him respecting our culture and making sure that it's the right time for both of us?"

"Well, honestly, guys aren't usually that sensitive or careful when it comes to sex. You show 'em a pussy, and they want in. You know, fuck now, and ask questions later."

I let out a much-needed laugh at her brash, no-nonsense way of putting it.

"I'm bein' totally serious! And I love men as much as the next girl, so I know how they tick pretty well."

"And how do they normally tick? I mean, he's the only guy I've ever dated, so I have nothing to compare him against."

"Usually, if a guy's not pressuring you into sex, he's either not interested or he's already getting it from someone else." She paused for a moment to look at her buzzing phone before sending the incoming call to voicemail. "So his break up with Karen may not be as complete as you'd like," she added.

"I was afraid you'd say something like that. I mean, I asked Michael about it and he said that he's with me now, but he can't just shut off his feelings for Karen."

"Girl, maybe that's exactly why he seems to trust you with Professor Morales so much."

"What do you mean?"

"Maybe Michael would feel too guilty forbidding you from getting any closer to Julien when he's still sleeping with his ex."

"Maybe," I said, as a cloud of doubt started to descend on me.

"But don't let that get you down, my Syrian sista'! You need to diversify your male portfolio a little, or you're going to have all of your emotional eggs invested in that Michael basket."

I chuckled at how she phrased her advice. "You really do like portfolio theory, don't you?" I said, trying to sound amused and lighthearted but realizing that my emotional unease was probably obvious to her.

"I'd just hate to see you get hurt," Maya added sincerely.

"I know," I replied, feeling somewhat comforted by her concern.

"Hey, cheer up – you're coming with me tomorrow night to another Julien party," she exclaimed, lightly grabbing my shoulders as if to shake me out of my low spirits. "Aren't you excited?"

"I guess… It'll be nice to take my mind off things… I'm really worried about my family in Syria."

"I hear you, girl. I hope it all works out for them. And maybe Julien can even help somehow. He knows – or can get to – just about anyone with any real power."

"It would be nice if he could do something."

Maya noted the time on her phone, gathered her things, and stood up. I did the same and we headed out of the room towards the stairwell.

"And you saw the kind of VIPs who showed up to his party, so it's not like he's the only elite person you'll be hangin' out with tomorrow night."

"I'm sure."

"So, maybe you'll run into someone else who can be helpful," Maya noted, stopping me for a moment so that we were looking at each other. "And I'm thinkin' you might be free to play the field a little, based on everything you've told me," she opined, with so much swagger, and such a raised eyebrow, that I had to chuckle at her.

We reached the stairs and started to descend them. There were no students around, so we continued speaking as openly as before.

"I'm bein' totally serious, Anissa… And trust me, none of those guys at the party – including Julien – will give you a hard time about poppin' that sweet cherry of yours, in case you get the urge again."

I laughed some more at her over-the-top style.

"You think I'm kidding, don't you?"

"I don't know, Maya. That's just not something I would do behind Michael's back – even if he still has feelings for Karen."

"Well, maybe you should have a chat with him about it. You know, just to clear the air and make sure everyone's on the same page."

"Yes, maybe I should. I was planning to Skype him anyway, as soon as I get home. So if I reach him, I may try to discuss this too."

The second piece of good news today was that, on my way back to my room, I saw an email on my phone from Michael, saying that he had landed and that he would try to Skype me in a few hours. So at least I knew that he had arrived safely and was thinking of me.

When we spoke, it was 2:15 a.m. in Damascus, which was his first stop. During our video chat, he looked and sounded very tired from all of the travel and jetlag, so I didn't want to keep him on too long, knowing how important it was to his safety for him to stay alert.

"How are things with your professor?" he asked. "Do you think he may want to help our cause?"

"Maybe." I shrugged. "I think it's going well."

He tilted his head just slightly, his expression curious. "Why?"

"Because he's acting like someone who likes me."

"In what way?"

"He was clearly trying not to pay attention to me in the last two classes. But then today Maya asked him if she could bring me to another party of his tomorrow night, and he said yes."

"That's good news," he said, releasing an exhausted but unconvincing smile.

"Listen, Michael," I said, shifting in my seat and bracing myself for a conversation that I both did and didn't want to have. "I know how tired you are, and how important this trip is, but there's something I really need to ask you. We don't have to talk about it much. But I just need to know."

He yawned. "Sorry, what is it? What's troubling you?"

"You and Karen – are you still seeing her in any way?"

He sighed, dejectedly. "Inās, I actually thought about this a lot on my flight over here."

"Thought about what?"

"Our relationship."

"And?"

"And I think it may best if we avoid any form of commitment at this point in time."

"What does that mean?"

"It means that we don't expect too much of each other right now. Things are complicated. I'm here and you're there."

"It's because you're still seeing Karen, aren't you?"

"No, I'm not. I mean, we still talk. She's doing so much to help the MCA – after just a week on the fundraising project, she already has a prospect who could make a six-figure donation." Michael seemed impressed by Karen's work and that bothered me in an admittedly catty way.

But I was more troubled by the feeling that he wasn't telling me everything. Maybe "avoiding commitment" wasn't such a bad idea after all. "And that's the only reason you're in touch with her?" I persisted.

"Well, that's not the only thing we talk about – we're still close. But that doesn't matter, Inās. It doesn't affect how I feel about you. She could never replace you. I hope you know that. And hopefully your professor could never replace me, even though you're getting closer to him." He scoffed and shook his head slightly, and I sensed the irony he was projecting. "For the cause. Only to help the cause."

"Michael," I sighed. "I'm not doing anything with him."

"I know, and I would never want you to. I mean, I know that I'm more involved with the cause than with anything else right now, but I do hope that we'll be in each other's futures. That's all I'm comfortable saying right now."

His waffling was confusing me. One minute he was suggesting that we should remain at a distance, and the next he was saying that he didn't want me getting close to anyone but him.

And yet, I still yearned to hug him and have him safely by my side. "So when are you coming back?"

"I don't know yet… I'm sorry, Inās, but you have no idea what the level of need here is. And I'm just one man, doing what I can on a tiny budget," he said, with frustration expressed in his clenched jaw. "We desperately need more cash to make a bigger difference. I think Karen will pull through for us. And maybe you will too. Your professor's political connections to members of Congress and other powerful figures could be critical. He can do more to assist us than anyone else I can possibly get to quickly, which means that basically everything is in your hands now." He touched the screen with his fingertip. "I'm sorry if this seems as if I'm putting pressure on you."

"What are you saying, Michael?" I suddenly felt daunted by the responsibility and confused about what exactly Michael wanted me to do with Julien. His finger dropped from the screen.

He sat back and ran his hands through his hair, clearly frustrated. "I don't like Julien, and he probably knows it. But you obviously have a spell on him and that presents a historic opportunity. You just have to continue being smart about how you relate to him. You have to ensure that he sees you like he sees no other woman."

"And what about us?" I asked, swallowing the lump in my throat that had formed out of hurt and anger.

"Inās, like I said, I want you in my future. I really do. But this is so much bigger than us. So whatever happens, whatever jealousies may develop along the way, they are nothing compared to the cause. You could be saving millions of Mideast Christians and other minorities. You could literally be helping to make world history by enlisting his support for the creation of a modern Christian state in the Middle East. So this isn't about you and me. Or you and him. It's about the promise that you made to your father to make a difference."

I sat silently in front of the glow of my laptop with Michael's face passionately pleading with me about the enormity of my mission. I subdued a tear from falling and tried to put aside my ego, so that I could focus on the bigger picture.

He sat forward as if he wanted to be as close to me as possible. "You are now in a position to do for Syrian Christians what they can't do for themselves – and what nobody else can do for them. So make the most of this opportunity. When you think the time is right, I want you to present Julien with a formal proposal. I'm going to email you the presentation that Karen and I produced for her potential donor, so that you can use that – it's for a $100,000 donation."

"I'm not going to use what she created with you," I snapped. Then I realized how irrational and jealous my reaction sounded, so I softened my tone with an explanation that happened to be true: "Your proposal would need to be customized so that it's as persuasive as possible to Professor Morales. And I know how his mind works better than the two of you do."

"Well, I can't argue with that," he conceded with a smile. "So just use what I email you as a starting point. It has a lot of facts, figures, and charts that will be useful to your presentation. But you decide what to highlight, add, or omit. And how much of a donation to request. It's all in your hands, Inās. And I have no doubt you'll make the MCA, and our whole community, proud."

"I'll try my best, Michael."

"Thank you, Inās. OK, I have to go now. It's not safe for me to be here after the sun comes up, and I desperately need to get a few hours of sleep before I keep moving. I'm thinking about you, and hoping for your every success."

"And I'm praying for your safety. Please watch yourself there. I want to see you back here soon."

"I will, Inās. I'll be in touch soon. Goodbye for now."

"Goodbye."

Chapter 41: Julien

Sunday, 3/30/14 at 18:42.

The last forty-eight hours have been full of journal-worthy moments. On both Tuesday and Thursday, I followed my plan of paying as little attention as possible to Anissa in class. Unfortunately, she responded in kind, and then I worried that I might have somehow lost her. So I decided, on Friday, to host a party the next night and invite Maya. At the end of my invitation text, I noted simply, "You can bring Anissa if you want." She knew me well enough to understand what this meant: Anissa should get the impression that her presence at my party was Maya's idea and not mine.

But I couldn't be sure if my forbidden obsession would even show up with Maya in the end, so I was delighted when the two arrived thirty minutes early, as I had originally discussed with Maya. As planned, Maya left Anissa alone with me so that she and I could chat a bit before the other guests arrived. We were in the kitchen.

"Funny seeing you here again," I joked, trying to put her at ease as I prepared us both a drink.

"Indeed. How is it that you continue to be in this place you call home?" she asked absurdly.

I played along. "That's a lot of nerve I have, isn't it? Perhaps I should try homelessness for a while."

"Maybe just for a night or two. It could give you a newfound appreciation for your digs. I mean, compared to my dorm room, walking in here makes me feel almost homeless. So I'm sure a night or two of sleeping on a park bench could do wonders for your return home."

I passed her a glass of cranberry juice and led her to the room next door, where we could admire the breathtaking view of the city below. "Does that mean that leaving this place depresses you?" I asked playfully.

"I guess it does. That might explain this strange habit I seem to have of showing up here!" she quipped, tipping her glass toward mine as if to say "cheers."

The banter was simply delicious and made her personality as irresistible as her looks, not to mention the way her lips caressed the rim of her glass. I involuntarily cleared my throat and looked back out at the view before continuing. "Well, I can't say that I blame you. I mean, I can think of worse habits," I said, almost as if I were confessing to some of them myself.

"I'll bet. Like maybe inviting over a much younger woman for a party that…" She looked around in every direction, as if to emphasize the absence of guests. "Doesn't seem to be happening… " Her irreverent insinuations stirred my need to have her even more.

I chuckled at her joke, hoping that she didn't catch any of the nervousness behind my laugh.

"You should know that I come from a very traditional family, so I don't normally put myself in this kind of situation."

Suddenly I felt self-conscious and potentially exposed, so I tried to play it cool and maintain my cover with a plausible explanation. "Well, Maya was so late last time, that I told her to come thirty minutes earlier than I asked all of the other guests to arrive, thinking that this might help her to show up on time, but – as Murphy's Law would have it – she was punctual this time and came thirty minutes early. But you'll see – there are more guests coming!" Fortunately, about twenty-five people had indicated that they would make it despite the short notice, so it was easy to correct her with confidence.

"I see," Anissa said, appearing to bite back a smug smile of skepticism about my claim. "Well then, I guess I should leave you to your final, pre-party arrangements so that you're ready to greet the other guests as they arrive."

"Yes, I probably should tend to a few other things," I began. "But… Now that I have you here, I was thinking that it might be nice to talk some time when I'm not busy hosting a party, teaching a class, or running a hedge fund."

"You mean like chatting during your office hours?" she asked coyly.

"No." I smiled. There was something maddeningly sexy about how she was forcing me to say more than I really wanted to say. "I mean something a bit more private and relaxed."

"Like what we're doing now?"

"Yes, but in a public place."

"I see," she remarked, her eyebrow rising just enough to suggest she knew exactly what I wanted: a date with her. And I was grateful that she had the good sense not to use that term – or make me do so – because that would have been so awkward that I might have just found a way to exit the conversation or abort the idea altogether.

"There's a fabulous restaurant, not far from the university, called

'The Lotus Flower.' Almost nobody knows about it, even though it has spectacular views and some of the best food you've ever tasted."

She took another sip of her drink. "Why do so few people know about it?"

"Because it's so exclusive that the owner has to know you and personally invite you. He prides himself on extreme discretion and never invites or approves reporters. And the use of smartphone cameras and video is strictly prohibited there."

"Why?"

"I think he's a bit of a Luddite. But he also believes that there should be spaces outside the home where people know they won't be photographed or filmed. And those rules are very attractive to members of the elite, since their privacy tends to be violated much more."

"Interesting," she responded, intrigued.

"Yes. It's basically where the wealthiest vegetarians eat out in Manhattan."

"Really?"

"Yes. Why don't we go there tomorrow night for dinner? It's a very beautiful, intimate setting where we can talk a bit more and get to know each other better." I couldn't help but swallow dryly.

"Why are you a vegetarian?" she suddenly asked me, as if she was gradually opening up to the idea.

"You'll have to take me up on my offer to find out," I smiled. "I'll have my driver pick you up from 115th Street and Broadway at 7:30 p.m."

And that's how we settled on our first date. Anissa is truly unlike any woman I have ever met: extraordinarily bright, beautiful, and charming. And she fled the Syrian Civil War with her goodness and innocence still intact. Literally. I could hardly wait to see her again.

About five hours ago, when I met with Lily for our weekly Sunday session, I managed to avoid mentioning anything about Anissa, despite my excitement about the dinner scheduled with her for later this evening. In fact, it almost felt as if I was being unfaithful to Lily – probably because I haven't been so open with anyone in a long time.

It's one thing to hide the dark secrets from my early childhood that I can't and won't tell anyone… But there's no similarly compelling reason why I'd have to conceal the details about my interest in Anissa. I guess I just don't want to feel judged by a woman who potentially interests me – especially if things don't work out with Anissa.

Even without the potential drama and complexity of mentioning Anissa in therapy, the session with Lily was still the same intense game of psychological cat and mouse that it usually is.

"I'm not looking forward to April 1," I told her at one point.

"Why not?"

"Areli, the psycho bitch who was harassing me, threatened her 'payback' for not coming to a deal with her."

"I thought you said you blocked her from your phone. That was…" Lily's face creased slightly into a look of confusion as she flipped through her yellow pad of notes looking for when I had said that. "About five weeks ago."

"Yes, I did. But she warned me in one of her texts – before I blocked her – that she would give me another month to come to terms."

"And she mentioned April 1?"

"She said that this would be an April Fool's to remember, or something like that."

"Well, maybe if you told me more about what happened, I could try to advise you."

"What's the point? She's going to do whatever she's going to do at this point. The best I can hope for is to learn from it and try to manage the fallout."

"Julien, when are you going to start trusting me enough for me to do my job?"

"I described my nightmares for you – something nobody else knows about."

"Yes, but now you won't open up about this Areli situation."

"Well, it's relatively minor and not worth discussing unless she actually makes good on her threat. And if she does, then I'll tell you whatever related background you want to know."

"And when will you tell me something about your father? I'm assuming that he was abusive to you and your mother, just from the fact that you avoid discussing him. But that's not much to work with."

I could have sworn I caught her trying not to roll her eyes before releasing a breath of frustration. "No, it's not," I conceded.

"And as an expert in psychology, you should know that the efficacy of my treatment is severely limited and potentially even incorrect because I'm lacking some key information."

"My father wasn't always abusive," I began. "But over time, he changed and went down a dark path that I don't think anyone saw coming. And in the end, he showed us both a side of him that would scar us forever."

"What else can you tell me about him? Or your childhood in Mexico?"

"Not much. I'm much happier with that stuff locked away."

"Can you even tell me what he did for a living?"

She placed the tip of her pen on her lip and narrowed her eyes at me. And again, I wanted to be that pen. "He worked as a security guard for a while. And then, after he was fired, he became a butcher."

"Do you think that's why you became a strict vegetarian?"

"Are you a vegetarian?" I shot back at her.

"No."

"Have you ever been to a slaughterhouse?" I challenged her.

"No."

"Maybe that's why you're still eating cooked animal flesh," My tone was deliberately speculative and somewhat judgmental.

"Somehow I never associated the two."

"Well, it's never too late. How about this: you show me some photos of your first visit to a slaughterhouse, and then I'll tell you more about my childhood."

"I suppose I could arrange a tour one of these days. But why would you link that to sharing about your childhood?"

"It might give you some valuable perspective on some of what I might choose to share. And it may also make you think about the cruelties that have to happen in order to feed your appetite for meat."

Her stare locked on mine. "I'll keep that in mind, Julien."

"Glad to hear it."

"You know what I've noticed about you, based on our discussions thus far?"

"What?"

"You seem to have a lot of compassion for animals. Your fund refuses to invest in companies that mistreat them. You're a strict vegetarian. You make large donations to animal rights groups. You take in a bird that you accidentally injured and try to nurse it back to health. And yet, with women, you seem to be far more distant, even reckless. You appear not to care as much if they get hurt – they're as disposable as the burgers you fault someone like me for eating."

"I beg your pardon? Women as disposable as burgers? That's an outrageously inappropriate and unfair judgment," I replied, as surprised as I was angry.

"I'm sorry, you're right. That didn't come out right," she said, apparently realizing that she maybe had felt some personal frustration about my womanizing ways and inadvertently let it slip out. "Obviously, that was wrong of me to say – I'm sorry." She continued, softening her tone. "But I do think that women are basically disposable to you and that you seem to empathize more with animals."

"Animals can't form intentions that we can judge as good or bad. They're pure and simple – just defenseless creatures trying to survive in a world that is increasingly hostile to them thanks to us. Humans, on the other hand, were given so much more power, intelligence, and freedom; and that makes the harm they often choose to cause sting a lot more."

"Yes, but maybe the women who have betrayed your trust in one way or another were responding to something in you, or some way that you related to them."

"Maybe. Or maybe I just haven't found a woman who's worthy of my trust," I replied almost bitterly, looking at her straight in the eye, so that she could ponder how much that answer might have been directed at her. And as my eyes connected with hers, my mind wandered to the beauty I was soon going to have dinner with, wondering if maybe Anissa was that special woman.

Chapter 42: Anissa

∾ Sunday, March 30, 2014 ∾

To My Dearest,

I need to try to sleep because I have to get up early tomorrow but, as usual, there's too much on my mind. To make matters worse, last night I slept only four hours, after endless thoughts about Michael being in Syria and what my date with Professor Morales would be like.

I spent most of the day going through the proposal that Michael had developed with Karen so that I could tailor it to Professor Morales. The document went through many revisions, and in the end I removed any explicit request for a donation. What I would ultimately give him, towards the end of our date, was more of an informational brochure (about the MCA's efforts in Syria and what they cost) rather than a solicitation. I didn't want him to feel pressured, or as if I expected something of him.

As planned, Professor Morales' driver picked me up and brought me to The Lotus Flower. We had what must have been the best seat in the whole restaurant – a private alcove on the terrace, which was covered by a retractable glass window that opened up in the summer.

A splendid, twenty-fifth-floor view of Manhattan enchanted us as we ate sumptuously healthy food with the stars above and the glistening lights of the city around us. We sat at the corner of the table, so that the New York skyline was directly in front of me and to the right of Professor Morales. As usual, he wore a stylish suit and tie. We were close enough to each other that we could easily hold hands.

When the waiter brought our orders, the plates looked more like works of art than dinner. "I almost don't want to ruin this by eating it," I remarked in awe. I took a fork in my hand, but hesitated to disturb anything with it.

"You can't have your Moroccan spiced chickpea cake and eat it too," he joked. "But trust me, you'd rather eat it than have it."

He started eating the herb-grilled, portobello-mushroom steak, and I finally enjoyed a bite of my dish, which was unforgettably delicious (as was his order, which I sampled). We also shared the mixed Mediterranean platter that he ordered in honor of my Middle Eastern roots; it included smoked hummus, eggplant caponata, baba ghanoush, almond tzatziki, grilled paratha bread, olives, slivered almonds, and olive oil. The food was so good that we spent the first few minutes just eating and savoring each bite.

"How are you liking your first year of college?" Professor Morales finally asked, pausing his enjoyment of the food. His question reminded me that the handsome man sitting next to me was very much an older gentleman. I joined him in taking a break from our feast.

"It's been a great experience so far – on many levels."

"I'm glad to hear it," he said, as he poured himself a glass of wine. "Would you like some or are you still waiting until you reach the legal drinking age?"

"I'll have a taste," I answered with a smile.

He smiled and offered me his glass. "Very adventurous of you."

"Yes, I've become quite the daredevil lately," I admitted, taking a sip from his glass. "Maybe after dinner we can scale our way back down the wall to the ground floor, rather than take the elevator." I handed him back his wine and licked my lips, which did not go unnoticed.

"Well," he began, clearing his throat as he accepted the glass. "I do that sort of thing only when I'm really drunk, so we'd have to notify the fire department in advance."

"Sounds like a plan," I replied with a chuckle. "So how did you like college? Did they have computers back then?"

He paused at my teasing, the rim of his glass resting on his lips. "We were just learning to use ink and paper, which turned out to be much more practical than etching our notes into stone."

I laughed. "Yes, I'll bet those cavemen right before your generation got really muscular just sharing notes with each other."

"Exactly..." We took a few more bites of our food and he resumed his answer. "In all seriousness, I really loved college. It truly is a special and unique time, but too many students don't realize it. Which is perhaps explained by one of Mark Twain's greatest quotes."

"And which quote is that?"

"Youth is wasted on the young."

"Oh, I love that!" I exclaimed, genuinely delighted and grateful to learn such a pithy pearl of wisdom. "It so perfectly captures the absurd condition of young people. Almost by definition, we're not really designed to value our youth during the only time that we have it. Although I feel as if my youth ended at the age of fifteen, so maybe I can relate to that quote more as an adult than most people my age can."

"Why at fifteen?"

"Because that's how old I was when things got bad in Syria."

"I see," he said, in a gentle, empathetic tone. But – as if he could intuit my conversational wishes – my professor skillfully kept our conversation from drifting into overly personal and depressing waters by returning to the original topic. "Well, I always try to remind students of how precious college is, and urge them to savor every moment. I really miss those years," he noted nostalgically.

"What do you miss most about them?"

"The social aspect."

"What do you mean?"

"College is probably the only time in your life when you're surrounded by so many smart, interesting, and accessible people. The spontaneous socializing that takes place countless times a day really can't be replicated in any other environment. You'll find, as you get older, that your friends become less and less available."

He seemed to be alternating between eye contact and beholding the rest of me. Strangely enough, I liked it. His desirous gaze made me feel singularly attractive because the admiration came from a man who had already seen so much beauty in his life. "In what way?" I asked.

"They'll get jobs. They'll start families. And soon, those people you could call on a whim and spontaneously meet, become increasingly inaccessible. Seeing them will require more scheduling – if you're even in the same city. And even talking on the phone will require more effort with each passing year, as your lives and calendars become increasingly dominated by pressures and commitments that were never present in college. I actually remember thinking about this in my late twenties, when I effectively gave up trying to chase down old college friends."

"What made you give up?"

"Well, on some level, it's similar to the psychological phenomenon of helplessness, where the will to try is lost. You get to the point where you just assume that your spontaneous call to a friend will go to voicemail or an assistant, and you decide not to bother."

I furrowed my brow and wondered sadly if the same thing would happen to me. "Why?"

"Because your own life has become governed by so many other things that by the time the friend gets back to you, the availability that you had when you called will be gone, and chances are high that the friend returning your call will just end up talking to your voicemail or assistant. And so an endless cycle of phone tag begins, and you know that it will probably just end with someone giving up. And, as you play all of this out in your head, based on the last few times you tried to call, you figure, 'What's the point? We'll just talk on someone's birthday or see each other at some mutual friend's wedding, or some such thing.' Unless, of course, you end up working in the same office or as partners in some venture."

"I was just going to mention that possibility."

"Yes, in that relatively rare case, you may very well continue to enjoy some of that spontaneous socializing that you had in college. But that is the exception that proves the rule, and at best you would have that with just a few people."

We took a moment to relish a few more bites from our dinner. The food really was extraordinary.

"The vast majority of the many interesting people you meet in college will quickly vanish from your life after graduation," he continued. "And the more time that passes, the fewer of those friends you will be in touch with, until you're down to a core few, and even those relationships will be enjoyed for fewer hours each year, and much of your preciously rare time together will be spent remembering the past, rather than creating dramatically new memories."

"Wow, that's kind of sad."

"It is. So enjoy it while you have it," he urged me, putting his hand on my shoulder for emphasis.

"I'll try," I said, my voice barely above a whisper as I glanced at his hand on me. "Although sometimes it feels like I'm carrying the weight of the world on me, so it's hard to savor the moment."

"The weight comes from what's happening in Syria?" he clarified, his fingers flexing mildly.

"Yes."

"I can imagine. And you must miss your family..."

"I do."

"When do you think you'll see your parents the next time?" he asked.

"They both died about two years ago."

His fingers tensed against my skin. "Oh. I'm so sorry," he responded awkwardly and regretfully. "You mentioned losing some family when you came to my office hours, but I assumed that they were far more distant relatives."

"Unfortunately, they weren't."

"I really shouldn't be asking you such personal questions so soon," he noted, taking his hand back. He seemed genuinely empathetic.

"No, it's OK, that was actually a perfectly normal question – I just have a very abnormal answer to it. And, like everyone else who asks me, you had no way of knowing that."

"That must get tiresome – having this sort of conversation about it."

"I'm used to it by now. If I choose to open up to someone a little, I get out all of the tough information right away. I tell them that my parents were in a horrific car crash on the last night that I saw them. My older brother died in the same collision."

"Does that mean that you just chose to open up to me a little?" he asked with a gentle smile.

"I guess it does," I smiled back. I quietly exhaled and pushed on with the false answer. "I knew it would be dangerous for them to be driving that night... And I wish I would have tried harder to stop them," I continued. "The fact that I didn't still haunts me... And since you're an expert in psychology, I might as well tell you that I still suffer PTSD from my last year in Syria."

"I can only imagine," he replied sympathetically. "You mentioned that you've been seeing a therapist, right?"

"Yes. Quite often my first year and a half in New York. And I still see her, though not as much as I used to. It's harder, now that I'm farther from her office and busier than ever with college pressures. But we developed some coping techniques that still work for me. And I did start a diary again, as you so helpfully suggested during your office hours."

"Well, I'm glad to hear it," he said, in a tone that suggested he was going to try to steer us back to a lighter topic. "I probably should have asked you this the very first time we spoke but... Is 'Anissa' a Syrian or an Arabic name?"

"Neither. My name in Arabic is Inās. But when I got to New York, I wanted to pick something more American-sounding, so I went with Anissa, which is the English version of my name."

"I see. And what does Inās mean in Arabic?" he asked, between bites.

"It just means Agnes, which means pure or chaste. She was a virgin martyr, venerated as a saint in the Eastern Orthodox Church," I explained.

"And in the Roman Catholic tradition as well," he replied with a smile of familiarity, as if it turned out that we prayed at the same church or something.

"You're Catholic?" I asked in surprise, as I enjoyed some more of the Mediterranean platter.

"Like any good Mexican-American, but not exactly a practicing one. Maybe more of a recovering one, you might say," he joked. "But I had enough of a Catholic education to remember that Agnes is the patron saint of chastity and girls, although I'm probably forgetting a few."

"Engaged couples, rape victims, virgins, and gardeners," I added. "There may be one or two more."

"And I don't remember the story behind her martyrdom," he admitted, which I took as an invitation to recount it to him.

"Agnes was martyred in her early teens during the reign of the Roman Emperor Diocletian, in 304 A.D. She was a beautiful young girl from a wealthy family and had many suitors of high rank. But she was so devoted to God that she refused even the governor's son, Procop, who had offered her lavish gifts and promises. Legend has it that she spurned him by saying, 'I am already promised to the Lord of the Universe. He is more splendid than the sun and the stars, and He has said that He will never leave me!'"

"She was quite the faithful romantic in her love of God. And at such a young age," he noted, his leg grazing mine for a moment.

"Yes. For refusing Procop, she was dragged naked through the streets to a brothel." I twisted a lock of my hair. "But an angel protected her in the place of sin."

"And then?" he asked, draping his arm around my chair for a moment.

"In the end, she was condemned to death. But Agnes was happier than a bride on her wedding day, ignoring those who begged her to save herself. She said to them 'If I were to try to please you, I would offend my husband. He chose me first and He shall have me!' And then she prayed and bore her neck to be beheaded," I concluded.

"And her memory lives on to this day – even at The Lotus Flower," he noted, skillfully returning us to the present.

"Yes, it does."

We took the final bites of our dinner, and then shared that slightly tired but thoroughly satisfied look produced by a hearty and delicious meal.

"Are you very religious?" Professor Morales asked.

"Well, I still have a lot of faith – it helps to keep me going at times. And I try to go to church as often as I can, although I've been going much less since I started college."

"But less church attendance doesn't mean less traditional, right?" he probed.

"Right." I had a feeling I knew where he was going with his question.

"That was the term you used to describe yourself at my last party, and I assume you meant something more than just a belief in chivalry."

"Definitely. I meant that I was raised with more conservative values in Syria. So I'm not like many of the girls that you see on campus, at your parties, or even at your office."

His hazel eyes peered right at me. "No, you're not. You're much more beautiful than they are," he said, as his gaze dropped to my lips.

I blushed a little and looked down for a moment. "Aren't you the charmer?"

"It's true."

"Well, thank you... But that's actually not what I meant by being different from them."

"Yes, I know. But why resist an opportunity to compliment your rare beauty?" He looked at me as if I were the only thing that existed at that moment, even as his cell phone started going off.

His seemed momentarily annoyed at the distraction, which forced him to focus on his phone for the few moments that it took to send the call to voicemail. "So tell me," he continued. "What did *you* have in mind when you mentioned that you're different from most girls?"

"Well, for one, I'm still a virgin. And – true to my name – I plan to save myself for my husband."

"Really?" He seemed impressed. "That *is* different. You don't hear about women waiting for marriage very often these days."

The waiter came by with another bottle of wine. He set it on the table, and took away our empty dishes.

"Living in New York hasn't made you question any of your traditional values and personal rules?" he asked, as he poured us both some more wine from the new bottle.

"Some things I've questioned, but not that."

"So when you date a man, how far will you allow yourself to go?"

He took a sip of his wine glass and put it down, resting his left hand closer to mine.

"Well, I haven't really dated much. Michael is the only one, and we didn't go very far," I explained, fighting an irresistible urge to walk my fingers closer to his.

"And you weren't even tempted with such a handsome man?"

"Of course I was – back when I thought he might be my future husband."

"And now you're not so sure?"

"I don't know. I found out that he's still close with the woman he was dating before he met me. And – even without that issue – I don't think Michael is very focused on finding his wife. He's too busy trying to build a new country for Christians in the Middle East."

"Well, he clearly has his priorities all wrong. I mean, who on Earth would try to found a new state in the Middle East rather than pursue Anissa?"

I laughed. "Yeah, well maybe once that country exists and he's its president, he'll have the time to do the small things like get married."

"And you're going to wait until then?"

"Well, I guess anything's possible, although I don't think so. But that doesn't mean that I'm having sex any time soon," I said, as if to warn him. "There's only one scenario I can think of where I might give myself to a man who wasn't necessarily going to be my future husband."

"And what scenario is that?" he asked, clearly intrigued, as he took another sip of his wine glass.

"A payment of one million dollars."

"What?!" He nearly spat out the wine. His expression was at once astounded and amused. "That was honestly the last thing I would have expected you to say!"

"Well, it shouldn't be that shocking. Haven't you heard those stories of women who put their virginity up for sale in auctions?"

"Yes, I have. And given that Michael is still potentially in the picture, the whole scenario reminds me a bit of that film, *Indecent Proposal*," he said.

I struggled to recall the name. "I haven't seen it."

"It's a nineties film about a billionaire, played by Robert Redford, who pays a million dollars to a cash-strapped couple, played by Demi Moore and Woody Harrelson, for the right to sleep with the beautiful woman for one night."

"Wow, you just made that million-dollar figure seem very unoriginal," I replied playfully. "I like to pride myself on originality and would hate to be accused of copying the number used in a movie. So now I'm thinking that I'd have to make it ten million dollars."

He laughed at my boldness. "At least you're not undervaluing yourself," he noted.

"But isn't that the first rule when valuing an asset?" I replied trying to seem as cute and innocent as possible.

"I just wouldn't have imagined that you'd ever think of doing something like that. But I'm glad to see that you still have some capitalist impulses," he added ironically. "We like people like that at my fund."

"Actually, if I were to do something like that, the ten million wouldn't be for me," I clarified.

His brow furrowed in confusion. "What do you mean?"

"I'd want the money to go, first and foremost, to the rescue of my remaining family in Syria, and then to the founding of Antioch."

"I can certainly understand the family part, but what's Antioch?"

"It's the historic cradle of Christianity. And the name of the new Mideast state for Christians that Michael is trying to build."

I handed Professor Morales the presentation that I had spent all weekend producing. He looked at it briefly, and then laid it down next to him on the table. "Is that what all of your activism has been about?" he asked.

"To a large extent, yes."

"But I thought it was mostly to stop the persecution of Christians…Although, I must admit, I haven't paid much attention to any political rallies, so pardon my ignorance here."

The waiter came by again. "Would you like some dessert?" he asked. The conversation was just now getting to the most important topic of all, so – even though I was full – I wanted to ensure that we stayed long enough for us to finish this next part of our chat.

"Yes, please," I replied. Then, turning to Professor Morales, added, "Unless you don't want any."

"No, we should absolutely get some dessert here. It's nothing short of divine!" he exclaimed. "Can you bring us the organic dark chocolate mousse and the tasting tray, so that she can sample a little of each item?"

"Of course. I'll be back shortly with that," he said, before walking away.

"You're in for a real treat… But I'm sorry, go on. You were

discussing the goals of your political group – stopping the persecution of Christians and building a state."

"Yes, we are focused on both goals, and they are intertwined. The reason why the Christians of the Middle East have been so persecuted is that they're such a vulnerable minority without any state to protect them. So a Christian state in the region gives them a voice, a safe haven, and a chance to live in dignity where they have been for millennia," I explained.

"Honestly, the whole Middle East has just looked like a big mess to me for the last few years," he said. "I mean, in nearly every country where the so-called 'Arab Spring' toppled existing regimes, chaos and/or radical Islamists took over. Look at Libya and Syria. Or Egypt – where the Muslim Brotherhood rose to power for a while," he observed.

"It's true. But at least the Egyptian army still had the respect of the people, so it was able to step in and correct the mistake of giving power to a former Muslim Brotherhood leader," I pointed out. "But that solution doesn't exist for Syria – its army is now toxic after carrying out Assad's genocide."

"So what do you think are the options for your country? It's not every day that I can solicit the informed opinion of a Syrian refugee about the situation in Syria," he added with a smile.

"At this point, I think we can expect the gradual breakup of Syria as a single country, much like what's been happening in Iraq. Without a secular strongman like Saddam Hussein to hold together Iraq's various ethnic, religious, and linguistic identities, the country stayed together only as long as the U.S. troops stayed there."

"Makes sense," he agreed.

"So in the end, Syria will Balkanize into a Sunni state, a Kurdish state, maybe an Alawite state, and – if we play our cards right – a Christian state."

"Well, as you pointed out, the same thing seems to be happening in Iraq, so couldn't you build your Christian state there too?" he asked.

I pushed my hair back so that my neck was more exposed to him. "Absolutely. The location for our state will depend on which diplomatic and geopolitical opportunities emerge in favor of its creation. Antioch could be in Syria, in Iraq, or even some contiguous territory that is taken from each of those disintegrating states."

"Interesting. So, to bring this back to your ten-million-dollar-virginity sale, you need that money – not for luxury handbags and expensive vacations – but to make history. You want to redraw the map of the Middle East so that Christians have a safe place to live in the region," he recapped, letting his arm graze my leg.

"Exactly. And this vision has completely taken over Michael's life, and mine too, to a lesser extent."

The waiter returned and placed before us a platter of assorted desserts and fruits, and the organic dark chocolate mousse. Professor Morales put some mousse on a spoon and raised it to my lips. "Taste this. It's pure paradise," he said with a seductive tone and an intense stare. I nodded my head slightly in consent and took in his spoon, letting the dark chocolate mousse melt in my mouth – a burst of bittersweet pleasure. I shut my eyes for a heavenly moment to savor the soft decadence. "Isn't that amazing?" he asked.

"It really is. It's so good that you almost wish you hadn't eaten something like that because then you know what you're missing."

"Exactly. That's how they get you to keep coming back here," he joked. "Anyway, I'm sorry for interrupting you with such temptations. What were you saying about your future state? It sounds funny to refer so casually to something so monumental."

"I know, I think the same thing all the time," I said in amusement, as I blotted my mouth with my napkin. "But Michael isn't fazed at all by the grandness of his vision. Nothing really seems to intimidate or frighten him. He's actually in Syria right now, risking his life for this project."

"Really? What's he doing there exactly?" Professor Morales asked, taking a small bite of the mousse.

"He's meeting with Christians living in Iraq and Syria, trying to expand the organizational infrastructure needed to create Antioch. He's also bringing them some supplies and other things they need to survive and stay in touch in a very difficult operating environment."

"Sounds serious."

"It is – he's risking his life for this. And people like my relatives in Syria desperately need security and protection from the growing force of domestic and foreign Islamists on Syrian territory."

"From what little I've seen about it on the news, the situation seems horrendous."

"They're some of the most ruthless barbarians you can imagine. These are Sunni extremists trying to convert, abduct, or murder Christians, Alawites, Shiites, Sufis, and even moderate Sunnis. So this is very much a life-and-death project for countless people, even though almost nobody knows about our plan for a new state yet. It hasn't yet received any major publicity."

"And your future state would be open to other oppressed minorities?"

"Yes, of course. The state would be founded as a Christian state, but it would be a Western-style, liberal democracy, and friendly to Western interests. There would be some legal protections to ensure that its demographics are always securely Christian, but the state would guarantee full religious freedom to all faiths and allow persecuted non-Christians to seek refuge within our borders – including moderate Sunni Muslims who are threatened for their religious or political views."

"Well, that should make it easier to get Western powers to support your new state." He inserted his fork into one of the small pastries on the dessert tray and ate it. "You know, I never really thought about it, but if you're sticking to the contiguous territory of the Middle East and North Africa, then that eliminates the tiny and mostly Christian island of Cyprus," Professor Morales began, as I sampled one of the desserts on the tray in front of us. "And then that leaves Lebanon as the closest thing to a Mideast Christian state."

"Exactly. And you can hardly call that a Christian state, even though about forty percent of the population is Christian."

"That's the highest percentage in any Muslim-majority state, right?" he asked, placing his arm around my chair again. The aroma of his aftershave sweetened the air with the smell of a distinguished man.

"Yes. And Lebanese Christians do have some political power reserved to them under the Taif Agreement. Although the Shiite Muslims arguably have far more real power because their militia, Hezbollah, is stronger than even the Lebanese Army."

"What's the Taif Agreement?" he asked with genuine interest. He seemed delighted to be learning from one of his own students. It felt comforting and exciting to be teaching the teacher, while nestled in his close presence.

"It was a 1989 accord negotiated in Taif, Saudi Arabia that helped to end the Lebanese civil war. The deal proposed a power-sharing arrangement that recognized the demographic shift to a Muslim majority," I explained. "And that helped to restore some kind of political normalcy in Lebanon."

"And how does that deal work?" he asked, taking a fig with his fingers. "Here, take one of these," he added, feeding me the small, sweet fruit. I smiled as I bit into its chewy deliciousness.

"Well," I mumbled, swallowing my mouthful, "before the agreement, Lebanon had a Sunni Muslim Prime Minister who was appointed by and responsible to the Christian Maronite President. After the Taif understanding, the Sunni Prime Minister was responsible to parliament, whose speaker is Shia. So the agreement effectively enhanced the powers of the Sunni prime minister over those of the Christian president."

"That sounds very complicated."

"It is. And that's probably why, for the last few years, Lebanon has been so politically dysfunctional."

"Almost makes the U.S. Congress seem unified by comparison," he joked. "And – from the little that I follow Middle East news – I do hear about the Syrian conflict spilling over into Lebanon. So who knows what that country's future even looks like…" he pointed out.

"Exactly. For many reasons, the new Mideast Christian state must be founded from scratch, and in a territory whose actual control is completely in question – like in Syria or Iraq."

"What you say makes sense," he began, "but doesn't that also mean that your new state will be doomed to instability, conflict, and territorial disputes?" he asked, moving some strands of my hair back, so that my neck was exposed again. I sunk my teeth into my bottom lip, trying to stay focused on the conversation.

"To some extent. But that's happening anyway," I explained, shifting in my seat. "Look at the Kurds, fighting to protect their rights and territory in northern Iraq. And the Shiites who defend southern Iraq. But once you have states that are strong enough to defend and enforce their borders, things get quieter. Look at Syria and Israel. We've been formally in a state of war for decades, but the border along our countries has generally been quiet for almost all of that time."

Professor Morales seemed to like that observation. "You make a good point. And it's consistent with the little that I do know about the Middle East: what counts there is strength because the weak are quickly crushed. But the strong get respect."

"Exactly. That's why the borders between certain enemy states can remain relatively peaceful. And once Christians have an official home, where they are not a vulnerable minority subject to the whims of the religious majority, I guarantee you that they will fight to defend its borders, because they will have a stake in its future and take pride in its success. Even if that state is just a tiny part of their ancestral land, they will fight to keep it. And any enemies around them will respect those borders. This state will allow Mideast Christians, for the first time, to seize our destiny and live in dignity and security in a region where we have lived for thousands of years."

"Well, I can see why you'd need a lot of money for that. Much more than the cost of expensive handbags and lavish vacations," he noted lightly.

"So maybe ten million dollars isn't enough," I quipped playfully.

"Probably not. But you don't want to price yourself out of the market either," he added dryly, as if to warn me not to push my luck.

"Very true," I conceded with an amused smile. "And what we need goes well beyond financing. We need power. Influential people who can help us to lobby the media and world leaders to support our cause."

"So you should be recruiting the Christian leaders of every denomination in Europe and the Americas."

"Oh, we will. The Christian diaspora will have a vital role to play in the birth of Antioch."

"As an Arab woman, you may be shocked to hear me say this," Professor Morales began, as if he were walking on eggshells suddenly, "but this sounds almost like what the Jews have done with Israel."

I offered him a reassuring smile. "Actually, Michael says that to me all of the time, so I'm finally getting used to the idea. And he says that we will need Israel's help in many ways."

"Well, they've certainly built a successful model that you can follow – especially with their high-tech economy," he noted. He seemed happy to switch the focus of our discussion from Mideast geopolitics to investment-related topics. "You know that they have more companies listed on the NASDAQ than any country after the USA and China?"

I noticed his eyes drop to my lips, and then down to my chest area. So I sucked in a deep breath, elevating my breasts for him. It felt like a bold move, but one he seemed to like, judging from his widening eyes. "No, I didn't know that," I explained, exhaling slowly.

"Yes… Well… The JMAT fund is actually invested in the Israeli tech sector, and it's performed quite well over the years."

"Interesting."

"Speaking of my fund, does this mean that you see your future more in international relations and political activism than in finance?"

"Well, for deeply personal reasons, the struggle for Antioch will probably guide my future more than anything else. But a career in finance could very well be the best way for me to help Antioch. I think my tour of JMAT helped to convince me of that," I added with a suggestive wink.

He gave me a serious look and put his hand on my shoulder. "Let's not forget that there's still a final and some more problem sets."

I released a much-needed laugh, as he brought us back to the inside joke we had established at the first party of his that I had attended. As important as all of the serious talk about my cause was, it had gotten a bit heavy and exhausting. So it felt good to return to a more familiar and playful dynamic. "Wait, you mean that even though I agreed to have dinner with you, you're still going to make me take this famously impossible final?"

"Call me a sadist, but I'm actually looking forward to giving you that exam," he confessed, putting his left hand on my right wrist.

"So that you can determine whether my midterm performance was an outlier? Or whether I'm an outlier?"

"Oh, I have no doubt that you're an outlier, or we wouldn't be here right now. But I am curious to see if you can repeat what you did on the midterm." His hand gently slipped off my wrist, aware of the implicit boundaries that hadn't been clearly lifted.

"Wow, I'm thinking that I need to head home and hit the books now so that I can start studying for it ASAP!" I replied in jest. "But first you have to keep your promise to tell me why you're such a strict vegetarian."

"Ah yes. Well, the answer is really quite simple: my father was a butcher and, after seeing him at work far too many times, I just couldn't stomach the sight – or even the thought – of meat anymore."

"Really?"

"See what a softie I am deep down?"

"Indeed," I chuckled at what I was about to reveal. "So I guess I should probably tell you that I really love eating meat."

He seemed amused by my bluntness. "Well, at least you didn't leave me wondering how you truly feel about the issue," he remarked ironically.

"Don't you love it when communication is simple and straightforward like that?" I gushed.

He smiled. "I do. And I'm actually really pleased to hear that you're such a proud carnivore."

"And why is that?"

"Because the virtues of vegetarianism will be one more thing that I can teach you."

We shared a laugh, and then he gestured to the waiter to bring him the check.

Chapter 43: Anissa

∾ Monday, March 31, 2014 ∾

To My Dearest,

I barely slept last night (I'm writing to you at 5 a.m. this morning) because I'm so confused about everything. I keep thinking about how much I enjoyed my date with Professor Morales, and how I'm going to see him in class tomorrow, and I can't decide whether to "play it cool" (as if we had never met privately outside of the classroom), go up to him after class and talk to him, or something in between.

I need an anchor to still my turbulent mind so that I can find my lost heart after the dinner date with Professor Morales. I'm definitely attracted to him, and there is something about the way we interact that feels magical sometimes. As crazy as it seems to me, I've even been thinking about offering my virginity to him in exchange for a ten-million-dollar donation to the MCA. That kind of donation could make such a huge difference to my family and community. And my virginity is probably the only thing that I can gift to a man who has pretty much everything. I can't stop thinking about this possibility now. And it's funny how the whole idea – and such a ridiculously large sum of money – suddenly seems more sayable now that we've joked about it.

On the other hand, I still feel drawn and loyal to Michael, who says he wants me in his future even though he still has feelings for Karen. But so many conflicting emotions and principles are buzzing about in my brain that they're turning me in my bed like a raft on a stormy sea.

Michael desperately wants a huge contribution to the MCA, but he would hate the idea of me becoming romantically involved with Professor Morales. I've always believed that I should save myself for my husband, but I also want to do everything in my power to help my family and people. So what is more important? If I use unfaithful means to secure a faithful end, have I been true to anyone?

And when I honestly question why I would even consider selling my virginity to Professor Morales, I know that some of the motivations are noble, while others are relatively petty. I guess I'm upset and insecure about the fact that Michael is still "close" with Karen (to use his term), and a part of me wants to outdo her in such an obvious way – and on this fundraising issue that matters so much to Michael – that she would no longer pose any possible threat or competition. I think I'm also drawn to the idea that I wouldn't have to wonder or worry about how and when to lose my virginity; instead, I could give it up for an unquestionably good and unselfish purpose (unlike those women who auction off their purity for their own financial gain). I also think that this personal sacrifice – compromising my morals about sex to try to help those I left behind – could also help me to manage my survivor's guilt. Somehow it gives my survival a greater purpose: by using my escape to help my family and community still suffering in Syria, it could almost be considered as part of some master plan that we all hatched together (as if I was randomly chosen to be the one who would escape and do whatever was necessary to bring everyone else out). And if so many helpless Syrian Christians must lose their virginity to armed Islamists who rape them, shouldn't I be willing to lose mine to my handsome and charming professor, if that could help them?

But those considerations are all related to my small world. The truly selfless and good motivations have nothing to do with which man I prefer, or my survivor's guilt, my insecurities about Karen, my desire to impress Michael, or my readiness to shed the awkward virgin status. The most important reason to give myself to Julien for a ten-million-dollar donation would be to help my family, and my people, in ways that could literally save lives. And, as Michael pointed out, I am in the incredibly rare and fortunate position to do for these vulnerable and downtrodden souls what they could never do for themselves. And if I were in Maria's shoes right now, and she were in mine, wouldn't I want her to do whatever she could to save me and Antoun, Uncle Luke's family, and however many other Syrian Christians she could help? Yes, I would.

But still, I've never felt so in need of a life compass, and there's no one who can guide me. Obviously, I can't consult with Professor Morales or Michael about decisions that involve or impact them. Uncle Tony is too removed from my situation to understand it, and I've never even talked to him about matters of the heart before. Maya doesn't share enough of my background and values for her advice to seem appropriate. Talking to Monique also doesn't feel right, even though she's the only person I've opened up to about the massacre of my family and other sensitive topics that I've shared with no one else. Maybe it's because she's much older and I'm afraid of losing her respect, since she might secretly judge me for considering a relationship with my professor – especially if I'm doing so for favors from him (however righteous my motives may be). My sister would have been the perfect adviser: we're close enough in age and values/background and she would understand my motivation to support the cause better than anyone else would, but we've grown more distant because of my infrequent calls and how different our lives have become. I also feel ashamed even discussing such "problems" with Maria when she's facing things that are infinitely worse. I don't want to mention anything that might highlight for her how much better my life is. So that just leaves you, My Dearest. I shall continue baring my soul to you, and hope that in the process, God will grace me with the wisdom to make the best decision.

If I'm being totally honest, part of me would want to explore a relationship with Professor Morales even if Michael weren't in the picture and there were no potential benefit to my community or family. My professor has many qualities that draw me towards him: his brilliant mind (from which I can always be learning), charm and confidence, handsome looks and elegant style, worldliness, dry humor and banter, keen understanding of human psychology, abundant wealth, and extraordinary social and political influence – with powerful friends from nearly every segment of society and the economy. All of this provides so much more comfort and security than I could probably find anywhere else. And I am definitely flattered by his subtle compliments, his clear attraction to me, and his appreciation of my qualities. Yes, the big age difference between us is awkward – but only in terms of how others might perceive it. Whenever I'm around him, I don't feel as if we can't relate because he's more than twice my age. On the contrary, it seems as if we understand each other surprisingly well – even though there is still so much about each other that we don't know. And, maybe it's not healthy or right, but – if I'm totally honest with myself – I'm probably also drawn to him because he has a very real and direct power over me: he will decide my academic grade in my favorite class and he owns the hedge fund where I dream of working after graduation.

On the other hand, I know that he's a notorious playboy and probably the most sought-after bachelor in Manhattan, so that could undermine some of the security he seems to represent. And he doesn't understand my community ties or concerns on any instinctual level. If he cares about my cause at all, it's mainly to please me; of course, that's still wonderful and I would be grateful for any help he decides to give, but I doubt that we could viscerally share the same feelings about the developments in Syria the way that Michael and I do.

Michael is truly a leader – possibly the founder and future president of a new country. He could very well become a historic figure and I am always inspired by his vision and determination. We share so many values and concerns and interests, and – if only because of our common culture – I think our families would get along much better than would be the case with Professor Morales (I actually know nothing about his family). And Michael irresistibly exudes masculinity in every way: his jawbone and rugged handsomeness, his muscular physique and fighting skills, and his deep and powerful voice. And he too is someone extraordinarily smart and educated, from whom I could learn so much – especially when it comes to international relations and Middle East history.

So I am torn about these two men, although I am still leaning towards Michael – mainly because of our strong communal connection, and maybe also because he was really my first crush ever. My first kiss. My first hope for our community. My Christian Hero.

But the same heroism that makes Michael so admirable and attractive – like embracing the dangers of Syria to help our people there – also makes him a far less secure "emotional investment." I have already suffered enough losses in that country, and can't imagine the pain I would feel if I were to choose Michael as my life partner, only to have him killed while doing God's work.

I wish I knew what to do.

And even if I were totally sure about which man I want in my future, it seems like whatever I do will leave some person or principle cheated. If I offer my virginity to Professor Morales for the sake of a big donation to the MCA, would I then have to hide this from Michael forever? Or would he ultimately accept and respect my decision in a way that wouldn't interfere with our future relationship? And if I slept with Professor Morales partly to impress Michael with the big donation that results, then does that forever taint any true and honest relationship I might hope to have with my professor? Would he forever be jealous of Michael, thinking that he's actually secondary to the Christian Hero in my life?

Then again, perhaps fidelity to the feelings of either man is entirely irrelevant. Maybe neither should have a say in this because my first duty is to my parents' wishes and the needs of my community. And if getting romantic with Professor Morales – even giving him my virginity – means a generous contribution that saves the remainder of my family and hundreds of Christian-Syrian lives, how could I not do such a thing? I can have Professor Morales require Michael to use part of the funds to save my family in Raqqa before using the money for anything else. How could I live with myself if ISIS slaughters what little remains of my family simply because I refused to do everything in my power to help?

Momentum is on my side now: my professor asked me on a date, we had a wonderful time, and – if I handle everything right – I could possibly secure a huge donation that makes all the difference to my family and my people. Tomorrow after class, if I can catch him alone, I could hint that I'm open to the exchange we joked about. A part of me wants to wait with this approach, but I also have no guarantee that tomorrow isn't my last chance to pursue the idea, while it's still fresh in his memory from a date we both enjoyed. As the supremely successful and attractive "catch" that Professor Morales is, he could become interested in some other woman at any moment. But my relatives and community need help now. In fact, they've needed it for years but nobody could give it to them, until maybe now. I think I know what to do. I knew the Lord would show me the way. Thank you God, for your grace and your kindness.

And thank you, My Dearest, for holding my hand while I walked through the thicket in search of the way. Now maybe I can sleep.

Chapter 44: Anissa

∽ Monday, March 31, 2014 ∾

To My Dearest,

I know that I wrote to you just seven hours ago (it's noon now) and I normally don't share things with you in the middle of the day before I've had much time to think about them – but I need you more than ever now. It feels as if so many momentous things are happening in my life, or maybe I'm just ill-equipped to figure it all out and make the best decisions along the way.

Today I spoke with Michael via Skype video again. It seems like every time I talk to him, I'm relieved that he's still alive – much like with my sister, brother, and uncle in Syria, with whom I also spoke today.

After reaching my family in Raqqa, I learned that Uncle Luke has been having some issues with a Syrian Christian in the city. His name is Ayman, and apparently, there's almost nothing meaningfully Christian about him. He's really just an opportunist using his sectarian ties to gain the trust of other Christians and profit from them in various ways. Uncle Luke told me that he made the mistake of lending him money a few months ago. After Ayman failed to pay him on time, Uncle Luke did some research and learned just yesterday that a few other Christians in Raqqa had lent him money and, when they tried to collect it from him, Ayman went to the Islamist authorities now ruling the city and falsely claimed that they had blasphemed the prophet Mohammed. This was the fastest way to avoid repaying his debts because armed Islamists would soon show up at the door of the accused, and the creditor was usually murdered on the spot or taken to some sham trial and murdered within a day or two. I begged Uncle Luke not to try to collect his debt from Ayman and he told me that he asked for his money back only twice and, after learning the truth about Ayman, he planned not to contact him again out of fear. I just pray that contacting him twice was not already enough to make him want to eliminate another creditor with a phone call to the ISIS police.

I asked Michael to see how he could help, but he said that he's barely had time to sleep and is constantly in meetings, or traveling between cities, often sleeping in different safe houses, so he just hasn't had a chance to see what he can do to help in Raqqa, but he said that he'll try. And he was thrilled when I told him about my dinner with Professor Morales.

"That's amazing, Inās. I'm so proud of how you're handling it. It sounds like you touched on all of the important points to make him see that this is a serious effort that's worthy of his support, but without sounding desperate."

"I tried. And I spent two days customizing the proposal for him, which I gave him at our dinner. So he has the details of what is needed and how to contribute."

"Great work! Just use your judgment about the best way to follow up with him, so that we don't lose momentum and can get his help as soon as possible."

"During our dinner, he definitely seemed a lot more open to the cause than he was on that first day we saw him on College Walk together."

"Well, that's not saying much," Michael quipped dryly. "But it sounds like there's definitely hope with him, and I couldn't be more grateful to you. If you were in Syria right now, I'd give you a massive hug. You'd also have a better sense of just how desperate the need is. So I'm really hoping you can score a big donation from him. And some political connections, once you're close enough to ask him for something like that."

"I'm doing my best, Michael." I felt guilty saying that, because "my best" now meant my decision to offer my virginity to Professor Morales, and that wasn't something I could tell Michael now (or maybe ever). And I felt even guiltier because Michael seemed so unsuspecting and happy for my success with Professor Morales.

"You have no idea how proud you make me," he beamed, bringing me back from my self-flagellating thoughts to the conversation.

"He actually followed me on Twitter last night," I reported, as if this could somehow make up for my potential infidelity.

"Really?" Michael asked in elated disbelief.

"Yes. I can't add him on Facebook because he already has the maximum number of friends possible. But I followed him on Twitter and, within an hour, he had followed me back. And I don't think he usually follows people back unless they're VIPs."

"That's huge!" Michael enthused. I saw his face light up in hopeful excitement in the Skype video chat on my laptop. "I think that might officially qualify you as a VIP. I mean, your tweets now reach someone who's extremely influential and whose followers include major policymakers, politicians, and others who could see your message if he retweets it. So this is actually a much bigger deal than you may realize."

I thought about the truth of what he said for a moment. "Wow, I better start coming up with some good tweets," I worried aloud.

"Don't worry, I'll help you," Michael reassured me with that confident wink that said, "We got this!"

I sighed and shrugged. "I just wish you were here so that we could celebrate some of these little victories together."

"I know. Me too," he replied.

"I really miss you," I confessed, finally releasing what I had kept inside for too long. I fought back tears of guilt over my secret decision to offer myself to Professor Morales after his class tomorrow, and then I suddenly started to second-guess myself, no longer sure if this was the right thing to do.

"I miss you too, Inās."

Chapter 45: Anissa

∾ Tuesday, April 1, 2014 ∾

To My Dearest,

I woke up this morning to some shocking news – a scandal involving Professor Morales! It seems like the entire campus has been talking about and sharing a story that appeared in the New York tabloids today. The headline read, "Columbia Prof in Underwear Selfie Scandal" and it was accompanied by some shirtless photos that he had taken of himself in the mirror, with the top of his Calvin Klein boxers showing at the bottom of the photo. I must confess that his chest actually looks much better than I had imagined it to be, although this is hardly how I would have wanted to find out! Anyway, here's what the article reported:

"Areli Smithpatrick, a twenty-year old Murray Hill resident who claims to have been the part-time lover of billionaire and Columbia University Professor Julien Morales, has today come forward with shirtless photos that probably leave the hedge fund tycoon wishing that this was some kind of April Fool's joke. But, unfortunately for the Ivy League lecturer who often appears as a TV commentator on financial news, the April 1st timing makes these photos of him no less real. The pictures, which show Mr. Morales taking photos of his naked chest with his cell phone, reportedly fetched five-figure offers from several tabloids vying for the exclusive and were, within an hour of publication, widely shared on social media. Areli, a self-styled 'full-time socialite,' claims that she dated the Latino-American financial powerhouse for about two months late last year after crashing one of his legendary penthouse parties. According to Ms. Smithpatrick, Julien Morales sent her those photos of himself in exchange for nude pictures of the party-goer nearly half his age. Repeated calls to JM Analytics & Trading, the $20 billion hedge fund owned and run by Mr. Morales, were not returned."

I genuinely felt sorry for Professor Morales, even if this was clearly the result of some very poor choices he had made. I also sensed an opportunity to get closer to him, although I still wasn't sure about my plan to offer him my virginity for a donation – especially after this incident. I was actually surprised that he even showed up to class, given how tempting it would be for students to discuss and joke about the scandal before, after, and maybe even during class. I felt terribly embarrassed for him, and his lecturing style seemed off – like he really just wanted to end the class early and hide in a cave somewhere. I also sensed some tension from Elise, although I couldn't tell if she was jealous, angry, mortified, or some combination of the three. But the energy that she projected provided further confirmation that our TA did indeed have some kind of secret relationship with our professor.

The lecture couldn't end soon enough and I was relieved when he concluded the class about twenty minutes early. He really didn't seem well, and I scowled at some of the students making obnoxious remarks just after our class ended early and we started packing up our things.

"Maybe we can analyze those selfies as a Psychology and Markets problem," one student jeered.

A female student in his circle of friends continued the joke: "Yeah, I wonder how much the used Calvin Kleins in those pics would sell for!"

Another added, "Seriously. Now we can assess how a shirtless selfie sent to a girl half your age affects your popularity in the market."

"Just drop it," I said to them. "Everyone makes mistakes."

"Oh, has he sent you selfies too? Is that why you're defending him now?" the young woman replied.

"No, she's just the teacher's pet," one of them opined.

"Is that the sound of grade envy I hear?" I retorted. "Grow up and move on. Every student seemed to like him before this happened. Cut him some slack – he's got enough people laughing at him in the city today. So those of us who benefit from his teaching can at least stay quiet if we're not going to support him."

I hoped – just for the sake of his morale – that Professor Morales could hear me defending him, but I couldn't be sure because he shuffled out of the classroom so quickly. I tried to catch up to him, and figured that he'd probably take the stairs, rather than wait for the elevator with students. When I got to the stairwell, I saw that I was correct about his exit path, and caught the top of his black-haired head below, as he descended the stairs, already a flight below me. I sped up my pace, but stayed far enough behind him so that he didn't notice me following him.

Once he was outside of Hamilton Hall, I shadowed him from a distance of about forty feet, until he was off campus, and there were no students around to see me approaching him. It was already dark out, so that made things easier. As I got closer, I thought about how humiliating this must be for him – not so much because his naked chest was now public knowledge, but because of what it said to everyone about his values, his self-control, and his judgment. Now everyone knows that he chose to take a needless risk that clearly backfired, and only in order to entice a woman clearly beneath him in every possible respect.

I caught up to him and continued at a brisk pace that matched his. "Professor Morales," I said gently, when I was by his side and close enough for him to hear me. A light breeze wafted a hint of his alluring aftershave toward me, prompting me to inhale deeper and savor the fragrance.

He looked at me, a bit annoyed – almost as if I was just another nuisance interfering with his escape from the public eye.

"Now's not a good time, Anissa," he said curtly.

"I know... I just want to say how sorry I am that you're going through this, and that I'm here to help in whatever way I can."

His walking pace slowed down a little. "Thanks," he replied curtly. I sensed that he probably just wanted to be left alone.

"I've tried to stick up for you each time I heard people speaking rudely about you today. And I'll keep doing that," I added.

"That's very kind of you, Anissa." He looked surprised to receive some unsolicited kindness. "But please don't. For your own sake. I'm toxic right now, and there's no need to sully your reputation by defending mine."

We stopped walking because we had reached his car – a black luxury sedan with dark, tinted windows. He opened the door and started to enter.

"Professor Morales," I began, not really sure what I was trying to say to him or what my plan was, beyond just flowing with the moment. He stopped and looked at me.

"Yes, Anissa?"

"I just wanted to tell you... " I froze up a little, nervous that I was obviously catching him at a bad moment.

"Look, I really don't want to be in public right now," he warned, quickly scanning his surroundings with unease. "If you want to talk, you can share my car and I'll have my driver take you back."

I, too, looked around to make sure there was nobody nearby who might see us together. "OK," I replied, getting into the back seat of the car next to him.

As we drove off, Professor Morales flipped a switch that completely sealed off the passenger area from the driver. "Quinn is completely trustworthy – he's been my driver for ten years. But now he can't see or hear anything back here, in case that makes you feel more comfortable," he explained.

"Thanks… But what I wanted to say really isn't that private… I mean, I just… I just wanted to tell you that I had a really nice time with you last Sunday night, but… " There was an awkward pause as I struggled to find the right way to phrase what I was trying to say without sounding as if I was somehow exploiting his current shame.

"But what?" he asked, with a tone suggesting that he was bracing for the worst.

"But I know that after what happened today, you may be viewing everything differently… So I… I also wanted you to know that it doesn't change the way I think of you."

His head jerked in my direction, as his eyes widened in surprise. "It doesn't?"

"Well, this woman obviously violated your trust, and I would never do something like that, so if anything, I think she's the one most at fault here… And, on some strange level, it makes me more comfortable around you."

His face displayed a look of detached disbelief. "Really?"

"Yes, really," I confirmed, as earnestly as I could.

"Anissa, your answers get more surprising by the moment," he responded lightly, with a hint of sad amusement in his tone. "How could this incident possibly make you more comfortable around me?"

"Well, it normalizes you a bit more. I mean, you make mistakes like everyone else."

He turned towards the window near him, as if to watch the passing buildings. "I guess I hadn't really thought of it that way," he mumbled.

"It's all about perspective – right, Professor Morales?" After getting to know each other better in a few informal settings and discussing things as intimate as losing my virginity, it felt odd to continue referring to him that way. But he was still my professor and I wanted to avoid the appearance of presumptuously taking liberties.

"I suppose it is," he agreed with a sigh.

"Did you try my suggestion of exploring new perspectives by sleeping on a park bench for a few nights before going back to your penthouse?" I asked, hoping to lighten his mood with a happier memory we shared.

He chuckled and met my gaze for a moment. "Oh, I just remembered something. Excuse me for a second." My professor took out his cell phone and I saw on its display that he was calling Raegan. "Hi, can you cancel my dinner tonight? Actually I need you to cancel all of my dinners and meetings this week… I know… Yes, I'm sure. Thanks, Raegan." He hung up.

"Where are we going, by the way?" I asked.

"Actually, I can drop you off now, unless you want to continue talking."

"No, I wasn't trying to get out. I was just wondering where we're going now that I just heard you cancel your dinner plans for tonight," I explained with a smile.

"Ah yes. I'm going to the Brooklyn Bridge. You're welcome to join me and then Quinn can take you back afterwards. Or if that's too much time away from your study schedule, I can drop you off now."

"Oh, I've never actually been to the Brooklyn Bridge. I'd love to join you, if you don't mind my company."

"No, I don't mind it. You seem to be a healthy addition to my perspective. And I enjoy our banter. So I guess we're going there together… It's a very special place, with a lot of personal significance for me."

I angled my body to face him more. "Why is that?"

"Maybe I'll tell you when we get there," he replied mysteriously. There was a slightly awkward moment of silence as I wondered why the bridge meant so much to him. "Do you know what my favorite, obscure piece of Brooklyn Bridge trivia is?"

I shook my head to indicate that I didn't. "No, but I'd like to."

A boyish yet handsome grin formed on his face. "To help finance the high cost of constructing it, in 1876, New York City rented out large vaults to wine sellers under the bridge's Manhattan anchorage. The vaults were consistently at sixty degrees – an ideal temperature to store wine. Anyway, on the walls of a vault, located underneath William Street and Park Row, is a fading inscription that states, 'Who loveth not wine, women and song, he remaineth a fool his whole life long.'"

"Really?" I asked, amused at the randomness of the inscription. "That's kind of funny."

"Yes. Really. And you know what's even funnier?"

"What?"

"I have loved all three and I seem to be a fool anyway," he explained drearily.

I gently touched his leg, offering what reassurance I could. "Don't be so tough on yourself."

"That's easy to say when you don't have a hard-earned empire to lose," he replied, before turning his head towards the window and looking despondently at the buildings passing us by as we drove. "But when the Dean might call you in for a disciplinary meeting that could jeopardize your expected promotion, or even your position at the university... When investors might leave your fund to disassociate themselves from scandal... When you can't publicly show your face anywhere in your city because you'll be ridiculed wherever you go, things are a little harder."

"You're right," I conceded. "I'm really sorry that you're going through this. I don't know how I would face any of those challenges. I honestly don't even know how you managed to show up to class today."

"I don't either. It was probably a stupid decision, but I wanted to face the storm head on. So I went to work as usual. And then to class. I thought I could keep my cool."

"And you did."

"Maybe. But it had a toxic effect on me. Seeing people at the office, and later standing up in front of the class, knowing that I was the laughing stock of everyone around me. That just made everything worse. And now I'm reeling from it all."

I hated seeing my professor so despondent. "I just wish there were some way for me to cheer you up."

"Me too," he said, in sullen resignation.

We sat quietly for a while as his driver kept us moving downtown, with the lights of the city's skyscrapers illuminating the night and passing by the darkened windows of his sedan. I thought maybe if I returned him to a happy moment that he and I had very recently shared, it might brighten his mood a little.

Finally, I broke our silence. "I hope this question doesn't seem inappropriate after what the tabloids did to you today," I began, but then stopped, suddenly unsure about continuing.

"Go on," he goaded me.

"Well, I was just wondering... What did you think of our dinner last Sunday?" I asked.

"I think you and Michael are working for a worthy cause and I applaud your efforts," he answered, somewhat mechanically – as if he wasn't at all emotionally invested.

"Is that the main thing you took away from our evening together?" I asked, trying to sound as disinterested as possible, even though I suddenly needed to know how he felt about me. I worried now that maybe we hadn't formed any sort of deeper connection than had existed between us before our dinner.

"Well, that was what we spent the most time discussing, but if you just mean how I liked the overall experience of sharing a meal with you, I enjoyed myself... Much more than I expected..."

My eyes locked on his. "Really?"

"Yes. Really. But unfortunately that leaves me in a bit of a quandary."

"Oh... Why?" I asked, dropping my gaze, as if everything was about to slip away.

"Well, there are some very compelling reasons why I shouldn't have allowed myself to enjoy our time together so much."

I released a pessimistic breath, bracing for the worst. "Because I'm just eighteen and still your student?"

"Those are the most obvious reasons – particularly after today's headlines. But the less obvious ones are my capacity to hurt someone who's already been injured quite a lot in her short life." Professor Morales diverted his gaze to the city passing us by.

"Do you think you'd hurt me?" I asked timidly.

"Well," he said, turning back to face me. "I don't have a very good track record with women. And the fact that you have so little experience with men only heightens the risk that you'd be hurt somewhere along the way."

"And you don't think you could treat me differently than the other women?"

"I find it ironic that every woman wants to believe that she is different from all of the other women before her."

I chuckled. "So our desires are pretty unoriginal, it seems," I concluded.

He matched my chuckle with his own. "As are male desires. We're probably even more predictable than women. But, based on all of our interactions until now and everything that I know about you, I'd say that there's a better chance that I'll treat you differently than there is with any other woman. But I still can't guarantee that."

His revelation shocked me. I honestly didn't expect him to admit that he did view me differently. And the truth was that I felt the same about him. He was so different from my other professors, and the other men I had encountered in life. Despite his obvious flaws, there was something essentially good about him, and his extraordinary intelligence came with delightful charm, a sophisticated worldliness, and handsome looks. And he seemed to suffer from a darkness that I wanted to understand and lighten. So I, too, was worried that he might somehow get hurt – especially with Michael in the picture. I also didn't know what to make of his warning about maybe hurting me. "So where does that leave us?" I asked, somewhat confused as to the direction of our conversation and whether there was a good outcome in sight.

"Well, the surest way for us to avoid hurting anyone would be to keep our relationship entirely… transactional," he stated, murmuring the last word awkwardly, suggesting that he was uncomfortable with the idea.

I gave him a reassuring smile and raised my arm so that I could casually rest my head in my hand against the back seat. "So by 'transactional,' I take it you mean, I sell you my virginity for a ten-million-dollar donation?"

He mimicked my posture and smiled in return, now looking a little relieved. "Yes… As you intimated at our dinner," he added, as if in his own defense.

"Well, it was all sort of a joke when we mentioned it over dinner. But, to be uncomfortably honest with you, yesterday I started to think that I should explore the idea with you more seriously," I admitted, turning red, as I suddenly felt embarrassed and ashamed. "Although I'm not so sure anymore – especially after today's scandal."

He placed his hand on my leg for a moment. "Don't feel bad about it," he reassured me. "Your motives are noble, and I'd probably try something similar, if I were in your shoes," he added empathetically.

"Really?" His candidness both relieved and surprised me.

"Yes. Although, honestly, I'm still a bit shocked at that figure," he noted in amusement. "But if I could somehow get comfortable with that number, and we were going to do this, we'd probably structure it as five million upfront, and five million after – as you would do in a commercial transaction."

I still couldn't tell if we were discussing the idea in purely theoretical terms or if he was actually now considering it. "So… that's how you'd want to do it?" I asked. "Because you care about me enough that you don't want to hurt me?"

He released a self-conscious smirk. "Yes, I think so. As funny as that sounds."

I liked that he cared about me but wondered if such an arrangement really would prevent me from getting hurt. "Why would a transaction be an emotionally safer approach?"

"Because we'd agree on exactly what we're getting from each other, so we'd expect no more and no less. And when everyone's expectations are met, it's much harder for anyone to get hurt."

"I guess that makes sense," I agreed, not entirely convinced that I might not develop feelings for him anyway.

He looked at me and released an ironic smile. "There's only one problem."

"What?"

"I've never in my life paid for sex and I don't plan on starting now, at a time when I need to pay for it less than probably any other man in New York, even when my brand takes a major hit, like it did today."

"But you're forgetting that I actually don't want any of that money for myself."

"True. And that's very helpful because – in my mind – that moves this from some very expensive form of prostitution to me just wanting to support something that you care about deeply," he said with a smirk that hinted of mischief.

I ran my tongue over the top row of my teeth and then gave him a smile of equal playfulness. "So why not just donate because it's the right thing to do?"

"Maybe I will," he suggested, finding a lock of my hair with his fingers. He momentarily studied it before letting it go and meeting my stare, his expression now conveying the seriousness of our discussion. "But remember that there are countless good causes out there. I can't make a meaningful contribution to all of them. Just like there are countless men out there, and you can't give your virginity to all of them. We all must make choices, and that is how we express our values."

I closed my eyes and whispered, "You make a good point."

"So if you choose me, then you have declared me more special to you than anyone else, because only one man can have that honor. And then suddenly your cause isn't just another one of a million charities out there competing for my surplus wealth. It is the nonprofit deeply cherished by that woman who values me so much, that she gave me her virginity over the billions of other men out there (including her future husband, probably)."

My eyes shot open. "When you add the word 'probably,' are you suggesting that you could theoretically be my husband someday?"

"Well, it isn't impossible because neither of us is currently married, right? And I did say that I could probably view and treat you differently than the women before you. I just can't guarantee it. And the odds that we'd end up as a married couple are rather diminished by the fact that you're extremely young to be getting married. And realistically, if I haven't found someone to marry by this stage of my life, I probably will never get married. But it isn't impossible, and – in that very remote scenario where it happens – I guess we would look back at this and laugh about how it all happened, and how you did indeed save yourself for your husband."

"That would make for an epic story!" I beamed. "And if it doesn't happen, then I will have done a great thing for a great cause. It beats losing your virginity among the cigarette butts on a sticky dance floor, right?"

"Talk about perspective!" he agreed in amusement. "Yes, selling it for a huge donation to a worthy cause would certainly be a better way to lose it."

"And you will have lived up to your last name, which means 'morals' – I looked it up the other day."

"Yes, it does. Although today has made it abundantly clear that I'm not guided enough by my surname."

"Well, that was today. There's always tomorrow," I reassured him, in the most humble but hopeful tone I could muster.

"Right. Listen, Anissa. I don't want us to discuss this idea of a transaction ever again. If I decide to help you, then you'll know because the Mideast Christian Association will receive a wire transfer of five million dollars. It may be anonymously sent, but you'll know it's from me. And then how you respond to such a donation will be entirely up to you. In a transaction, the contract would stipulate that such a payment triggers your duty to perform, and once you do, then that would trigger my duty to pay the balance. But we're not going to have a contract."

"Because maybe you'll just support the MCA for being a worthy cause?"

"Yes. Maybe I will. And because you really are different and special, so I don't like the idea of having something as cold as a contract with you."

"It would feel very strange to me, honestly," I admitted.

"I can imagine… It's not exactly a trophy. And if I were to bring you into my bed, I wouldn't want to think that you came to me because you were under some formal obligation to do so."

I felt slightly aroused when he mentioned bringing me to his bed. "But you're the one who claimed that making it transactional would protect me from getting hurt," I reminded him, now confused.

"Yes. I know. I'm full of contradictions today. I'm quite confused after all that's happened, and hopefully the Brooklyn Bridge will help me to clear my head… The truth is, I really wasn't planning on seeing anyone after class today, much less having you ride with me in my car, so my head's a bit muddled at the moment."

"I'm sorry – I did want to talk to you briefly after class. But I wasn't planning on joining your car ride… It just sort of happened."

"I know. I was there when it happened," he noted absurdly, to my amusement.

A little later, we arrived at the Brooklyn Bridge. His driver dropped us off on the Manhattan side of the East River, by the entrance to the pedestrian walkway. Even with our coats on, it was a bit chillier because of the stronger winds in the bridge area. As we walked towards Brooklyn, suspended over the water, I admired the nighttime Manhattan skyline around us. And I marveled at the bridge's cable arrangement above us, which formed a distinctive web-like pattern. I also wondered what it would feel like to reach out and hold my professor's hand.

"Do you know anything about this bridge?" he asked.

"Only that it connects the boroughs of Manhattan and Brooklyn, and it's more beautiful than I had imagined," I confessed, enjoying the unique moment we were sharing.

"It's a hybrid cable-stayed/suspension bridge – and one of the oldest bridges of either type in the United States. It was completed in 1883 and spans about 1,596 feet. It was the first steel-wire suspension bridge ever constructed."

"What are its towers made of?" I asked.

"Limestone, granite, and Rosendale cement."

"It's truly splendid – the whole thing."

"Yes, it is," he agreed.

"And it reminds me of what I love so much about this city," I remarked.

"And what is that?"

"Manhattan is one big monument to human potential."

"It really is," he concurred, admiring the bridge with me.

"It's full of these grand structures that are possible only thanks to our greatest virtues – intelligence, planning, cooperation, vision. Things that you almost forget exist when evil, terror, and war ravage your country and become the normal state of affairs," I pointed out.

"Well, I'm glad that New York could serve as your bridge back to civilization," he replied.

"Me too… I'm extremely fortunate… And grateful."

We walked in silence, relishing the breathtaking views and glittering horizon around us.

When we reached the midpoint of the bridge, Professor Morales stopped and faced the water, leaning on the handrail. I stood next to him and did the same.

"What I'm about to tell you, very few people know," he began. "Maybe only two of the therapists that I've had, and my journal."

I was silent for a moment, not sure what to say or how I had earned this honor.

"Do I have your word that you'll never tell a soul what I'm about to share with you?"

"Yes, of course," I said.

"For some reason, I feel like I can trust you – even on a day when I should be trusting no one."

"Why do you trust me so much?" I was suddenly very curious to know.

"Since the very first day that we met, I've always sensed a basic goodness about you. And I know that you've been through far worse in your short life than what I've been through in over twice as many years. So you have more perspective than most people. And for that reason, you're undoubtedly more sensitive in many respects. Beyond all of that, I've seen and admired how much you are driven and guided by very high ideals. You're also not a social climber, as far as I can tell. Your motives are pure."

My fingers clutched the Syriac cross on my necklace. "When you come to a new country with so little, all you have is your character."

"Exactly."

There was another long silence, almost as if he was still deciding whether to open up to me. As I waited, I let go of my necklace, noticing the ambient traffic noise in the background and the sound of a boat on the river sailing towards us.

"Seeing those articles about me all over the Internet and on campus today was a painful fall," he finally began. "I'm not sure how far the descent is, because I'm still falling. But I've hit rock bottom about half a dozen times in my life," he admitted somberly, while looking out into the horizon ahead of us. "And, on a few of those occasions, when I was living in New York, I found myself on this bridge, more or less at this midpoint where we are right now, just staring at the East River... There's something very powerful about just stopping everything in your life to contemplate how it's all in your hands, at any given moment... Time seems to slow down and speed up all at once, as you realize that every moment is a choice, even if we normally aren't aware of it... Life can continue... Or it can end... It's a very powerful choice. And during those moments of dark nihilism, I stood here and felt that choice... And the longer I stood here, struggling with that choice, the more a certain vertigo took hold of me, almost daring me to stumble irrevocably over the edge."

"You don't mean vertigo from the height above the water, do you?" I asked.

"No. I mean the vertigo of choice – the dizziness and heaviness of actively choosing between life and death, after some existential despair reminds you that you actually have a choice... Because that is when you're most alone... When you come to this bridge by yourself at night, there's really no one who can stop you."

"Well, it's pretty hard to force someone to live, if they're in full control of their faculties and mobility," I agreed. I felt a deeply personal confession bubbling to the surface, but couldn't suppress it for some reason. "I've been there too... " I took a hard swallow. "At the precipice... A few times... "

"I'm sorry to hear that," he said, lightly putting his hand on mine. "But after all you've been through, that doesn't surprise me."

I looked out onto the river, and fixed my eyes on the movement of the water for a moment. "Yes. It's a very lonely place..." I turned to look back at him. "But maybe if you know that someone else stood there too, and came back from it, you feel less alone when you're standing there."

"Maybe," he said sadly, as he removed his hand. "But when the darkness finally brings you to the point where no one can really stop you, and you're peering directly into the end of your life, the freedom of the moment can knock you off balance. Which makes you grip this rail even tighter. And holding it so tightly reminds you of its purpose, and the fact that you're not supposed to go over the rail – because life is meant to be protected, not discarded."

We stood out there for a bit longer, but it was getting cold, so Professor Morales walked me back to the Manhattan side of the bridge, where his driver was waiting.

"Quinn, please take her back to the university," he instructed his driver, through the open window. He then opened the passenger door for me. "Goodbye, Anissa. Thanks for listening."

I paused before entering the car. "Aren't you coming too?" I asked, wanting to wrap him in my arms to ease his troubled soul. I hated seeing him this distraught… If my touch or warmth could provide any form of comfort, I wanted to gift that to him.

"I'm not ready to go back yet. Don't worry, Quinn will return for me after he drops you off."

"Are you sure you're OK here alone?" I asked, full of unease.

"Yes, Anissa. Aloneness is part of my coping ritual – like all of the other times that I've come here. But thanks for your concern."

Chapter 46: Anissa

∽ Tuesday, April 8, 2014 ∾

To My Dearest,

    The last week has been marked by an ominous uncertainty about Professor Morales. I never actually got his phone number, so there was no way even to try calling him. There was something so solid and certain about the way he had told me at his party that his driver would pick me up for our dinner date at 7:30 p.m. the next night, that it didn't occur to me to exchange numbers with him then. And after our date, which didn't even end in a kiss or anything like that, it seemed odd to ask for his number when I'd be seeing him in class two days later. So all I could do to confirm that he hadn't jumped off that bridge the night I left him there was to collect and assemble the other available clues.

    Unfortunately, those clues did not bode well for seeing him again. The first bad omen happened during my car ride with him, when he instructed his assistant to cancel all of his dinners and meetings for the rest of the week. And then, of course, there was everything he told me on the Brooklyn Bridge. Even the way we parted gave me a bad feeling: he didn't say "I'll see you in class," or "see you on Thursday" or anything else that implied a next time; instead, he said "Goodbye, Anissa."

    On top of that, he missed class last Thursday without any notice – which was very unlike him. The students just sat there, joking amongst themselves for about twenty minutes, waiting for him to show up, before they finally concluded that he wasn't coming. After class, I called Maya to share my concern about him, and asked her to let me know as soon as she was able to reach Professor Morales.

    Beyond those troubling signs, he hadn't tweeted anything since March 31. Every day I went to his Facebook profile, which I could still view, even though we weren't connected as friends, just to see if he had posted anything, which might at least indicate that he was still alive. But there too, each day that I checked, I saw no activity in April.

    By Friday, I decided to go the JMAT office, to see if I could get some answers there. But the security guards wouldn't let me into the building without a visitor pass and they had no information for me. When I tried calling the JMAT office, they told me that the firm doesn't release any details about Mr. Morales or any other employee, and then I realized that they had probably been deluged by calls after the scandal, so it would be even harder to get any information out of anyone there.

I knew it was a long shot, but I also tried going to Professor Morales' university office hours; of course, he wasn't there either.

On Saturday, desperate for any hint that Professor Morales was still alive and increasingly concerned that I'd find none, I tried going to his apartment building. But the doorman was utterly unhelpful.

"I work here only certain shifts," he explained. "So he could have easily come and gone when I was off duty."

"Well has he come or gone while you were on duty?" I asked.

"I'm sorry, ma'am, but the building has extremely strict rules about the privacy of our residents, so I'm afraid I can't tell you what you want to know."

"Not even when he last came in or out or if he's even here?" I persisted.

"Sorry. All I can do is accept a note or a package from you and give it to him the next time I see him."

"OK, can you buzz him to see if he'll receive a visitor right now?"

"That I can do," he said politely. He picked up the building's internal phone and pushed some buttons. We waited. Finally, he put the phone down. "Sorry, there's no answer."

As I was leaving his apartment building, I again called Maya to see if she had been able to reach Professor Morales. But she told me that her calls were still going straight to his voicemail and her texts continued to go unanswered. This time I asked for his phone number so that I could call him directly, but she refused to share it, saying, "He would kill me if I ever gave out his number like that without his permission. And you'd never get through anyway. If he's not responding to my number, he definitely won't answer an unknown number."

By this morning, I feared the worst and wasn't even sure whether there was any point to going to his lecture this evening at 6 p.m.

Meanwhile, Michael was supposed to call me today at noon my time to update me on the latest and show me that he was still alive, even though he's scheduled to fly back from Syria tomorrow. I'm sure he was also eager to hear if I had any update on Professor Morales, since – when Michael and I last spoke (two days ago) – I told him that I was worried we might never see or hear from my professor again.

But I was waiting by my laptop for many hours past noon and

Michael still hadn't logged onto Skype or contacted me in any other way. As it got later, I became increasingly distressed, thinking that I've now lost both men. In an attempt to amuse myself with some dark humor, I wondered if, unbeknownst to me, I carried some kind of evil omen that kills off the men in my life.

And then, almost six hours past the time he was supposed to call, just as I was descending into a dark despair of worst-case scenarios, I got an email from Michael. I was so relieved. Just the fact that he emailed me at all lifted a huge weight off my shoulders. But then what he wrote in his email just blew me away:

"Inās, so sorry I couldn't get in touch sooner. Some unexpected issues arose and I may now have to stay in Syria for a bit longer – including to help your relatives in Raqqa. But guess what??? A donation for five million dollars was wired into the MCA bank account this morning. Yes, you read that correctly. Five million dollars! AMAZING WORK, BABY!!!"

I let out the hugest sigh of relief and just smiled in unbridled elation, staring at his email and rereading it. I must have gone over that email about twenty times before realizing that I was officially late for Professor Morales' lecture.

TO BE CONTINUED IN...

Anissa's Redemption

...the next book of ***The Syrian Virgin Series***.

About the Author

Zack Love graduated from Harvard College, where he studied mostly literature, psychology, philosophy, and film. After college, he moved to New York City and took a corporate consulting job that had absolutely nothing to do with his studies. The attacks of September 11, 2001 inspired him to write a novelette titled *The Doorman*, and heightened his interest in the Middle East. A decade later, that interest extended to the Syrian Civil War, which provided the backdrop for his latest work. In late 2013, Zack began releasing his unpublished works of fiction and became a full-time author. He has published comedy, psychological and philosophical fiction, and romance. Zack enjoys confining himself to one genre about as much as he likes trying to sum up his existence in one paragraph.

Author links:
–Facebook: https://www.facebook.com/ZackLoveAuthor
–Twitter: https://twitter.com/ZackLoveAuthor
–Website/Newsletter: http://zacklove.com/about-me/newsletter/

And if you need a good laugh after such a heavy read, check out Zack Love's extremely objective review of his own book on Goodreads (where you can also connect with him):
http://tinyurl.com/epicGRreview

Other Works by Zack Love

Anissa's Redemption
(a novel – the sequel to *The Syrian Virgin*)

Anissa Toma fled war-torn Syria after narrowly escaping the massacre of her Christian family by Islamists. Fortunate enough to rebuild her shattered life in New York City, the young refugee gained admission to an elite college, where she excelled. Her beauty, brains, and purity soon captured the interest of two powerful men: Michael, an activist working to establish Antioch, the first Mideast Christian state, and Julien, her professor and one of the city's wealthiest bachelors.

As Anissa's saga continues, the refugee-turned-rising-star must navigate between Michael and Julien, while trying to help her surviving relatives and other vulnerable Christians in Syria. As she gets closer to both men in a complex and evolving love triangle, can she unlock Julien's traumatic childhood to open up his heart? Or will Julien find greater solace from his nightmares and other demons in the sessions with his intriguing therapist? What will Michael do for Antioch and for Anissa, and what will Julien's role be? How far will each person go to help Anissa's remaining family and other persecuted Christians at risk in Syria? Find out in this stunning sequel to *The Syrian Virgin*.

Sex in the Title
(a novel – romantic comedy)

New York City, May 2000. The Internet bubble has burst and Evan, a computer programmer, is fired with an email from his boss. The next day, his girlfriend dumps him, also via email. Afraid to check any more emails, Evan desperately seeks a rebound romance but the catastrophes that ensue go from bad to hilariously worse.

Fortunately, Evan meets Sammy – someone whose legendary disasters with females eclipse even his own. To reverse their fortunes, they recruit their friends – Trevor, Yi, and Carlos – to form a group of five guys who take on Manhattan in pursuit of dates, sex, and adventure.

When Evan, a closet writer, falls desperately in love with a Hollywood starlet, he schemes to meet her by writing a novel that will sweep her off her feet. Sammy knows nothing about publishing but is confident of one thing: Evan's book should have the word "sex" in the title.

With musings about life, relationships, and human psychology, this quintessential New York story about the search for happiness follows five men on their comical paths to trouble, self-discovery, and love.

Stories and Scripts: an Anthology
(a collection of stories in various genres)

Thought-provoking, dreamy, sad, and hilarious, this collection of works takes the reader on a diverse and unforgettable literary journey through a variety of topics, themes, and emotions.

The anthology totals about 73,000 words and contains a novelette, four short stories, a theater play, and a screenplay. These seven spellbinding stories spanning several styles and genres include a dramatic romance, a satire of the mega-rich, a somber and soulful reflection on the problem of evil, humorous dating adventures, and stories driven by philosophical musings.

Printed in Great Britain
by Amazon